Division One: A Very UnCON-ventional Christmas

by Stephanie Osborn

Chromosphere Press

Huntsville, AL

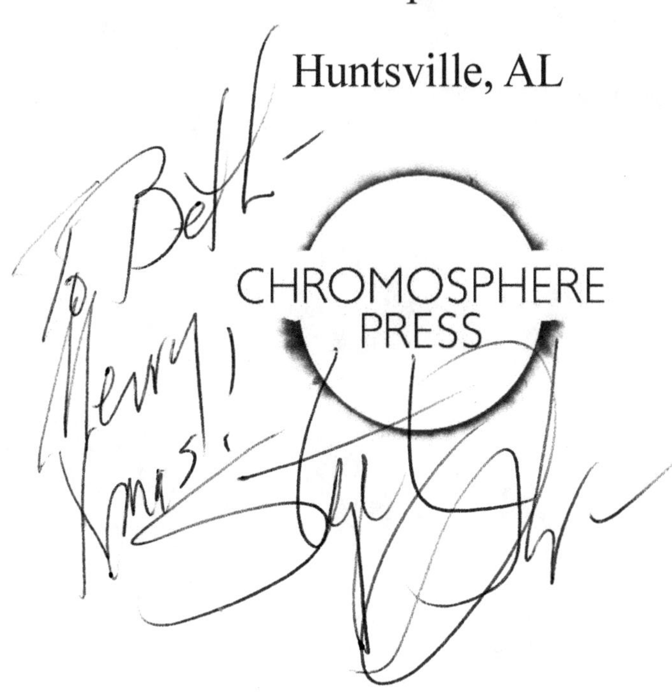

A Very UnCONventional Christmas

ISBN 978-0-9982888-5-7 (print)

Fiction

First electronic edition 2017

Chromosphere Press
P.O. Box 3412
Huntsville, AL 35810
www.chromospherepress.com

Table of Contents

Chapter 1

Echo heard a small commotion in Omega's quarters next door as he unwound for the day; it sounded to him rather like large boxes being thrown around. So the stereotypically tall, dark, handsome, and enigmatic Agent wandered over to the 'back door'—the connecting door between partners' quarters—to see what was going on next door.

In the next apartment, a statuesque blonde with a long, platinum-blonde French braid sat in the middle of her living area floor, humming Christmas carols to herself, and surrounded by a pile of what looked like foliage. Storage boxes were indeed scattered around the room. Echo knocked on the door frame.

"Meg? What on Earth are you doing?"

She looked up and smiled happily.

"It's December first, my dear sir. What do you think I'm doing?"

"Trying to build a compost heap, it looks like."

"Well, if Fox had let me have a REAL tree, it would already be up, and I'd be decorating it. AND the room would smell terrific. But he said no, it was a potential fire hazard, and too messy. So I'm stuck here trying to assemble something that's worse than the hypercube puzzle."

"Are you suggesting we change the test sequence for Alpha Line admission?" Echo grinned. His partner matched his grin.

"Well, it wouldn't be as big a power draw, that's for sure." Omega stuck another branch in the trunk of the tree. "I kinda wish I'd gotten one of the kind where the branches are attached and fold up for storage, 'cause then I could just set it up in the stand, maybe shake it a little bit, adjust a branch here and there, and it'd be ready to decorate. But it's too late now, I guess. You wouldn't want to give me a hand here, would you?"

"Well...I don't do Christmas much..."

"Oh...um, well, never mind then. I just called Romeo and India to come help decorate, and they'll be here in a few. They can give me a hand." She returned to intently studying the tree puzzle. But there was now an odd, slightly pinched look around her bright blue eyes. Echo drew his brows together in concern.

"Meg?"

"Hmm?" she answered without looking up.

"Something wrong?"

"No." But she still didn't look up.

"C'mon, Meg, don't—"

There was a knock at her front door.

"Come on in, y'all," Omega called, getting up and quickly brushing past Echo on her way to the door. "Welcome to North Pole Central!" A handsome young black man, slightly under six feet tall, with a military crew cut and a muscular build, accompanied by a slim, attractive Afro-Asian woman with short black hair and almond-shaped amber eyes, came in, laden with bags of groceries, cheerily greeting Omega.

"Hey, pretty lady! It's the Christmas thang!" Romeo exclaimed.

"Yeah, don'tcha just love it?!" Omega responded with a smile. "What's in the bags?"

"Here, Romeo, give it to me. Mind if I use your kitchen, Meg?" India asked, taking Romeo's bag with her own.

"No, that's fine. Go ahead."

"See, I figured, if we gonna get together an' deck the halls," Romeo explained, "we needed the appropriate refreshments. So I talked India into..."

"Making mulled cider," India finished for him, sticking her head out of the kitchen.

"Oh, that sounds wonderful!" Omega exclaimed, all but clapping her hands in delight. "My mom...used to make it for Christmas..."

"Bet YOUR folks did Christmas in a big way too, huh?" Romeo asked.

"Yeah..." Omega's face held a faraway, bittersweet expression, as Echo watched the interaction closely, suspecting something was in the wind, but having no idea what, as yet. "Yeah, they did. Need any help finding anything, India? I've got a fresh batch of homemade shortbread to go along with the cider..." Omega headed to the kitchen, and Romeo sat down in the middle of the 'compost heap.'

"Echo, my man. Siddown here an' let's us put this tree together."

"I...don't think so."

"Whaddaya mean, 'don't think so'? Oh, man, you're not like, Jewish or something, are ya? Like Fox? 'Cause I sure didn't mean to offend you..."

"No. I observe Christmas. I just...quit celebrating it."

"Damn, skippy. You sound like India. She don't get into Christmas much either. Says it's one a' the peak seasons for shit goin' down in an emergency room. I hadda pull out all th' stops just to convince her to come over with me, never mind th' cider. Well, me an' Meg 'll just haveta make up for the both of ya."

"Looks like you two can more than manage that."

"Mmm...smell that?" Romeo said, sniffing, as a delicious, spicy-sweet odor wafted through Omega's apartment.

"Yeah. Smells good," Echo admitted.

"Hey, guys," Omega called from the kitchen. "We've got authentic, homemade Scottish shortbread from my grandmom's old family recipe, and India says the cider 'll be ready in a few minutes. We got chips an' ranch dip, too, and I can make a pot of coffee if anybody wants it, or you can just use the pod brewer if you take a notion. I can also throw together some sandwiches if you're really hungry. Who wants something?"

"Abso-damn-lutely!" Romeo called back. "Echo?"

"...I could be talked into it."

* * *

Later that evening, the tree was up, and Omega's apartment rapidly began reflecting the Yuletide spirit of its occupant. Overstuffed hot roast beef sandwiches, along with the cider, chips and dip, and shortbread, had made for an early but ample dinner for the four. India mostly handled the food, and Echo bent his personal rules sufficient to carry food trays and decoration boxes as needed or requested. Romeo pitched in enthusiastically on decorating alongside Omega, completing the tree assembly and climbing up on a stepstool to place the star on top.

"Might've known," Echo remarked with a grin as Romeo positioned the ornament.

"Known what?" Omega asked, noting the grin. "No, turn it clockwise a bit, Romeo. About...twenty degrees?"

"Might've known you'd have a star on top," Echo replied as he sipped mulled cider and reached for another piece of shortbread. Omega noted with some hidden satisfaction that her partner had consumed more of her homemade shortbread than any two of the other three agents there. Then again, she considered, he was considerably taller and broader than, but was every bit as active as, the other three, so unwanted poundage was highly unlikely.

"Of course," she responded with a chuckle. "You expect a former NASA astronomer and astronaut to have anything else on her Christmas tree? That's perfect, Romeo. Right there. Okay, India, it's our turn."

"Turn for what?" India asked.

"Decorating. Tree ornaments are in that box over there." She pointed. "Hand it over here, would you, Echo?"

"Sure, Meg. Hang on a sec..." Echo shoved the remainder of the shortbread cookie in his mouth and sat down his mug of hot cider before reaching for the box in question, cheeks bulging.

India was somewhat reluctant, but Omega and Romeo's enthusiasm was infectious, and soon she was laughing and hanging ornaments along with them. Romeo and Omega fearlessly clambered up on the furniture in their efforts to hang garlands over doors and across ceilings.

"Echo?"

"Yeah, Meg?"

"I got a job for you. Here. Wreath. Hanger." She held out both objects and pointed. "Front door."

"...No..." His voice was very quiet.

"Aw, c'mon, Echo, it's just a wreath." She studied his face for a moment, seeing something in his dark eyes, something that looked—to her, at least—like carefully-hidden pain, and acquiesced. "Okay, never mind. I'll get it." As she passed by him on her way to the door, she murmured, "You okay, hon?"

"Mm-hm."

"All right. Sorry. More cider—and coffee—in the kitchen..."

"Shortbread?"

"That, too."

* * *

So Echo had hung around, sipping hot spiced cider, munching shortbread, and watching, mostly, although Omega had finally managed to coax him into hanging just one ornament on her tree.

"...Just one, Echo. And I won't bug you about it any more, I swear I won't. See, my family had this tradition: nobody had to decorate that didn't want to. But everyone had to put ONE ornament on the tree. No more, no less. And no exceptions. That way, the tree kind of belonged to everyone. I'd really like for this tree to be like that, too."

This time Echo saw something in Omega's eyes—old pain, mingled with a kind of wistfulness that amounted, in Echo's mind, to almost desperate pleading—and capitulated. *Thaaaaat...*he thought in some concern, trying not to wince as he met her gaze. *That's...not good, that look. Yeah, I can do this for her, just the once. Especially if it gets rid of that look in her eyes.* He nodded his acquiescence, and moved to the big box of ornaments, secretly noting the way his partner's face lit up at his response. *There we go. That's better.*

He had rummaged around in the ornament box, among the year-dated decorations and the old keepsakes from her childhood, and come up with an ornament he didn't understand.

"What's this?" he wondered, holding it up.

'This' was an eight-inch-long, square, oxidized iron spike, carefully nestled in a red-velvet-lined box. A red ribbon loop was tied around the top of the spike.

"Oh, that's a special ornament," Omega said softly, with a smile. "I put it on every year. It's a reminder."

"Of what?"

"Of the rest of the story. Christmas is only the beginning of it, you know."

The others nodded, comprehending, and Echo extracted it from its box and carefully hung it on Omega's tree.

When they were finished, Omega served more of India's cider, dimmed the lights, and turned on the tree. The room glowed with soft, flickering, multicolored light.

"NOW," Omega said dreamily, "it's Christmas..."

* * *

"Meg?" Romeo's voice came over the cell phone the next morning. "You finished with your Christmas shoppin' yet?"

"No; as a matter of fact, I was just getting ready to go do that," Omega said, sitting on the sofa in her den.

"Echo goin' with ya?"

"...No."

"Mind if I join ya? I need a favor," Romeo asked.

"Sure. C'mon. Glad of the company."

"Okay, thanks! I'll be 'round the corner in a few, then."

Omega gathered up her black overcoat and called hopefully through the back door, "Echo? Romeo and I are going Christmas shopping..."

"Have fun."

"Are you SURE you won't come along?"

"Positive."

"All right. See you later..."

She sighed inaudibly, shrugged, and headed out the front door of the apartment to meet Romeo.

* * *

A few minutes later, there was a knock at Echo's door. When he opened it, India stood there in her overcoat.

"Grab your coat and let's go for a walk," she declared.

* * *

"...So I was wondering if you'd help me out, ya know, gimme that female point of view. This'll be our first Christmas together. So I want it to be something really special."

"Sure, Romeo, all you had to do was ask. Maybe you can help me, too," Omega said as they walked along the snowy sidewalk.

"Howzzat?"

"I haven't a clue what to get Echo. What do you give a man who neither needs nor wants anything? He's so minimalist..."

"Yeah, girl, I hear ya. India an' I got the same problem, tryin' to figure out what to get him. I mean, have you noticed the man's apartment? Bare minimum of furniture, no pictures, no knickknacks, no mementos. Not even a damn houseplant."

"Yeah, I know, Romeo. But I think I do understand it. You and India CHOSE this life, chose to be part of the Agency. Echo and I didn't, really. We sort of became Agents by default. We didn't GIVE UP everything, we LOST it. And when you've...lost everything, you can tend not to want to... get attached. That way, you can't lose it again."

Romeo mulled that over for a while.

"You're not like that," he finally pointed out.

"Romeo," she said quietly, looking away, "you have no idea. Not all losses are material...and not everyone handles them the same way."

"Sorry, Meg," Romeo apologized gently. "Guess I stuck my foot in that one, huh?"

"No, Romeo, it's my fault. Just kinda, I dunno, overlook my moods, if you don't mind. I'm...a little hypersensitive right now. Maybe a lot hypersensitive, from time to time. This season of the year...I anticipate it the most, and I dread it the most. My family was killed right before Christmas. And this year...well...first year in the Agency and all..."

"Oh, man! I'm sorry, girl. I didn't know...didn't think about..."

"It's okay. That's why I told you. I just have to get through it." Omega was matter-of-fact. "And, um, if you want to go ahead and tell India, sorta as a heads-up, I wouldn't mind."

"Oh, uh, okay. Yeah, I'll tell 'er. Um." Romeo broke off, uncertain. "Uh, so, did you like the Macy's display?" he asked after an awkward pause, trying to change the subject and cheer Omega up.

"Yeah! It was great!" She smiled, but there was still the residue of shadow lurking in the sapphire gaze.

"You seen Rockefeller Center yet?" he tried again.

"No. That's where the big tree is, right?"

"Yeah! C'mon, let's go take a look! You have got to see it!"

* * *

Romeo and Omega strolled down the crowded promenade, and she exclaimed with delight over the heralding angels and other decorations along the way. But when they got to the plaza itself, she tilted her head back, and looked up...and up...and up.

"Damn, Romeo! HOW big did you say this tree was?!"

"'Bout ninety-three feet this year, they say," Romeo replied.

"Wow. I'm glad I didn't haveta check THOSE strings of lights," Omega murmured.

"I agree with you," a voice remarked behind her, and Omega turned to see a man wearing a black Suit, black overcoat, and the same kind of wrap-around, 'special' sunglasses Omega had in her jacket pocket. He extended his hand. "Hi. I'm Sierra."

"Omega," she said, shaking his hand. "This is Romeo." The men shook hands.

"Partners?" Sierra asked.

"No," Omega replied. "Echo is MY partner—"

"An' India is mine," Romeo finished. "The Alpha One and Two teams."

"Ah yes, Alpha Line. The Agency's front line," Sierra remarked in an odd tone. "Nice to meet you. On a mission?"

"Sorta," Romeo grinned. "Christmas shoppin' for our partners' gifts. You?"

"Mmm...picking up a message," Sierra replied in an oblique fashion, and Romeo and Omega gave him knowing looks.

"Don't let us keep you, then," Omega told him. "See you around, Sierra. Come on, Romeo, let's let the guy work."

"Later, m' man," Romeo told Sierra.

"Be seeing you." Sierra moved off.

"Hey!" Romeo exclaimed then, grabbing Omega by the hand and dragging her down some steps, "let's hit the ice for a few!"

"Romeo! Are you crazy?!" Omega responded, pulling back. "I'm from the deep South, remember? I've never seen this much snow before in my life, except in Antarctica! I SURE don't know how to ice skate!!"

"Ain't no thang! I'll teach you!" Romeo encouraged, already renting two pairs of skates. He handed one pair to Omega, who shrugged good-humoredly, sat down on a bench and removed her shoes, then began gamely lacing the skates onto her feet.

Romeo was already on the ice by the time Omega wobbled over to the edge of the rink. He was quite good, and Omega guessed he'd probably played hockey as a boy. She hesitated at the edge of the rink, not entirely certain what to do. Romeo came gliding up to her, stopped, and held out his arms.

"Okay, Meg, just take my hands and follow me. I've gotcha," he said reassuringly, wrapping his gloved hands around her wrists. "It's like walking, sorta." Tentatively, she stepped out onto the ice, following Romeo awkwardly as he skated backward with fluid grace.

"Romeo," she said, in a mock threat, "if I break my fool neck here, IT'S YOUR FAULT!!"

Their laughter floated out over the ice rink, as Romeo slowly picked up the pace, forcing Omega to gradually begin gliding across the ice.

* * *

The sound of familiar laughter drew the attention of another black-clad couple drinking coffee and surrounded by shopping bags at the café overlooking the plaza.

"Look, it's Meg and Romeo!" India pointed. "He must be teaching her to ice skate."

"Yeah," Echo agreed. "Romeo must've played hockey as a kid. Looks like they're having a good time."

"That's great. She needs this." India smiled.

"How so?"

"She's had a rough year, Echo. You know that. Getting absorbed into the Agency whether she wanted to or not. Nearly getting killed by a psycho telepath. Almost being forced into killing you. Finding out her whole life was engineered by that telepath just to get revenge on you. And this is her very first Christmas with us. The other night, when she and I were talking in the kitchen, I found out a few things in the course of our conversation, and read between the lines on a few more things. Christmas is a hard season on her, Echo. She seems to miss her family most this time of year, though I'm not sure why. I THINK she's...homesick, is maybe the closest word I can come up with. Lonely. I kind of got the impression she's trying—both consciously and subconsciously—to recreate, with us, some of her family's holiday traditions."

"Well, I'd think that's good. It shows she's accepted being here."

"Yes, that's true. But I suspect that it's still painful. The differences probably only serve to make the loss more noticeable."

I can sure understand that, he thought. "Mmm. So what is it you want us to do? What is it you want ME to do?"

"I'm not sure there's anything to be done, Echo. Except try to be understanding; maybe cut her a little slack, if things get rough. I was only giving you a head's up that something's in the wind, not trying to give you a hint about anything. She's pretty much got to work through this herself. No one can do it for her."

* * *

As they progressed down the ice, Romeo gradually slid his hands farther and farther down toward Omega's fingertips, as she developed more confidence in her movements on the slick surface. Finally, only their fingertips were touching. Romeo dropped one hand away. Then he eased the contact on the other.

"Oh. Ohh...No! Don't do it!" Omega warned.

"Too late." Romeo grinned and dropped his other hand. "Just keep goin' like you have been. That's it! You're doin' great!"

Omega swept out over the ice, an astonished smile on her face as she realized she was 'soloing.'

"Hahah! This is fun!" she cried, and they laughed. After a few more moments of gliding smoothly across the ice, Omega said, "Romeo...I got a question."

"Shoot," he said, pacing her.

"Now that I'm going...how the hell do I STOP??"

"Do you think you can balance on one skate blade? Maybe enough to drag the toe of the other foot behind you, and kinda dig in the teeth on the front of the blade?"

"Um, no, not really, not yet..."

"Relax. It's easier than you think. Just—"

"On one skate?! No!"

"Ease up, girl, it's okay. All right, then do it like this. Watch," and he leaned back slightly as he smoothly turned his skates against the direction of motion, coming to a halt.

"Oh boy. Well, at least that's on two feet. Okay, here goes..."

Omega did fine until her skate blades hit a little ridge of ice. Then her feet flew out from under her, and she landed spread-eagled on her back, spinning across the ice. Romeo sprinted after her, knelt down beside her...

* * *

In the café, Echo and India had been watching Omega's successful solo run when they saw her fall. Echo instinctively started up, concerned for his partner's safety, but India grabbed his arm, pulling him back down into his seat.

"Sit down. She's okay."

"But..."

"Let her learn. It wasn't a hard fall. And Romeo's there."

"True. But his form's a little sloppy..."

Just then, they heard Omega's laughter resounding across the ice, and barely made out her voice.

"THAT didn't go at ALL according to plan, did it?" She still lay, prone on the ice, but was laughing hard enough to visibly shake. Echo relaxed.

"No, but that's okay." Distantly, Romeo's voice reached them. "Let's just try it again."

"That's the trick, isn't it?" She sat up, and laughed once more. "First I have to stand up on this stuff before I can fall down again!"

Echo and India watched, amused, as Omega struggled to get back to her feet on the ice. It turned out not to be as easy as Romeo apparently hoped; she took Romeo down with her, twice out of her first four attempts. A third effort saw her land hard on her behind with a grunt so loud that the wincing couple in the café could hear; on the fourth attempt, she nearly anted her face into the ice, avoiding it only because of her training and athleticism.

A fifth attempt saw her almost get upright, holding tight to Romeo's hands, only to have her feet slide out from under her...right between Romeo's legs. Pivoting from his shoulders like the bob at the end of a pendulum, she shot off on her back behind him, feet first, and Romeo had to spin and sprint after her.

After several more hilariously-missed starts into the bargain, she finally managed to gain her feet, with a lot of help from Romeo. But by the time they were BOTH upright, they were laughing so hard they couldn't do anything except stand there and hang onto each other so Omega wouldn't fall back down...again.

"They're like a couple of kids," Echo observed with a slight smile, a hint of affection hidden in it.

"Yeah. That's one of the things I love about Romeo; he can be so playful. And yet he can be serious when he needs to be. He's a lotta fun to be around. And Meg—for all that she has this genius intellect, and is a good eight or ten years older than Romeo and I think about three or four years older than me, her basic personality can be really very simple, almost childlike at times. At other times, she's one of the most complex, sophisticated individuals I know. Present company included. In fact, at those times, you're a lot alike."

"Yeah. Maybe. But I still think I should make sure she's not hurt."

"Echo, do you really think Meg would be that uninhibited and carefree if she knew you were watching?"

Echo shot India a startled, slightly pained glance.

"What do you mean?"

"Echo, you're not just her partner. You're her teacher, her mentor. Her role model. Her hero, like I told you and Fox back during Slug's attack. Look, Echo, it's like this: to her, you are not ONE OF the Agents; you are THE Agent. Romeo has a little bit of that same mentality, by the way."

"Well...I AM one of the Originals, I guess..."

"Exactly. And you—THE Agent, one of the Originals, or in her mind, THE Original—you respect Meg, and she knows that and appreciates it. In turn, she looks up to you, and wants to keep that respect. She wants to meet your standards. But I think, given her drive and perfectionism, that what she's really trying to meet is HER VIEW of your standards, which are even higher."

"Are you saying I inhibit her from being herself?"

"No, not at all. She seems very comfortable around you, and she's told me on several occasions that you're the best friend she's got. No, I think she's being herself. But that doesn't mean she thinks she meets with your approval. Or even with her own."

* * *

Down on the ice, Omega had finally gotten the hang of stopping while remaining upright, her innate athletic ability and coordination standing her in good stead. Now, she and Romeo were involved in a spirited game of tag.

"Gotcha! You're it!" She came zooming by and slapped her companion on the shoulder. Romeo sprinted after her, and she picked up the pace, pushing her limits. She yelled over her shoulder, "Betcha didn't know you were training the next Olympic gold medal speed skater!"

"You wish!" He laughed, and pushed a little harder.

As Omega turned her head back around, she watched in horror as a little boy on skates, only around five or six, fell hard on the ice, sliding right in front of her. The entire world seemed to slow down.

* * *

In the café, unseen by the pair on the ice, Echo watched as Omega leaped into a full sprint, just as a tiny child fell hard in front of her. His breath caught in dread and dismay.

The whole ice rink seemed to stop.

Horrified but helpless to intervene, India and Echo both came to their feet.

* * *

No room to stop—too fast to turn—what the hell did I think I was doing, first time on skates?! Omega had just time to think. *Stupid, stupid, STUPID!*

Out of ideas, Omega put everything she had into one desperate, powerful forward leap.

"Ohh man! This is gonna huuurrt..." she told the air as she left the ice.

She cleared the child in slow motion, pulling her feet up to avoid hitting him with the skate blades, then began worrying about landing.

"Meg! BALANCE! Maneuver Foxtrot-Four!" she thought she heard a familiar voice call in the near distance, but she didn't have time to analyze it, only obey it. Quickly she found her center of gravity and got her body distributed properly around it. *Maneuver Foxtrot-Four...* She pulled her feet under herself, arms out, leaning just slightly back, as she neared the ice and the world accelerated back to normal speed...

"Uuff!" Her skates hit hard, but straight, the impact jarring up through her body and knocking the breath out of her. Her knees bent deep, absorbing the shock; her arms flew out and forward, her body crouched low. Miraculously, she stayed upright. It wasn't graceful; it wasn't polished. But it had worked.

Her forward momentum gradually slowed, and she rested her hands on her bent knees, breathing hard, as she came to a stop. Romeo rushed up.

"Meg!? You okay, girl?" Romeo was leaning over her.

"Yeah," Omega said, panting. "Whoa. Gimme a minute." She slowly straightened up. "Is the little boy all right?" she asked.

"I think so. Wanna go check?"

"Yeah. But I'm just a little wobbly-kneed at the moment. Hang on a second."

"Here. Lean on me," he offered. "I won't let ya fall."

* * *

Still unseen by the pair on the ice, Echo and India watched from the café as Romeo pulled Omega's right arm across his shoulders, and put a steadying arm around her waist.

"Damn. You think she's hurt?" Echo wondered, worried.

"She's gonna know it tomorrow, probably, but no, I don't think she's hurt, not seriously, anyway," India decided, scrutinizing the other half of Alpha One with a professional physician's eye. "I don't see her limping or anything, and her stance is even."

"What's wrong, then?"

"Ooo, I think I know. She's shook up," India observed, voice soft. "See her trembling? All the way from up here?"

"Yeah, I do. I'm a little surprised at that," Echo murmured, concerned.

"I'm not. I'm betting that's the first time she's ever been on ice skates before, by the look of things. And the adrenaline surge from a stunt like that last bit? It's probably got her ringing like a church bell. I know it would, me."

"Mm. Yeah, good point."

They continued to watch as the pair on the ice skated slowly over to the little boy, and Omega knelt in front of him.

* * *

"Are you all right?" Omega asked, kneeling in front of the boy.

"Uh-huh. I'm fine," the child replied, unconcerned. "That was way cool. Are you gonna do it again at the toy store?"

"Uh, no, dear, I don't think I'm gonna be doing THAT again for a long time." Omega shot an amused look at Romeo.

"Oh. I'll see you at the toy store, then. I want YOUR action figure. You're pretty."

"Thank you, honey. But what makes you think I'll be at the toy store?"

"You're one of the *Black Suits*, aren'tcha? Like the action figures."

"Do you know what he's talking about?" Omega looked up at Romeo.

"Nope."

"Oh, I am so sorry," the little boy's mother gushed as she hurried up then. "Is everything all right? Nobody's hurt, right? I know it must've spoiled your break from the store, too. You're really very good—you two look JUST LIKE the action figures. Especially him." She pointed at Romeo.

"Um, thank you, ma'am," Omega responded, at a loss.

"Uh, ma'am?" Romeo asked. "We've been working so hard...and then we took a break...we, uh, haven't had a chance to look at the action figures yet. Are they any good?"

"Oh, yes," the mother responded with a broad smile. "So imaginative. Galactic government and alien law enforcement, all in black, with such futuristic weapons! Bobby, do you have your Agent Five with you?"

"Yeah, Mommy. He's my favorite."

"Show it to the nice lady."

Bobby reached into his coat pocket and pulled out a little action figure, dressed in a black suit, white shirt, and black tie, and handed it to Omega. Omega's blue eyes fairly glazed over in shock, and she handed it up to Romeo, who murmured under his breath, "Uh-oh."

It was a perfect, miniature replica of Echo.

* * *

As Romeo and Omega walked through the front door of the flagship toy store on Fifth Avenue, she turned to him and said, "Okay, I guess you're the more experienced agent here. I know I'm officially the chief's assistant, but I'm gonna defer to greater experience, and that's you. How shall we do this, ranking field agent?"

"Huh. I guess I am. All right. If you're sure, girl."

"I'm sure."

"Okay, whassay we check th' displays up front first. I'm thinkin' the new stuff oughta be there. If it ain't, you fade left an' I'll go right, an' we start hittin' the aisles. Go from the outside in, an' meet in the middle."

"Works for me."

As they entered the main floor, Omega looked up...way up.

"Uh, Romeo? I don't think we have to worry about finding the toys..."

"Damn straight, skippy. You got that right," Romeo muttered, staring in something akin to horror.

The *Black Suits* display was mammoth. Romeo and Omega were shocked, not only at the size of the display, but at the crowd surrounding it, grabbing armloads of toys and taking them to the checkout counter. As they approached, they tried to get a look at the various action figures and other accessories. Suddenly a childish voice rang out in a high treble.

"Mommy! LOOK! It's the REAL *Black Suits*!!"

Abruptly, the two Agents were engulfed in a wave of delighted, screaming children.

"Agent Eighteen! Can I have your autograph?"

"You're pretty!"

"Can I be a Black Suit? Huh? Please? Can I?"

"Hey! Hey! Hey! Hey!"

"I wanna hug!"

"Where's your memory-thingie? Can I play with it?"

Before they knew what was happening, Omega held a little girl in her arms who was playing with Omega's braid, and Romeo had another child riding 'piggy-back' while wielding a toy ray gun. Still other children hugged the legs of the pair, clung to their hands, and generally tried to get as close to the Agents as they could. Beaming parents stood just behind the horde of children, remarking on how very good the 'PR actors' were, and how creative the entire franchise was.

"Aren't they just adorable?"

"Wish I had my camera."

"Look, the lady is holding my Julie."

"These are really good. I'm going to get Nicky the complete action set for Hannukah."

Omega glanced at Romeo, overwhelmed.

"Oh, wow," she murmured with a faint smile, and Romeo grinned.

"The kids are cute, huh?"

"Yeah. Sometimes I..." she broke off. "Romeo, this is fun, but we gotta do something, and fast. They RECOGNIZE us. Can you imagine what must be happening to the Agents on the street?"

"Oh, shi—" Romeo caught himself, given the children all around them, then tried again. "Oh, man. You're right. We gotta get this back to Fox. An' if we can bring in as many of the different kinds o' toys as we c'n get our hands on..."

"Uh-huh. He'll be able to see the size of the problem. 'Cause I don't think he'll take it seriously otherwise—I mean, it's toys! But how do we get out of this mob of children? They're crawling all over us," Omega said, smiling down at one little boy who had an obvious crush on her. He immediately turned six shades of pink and ran back to his mother.

"Hang on, girl. Got me an idea," Romeo said, raising his hand and signaling the store manager by the counter, who was watching the scene with delirious joy. Immediately the manager began organizing his staff into what the Agents usually termed an 'extraction team.' Within moments, the two operatives were safely ensconced in the storeroom in the back of the store.

"Wow. The Agency did NOT prepare me for THAT," Omega said with complete sincerity.

"The PR firm should've warned you," the manager told her, misunderstanding as she had intended. "These toys are HOT."

"I can see that," Romeo remarked, peeping out the storeroom door at the crowd thronging the storefront. Turning back to Omega, he looked her in the eye expressively as he said, "Sweetheart, I'm sorry. I just don't see how we can do it. I am NOT fightin' my way through THAT again, even for the kids' Christmas. That was WAAAY th' hell too much."

Omega caught on, and went with it.

"Oh, but honey," she pleaded, "you KNOW how much they want 'em. Especially since we got this gig. They've been telling everybody at daycare that Mommy and Daddy are *Black Suits*."

"Aw, that's cute, " the store manager said, grinning. "They sent a couple to do this. Hey, look, maybe I can help youse guys out of a jam. We got lots more *Black Suit* stuff in those boxes behind you. Pick out what you want, I'll ring it up out front, and bring it back to you. Then you can call it a day, sneak out the shipping dock, and go home."

"Oh, would you?" Omega exuded charm. "It would mean SO much to the children..."

"Sure, no problem," the manager replied, lifting the flaps on a couple of already-opened boxes. "We got this batch scanned and in our inventory list this morning, they're just not up on shelves yet. It's a good selection of the toys, too. Here ya go. How many kids youse guys got?"

"Two," Romeo said.

"Three," Omega said simultaneously. They looked at each other blankly. *Whoops.* Omega blushed, then patted her belly. "Oh! Um, well, there'll BE three soon. I was saving the news 'til Christmas, but...Surprise, honey."

Romeo looked startled; then, coming rapidly up to speed, he caught Omega under the arms and spun her around, grinning, just before pulling her in for a bear hug.

"Nice save," he murmured in her ear. Then, in a normal voice, he told her, "Cool, sweetheart! Pick out some neat toys for the other kids an'..." he gave her a sly grin, "we'll go home an' celebrate..."

The store manager was grinning from ear to ear as a pink-cheeked Omega bent over the boxes and said demurely, "All right, honey; it'll just take me a minute..."

Chapter 2

Romeo and Omega returned to Headquarters sporting several bags each from the toy store. When they walked into Omega's apartment, Echo, India, and Fox were waiting.

"What's this all about?" a mildly-irked Fox demanded to know. "It had better be good. I've got a diplomatic visit from the Prime Minister of Lambda Andromedae III to prepare for, and I need to be in my office working on that."

"Oh, it's good, Fox. We've got a big problem, right here." Omega dropped the bags on the couch, as Romeo followed suit.

"TOYS?! Oy vey! You dragged me away from planning a diplomatic visit for TOYS?"

"Yeah, Fox. But not just any toys," Romeo responded.

"Look," Omega said, and began pulling out items. "They call this a particle blaster," she said as she displayed a toy version of a proto-cyclotron blaster. "This is a 'Model Four Disintegrator,'" she added, while holding up a toy tachyon splitter rifle, nearly full-sized. Romeo held out a plastic Winchester & Tesla Mark II death ray, sized for smaller hands.

"Here's what they call a 'Fusion Zapper,' and this," he said, holding up a fake brain bleacher, "is an 'Un-memorizer.'"

"All right," Fox responded, "this is interesting, and a bit troubling, but it's not PERFECTLY identical, and is probably just residual déjà vu from someone who was brain bleached..."

"No, Fox," Omega said, shaking her head. "Take a look at this, y'all." She pulled out a handful of action figures in plastic bubbles on cardboard backs. "Here are Agents Five, Nine, and Eighteen," she said, handing the miniature likenesses around, "and here is the Director—Agent Six," she added, handing Fox the action figure of himself. "There are others. Granted, it seems only to be Headquarters agents, at least so far, but damn. Look at the resemblances! Also please to note that the numbers are correct, relative to the letters of the alphabet corresponding to your code names."

They all looked at the toy representations of themselves, then at each other.

"Okay," Fox admitted, "we've got a problem."

* * *

"Where's YOUR action figure, Meg?" India asked, staring at the array of toys that now covered Omega's couch.

"So far as Romeo and I could tell, I don't have one," Omega responded with a shrug. "Either I'm too new and the perps don't know me yet, or maybe they just couldn't figure out how to work a Greek letter into a numerical system based on the Roman alphabet."

"Or maybe they didn't have enough lead time, once you came on board the Agency, to design one," Echo speculated.

"What were you doing at a toy store? How did you find out about this?" Fox asked.

"I took Meg skatin' at Rockefeller Center on our day off, and she ran into a little boy who thought we were LIVE action figures," Romeo explained.

"'Ran into'...literally?" Echo queried, his face expressionless, a faint gleam in his eye. India elbowed him.

"Almost," Omega responded, then paused, dimly remembering a distant, familiar voice calling instructions even as she went airborne. Her brow furrowed for a moment, then she mentally set the matter aside for later, and continued. "He showed us his action figure toy, and both of us recognized it as you, Echo. His mother told us where they got it, so we hightailed it down there—and nearly got mobbed."

"What?!" Fox exclaimed in shock. "Why?"

"These toys are the biggest thing since *Frozen*, Boss," Romeo answered. "Everybody thought we were PR actors doin' a promo, an' the kids crawled all over us."

"Literally," Omega added. "I had one child in my arms, Romeo had another on his back, they were trying to climb up our legs..."

"I hadda keep little hands outta my pockets an' offa my stuff," Romeo continued. "One kid nearly got his hands on my Winchester & Tesla, when he found it in my backup holster."

"Me too," Omega averred. "Only it was my force cuffs, in my jacket pocket."

"Oh, no," India said softly, her eyes widening as she grasped the implications.

"Oh, yes," Omega said grimly. "The Agents are now recognized across the city, and this toy line is about to go nationwide for Christmas. Our anonymity is shot."

"And with the Prime Minister coming in..." added Echo, now understanding the magnitude of the problem.

"Exactly."

"Break out the shovel, guys. We in some deep shit," Romeo finished.

* * *

Omega drifted over to Echo's side as Fox pulled out his cell phone and began issuing orders. She watched Fox intently as she remarked, offhanded, "By the way...I want to thank you."

"For what?" Echo asked, mildly puzzled at the non sequitur.

"Let's say...for always being there to help me land on my feet?"

"...Ah. You're welcome." He grinned slightly, realizing he'd been caught.

"What on Earth were you doing there?"

Echo drew her away from the others and dropped his voice.

"Getting a cup of coffee with India. We didn't know you and Romeo would be there too. She asked me to help her Christmas shop."

"Oh...so, does Romeo have some competition there?"

"Not that I know of. Why?"

"You turned down my invitation to go Christmas shopping." She shrugged. "Just thought maybe you got a better offer."

He glanced at her, trying to read her expression. Her face was emotionless as she watched Fox.

* * *

"Nah. Actually, 'ask' isn't what India did. She flat-out wasn't going to take 'no' for an answer. She wanted a male opinion while shopping for

Romeo's gift, and I was gonna be the male giving the opinion. Whether I wanted to or not." There was a hint of thinly-disguised irritation in Echo's voice, to Omega's knowledgeable ear.

"Oh. Hah! That's funny. That's exactly why Romeo wanted me along."

"You looked like YOU were enjoying yourselves, at least."

"Yeah! It was fun. I've never ice skated before. Come to think of it, I've never seen that much ice before. Well, except in Antarctica. And that's kinda different," she made excuse.

"Don't forget all the snow in Stockholm last month."

"Yeah, but the waterways weren't frozen."

"True. Wanna go again sometime? Ice skating, I mean. I think we both had enough of Antarctica to last a lifetime. Stockholm, I'm game for, I suppose. We can always visit Nick."

She shot a slightly surprised glance at him. He was looking down at her with the barest hint of a smile.

"Sure!" she decided. "Assuming today's escapade hasn't left me too stiff to crawl out of bed tomorrow, I'd love to go again."

"Meh; don't worry if you're stiff. I know a few tricks for that. Just come get me in the morning, preferably before breakfast, and I'll help you out. Matter of fact, I think I'm gonna go ahead and schedule our day tomorrow to accommodate it; you came awful damn close to a bad wipe-out today. Alpha Two can fill in for anything really serious that comes up first thing. We'll get you limbered up, and THEN take to the streets."

"Okay, thanks. I appreciate that, an' I'll take it! And yeah, I did almost wipe out bad. I could just see me landing on the ice with one part of me sliding one way, while another part went someplace else. All while still attached."

"Yeah. Been there, done that, and it doesn't feel good at all. Funny how nobody actually gives you a t-shirt for it, though."

"Yup, I HAVE noticed that, now you mention it. Which is a shame. A body could at least use the durn things to wear for working out in the gym. I'll likely be taking you up on all that limbering up in the morning, though, 'cause I'm already gettin' pretty stiff. My back is startin' to hurt, too."

* * *

"Well, shit. I was hoping I'd managed to catch you with a maneuver instruction before you actually pulled anything."

"Nah. I was flailing through the air too much for that. Prob'ly looked like a stupid helicopter."

"Yeah, I guess you were, at that, baby, but I didn't think you looked like a helicopter, OR stupid. You looked to me like somebody who was trying desperately not to hurt a child, and a pretty little one at that. To be honest, I doubt Romeo OR I could have come to a stop fast enough to avoid hitting that kid; he was just right there, and there's momentum and inertia and shit to contend with. So you done good." He glanced at his chronometer, considering. "Mm, okay. Look, why don't you come get me a little while before you get ready for bed, and I'll go ahead and get you started on my next-day protocol tonight. And I think you should probably start THAT with a good soak in the tub with your 'lavender bubble-bath shit.'"

Omega laughed softly.

"You are never gonna stop calling it that, are you?" she wondered between chuckles. Echo grinned.

"Nope."

"Okay. Sounds like a plan. You know, I didn't know you ice skated."

"I've done it once or twice. Enough to know what I'm doing. So you wanna go skating with me sometime, or not? Wait, you said you would, if the stiffness didn't put you off, didn't you?"

"Yeah. Just don't laugh at me too hard."

"Why not? You and Romeo were laughing like two kids."

"As the father of my baby, he's allowed." Omega grinned.

"WHAT?!" Echo felt his face freeze in shock. Whatever she meant, he decided immediately that he didn't care for the sound of it.

"Toy store managers are awful damn easy to fool, when you get down to it. And Romeo thinks almost as fast as you do, coming up with a cover." Her grin grew wider. "Besides, I said, 'laugh AT,' not 'laugh WITH.'"

Echo grinned in comprehension.

"Oh, okay. I'm 'with' you, then," he chuckled. *Well, that's all right,* he thought. *I really didn't wanna deal with THAT complication to our partnership. Let alone the Alpha Two partnership.* "No problem."

* * *

"All right, ladies and gentlemen, that's taken care of." Fox closed his cell phone. "I've assigned every available agent to round up the toys and contain the situation. And I want to thank you two for bringing it to our attention."

"Hey, Fox, no prob," Romeo replied.

"Fox," Omega said hesitantly, "are you SURE it's contained? I mean, the scope of this...a nationwide toy campaign at Christmas..."

"Don't worry," Fox responded, "we'll have them off the shelves by the end of the week. What I'm more concerned about is how they got there."

"What?" Omega asked, confused.

"It's too detailed. Did you read the story line on the back of the action figure packs?" Fox asked her.

"Yes. It nailed us. Secret organization, galactic government, interstellar trade, alien immigration, and law enforcement...everything. All of the figures are even recognizable agents," Omega answered him.

"Fox, are you thinking—" Echo began.

"Yes, Echo, I am. And I can't come up with any other logical conclusion. We have a mole in the Agency."

* * *

Later that night, Omega knocked on the frame of the back door, and Echo looked up from his book—he was stretched out on his couch rereading Dickens' *A Christmas Carol*, a little personal annual tradition he'd begun some years earlier—to see her standing in the archway, wrapped in her long black terry robe.

"Okay, Ace," she told him. "I've had a nice long soak with the lavender bubble bath. It helped a little, but my back and shoulders are still hurting. Now what?"

"Oh," he said, remembering. He put aside the book and stood, coming to her. "You trust me to stretch you out a little?"

"Of course." Her expression was open, accepting, and undoubting. Something inside Echo warmed in that moment.

"All right, then. I'm assuming you've got nothing on but that robe?"

"Um," she flushed, "yeah. Why?"

"'Cause if you had on full pajamas, I'd do this stretch differently. But we'll do it so it preserves your privacy. Give me your hands, and bend over from the waist...easy, easy...bend your knees a little, lean your butt up against the door frame, and put your weight on it. Good. Now try to just relax, and let your body hang from your hips on the bottom, and your hands in mine on the top. I'm going to stretch out that low back. Tell me if it hurts, or gets to be too much. Keep your weight leaning against the door frame. There ya go."

As Omega obeyed his instructions, Echo very gently tugged on her arms, gripping her hands firmly. As her muscles loosened, he slid his hands up until they grasped her wrists, and continued a gentle, assisted stretch.

"Mmm," she said after a few moments.

"Feels good?"

"Yeah. But boy, is it tight."

"Where?"

"Shoulders, at the moment. Like, through the shoulder blades. Across 'em, kinda."

"Okay, let's ease you back up and we'll do something about that."

Echo helped her stand upright once more; he didn't want her stressing that low back until he'd gotten her muscles more relaxed. Then he showed her how to bring one arm close across her chest and hold it, stretching the upper back and shoulder, one side at a time.

"How's the rotator cuffs after what you were calling your helicopter mode?" he wondered.

"Decent," Omega noted. "So far, they're not complaining."

"Good. The work we've been doing in the gym must have 'em in good shape."

"I'd have thought my back would be in better shape."

"Well, your back took a pounding from the landing, for one; your skates hit the ice awfully damn hard, baby. India and I could both see the ice chips fly from the blades, all the way from the café. Plus, it wasn't like you had a chance to mentally prepare for it, or plan, or much of anything, really."

"Yeah. Thanks for calling out a good maneuver—I'd drawn a complete blank, and there were only a couple of phrases going through my mind."

"I'll bet one of 'em was, 'Dammit.'"

"It was! Another one was, 'Don't hurt the kid don't hurt the kid don't hurt the kid.'"

"Interspersed with, 'Oh shit'?" Echo grinned. Omega laughed.

"Boy, do you know me! Pretty much, yeah. The litany really went, 'Oh shit! Don't hurt the kid don't hurt the kid don't hurt the kid! Dammit! Oh shit!' Over and over...until I cleared the kid. Then it was just, 'Oh shit oh shit oh shit!' until I heard you call."

"And after that?"

"I knew what to do, then. I started concentrating on getting into that position to land."

"Good. It's amazing how much the world slows down when crap happens, isn't it?"

"Amen to that one," Omega vouched.

* * *

Echo ensured his partner was thoroughly but gently stretched out, then he gave her a pain reliever and muscle relaxer that the medlab kept available for Agents' use—and which consequently always resided in his bathroom's medicine cabinet—and sent her straight off to an early bed.

The next morning, he slipped into her bedroom—she had given him permission to do so, the night before—and gently woke her, helping her out of bed, dismayed to see how stiff she was in despite of the previous night's prep. He promptly sent her into the bathroom for a long, hot shower.

While she was in the shower, Echo called Fox.

"...So yeah, I'm afraid if we push it today, we could end up injuring her bad enough to take her off duty for weeks, instead of only a day or two."

"Fair enough," Fox replied. "I see nothing of immediate importance that I'd need Alpha Line for, anyway, especially given that we already have Alpha Four and Six off on assignment, and Alpha Five has gone back to Geneva for some wind-up kinds of things on those last few cases they worked before joining your department. So if something comes up, I'll use

Alpha Two. I'd much rather have you and Omega both available when the Lambda Andromedan contingent arrives, frankly."

"You think that Four, Five, and Six will get back in time for that?"

"Knowing those assignments, I doubt it—running security for the renewed negotiations between the Caltorians and the Ulyffon Alliance? There's no telling when they'll get back to Headquarters! And the main case that Five went back for was that rogue K'hardugsin. And you know how difficult the K'hardugsin law enforcement can be."

"Yeah, good points, and I knew all that—I approved the assignments, after all. I'm afraid I'm not awake enough to be thinkin'. Like Romeo sometimes says, I can't brain yet. Especially before my morning caffeine."

"Not to worry, old friend, about any of it—I'm not out of my quarters yet this morning, either. Anyway, it'll probably just be Alpha One and Two for the Lambda Andromedan security. But that's all right; the four of you should be plenty, given you're the two most experienced teams in the department, relatively speaking. So let's get Omega patched while we can."

"All right. We're available for major emergencies, of course, Fox, but..."

"No, no, I totally understand, Echo. Shit happens. Take care of your partner. That's why we assign newbies to experienced Agents. Have you taken her to the medlab? Are you putting Omega on sick leave?"

"No, I thought we'd do 'office' type work today. You keep wanting me to do that shit, so today, you got it."

"Good man. And the medlab?"

"I think I can handle it without taking her to Zebra. But if things look to be more serious than I think they are right now, I'll get Meg to the medlab straight off."

"All right, alter khaver. Keep me posted if anything changes."

"As always."

* * *

The hot shower was succeeded by another stretching session, and a good breakfast, heavy on the protein, for recovery. Then Echo took Omega to the gym, where their workout that day consisted of cardio and very light weights, mostly intended to warm and limber the muscles.

But when Omega stilll showed signs of difficulty in her low back, Echo shook his head.

"Go back to the locker room and shower, baby, then head for the massage room. I'm gonna see about getting you some therapy on that back, before you tear something. And if that doesn't work, we're going to the medlab."

"Um..." Omega turned a bit pink, looking sheepish.

"What?"

"I, uh, I've never had a massage before. What...?"

"Oh," Echo said, comprehending: Omega was confused about how she should prepare for a massage. "Take a hot shower to keep as loose as you can, then dry off. Wrap the towel around you, and go into the massage room—there's a labeled door into it, opening off the men's and women's locker rooms. It'll be locked if it's occupied, but I don't think it is, right now. Knock, just to make sure, though. Ditch the towel and lie face down on the table; your face goes in the little padded ring, and the bolster goes under your ankles. Pull the sheet over you, and wait for the massage therapist to come in and work on you."

"Just the sheet? But I'll be..." The pink in Omega's cheeks turned darker. "You know."

"Nobody's gonna see anything," Echo explained. "That's what the sheet is for. It keeps you warm, but it also covers up everything that's not being worked on."

"Do I gotta...?"

"Well, I can take you to the medlab, but there's a good chance that Zebra will just prescribe massage therapy anyway, if there's nothing serious wrong." Echo paused, mildly concerned. "What's the matter, baby? Most people like getting massages."

"It...I'm...embarrassed," she admitted to him, staring at the floor. "And annoyed with myself 'cause I'm hurt and have to stand down for the day. I'd much rather be useful than sit around on sick leave. Not to mention, I know you prefer to be active, and this kinda throws a monkey wrench in everything."

"No, you're not on sick leave, though if we have to go to the medlab, you might be," Echo explained. "India and Romeo are gonna handle the field work today, and you and I are gonna play department chief and assistant, and do administrative stuff, which needs doing anyhow. I thought, once we got done here, we'd spend the day looking over the Alpha Line applications and weeding through 'em, maybe talk over some of those testing and training ideas you've been coming up with. Besides, I'm thinking we need to start icing that back, and this way, I can see that you do it properly—you tend to get that absent-minded scientist thing goin' when you start working on something, and then you forget to put the ice on regularly."

"Oh. Okay. Will...I mean, so it feels good?"

"Most people like it, yeah. Deep tissue massage can be a little painful at times, and at least some of this might be, 'cause it looks like you've kinked yourself up but good, but it'll feel better after."

"All right," Omega sighed. "Let's try this, I guess."

"There's my pal."

* * *

Omega followed instructions, taking a nice hot shower and letting the spray hit her back, before drying off and slipping into the massage room. No one else was there, to her relief, and she quickly crawled onto the massage table and pulled the sheet up to her neck, before settling down on her belly, hooking her feet over the bolster, and resting her face in the padded ring. Then she tried to relax, listening to the soothing electronica music that wafted from hidden speakers, floating through soft, lavender-scented air.

After a few moments, she sighed, and she felt her body sag into the padded table—at least, as much as her tight back would let her.

A couple of minutes later, the other door opened quietly, and Omega sensed another human enter the room. Soft footsteps made their way around the room, pausing as the sounds of both doors being locked reached Omega's ears, before those same footsteps moved to the side of the table. Two hands came to rest on her sheet-draped shoulders for a long moment, soothing. They patted gently, then squeezed lightly.

"Um," Omega murmured, "did Echo tell you that I, um, I'm a rookie at this?"

"Mm-hm," came a soft, male reply. The hands patted again.

"Okay. I, uh, I'm a little ticklish, but right now my back hurts enough that I don't think you COULD tickle me..."

This time the hands squeezed again, very very lightly, before the sheet was tugged down from her shoulders and folded just below her hipbones. The hands tucked the edges of the sheet firmly under her body and thighs, then positioned rolled hand towels along her sides, immediately under her armpits; Omega was grateful, because it meant there was much less chance she would inadvertently flash the therapist with her breasts, simply by shifting position.

The hands left her skin briefly, and she heard a slight gurgling sound over the soft music. Seconds later, the hands were spreading warmed oil across her back, ensuring her skin was well lubricated. Hand-over-hand strokes worked from her right side at the hip, up to her shoulder, before the therapist switched sides and repeated the process. Then he came to stand at her head, sliding his hands down the length of her back several times, pressing in with the heels of his hands, and she stared down at well-groomed bare feet encased in black sandals.

Everything here is black, she thought with a hidden grin. *If we wear it, it's black. Or white,* she amended, thinking of her shirts. *Then again, it's kind of almost urban camo, the way it works, so hey.*

Strong, skilled hands worked deep into her back, easing the muscular tension there and soothing offended muscles. *This really does feel good,* she decided, and Omega found herself relaxing under the therapist's ministrations.

One thing that flatly refused to relax, however, was her lower back on the right-hand side.

"Mm," the therapist noted, gentle hands probing the area.

"Unh," Omega grunted in discomfort, shifting position a bit in reaction.

"It still hurts, huh, baby?" Echo's voice murmured, and Omega blinked, shocked.

"ECHO?!" she exclaimed. "Are you in here?"

"Of course," he sounded amused.

"How long have you been in here?"

"The whole time, Meg."

"But...but I only heard the therapist come..." She turned her head, then without thinking, started to push up.

"No, no," he said, as a strong male hand splayed itself between her shoulder blades and pushed down. "You need to stay right there unless you intend on giving me a really good look at, um, your assets. I planned this out to try to minimize your embarrassment, and that's a good way to undo all my planning."

"YOU'RE the one who's been working on me?!"

"Yeah," Echo murmured, continuing to gently knead her low back. "Hey, relax here! You got all tensed up again! I figured, as nervous and embarrassed as you were about the whole idea, that maybe having someone you knew and were comfortable with working on you was better than bringing in a stranger. Was I wrong?"

"Uh..." Omega felt her skin heat as she flushed. *Oh man. How do I explain THIS one...?* she thought. *That I wasn't expecting the hands on my naked body to be those of the man I'm crazy about, but that I don't dare tell...?*

"Huh. Judging by the blush all over, I guess I WAS wrong. Sorry. I was just trying to help."

"No, no," Omega offered, thinking fast. "No, you weren't wrong, hon. I just...wasn't expecting it to be you. I had it in my head that this was some, um, I dunno, a detached, disinterested, highly-trained therapist, and..."

"Well, I'm trained well enough," Echo noted, continuing to work on her back. "I took the training after X-ray got himself hurt about eight years ago, so I could help him out when we were away from Headquarters, while he was recuperating. I even helped out on Romeo a little after he busted his leg—the medlab wanted me to help ensure good circulation to speed healing, especially with the meds they were giving him. So—at least as far as the Agency is concerned—I really am a certified massage therapist. But disinterested, I'm not. I'm VERY interested in getting you back to full function. Baby, you got a really badly knotted muscle back here."

"Wow. I had no clue, Echo, about all that training. I didn't even know you COULD get that kinda training here."

"Yeah, you can, and a lot more besides. How do you think I got my degrees?" he pointed out. "Wasn't like I could just go down to the local university and take classes. In fact, I keep meaning to let you know—there's been some requests outta Division One University for you to teach an astronomy course."

"Really?"

"Yeah."

"Sounds like fun."

"Okay, I'll pass it on. How's this?"

"Unh. Dammit. It hurts enough for twelve people—ow! Stop poking it! What are you doing?"

"All right, that tells me what's going on in there. Lie flat, try your best to relax, and breathe through it," Echo instructed. "I'm pretty sure I can work this out, but you need to trust me and let me work, and not tense up even if it hurts some."

"Okay, I'll try. What are you gonna do?"

"Usually a knotted muscle is basically just a chronic, low-grade spasm or cramp. There's places in a muscle kinda like a trigger point where, if I can apply pressure long enough, the muscle reflexively relaxes. I'm gonna try and do that. But it's gonna hurt before it feels better. Do you know what I mean when I say to breathe through it?"

"Yeah, I get it."

"Nice and slow and deep. I'll apply pressure during your inhale, and hold it during your exhale. Keep it steady."

"I'll do my best."

"I know, baby. Just hang on. If this doesn't do it, I'll be surprised. I'll also be taking you to see Zebra."

"All right..."

Omega relaxed as best she could, and as Echo's strong fingers pressed into the flesh of her back, she took a slow, deep breath, trying not to grunt in pain, and let it out again, just as slowly. As she inhaled, he increased the pressure slightly; as she exhaled, he held it. Then they repeated the process. They kept this up for several more seconds, Echo pressing deeper and deeper with each inhalation, before Omega felt the muscle loosen at last.

"Ohhh," she sighed in relief. "Finally!"

"Amen to that," Echo agreed. "I was starting to get concerned."

"So what happened? What did I do to myself?"

"I'd say you probably hyperextended a little, at least on this side, and royally pissed off the spinal erectors," Echo decided, gently kneading the newly-released area, before sliding his hands firmly up her back and winding up the massage. "Maybe a slight sprain, maybe just a bit of a pulled muscle. We'll ice it, off and on today, get plenty of fluids in you—which you should always do after massage therapy, by the way—and you ought to be a lot better by later today. Don't be surprised if you bruise a little in that area, though. I had to apply a LOT of pressure to get it to loosen up. Which is why I'm ending this now; if I do much more, you're gonna be too sore to move, just from the massage."

"I gotcha," Omega murmured. Echo pulled the sheet back over her.

"Okay, I'm gonna leave and go back into the men's locker room, and put on my Suit," he told her. "You lie there for a few minutes and just unlax. Don't go to sleep, though! I don't want to have to come back in here looking for you, let alone have you roll off the table in your sleep—it'd mess you up, all over again! And when you do get up, go slow. You'll be surprised how disoriented you'll be."

"All right," Omega agreed, and listened as his footsteps retreated. The door opened and closed, and he was gone.

She took a deep breath and let it out in a long, discouraged sigh.

* * *

The day was generally quiet, and even Alpha Two only performed some routine patrols. Alpha One, however, got a good bit of paperwork done, identifying and prioritizing a slate of in-house candidates for departmental membership, and updated the Alpha Line training protocols as well.

Roughly every hour to hour and a half, Echo rose and fetched a chemical cold pack from a kit which he'd deposited earlier, in the corner of the meeting room which had been assigned to Alpha Line agents, next to his desk. He would put it on his partner's back under her Suit jacket, then set an alarm on his wrist chronometer for fifteen minutes at a go. He also ensured she got up and moved around the room after removing the cold pack each time. He refused most of her requests to go get coffee, fetching bottled water for her instead.

"Trust me, baby," he told her, after her fourth trip to the ladies' room. "You will feel much better later for the water I'm pushing in you now."

And by the time they got off shift, she had to admit, she did.

* * *

When a much-improved Alpha One cut through the Core the next day on their way to check on the Alpha Line assignment listings in the department's specially-assigned room off the Core, the lights between the floor tiles around them turned deep red, flashing in the *urgent* signal.

"Fox wants us," Omega noted, spotting it. "Like, five minutes ago."

"Yup. Let's go," Echo agreed, veering off toward the ramp to the Director's Office.

* * *

"Come in and have a seat, both of you," Fox said as they came through the door. "Echo, you're a department chief now; sooner or later, you have GOT to set up in that corner office I made for you in the Alpha Line room, and establish some regular office hours, so I know when I can reach you. I liked knowing where I could find you, yesterday."

"Make it a lot later than sooner, Fox," Echo said, shaking his head. "No offense, but I didn't take the position to sit all day in an office. And you know you can always reach me—or Meg—on our cells, wherever and whenever."

"I know; it would just be simpler to be able to walk across the Core, sometimes. Not to mention give me a chance to stretch my legs once in a while. Anyway, I have something I need you to do, and I figured either Alpha One or Alpha Two should get the follow-up. And since Alpha Two is already on assignment and they filled in for you yesterday, and since Omega was part of the discovery, Alpha One gets the job."

"Sure, Fox. What's up?" Echo tossed off, as Omega's eyes widened.

"Um, Fox," she suggested, "maybe you might wanna give one of the other Alpha Line Agents a call, send 'em in with me instead of Echo..."

"What the hell?" Echo grumbled, turning to his partner with a scowl. "You tryin' to ditch me, Meg?"

"No, tryin' to protect you, Ace," Omega murmured, meeting his annoyed brown gaze with a worried blue one. "If I correctly read Fox's statements just now, I don't think you're gonna like this one at all."

* * *

"I expect you did read me correctly, Omega," Fox agreed. "As to whether or not he likes the assignment, it doesn't really matter. Echo is an experienced Agent. He knows how this works."

"Damn straight," Echo declared, still irked. "I doubt there's anywhere you can go, Meg, that I can't deal with—and go right in alongside you."

* * *

"Ladies' room?" she tried, pert.

"Try me," he declared, leaning forward slightly and raising an eyebrow.

"Not if I have to GO," she protested. He folded his arms, staring down at her.

"I repeat—try me," he said.

"Good," Fox said, as Omega threw up her hands. "Very good. Then you certainly won't mind going back to the toy store with her to follow up."

* * *

"No, I—what?" Echo did a double-take.

"Told ya," Omega murmured. "You aren't gonna like it. At. All."

"That's as may be," Fox noted, overhearing the soft aside, "but it's necessary all the same. Echo, I want Omega to take you and go back to the toy store where she and Romeo first found the *Black Suits* toys. I want Alpha Line's most experienced Agent having a look-see. It seems to be the focal point for the marketing push here in New York City, and I want to stay on the lookout for any new toy styles. In particular, I want you two to keep an eye out for an action figure based on Omega, since hers evidently hasn't come out yet. That speaks to me of a second wave marketing release. Now, that could be waiting for a film release, which we think is coming—I'm trying to get a line on that—but it isn't gonna hurt to keep a watch on things.

Hopefully, we'll be able to scotch it before it happens, but barring that, we'll need to put our own spin on it, so we need as much intel as possible."

"Shit, Fox—"

"Echo," Fox interrupted the senior agent, "did you or did you not just finish telling your partner that you could handle going anywhere she could go?"

"I did, but damn, boss!"

"Are you telling me that the chief of Alpha Line is afraid of some children?" Fox raised an eyebrow.

"Hell no! I'm not AFRAID of 'em. I just...don't like...I'm not used to..." Echo tried to figure out how to explain.

"Then get used to it, old friend," Fox said, as the other eyebrow joined the first. "I may not have kids of my own, but I had plenty of nieces and nephews for the experience, back in the day before the world went temporarily insane. I swear to you, they don't generally bite. At least, once they're past a certain age."

* * *

"'Generally,' Fox?" Echo said, a hint of bitterness in his tone.

"Generally," Fox repeated, expression bland. He met Omega's gaze, and the hazel eyes of the Director twinkled at her...and her alone; his face was averted such that Echo could not see the look in his eyes. Her own eyebrows shot up in surprise as she grasped his unspoken message.

Waitaminit. Fox WANTS to throw Echo into the deep end of the pool? Why the hell would he do that? Is there something going on I don't know about, or is he just determined to make sure Echo's ready for anything, next time some alien kid gets lost? What gives, anyway?

She happened to be looking right at Fox as she considered this, and the hazel eyes twinkled even more, as he watched her process the information. But the Director of the Division One Agency gave away nothing to his junior field agent.

Oookay, she thought, mildly frustrated. *No hints on this one. I guess I'll find out whenever the time is right.*

"Omega?" Fox said then, interrupting her train of thought. "From the various reports I've gotten, you deal with children quite well. Can you take your partner in hand on this assignment?"

"I, uh, I'll try to, sir," she murmured.

"Good."

"Um, sir, do you want us to do this undercover?"

"I don't think that will be necessary, Omega." Fox glanced at the chronometer on the wall. "All right, you just came on duty for this shift. Take your time preparing, but I expect a report on my screen not later than second lunch today. That gives you ten hours, and the store opens in one. Alpha One is dismissed."

* * *

"Don't we need disguises or something?" Echo wondered as they approached the front of the toy store on Fifth Avenue.

"As long as we show up in our Suits, they're gonna think we're *Black Suits*, whether we actually look like the toys or not," Omega told him. "But we weren't given permission to do otherwise, so we'll have to fudge it. Look, Echo, it's like Fox pointed out, I don't have an action figure yet—I mean, that we've seen yet—but they were still crawling all over me every bit as much as they were Romeo."

"Shit. So that's why you kept asking about undercover, even after Fox dismissed us."

"Yeah. And why I tried to get you out of it, Ace," she murmured, reminding him. "I'm sorry it didn't work. And I would never just ditch you, unless I was seriously protecting you from something. Next time, try to remember that I might have a legitimate reason for doing a thing like that, an' work with me, please."

Echo sighed, grasping that she was right. His shoulders slumped for a moment, and he manned up to do the right thing by his partner and buddy.

"I know, and I'm sorry, Meg," he apologized. "You WERE trying to get me out of it, and I appreciate that now. In several senses of the word," he added. "The truth is, it stung to think you were trying to get rid of me, so I fought it. It was my own damn ego that marched me right into this, even over all your efforts to get me off the hook." He paused, squaring his shoulders, steeling himself for an onslaught of children, then gestured at the door. "Well, let's get going. The sooner we start, the sooner it's over and done." He held the door for his partner, as befitted a proper Southern gentleman for a proper Southern lady, and they entered the store.

* * *

The display, as Omega already knew and Echo soon found out, was near the center of the store, toward the front. But as soon as they entered the store, the customers spotted them. The first kids arrived at their sides before they could even reach the display...even escorted to it by grinning store employees, as it turned out.

Oh, that is so not good, Omega thought, remembering what happened two days before, when she'd been there with Romeo and they'd been mobbed. *Echo will NOT take well to THAT. He doesn't have the same personality or liking for kids that Romeo's got. It's only a matter of time before Romeo and India decide to have a few, I expect. Which is gonna complicate life in Alpha Line.* She shook her head. *Focus, girl. You gotta figure out how to get Echo through this.*

Little hands reached up for Omega's, and instinctively she picked up the smallest child, hefting the little boy to her hip, before taking several more tiny hands in her free hand and leading them toward the display. She shot a glance at her partner, to find that he already had a child holding each hand, a third riding his left foot with every step, and a fourth holding his right leg.

But to her surprise, Echo was...grinning. The child on his left foot was a little too heavy for him to readily walk, so he assumed what Omega considered something of an Igor-shuffle, dragging that foot—and the child riding it—along as he went, without so much as a word of complaint. She took a closer look at the little boy, and discovered that he was handicapped when she spotted the brace he had on one leg.

Just then, Echo reached down and picked the boy up, swinging the child up to his broad shoulders.

"There you go," he murmured to the child. "Is that a little better?"

"Yes sir," piped the lad, who suddenly hugged Echo hard around the neck; the male Agent turned red-faced from nigh-asphyxiation. "I'm way up high now! Thank you, Agent Five!"

"You're welcome, son," Echo replied, moving forward again.

* * *

About the time Echo had gotten the boy with the brace settled on his shoulders, caught his breath after nearly having it hugged out of him, and started on after Omega, who had paused and looked back to see what had become of him, the Agent felt a light touch on his thigh. Glancing down to see what it was, Echo froze, stunned.

Looking up at him was a shy little girl. She MIGHT have been all of five years old, if that. She had white-blonde hair in two short little braided pigtails, a wide—if somewhat timid—smile, and the biggest, brightest blue eyes he had ever seen...

...Since Meg last looked at me, he thought absently, transfixed by the adoring gaze of the small child. *It could be...it's exactly how I would have pictured her at that age. Damn. This kid's adorable, too.*

Without another moment's thought, let alone having fully processed the ones he'd just had, Echo scooped up the moppet in his right arm, perching her on his hip, as he looked up to locate his partner and continue the last few feet to the huge toy display.

* * *

Omega watched in astonishment, both platinum-blonde eyebrows ascending as high as they would go, as, with one child already perched across his shoulders, Echo lifted another into his arms, resting the second child on his hip. More children stepped in, holding his free hand and hugging both legs, but to her surprise, he didn't seem to notice—or mind—as he murmured something to the little girl, and listened as both the girl and the boy responded.

The girl whispered something in his ear, and Echo nodded. She whispered something else, and the Agent nodded again, then bobbed his head in Omega's direction. The girl looked up, saw Omega, and giggled, then whispered again in Echo's ear. The boy on his shoulders evidently heard and agreed, because he wiggled and bounced, nodding enthusiastically;

Echo freed his left hand quickly, putting it up to steady the lad, before reaching back down for the hands he'd had to drop to do so.

I...have absolutely nothing to do, to achieve whatever private agenda Fox had in mind for Echo, Omega decided, watching in amazement. *I didn't think he liked kids, or at least considered himself too tough for 'em. But THAT sure doesn't look like it. Maybe he's just not used to 'em. After all, he was barely more than a kid himself when he got drafted into the Agency, and it ain't like there's a lotta children running around Headquarters, most of the time. But I'll say one thing: The last time I saw anything that cute, Echo was getting hugged by an alien toddler.*

Just then, Echo made it to where Omega stood, surrounded by her own contingent of admiring small humans, and he looked at her and grinned.

"Meg, I got some folks I'd like you to meet, here. This little lady," he introduced the child in his arms, "is Amie, and this young stalwart," he indicated the boy on his back, "is Randy. Down here," he managed to wave the hand under Amie at the children clustered around him, "are Pete, Mike, Janet, and Andy. Kids, meet my friend Meg."

"Hi, Meg!" said the two tykes Echo was carrying, immediately followed by a chorus of the same from about his knee-level. She grinned.

"Found some new friends, huh, Ace?"

"Looks like it. I already told 'em to stay outta my pockets, that it wasn't nice to go poking around in other peoples' stuff, and they're all behaving." He eyed the children around Omega. "You hear that, kids? Let Meg's pockets alone, too. Her things are her own, and they aren't toys."

"Yes, Mr. Agent Five," came the Greek chorus of tiny voices again. Amie tucked her face into Echo's neck, snuggling in—not unlike a certain alien toddler, Omega observed. But this time, Echo seemed okay with it. *Or maybe just more used to it,* she considered.

"You actually look like you're having fun," she decided.

"Well...this wasn't so bad, after all," he concluded. "They're kinda cute."

"I dunno how come, but there don't seem to be as many here today," Omega said, looking around...

...Just as an announcement came over the store's loudspeaker.

"LADIES AND GENTLEMEN, CHILDREN OF ALL AGES! THE *BLACK SUITS* HAVE ARRIVED FOR THEIR PROMOTIONAL TOUR! FOR ALL YOU LITTLE ALIENS OUT THERE, YOUR FAVORITE ACTION FIGURES ARE HERE IN THE FLESH! COME TO THE TOY DISPLAY IN THE CENTER OF THE STORE AND GET UN-MEMORIZED BY YOUR VERY OWN *BLACK SUIT*!"

"Uh-oh," Omega murmured, glancing around, as children and parents seemed to emerge out of the woodwork, descending on the suddenly-besieged Agents at speed. "THAT'S how come—they didn't know we were here!"

Seconds later, they were surrounded, and kids were starting to try to climb the couple, as well as the display beside them. Echo AND Omega had hard work to keep inquisitive hands off weapons and more.

"Well...SHIT," Echo said, with feeling.

"Mistaw Agent Five!" little Amie hissed, shocked. "You said a BAD WORD!"

Omega hid a snort in her hand, and Echo flushed, looking chagrined.

* * *

Within moments, a cascade of packaged toys nearly buried Omega and several children beneath it, when one small herd of kids tried to climb over the display to get to the '*Black Suits*.' But when several unruly children tried to climb straight up Echo's back—using his weapons, hidden beneath his jacket in the small of his back and under both arms, as foot-and hand-holds—THEN grab Randy's leg brace and try to pull the boy off Echo's shoulders to take his place, the Agents had had enough.

Echo set Amie on her feet on the floor, with whispered instructions to run to her parents, then he swept Randy down and gave him the same instructions, patting them gently on their backs as he sent them off, running through the crowd. Omega quickly divested her arms of clinging children as well, as Echo fairly raked the rest from his long, muscular form. Then he turned to Omega.

"Run!" he exclaimed, pointing down an aisle.

Omega spun and ran like the wind, dodging and leaping around thronging kids, as Echo turned the other way and mimicked her performance.

With squeals and shrieks of delight, hordes of children joined the imaginary chase, streaming after them, parents right behind.

* * *

Omega, having already learned that the safe zone was in the storage area in the back, headed straight there, bursting through the door marked EMPLOYEES ONLY with no hesitation. Several children tried to follow her through, but their parents saw the sign and grabbed them before they could get past the threshold.

In the storage area, several employees looked up to see who had just barged in, then grinned when they saw the female Agent.

"Hey, you're back," one of them said. "I remember you from the other day! Did they send your husband back with you?"

"No," Omega said, "Joe, wasn't it?"

"Yes, ma'am, that's me!"

"No, Joe, today the Agency sent me back with my best friend. Only problem is, he's not used to kids. And, um," Omega thought fast, "he's a veteran, and, uh, he kinda didn't take it so good when the announcement went out and the kids just came at us like a wave."

"Oh, SHIT!" Joe exclaimed. "Where's the manager? Where's Bob? Jim, run get Bob! We gotta get the other PR guy outta there fast, before he knee-jerks and hurts somebody!"

"Oh, no no no, he's not dangerous," Omega lied through her teeth, because Echo was plenty dangerous if it was necessary for him to BE dangerous, "it isn't PTSD or anything like that. He just kinda—" She shivered despite herself, and it was no act. "Wow. You just had to be there. We had a good-sized group of kids around us, ten or twelve maybe, and we were doing fine. But when that announcement went out, and they came from the four corners? And then knocked part of the display down on top of us?" She shook her head. "Well, I don't mind telling you, we RAN."

"So where is he?" Joe wondered, as Bob, the manager, hurried up alongside Jim.

"I dunno," Omega admitted. "He ran in a different direction from me."

"Well, hi there," Bob said with a grin. "They sent you back!"

"Bob," Joe said, "we got a situation. They sent a different guy with her, and..."

Joe took Bob and Jim off to one side to explain the situation. Omega got out her cell phone and tried to contact Echo via text message, but he didn't answer.

* * *

On the floor of the store, Echo had managed to find another display big enough for him to hide behind it, this one in a back corner. Peering around it, he saw another herd of children headed in his general direction, several parents egging them on.

"C'mon, Julie!" one adult said. "We have to find him, so you can get his autograph. If he's going to come to the store, you are surely going to get his autograph!"

"But Mommy, won't it just be a number?"

"That doesn't matter, honey! It's the principle of the thing! No child of mine is going to be overlooked or ignored!"

"Damn straight!" another mother declared. "Terrell, we gonna find that dude! We gonna MAKE him give you an autograph!" Several other parents agreed, and the herd charged onward.

Echo pulled deeper into the shadow of the display as they neared, tucking his head and briefly flipping up his Suit jacket collar to help hide his face and shirt, and the gang of children and parents passed by the rack of toys, failing to notice the cranny behind it which shielded the ninja-like Agent from their sight.

Once they were gone, Echo studied his surroundings, then gave the display behind which he sheltered a careful examination. There was a sturdy aluminum framework underneath it to support the weight of a whole selection of remote-controlled vehicles, and he quickly discovered it was firmly attached to the store shelving in back, and thence to the wall.

All right, he decided, starting to climb it, *if they're gonna hunt me down like a pack of Betelgeusian snorkle-raptors on the prowl, I might as well use the same tactics to escape. Isn't like I can shoot 'em, anyhow. Dammit.*

Within seconds he was at the top of the display, crouched low. Echo was actually more visible there, as he had little to no cover. On the other hand, he was well above the eye level of the kids, and none of the adults appeared to be thinking to look up.

I'm safe here for a few minutes, he thought. *Let's get the lay of the land.* He studied the layout of the shelves, the locations of the cashiers, restrooms, and the various employee doors. Then he started locating the various 'brat packs,' as he had begun thinking of them, and determining movements. *Damn, it's worse than playing a video game. I gotta run the maze just so, and find the right exit, or the little monsters are gonna get me. And where the hell is Meg?*

Just then, his cell phone dinged a loud text alert.

The nearest brat pack heard it and glanced around, trying to follow the sound.

Echo flattened himself on top of the shelf, behind several boxes of doll houses.

* * *

"All right, ma'am," Bob told Omega, "everything's all right. We're gonna go out and sweep the store and rescue your friend, wherever he got himself off to. It'll be fine. You stay here, and we'll be back soon."

"Okay," Omega agreed. "Thank you! I'll keep trying to reach his cell with a text. If I get through to him, where do you want me to tell him to meet you?"

"Tell him to just try to stay put, and we'll find him," Bob said. "With all the kids out there, he won't be hard to find if he does that."

"Oh boy," Omega murmured, as Bob and his chosen extraction team set out to rescue Echo.

* * *

Hidden for the moment, but unable to go any farther until the brat packs shifted position, Echo had the presence of mind to pull out his cell phone, put it on vibrate, and check the text message. *It's Meg,* he thought, reading it.

Ace, where r u? U ok?

He swiped the tip of his index finger across the screen, spelling out a reply.

Hiddn bhind boxes on top of a shelf.
OK but pinned down.
U safe?

He waited several moments, then the device tickled his hand as it vibrated an incoming message alert.

Im fine. In back in storeroom.
Store sending extract team, looking 4 u.
Get down & meet them. Theyll take u 2 me.

Echo peeped around a box and saw a team of employees emerge from a door on the back wall of the store. They moved straight for the *Black Suits* display, where they organized themselves and began a systematic sweep of the store.

All right, that would be them, he thought, looking about himself and sizing up what was around him. *So behind that door has to be where Meg is. I can't let 'em catch me up here, but damn if I'm gonna let 'em find me cowering behind a stack of toys either. On the other hand, if I go back into the herd, it's only a matter of time before someone bumps the wrong button on one of my blasters, or more likely, my Winchester & Tesla. And then SOMEbody is gonna get hurt. If it happens to be my Winchester & Tesla—which, given the way they were climbing on me, is likely—it's apt to be ME that gets hurt. And I like my ass the way it is; I've worked hard enough for these damn glutes.*

He studied the layout of the interconnected shelving for a few more moments.

Aha. There we go. If I follow this aisle down to the end, then take the left bend, I can get in behind 'em, one aisle over from the rear wall, where they came in. If Meg is in the room they came out of, I'll just get her and we'll go out the loading dock or something. Hell, I've had enough of this. Fox can come get his own damn information, and see how he likes it.

Echo started creeping along the top of the shelf, doing his best to keep out of sight behind various boxes and items of inventory, and hoping nobody thought to look up.

* * *

Once she ascertained that Echo was all right and more or less out of harm's way, if in an awkward position apt to make him look crazy if he got caught there, Omega began looking around the storeroom. No one else was in it, the rest of the staff having been recruited by Bob for the extraction team, so she decided to check out the latest shipment of inventory—it should, she considered, prove fairly easy, with no one in the store the wiser.

A couple of quick taps to her cell phone screen activated an app that put paid to the rudimentary security in that part of the store, including the cameras.

Pulling a small lighted device—which she had developed jointly with Madrid, head of the weapons lab—out of a warp pocket, she flipped it on and ran it over the packing tape of the nearest sealed shipping carton; the tape came loose, and she opened the box, looking inside. Coming up with nothing she had not already seen, she closed the box, put the tape back in place on the flaps, and toggled a switch, running the device back over the tape, leaving it sealed once more. Then she moved over to the next carton and repeated the process.

* * *

Echo got to the end of the last aisle, glanced around to be certain no one was watching, then began to ease his way down, one shelf at a time, to the floor.

Okay, I'm this far, he thought, as his feet touched the floor. *Another ten feet to the left, around the end cap of the shelving, then through the door, and I should find Meg. Then we can get the hell outta here.*

He turned...and stopped dead.

Two small moppets faced him.

He was cornered.

Damn, he thought.

* * *

Omega finished going through boxes, and made sure there was no sign she had tampered with them. Then she turned off the security jamming app, stacked several of the boxes into a chair shape, and sat down to wait for her partner.

* * *

"Mistaw Agent Five, are you weaving?" little Amie said softly, holding Randy's hand. "Awen't oo going to teww us goo'bye first?"

Echo blinked, recognizing the little ones he had carried through the store. *Forget escape,* he thought. He went down on one knee in front of these two.

"Are you going to tell anyone else I'm here?" he wondered.

"Oh no sir, Mister Agent Five," Randy declared. "We saw how dey treated you! Dey wasn't very nice! But you are." The boy hobbled forward and reached up to wrap his arms around Echo's neck. The hug this time was much gentler; Echo no longer feared for his larynx.

"'Es," Amie agreed, stepping up for her turn at a hug. "We wuv oo, Mistaw Agent Five."

"Why don't you two call me just..." Echo pondered briefly; finally, with considerable regret, he settled on, "just Five?" *And that way I don't haveta brain-bleach 'em,* he thought.

"All riiiight!" Randy hissed with a huge grin.

"'Es!" Amie averred, smiling. "I wuv oo, Five. Oo be good, okay? Don't say any more bad words!"

"I'll try to do better, Amie," he told her.

"Pinky pwomise?" The little imp held out her finger.

"I dunno if I can do THAT," he grinned. "This *Black Suits* job is kinda hard, ya know. Sometimes a guy has to let off a little steam."

"Oh, I see," the solemn child told the Agent. "Oo gots 'a take care ob awl da bad awiens, wight? An' dey makes oo mad, sometimes. 'Cause dey is bad."

"Right."

"Wike my mommy says, oo gibs dem what for?"

"I do. Every chance I get."

"Oo do dat, den!" Amie grinned, then she and Randy gave the Agent another round of hugs.

"Okay, Five," Randy said, "you go find your friend Meg, an' we'll run 'cross da store an' tell ebrybody you's over dere. Dat way, nobody will fink to look for you here."

They scampered off, hand in hand, and Echo stood, watching them go.

Those kids, he thought in amazement. *For all the world, little Amie has got to be related to Meg some way, even if only distantly. And that Randy... he could've been me, especially if the staph infection in my leg hadn't cleared up properly when I was so little.* He shook his head in wonderment. *I need to keep my eye on those two. We might just have a couple of damn fine Agents in about fifteen or twenty years.*

Finally he turned toward the door marked EMPLOYEES ONLY.

* * *

The door opened abruptly, and Echo came through...alone.

"THERE you are, Ace!" Omega exclaimed, jumping up. "I've been a little concerned."

"The only problem was that I should have followed you," he said, offering her a wry grin and a shrug. "You're not a rookie any more, and I really need to quit treating you like one when it counts. Fox gave YOU the lead on this, because you've been here before. I should have followed it. Instead, from force of habit, I usurped it."

"I...he did?" Omega said blankly. "When did he do that?"

"Yeah, remember what he said about you taking me 'in hand' and coming here? I didn't recognize it either until I realized my notion for us to split up was the wrong idea. Then it hit me in the face like a cream pie. The lead dog got in the way again." He glanced at all the boxes. "You check 'em already?"

"Yup."

"Anything?"

"Lotsa things. There's crap-tons of *Black Suits* toys in 'em. Nothing NEW, though."

"Good girl. I guess I was the diversion on this mission, huh?"

"Hey, Ace, whatever works." She grinned, unaware of how much she looked like a certain tiny tyke with blonde pigtails in that moment, or of the warm reaction it generated in her partner. "You ready to go?"

"Oh HELL yes."

"C'mon, then. The loading dock is this way." She turned toward the exit.

"Lead on, baby. I swear, this time, I am on your ass like the tail on a dog."

Mildly offended at the simile, Omega turned around and gave Echo a cross-eyed, slightly scowling glance at that remark.

"I've definitely heard more complimentary phrases with respect to my posterior," she noted, and he laughed.

"Sorry," he said, seeming a bit sheepish. "You know what I mean."

"Yeah, yeah," she grumbled. "Let's go."

* * *

India had already completed getting ready for work and was channel surfing while waiting for Romeo to finish dressing. The female agent found it amusing...in a vaguely annoying sort of way...that she was always ready before her partner.

And they say women are the fashion plates, she thought with affection. *But Romeo...he's not vain, not really. But he does like to have everything just so. I guess it's the whole military spit-shine thing. And that...takes time. Unfortunately, there's never anything on worth watching this time of day, while I'm waiting.*

She clicked the remote, allowing herself a moment on each channel to evaluate. At least she had control of the remote, for the time being. Romeo channel surfed so fast it made her dizzy sometimes.

Has to be a man thing, she thought with a smile. *Meg has the same complaint when she and Echo watch together.*

*Weather...*click.

*Talk show...*click.

*Infomercial...*click.

*News...*click.

*Another infomercial...*click.

*Cartoon...*click.

Wait a minute...back up. Click.

India watched the program for a few moments, then grabbed a blank flash drive and slammed it into the port, pressing <RECORD>.

"Romeo! Get in here!"

"Hang on a minute, India, I'll—"

"NOW!!"

Romeo ran into the room, no shoes, no socks, shirt unbuttoned, trousers unzipped.

"What?!"

"Look." India pointed at the television.

"Oh, man. This...is...baaad."

"I'm recording it."

"Good. Beep Echo an' Meg. Tell 'em to meet us in Fox's office five minutes after this ends. I'll be good to go in two."

"Gotcha."

* * *

"So there you have it. The *Black Suits* are now a Saturday morning cartoon, in addition to the toys," India finished, as the multimedia recording ended. "And you saw the commercial for the new live-action movie that's in production. These Williamson and Rogers guys look an awful lot like some of our agents." India looked pointedly at Romeo and Echo.

"Except for Echo's age," Fox agreed. "He's at least a good decade or more younger than the actor playing the character based on him, I'd think. Still, it makes me wonder if they might be distantly related or something."

"Good casting," muttered Omega. "With excellent makeup artists."

"Yeah, probably. But we've got a major publicity blitz here. How's the toy containment going, Fox?" India followed up.

"Not as well as I'd hoped," Fox admitted. "Romeo was right—these toys ARE big. The manufacturer is putting them out in massive quantities, so sweeping the stores alone does no good. As soon as we get the stores cleared, more shipments come in."

"I gather this whole thing is NOT coming out of our Los Angeles Office, then?" Echo queried.

"No, it's not," Fox confirmed. "It would be a lot more vague, and the agents a lot less identifiable, if it had. But I did check. And Juliet, the L.A. Office chief, said positively it did not come from them."

"Damn."

"Exactly. The good news is, that office IS going at it from the legal end already," Fox noted. "Trademark and copyright infringement on a concept that came out of 'our' production company, that ostensibly got stuck in something called 'pre-production hell.' Which, I gather, means it was a property that got started, but never made it to film or something. We were smart enough to trademark, not only our own actual items, but all kinds of variants, as being 'prototypes' of one sort or another—the concept we had behind the idea was more or less that of the Agency hiding in plain sight. So we CAN go after this film production, and probably do so successfully, but the legal approach may not work in time to save our secrecy, let alone help with the upcoming diplomatic visit."

"I suppose, in a backhanded sort of way, we should be flattered," Omega considered. "Or at least, Y'ALL should be."

"If you say so, maybe. But it's sure as hell not helping the organization," Echo responded.

"No, it's not," Fox agreed. "And with the Prime Minister arriving so soon, we have got to lock this down."

"Well..." mused Omega, "SOMEBODY has to be 'designing' these. Maybe..." she looked over at Romeo and Echo, and her eyes went wide, then narrowed. A smile slowly spread across her face. "Yeah...oh, yeah!!"

"Uh-oh. You like the sound of that?" Romeo asked, looking at Echo. Echo studied Omega's face, then glanced back at Romeo.

"No."

"What did you just come up with, Omega?" Fox asked.

"Look, guys. We need to track down the source, right?" Omega verified.

"Of course," Echo responded.

"And to do that, we need a foolproof way to get deep into the toy company."

"Yes," Fox agreed.

"How would you two like to be movie stars for a day?" She grinned widely.

"Ooo! I LIKE th' way you think, girl!" Romeo declared.

"Tell me more," Fox noted.

"Shit," was all Echo said.

* * *

"Okay, here's the plan," Omega explained. "Echo and Romeo are Rogers and Williamson respectively, and India and I are PR types, assistants to the stars, as it were. This is a publicity appearance, the stars of the movie and their entourage—we'll probably need some other agents in disguise to act as managers and media and drivers and stuff, Fox—showing up in costume to promote the movie and look at the toy line," Omega explained.

"I REALLY like the way you think," Romeo said, grinning. "Me—a movie star."

"Echo?"

"Mmm."

"No good?"

"No, it might work. I just don't normally do such high-profile activities. I prefer my privacy."

"In this job? I can't imagine why," she teased. He only shrugged, turning to the Director.

"Fox?" Echo asked. "What do you think?"

"I don't know, Echo. It IS awfully high-visibility."

"Hey, if y'all have a better idea, go for it," Omega responded agreeably. "It was just a thought. But 'high-visibility' is our whole problem. I figured we might as well use it."

"You have a point," Echo admitted, and paused to consider. "All right," he finally sighed, "I'm in."

"Fox?" Omega pressed.

"You've had some damn good ideas in the past, Omega. I'll go along with this one, too."

"But what about Echo's age?" India wondered. "He's way too young to pass as that actor, isn't he? That Rogers guy?"

"And in my opinion, he doesn't quite look his real age, anyway. It's more his bearing that comes across as older due to his experience, I think." Fox shrugged, with a wry grin. "Especially after so many years hanging out with alter trombeniks like me. Don't worry, though. I have something that'll take care of that, as well," he declared, enigmatic. "Give me some time to arrange the logistics. I'll line up the 'media,' like Omega recommends. And I'll check to make sure the real Hollywood types aren't actually doing it. It would be awkward if both groups were to show up simultaneously."

"Good point," Omega acknowledged, grinning with mischief. "But it WOULD be interesting..."

* * *

"Meg? What's taking so long?" Echo knocked on her closed bedroom door in some annoyance. "If I've got to do this, let's go ahead and get it over and done with."

"Be patient, Echo," Omega's voice filtered through the door. "India and I decided we needed to look the part as much as you and Romeo, so that means a few extra steps getting ready today. Come on in. I'm just finishing my makeup."

"I didn't know you wore makeup," he said as he opened the door.

"Normally, I don't wear much. Today, it's one of those extra steps," she said, deftly applying lipstick with a brush in the bathroom mirror. She finished and stepped out into his full view. "There. What do you think?"

He blinked in surprise as he got a good look at his partner. She wore her usual black Suit jacket and black tie, but instead of Suit trousers and menswear shoes, she wore a black miniskirt and stiletto-heeled black patent pumps, which showcased her long legs and placed her gaze only a couple of inches below his own eye level. Her white shirt was buttery-soft silk, the necktie worn loosely looped like a scarf, the collar open to expose a considerable hint of decolleté. Her platinum blonde mane—usually French-braided and often wrapped into an updo and out of the way—today was down, loose and full, swept back from the right temple, but draping provocatively across her left cheek. Her pale face was flawless, the makeup subtle, with softly pouting mouth and riveting, smoky eyes. Echo looked her over slowly from head to toe, his dark eyes tending to linger for the briefest of moments on the full red lips, then he nodded silently.

"May I take it I clean up nicely?" Omega asked with a smile as she watched his inspection.

"You'll...do." Echo kept his expression carefully neutral; he didn't want to offend her with an accidentally-inappropriate remark. He hadn't handled things well with her at the toy store, and he knew it. He also knew she had been mildly irked by his comments, and he hoped to avoid a repeat performance. *After all,* he considered, *I LIKE getting along with my best pal. I just probably better not tell her how easy on the eyes I think she is. Especially right now. Whoa.*

"Wow. Thanks so much for the enthusiasm." Her smile vanished. Her expression fell and her face closed. He blinked, startled by her reaction.

Well, shit, he thought in dismay. *Back in the doghouse. I thought she was offended by the 'tail on a dog' remark the other day, but today she was...fishing for a compliment? Maybe the other day she was offended by... aw shit. Did she seriously think I was comparing her to a dog...? Surely not. She can look in the mirror and tell otherwise...can't she? Or is it more that SHE thinks that* I *think she looks like a dog...?*

A knock came at the door just then, interrupting his musings.

"Come in!" Omega called, as she walked into the living area. Echo slowly followed her, still observing the transformation and puzzling over what he should have said...and why.

India entered the apartment first, attired similarly to Omega, and just as knock-'em-dead in an auburn wig and green contact lenses to make her less recognizable. Romeo followed, watching India with appreciation, and when he got a full view of Omega as well, he gave her a long wolf whistle.

"Pretty lady, you are tooo fine," he declared.

"At last," Omega grinned at India, "a man who APPRECIATES a woman's efforts." She deliberately ignored Echo.

India grinned back, and together they leaned over and kissed Romeo, one on each cheek. Echo watched with tight face and folded arms—along with a distinct sense of annoyance and a certain amount of determination—as Romeo suavely offered each woman an arm.

"Ladies? Shall we?"

They laughed and took his arms.

"'Mr. Williamson,' I'd be delighted," Omega responded. "Are you ready? Y'all HAVE done your homework, right? The videos, interviews, and stuff?"

Echo just stared at her in disbelief.

You have to ask? he telegraphed, using their secret codes.

Omega met his gaze then, and quickly cut her eyes sideways, toward Romeo. Only Echo saw the surreptitious communiqué, and he blinked once in acknowledgment.

Aha. It isn't me she's worried about; she trusts me to know my stuff. It's Romeo getting off on the attention and getting cocky as a result that she's worried about. She's just being diplomatic and addressing both of us.

"You know it, lady. Williamson is one cool dude, 'cordin' to his dossier," Romeo replied, confident. "I'm down with it."

"All right then! 'Mr. Rogers,' are YOU...ready?" Omega asked meaningfully.

"Yes," Echo said, brusque.

"Then let's go do it!"

Chapter 3

The wintry wind howled between the buildings, swirling snow about, as the Agent 'chauffeur' opened the rear door of the limousine to let Omega and Echo out. Five minutes before they'd arrived, Echo had activated the device Fox had provided: a solid holographic projection disguise, only recently miniaturized small enough to use as personal camouflage. It instantly created the illusion that Echo was the spitting image of the actor Rogers, despite the decade or so age difference—which Omega had explained as probably due to casting an actor that looked as much as possible like Echo, regardless of relative ages. "Which," she had pointed out, "can be modified, at least to a point, with makeup."

Behind them, in another limousine, Romeo and India repeated the scenario, while other agent 'media' swarmed around them.

"Ohh," Omega moaned under her breath, just as a strong, frigid blast swirled around them, flapping the tails of their overcoats about their legs. "I'll be glad when this is over so I can crawl back into my nice wool trousers. There is a NASTY wind chill out here. I think my legs are turning blue."

Echo glanced down to survey those shapely extremities.

"They look just fine to me," he noted.

"Yeah, well..." Abruptly she did a double-take, wondering if that had been a compliment, and scrutinized Echo intently. But Echo's attention was already elsewhere, playing to the faux media. "...At least it isn't Antarctica," Omega finished, slightly bemused.

A small crowd was beginning to gather around the entrance to the toy company as Romeo and India maneuvered their way up to Echo and Omega.

"Let's get this show on the road," Echo said, and they made their way to the main entrance, with the help of Agent 'security.' Inside, they were met by a vice-president from the toy company, who had apparently been hastily summoned, judging by how he was still in process of adjusting his tie and suit coat.

"Mr. Rogers! Mr. Williamson! My name is Browning," he gushed, shaking their hands warmly, "what an unexpected honor! We're so glad to have you visit us..."

"Unexpected?" Omega was brusque, crisp and efficient. Consequently, her normal Southern accent was damped down almost to nonexistence. "Publicity was supposed to have this set up weeks ago. Do you mean to tell me no one notified you that we were coming?"

"No...no...I'm afraid there must have been some miscommunication..."

"Barbara," Omega turned to India as she spoke, "make a note to inform Stephen of this, would you? This just will not do. It's the third time! If this is the way that firm handles things, we need a different publicity company." India nodded, pulling and activating her tablet and making annotations on it. Omega turned to Echo. "Mr. Rogers?"

Echo shrugged and looked at Romeo, who nodded.

"We're here. Might as well keep goin', I guess," the younger Agent said.

"Agreed," Echo said, letting his natural Texas accent flow all over the lone word.

Omega turned back to the vice-president.

"Then let's get on with the tour," she said.

* * *

As the tour progressed and word spread through the company, more and more people joined the entourage—managers, designers, creative consultants, and more—all intent on getting as close to the 'stars' as possible. The Agents were growing increasingly uncomfortable—except for Romeo, who was eating it up. But when an actual, real-world reporter approached Echo, mini-recorder in hand, the limit was reached; how she had gotten through the invisible perimeter the other agents had set, Omega had no idea.

"Mr. Rogers, may I...?" the reporter began.

"Maybe later, at the press conference," a terse Echo responded, cutting her off, and looked over the woman's head at Omega. Their eyes met, and she understood.

That's a 'get me the hell outta here' look if ever I saw one, and from Echo, no less, she realized. *Time to extract. At least from that reporter.*

Already working her way toward Echo, she whipped out her cell phone, activated it, and said, "Hello?"

"...Fox here, Omega."

"What's that? Oh, yes, Stephen. Of course. Yes, yes, I'll tell Mr. Rogers right away."

"Omega, what—" Fox's voice cut off as Omega closed the cell connection.

"Mr. Rogers? Excuse me." Omega worked her way through the small crowd that surrounded her partner and took his arm. "Excuse me, please. I have a message from Stephen..." She skillfully extracted him from the small group and drew him off to one side, watching his face relax marginally.

* * *

In his office back at Headquarters, Fox laid the phone down on his desk, staring at it in puzzlement.

"Oy! What the hell was THAT about?" he wondered. "And who the blazes is Stephen?"

Then he glanced at his wrist chronometer and realized where Omega and her partner likely were.

"Ah! That must be it," he decided. "She needed a diversion, and the phone must have automatically routed to the most recent number in the call list." He shook his head, a slight grin on his face. "I'm looking forward to reading THAT mission report..."

He chuckled to himself, then returned to his paperwork.

* * *

"Hang in there," Omega encouraged Echo in a murmur, as they stood in a corner, away from the worst of the circus. "Y'all are doing great. Next stop is Design and Development. We should find out all we wanna know, right there, about who's doing this."

"Good."

"Echo, I know this isn't pleasant. It's even worse than the toy store was. I'm kind of sorry I thought of it. But try to loosen up a little. You're gonna give Mr. Rogers a reputation for...I don't know, disliking interviews or something." She glanced over at Romeo, surrounded by people, and pulled a wry face. "Although I've gotta admit, if the poor man has to put up with THIS sorta...shit...very often, I for one wouldn't blame him if he decided to take up residence in the middle of the Gobi Desert..."

"I'll stick with the Agency," Echo agreed.

"No movie career, huh? All right, I can live with that. Ready to dive back into the fray?"

"Do I have a choice?"

Omega studied Echo, considering. Then, motioning India over, she told him, "Let me see if I can run a little interference. Stay put. I'll be right back."

"I'm not moving from this spot," Echo averred. "Trust me on that."

* * *

After a brief conversation with India, Omega turned back to Echo.

"All right," she said softly, "let's go. Stay behind us, and we'll grab Romeo on the way past." India and Omega pressed forward, ahead of Echo, into the cluster of people, India on the left, Omega to the right.

"Excuse...excuse me...may I have your attention, please? Thank you all very much for coming, but Mr. Rogers and Mr. Williamson are on a tight schedule," India called in an authoritative tone. "We've just been informed they have a plane to catch this evening. We need to finish the tour, but we need to keep it short so they can make it to JFK on time. So if you'd all be so kind..." She pointed at two of the 'media,' who were in fact really agents in disguise. "You...and you. Come with me. The rest of you may go." Slowly the group began to disperse.

"I apologize," Browning said, shaking his head. "Had we known in advance...security..."

"That's all right, Mr. Browning," India told him, as Romeo joined them. "We can handle it. Let's just continue the tour."

"Yes, let's go on, please," Echo agreed, once more laying on the Texan accent with a trowel, while maintaining a high-functioning vocabulary; it made for a fascinating contrast, especially to Romeo's more relaxed, laid-back, almost-but-not-quite-'hood persona and dialect. "Ah'm extremely interested in seein' the design work for the *Black Suit* line. Very... imaginative."

"Of course, of course. Right this way, then, gentlemen...uh, and ladies."

* * *

"And gentlemen, may I present David Harwood, the designer of our *Black Suit* toy line." Browning moved back as Romeo and Echo stepped forward, hands extended.

"Pleased to meet you, Mr. Harwood," Echo murmured politely.

"Quite a toy line you got there," Romeo said.

"Um, thank you...thank you very, uh, much," the toy designer said, appearing—and sounding—rather diffident. He was obviously somewhat overwhelmed by the interest the two 'celebrities' had taken in him and his work.

As Romeo took over questioning the designer, Echo busied himself with a surreptitious, detailed study of the various models and sculptures scattered around the man's work area, under cover of simple and somewhat indifferent curiosity. His eyes widened as he spotted a work in progress: a tall, shapely, athletic woman in a black Suit, platinum blonde hair hanging down her back in a long French braid. The sculpture was in process of modification, however, and had he not known his partner as well as he did, it might not have been recognizable—the face was incomplete. He glanced at the agent designation on the base; it was the Roman numeral XXIV.

Twenty-four, he thought. *Which corresponds to the Greek letter omega. It's her. It's Meg.* Picking it up, he caught Omega's eye, swept his gaze over the figurines, looked down at her image in his hands, and then looked back at her. She blinked an acknowledgment, her own eyes widening.

"Mr. Rogers, don't let me interrupt," she said quietly, motioning the Agency photographer over, "but this is a perfect photo op..." Echo nodded, and turned back to Harwood as the digital camera began to click.

"Very creative work here. Ah'm impressed, son. As one...artist...to another, mind if Ah ask where you got the idea? The inspiration?"

"Well..." suddenly Harwood seemed decidedly uncomfortable as he noticed the sculpture Echo unconsciously fingered lightly in his hands, "...actually, a...a friend of mine...suggested it to me."

"Really? Some of mah best...performances...have come as a result of a friend's idea," Echo remarked, maintaining a straight face while throwing a glance over Harwood's shoulder at Omega. Omega bit her lip and looked away, eyes twinkling. *Gotcha,* he thought with carefully hidden amusement.

"Um, yes. We were talking over dinner one night, and he told me some cockeyed story about a secret galactic government agency that polices aliens, handles UFOs, interstellar diplomacy, interplanetary trade agreements, all that sorta thing—a kind of secret government. The whole urban myth, brought to life. Said some of 'em were even aliens themselves. Sounded like he'd been watching too much of that show on the historical network, if you ask me. But I got to thinking afterward, and decided it would make a really cool toy line, maybe even a cartoon. So I got back with M—" he shot a quick, anxious look at Browning, then continued, "m...my friend, and told him my idea. He thought it was great, promised to help, and started providing me with all these diagrams and sketches. He's a real conspiracy...theorist..." His voice trailed off; Harwood had just gotten a good look at Omega, and his already-shaky composure vanished altogether as, nervous, he glanced back at the figurine Echo still held. He gaped at the agents.

"I guess so," Romeo remarked. "Sure sounds like one."

"Ah was wondering," Echo ventured, "if you'd be willing to sell this one to me when you're finished? Ah'd like it for my study—as a memento, sort of." He gestured with the statue.

"Uh, well," Harwood stammered, "it-it's as f-finished as it's gonna g-get, Mr. Rogers."

"Why? It doesn't even have a face yet."

"That's one t-that we decided not-not to put into p-production. M-my friend told me th-the ag-agent wasn't...wasn't real...was a...a ringer. You-you, uh, y-you can..." he glanced at Browning, who nodded, "um, can h-have it." Omega blinked as Echo caught her eye. He nodded his thanks to Harwood.

"Consider it a little souvenir of the tour," the vice-president added with a smile.

"Well, thank ya, very much, both of ya. Mind telling me who your friend is?" Echo tossed off laconically as he slipped the little icon into his pocket. "L.A.'s always on the lookout for good, creative design teams, and you and your friend sound like you'd fit the bill. George or Rick might have something open..."

Harwood opened his mouth to reply, but Browning stepped in.

"I'm really very sorry, Mr. Rogers," Browning observed, voice firm, "but you're asking about proprietary company information. And David is a valued member of our staff. We'd hate to lose him."

"Oh, okay, no problem. Didn't mean to step on any toes. But David, if you ever change your mind and decide you want to do Tinseltown, look me up, ya hear?"

"Y-yes sir, Mr. R-Rogers. Thank you, sir..."

* * *

Back in the limo at last, Echo and Omega fairly collapsed in the back seat, mentally—though not physically—exhausted.

"That was way the hell much. I wonder if Romeo and India are this beat," Omega wondered with a sigh. Echo glanced out the back window.

"India is, anyway," he observed.

"Well, that's over with. As soon as we get back, I'm heading home and wrapping up in a blanket for an hour or two. I am FREEZING in this little skirt."

"Romeo would probably say you were holding the thermometer upside-down. Here," Echo said, removing his overcoat and draping it across her lap as she blinked in confusion at what sounded like yet another compliment on her appearance—from Echo, no less. As she gratefully snuggled down under his coat, he leaned over the front seat and said, "Charlie, crank up the heat a bit, would you? Meg got kinda bad frostbite on that Antarctic mission this past summer—well, it was winter down there—and I think maybe it's left her a little sensitive to the cold."

"Sure thing, 'Mr. Rogers,' sir!" Charlie grinned at them in the rear view mirror, even as he nudged the automobile's thermostat toggle higher.

"All right, enough of this 'Mr. Rogers' shit. Damn. I am never going to see another movie again for the rest of my life."

"Aww," Omega said in a tone of mock-disappointment. "And here I thought we were gonna see the latest *Trek* sequel on our next day off."

"I don't think so."

* * *

Much later that evening, an off-duty Omega—now clad in wool-blend trousers, to her considerably-increased comfort—walked out onto the ice at Rockefeller Plaza with gingerly tread, lightly digging in her toe picks with each step to secure herself until she was certain of her stability. Then she began a slow lap of the rink to get warmed up.

As she passed by the base of the gigantic Christmas tree, she dared to look up at it. It was even more beautiful at night than it was in the daytime, she decided, as the strings of colored lights were far more visible in the lower light levels. Moreover, the twinkling, multicolored lights reflected softly in the ice all around, giving a fairyland aspect to the entire plaza. She glided along rhythmically as Tchaikovsky played somewhere in the background, picking up speed gradually, happy and relaxed for the moment.

"Gotcha."

"Woop...!"

Omega accelerated unexpectedly, as she felt an arm slip around her waist and her gloved hand caught. She gasped as she was swept fluidly across the ice.

"Echo!! I had no IDEA! I'm not this good! I'm just a beginner!"

"Take it easy," he murmured in her ear. "I'm not, and I won't let you fall."

"But Echo—"

"Shh. It's okay, baby. Look, Meg, have you ever...ballroom danced?"

"Oh, yeah..."

"You know how you follow your dance partner's lead by reading his body?"

"Yes."

"It's the same thing here. You already do it in the field with me; you can do it on the ice, too. Relax, read my body language, and trust me, baby. I know what I'm doing."

Omega did her best to relax, then she reached out mentally, slowly becoming aware of Echo's moves, just as she did when they were training. Gradually she began to anticipate his turns and direction changes as they glided across the ice.

"Good," he murmured approvingly. "You're gettin' it. Now let's have some fun."

He released her hands and pushed against her side, forcing her away from him. He caught her right hand just before she moved out of reach, and pulled her after him as he swung about to skate smoothly backward. They moved across the ice in a graceful curve, in perfect time with the music.

He pulled her back in against him, and gloved hands went to her waist. Omega's breath caught as she grasped what he was about to do.

"Echo...you're NOT gonna—oh, good grief..."

Omega was suddenly high in the air, sitting on Echo's shoulder as he spun across the rink.

"Arms in the air; make a graceful Y with 'em. Think...think muse, here. Flowing and elegant."

"Oh, shit." She obeyed as best she could, waving her arms slowly through the air as they moved across the ice.

"TRUST me, Meg. Just like in the gym. Pretend it's a workout."

"You're not the one here I don't trust..."

"Right foot down, left leg straight out behind you. Point your toe. Lean forward and arch your back." He lowered her to the ice facing him and pushed her away as she followed his instructions. Her arms automatically, fluidly, swept outward, swanlike, to keep her balance as she moved away from him, gliding backward across the ice. Meanwhile, Echo moved in the opposite direction, athletically executing a flawless double axel.

As Omega slowed, she gradually straightened up, and Echo sailed up to meet her, catching her and gently propelling her backward.

"Echo, there's about a bazillion people standing around the rink, watching..."

"Is that a technical term?" He grinned. "If you're nervous, pay attention to your partner and ignore 'em. Big deal anyway. They'll just think it's a Christmas promo for the damn movie. We don't want to give Mr. Rogers a bad rep, remember? I wonder if HE can skate..."

"He can now, whether he knows it or not."

"Yep."

"But what if I fall?"

"I pick you up and we keep going."

"But—"

"Quit worrying, Meg. You're way too nervous, baby. You didn't mind falling when you were skating with Romeo. You thought it was funny." He pivoted again and skated backward beside her.

"That...was different."

"Why?"

"Romeo isn't my department chief, for one thing."

"Meg, you're not 'on,' here. This isn't a test; it's not a mission. You don't have to impress ANYBODY. Quit thinking of me as your boss all the time. I'm only gonna stand on that kinda formality when there's that kinda formality that needs to be stood upon; do you get me? So relax. FOX is the boss. WE are two good friends, who happen to be partners, having fun together off-duty. Enjoy it. If you're looking for my approval, you should know you earned it a long time ago. And that won't change if you fall flat on your face and knock me down with you." He grinned at her, encouraging, and she bit her lip, considering.

* * *

India was right, Echo thought, watching his partner. *She does have a different attitude around me. Dammit. I hoped we were in a better place than this, her and me. Then again, I can understand WHY Meg has this attitude; it's just...well, she doesn't NEED to. I'll just have to pay closer attention and ensure she knows she can relax around me. Hopefully that little speech is a good start.*

Omega intently studied Echo's calm, smiling face as he spun them back around to skate forward; he saw her nod to herself, and realized she finally understood...and tacitly agreed. *Great!* he thought, relieved. *That's more like it. Maybe that took care of it, right there.* Then he sensed her body slowly, subtly change, relaxing in his arms as they rounded the end of the rink.

As they skimmed swiftly along the ice beneath the huge Christmas tree, she dared to tilt her head far back to look up at it for several long moments. He glanced down at her to check her expression, concerned she was still worried, and saw instead the tree's lights reflected in her wide, shining sapphire eyes and sparkling, multicolored, in her silvery hair.

Damn, he thought briefly, with a smile. *Talk about a sugar plum fairy. I don't need to go to dreamland to find one—I got my own, right here.*

He caught her hands in his as he moved in front of her, turning to skate backward again, holding her at arm's length, content to study her face. She looked from the tree down to his face and smiled then, completely at ease.

There's my girl, he thought, pleased. *We've got this. We've always got this.*

"Ready for our big finish?" he grinned then.

Her laughter rang out like Christmas bells.

"What, exactly, did you have in mind?" she asked.

* * *

Some time later, when Omega had begun to tire from the unaccustomed activity, they got a table in the café overlooking the skating rink, the same one from whose vantage Echo and India had watched their partners skate a few days earlier, and ordered hot coffee—although Omega opted for a mocha with whipped cream instead of her usual basic, in honor of the season. "It's sorta like hot chocolate, but with caffeine," she'd explained, when Echo had given her a puzzled glance.

When their hot drinks arrived, the pair settled in with companionable sighs, content to people-watch as they rested and sipped their beverages.

"Nice night," Echo decided.

"Yeah, it is."

"You have fun skating?"

"It was a blast!"

"Good. We'll do it again, next time we have a free evening."

"Okay, great!"

They fell silent for a while, as Echo's dark eyes took in everything without appearing to do so, and an eager Omega sought out all of the Christmas decorations, both storefront and street-side.

* * *

"I love this," Omega abruptly confessed with enthusiasm, looking around the plaza. "It's like..." she laughed then, a delighted, suddenly-shy laugh, "it's like when I was a very little girl, and Toyland was a real place, under the huge Christmas tree," she waved at the tree in the Plaza, "populated by dolls and teddy bears and toy soldiers, with a magical model train that went anywhere my imagination could take me..."

Echo drank his coffee, and wordlessly looked across the decorated plaza, showing no reaction—though his gaze darted hither and yon, dark eyes seeming to choose targets in their surroundings according to her comments. Omega risked a glance at him, feeling her cheeks reddening.

"Um. Sorry."

"Mm? For what?"

"I'm being ridiculous."

"No, you're not being ridiculous."

"What would you call it, then?"

"Reminiscing."

"You don't mind?"

"I kinda get a kick out of it, actually."

"Huh?"

"I keep picturing this little bitty blonde kid with huge blue eyes and braided pigtails." He paused, considering, then added, "Bouncing up and down and squealing in excitement."

Omega rolled her eyes, rueful.

"You wouldn't be far wrong, if the truth be told," she informed him.

"Figured as much." He nodded to himself, the beginnings of what might have been a satisfied smile disappearing into his coffee mug as he raised it to his lips.

Just then, a waiter came up with a message on a tray. Echo picked it up and looked at it, then sat up straight, all signs of the relaxed demeanor he had had vanishing, to be replaced immediately with mission-level intensity. Omega realized something was up, and went on alert herself.

"Who sent this?" Echo asked the waiter, tone verging on sharp.

"Over there, sir." The waiter gestured to another table.

"Tell him to join us, please."

"Echo? What does it say?" Omega asked, as the waiter left their table.

Echo flipped the note across the table to her. She picked it up, and read: *Agent?* Echo moved his chair around the table, close to Omega, thereby positioning the open chair across the table from the two of them, and creating an obvious united front—called Alpha One—in the process.

* * *

As the gentleman from the neighboring table joined them, he bowed slightly before sitting.

"Oon chucka bih?" he murmured.

"Indoy chu," Echo glibly responded, then turned to Omega. "Erikian."

"Um," Omega murmured, "I hope nobody minds my asking, but... what, or rather who, is an Erikian?"

"Not at all," the gentleman remarked. "Are you familiar with the inhabitants of the Zeta Reticuli system? The Glu'gu'ik?"

"I am," Omega averred, shooting a veiled glance at Echo, and he quickly stifled an unwise—and very undiplomatic, on several levels—snort at the expression in her sapphire gaze.

"Yes, we both are," Echo agreed. "We've...had dealings with them, my partner here and I."

"Well then," the Erikian observed, "Erikians are around a third of a meter shorter than Glu'gu'ik, on average. And we have pale green skin, rather than gray. However, it is believed by many of our erikopologists that we are an offshoot of the Glu'gu'ik, possibly from an ancient colony. Our planet is larger and more massive than theirs, and our star a different spectral type, so over time, the environmental differences would be expected to produce the biological changes we see."

"And they wear environment suits on Earth, Meg," Echo murmured.

"It's really kinda like the suit of electronic armor that guy in the comic books wears, actually, rather than what Ho'd'ni used. Our atmosphere is a little different from theirs, so they need higher pressures and a different mix of gases. Think lightly armored space suit, I guess. Only disguised."

"I...see..." Omega murmured, thoughtful. "Do you have the same ability to manipulate the quantum foam as the Glu'gu'ik?"

"Not so much, in all honesty," the man said. "It seems that either that was a more recent evolutionary development, or the need for a more hands-on technology on Eriki sort of...devolved that ability. And I, for one," he added, "do not especially regret the fact."

"Oh..."

"The cogs are turning," Echo observed with a fond smile. "What comes out of her mouth next will probably surprise us all."

"Excellent," the Erikian said, then noted, "I gather your lovely partner does not speak my language?"

"No. Not yet."

"Very well, then. I shall be happy to converse in your tongue so that she does not feel...what is the word? Abandoned?"

Echo registered the twinkle in Omega's eyes at the Erikian's courtliness, and realized she had decided to play along when she unleashed her full, Scarlett O'Hara, thick-and-sweet-as-molasses accent. He sat back and listened, hiding his own delight at her soft intonations.

"Why, thank ya very much, suh," she declared. "If this is what all Erikians are like, Ah shall make it a point to learn your fascinatin' language."

Echo smiled to himself as he watched the Erikian's pleased reaction. If the unknown being wasn't already in their corner, he was now.

"Now, what did you need, sir?" he asked the Erikian, unable to completely help the slight Texan twang that lilted his own speech, after listening to his partner.

"My Earth name is Kartchner," the Erikian said. "Charles Kartchner. My assumption was correct? You are Division One Agents?"

"How many other Terrans can speak Erikian?" Echo replied, the irony in his voice dry as dust.

"True..."

"I'm Echo, and this is my partner, Omega. We comprise the Alpha One team."

"Ah! The premier Alpha Line team! Very well, then; I am indeed favored to have encountered you. So. Based on your earlier explanations, you are already aware of my real nature, and that of my...environment suit."

Echo and Omega both nodded, Omega rather more hesitantly than her partner.

"Good. But are you also aware that my...suit...can be adjusted so that I may view different spectral regions?"

Echo nodded, but Omega cocked an eyebrow.

"Interesting," she murmured. "But not surprising, I guess."

"You are still relatively new as an Agent, I infer?" Kartchner smiled.

"'Fraid so. I'm workin' on it, though."

"Very good. Agent Echo is well-known in galactic circles; he has an excellent reputation. You are fortunate to have so experienced a partner."

"I am," Omega agreed. She shot an affectionate smile at Echo, who allowed his normally-sharp gaze to soften and warm in response.

"But I digress," Kartchner said. "I was enjoying your holiday decorations...I have never visited Earth at this season before...and observing them at different frequencies, when I realized that the...what do you call it? Holiday bush?"

"Christmas tree," Echo supplied, as Omega suddenly fought desperately to maintain a straight face. Fortunately Kirtchner did not notice, though Echo did, and bit his lip to hide his amusement.

"Yes—that is it. The tiny incandescent radiators on the Christmas tree are emitting a modulated signal."

Echo sat back in surprise at that, letting out a silent breath.

"What the he—! The lights are blinking a message?!" Omega exclaimed, managing to keep her voice low.

"I believe that is what I said, yes."

"What did it say?" Echo asked.

"I am unfamiliar with the particular code being used, so I fear I cannot determine that," Kartchner told them.

"All right..." Omega thought rapidly, "single or multiple wavelengths?"

"So far, I have detected only one wavelength."

"And that would be—?" she pressed.

"One moment. I will use the onboard computer to convert," Kartchner said. "There. Your photonic wavelength unit is named after a deceased Terran, I believe...his name escapes me..."

"Angstrom," Omega supplied.

"Angstrom! Yes. The signal is occurring at one thousand two hundred fifteen Angstroms."

"1215...Echo, that's the Lyman Alpha line, well into the ultraviolet. Whoever the signal is for, it isn't for a human."

"Yeah, you're right." Echo pulled out his cell phone. "Fox? Got a good one for you. The Christmas tree at Rockefeller Plaza is being used as a signaling device. Yes, you heard right. Have the Communications Department scan it at a wavelength of..." he looked at Omega. "What was the wavelength again, Meg?"

"One-two-one-five Angstroms. The Lyman Alpha spectral line."

"Did you hear that? Yeah...One-two-one-five Angstroms. And put the Alpha Three Enigma Team on it, on my orders. Also make sure Communications runs a full spectral sweep on the tree and surrounding area, just to verify there aren't any other frequencies being used, or signaling devices in operation. Yeah, that'll do for now." Echo deactivated the cell phone and returned it to his pocket. "Well, partner, looks like playtime's over. Let's go."

* * *

When Alpha One arrived back at Fox's office, the Communications department, working in conjunction with the Enigma Team, already had the decoded signal displayed on one of the wall screens:

Two Days

Eight Days

"Well, that's interesting," remarked Omega to her partner as they moved to take chairs across from Fox.

"Yeah," answered Echo. "Two dates with seemingly no connection—

the Prime Minister's arrival, and Christmas Eve. At least, I assume it's Christmas Eve. I guess it depends if you're supposed to add the days together or run 'em in parallel."

"There's more, you two," Fox remarked as they sat down. "We reviewed our satellite data of the plaza for the last couple of days. Yesterday's message read, 'Three Days—Eight Days,' the day before, 'Four Days—Eight Days.'

"So add 'em together," Echo concluded.

"Right," Fox agreed. "It's a countdown."

"To a double event," Omega expanded on the idea as she considered it. "I'll bet a body part that's it—the second timer doesn't begin until the first has wound down and the first event executes."

Fox and Echo listened to her brainstorming, intrigued.

"So you're saying another countdown of eight days should be triggered by the Prime Minister's arrival on Earth," Echo remarked.

"That's what it looks like to me," she averred. "So yeah, the Prime Minister's arrival, and Christmas Eve. Whether those events are actual correlations, or just coincidences, I dunno."

"Well, the Prime Minister's arrival almost certainly has to be the first event," Echo decided. "Then we got eight days from that."

"But eight days to what?" Fox wondered. "What the hell does Christmas Eve have to do with it? Surely that one is a coincidence...isn't it?"

"That's today's jackpot question, isn't it?" Omega asked, and shrugged.

"And here's another, just as important: Who was the message for?" Echo asked.

"And who sent it?" Omega followed up. "At least it's not toys."

"No," Fox replied with a sigh. "But it's getting more and more difficult for us as the *Black Suits* become increasingly popular. Field agents are getting tense."

"Let's see," a wry Omega said, ticking off fingers. "We have a planetary head of state arriving imminently. We have a coded countdown apparently tied to said potentate's arrival. We have a complete loss of anonymity of the undercover organization responsible for providing security to the minister. The field agents are tense? I can't imagine why..."

Chapter 4

One Day—Eight Days

"Echo?" Omega knocked on the back door's frame.

"In here."

"Bedroom?"

"Yeah. C'mon in. I'm dressed."

Omega wandered into Echo's bedroom, and sat down on the foot of the neatly-made bed, as Echo fastened his shift cuffs, flipped up his collar, and began tying his tie in front of the dresser mirror. Arrayed before him on the dresser were several weapons, a comb, a hair brush, a bottle of cologne, and a lint roller. The barest hint of bergamot mixed with several aromatic woods wafted through the room, and Omega realized he had applied the cologne only moments before she had called to him. She smiled to herself, and surreptitiously inhaled the scent of her partner, enjoying it.

"Ready in a minute," he told her.

"Take your time. I woke up early today."

"Breakfast? I can pull one of those egg-and-cheese casserole things from the freezer and pop it in the oven. Be ready in about five minutes."

"That sounds pretty good." She smiled.

* * *

Echo eyed Omega in the mirror.

"You look like you're feeling a lot better today than you did after the last time you went skating."

"That's an understatement." Omega laughed. "By the way, I don't think I ever properly told you how much I appreciated your taking me downstairs to the gym and helping me work out the stiffness last time, instead of one of our usual, high-intensity workouts. Not to mention all the other stuff you did—the stretching, and the massage, and stuff. It helped—a lot."

"You wouldn't have been much use in a skirmish in the condition you were in." Echo grinned.

"And THAT'S the truth. I think it wouldn't have been too bad if I hadn't been trying to combine speed skating with track and field."

"Look at it this way. You may have created a new Olympic sport: Parkour on ice."

"Mm, oh-kaaaay. Winter or summer?"

"Good question." He chuckled.

"You're really good on the ice, Echo. I had the distinct feeling last night that you had to hold back a lot on my account."

"Mmm..." Echo hedged, wondering how to answer without possibly embarrassing her or making her feel inadequate. *Especially as hard as it was to get her to relax and quit worrying about looking bad in front of me,* he considered. *But I got nuthin' for an out at the moment...*

"Uh-huh," she responded in a knowing fashion, and he realized he hadn't fooled her for an instant.

Damn it, he thought, mildly chagrined.

* * *

"...I suspected as much," Omega mused. "You know, I wouldn't have thought about you figure skating."

"Why not? I've been doing it for several years now. It's a good workout. It takes quick reflexes, coordination, and strength. And I enjoy it."

"It's just a side of you I've never seen. A more...artistic...side."

"You think you know all there is to know about me?" Echo asked her, a sharp edge to his tone. He snugged the tie knot up near his throat, leaving it loose, then flipped his shirt collar down over it.

"No." She grinned, rueful. "I know better than that. Just the opposite, in fact. I only meant you keep surprising me. There's a lot of facets to your personality. It keeps me guessing. Churchill, you know."

"What?"

"'A riddle wrapped in a mystery inside an enigma.' That's my partner."

"Well...good," he said cryptically, with a slight smile, tightening his tie and positioning the knot comfortably. "'Predictable' is a killer. Especially in this job. You show some promise on the ice, too, by the way. And you looked like YOU enjoyed it as much as I did—AFTER I got you to settle down."

"...Yeah." She managed to stifle the sigh.

* * *

Echo studied his partner carefully in the mirror. He had seen the brief flicker of despondency that had crossed her face as she answered, and it bothered him. *Damn. I guess it's gonna take more than the one speech to conquer this one,* he considered. Finally he decided to tackle it head-on.

"Meg, do I intimidate you?"

"Isn't that what Agents do?" She smiled the same rueful smile. "Intimidate people?"

"Civilians, yes, when necessary. Partners, NO."

"Don't worry. Intimidation implies fear. I trust you, remember? Trust and fear are mutually incompatible."

"Are they?" an enigmatic Echo replied, allowing the faint hint of what might have been skepticism to creep into his deep tones. He picked up his blasters from their resting place on the dresser top, and slid them into their respective shoulder holsters. "Then what?"

"I guess I can't help...comparing myself to you," Omega confessed, and this time Echo heard the sigh he had only suspicioned before. "Since I know now that I was bio-engineered against my will to be an Agent, sometimes I wonder—could I keep up with you otherwise? Would I even be able to do this job at all if it was...JUST me? Without all of the...'improvements'? Could I have done...ANYTHING of what I've done, in the last two decades?"

Damn. Looks like India was right about that, too, he thought in some dismay, shrugging into his dual shoulder holster. *In spades, and then double down on it. That remark about 'improvements,' though...that's something not even India's picked up on. And I can't say that I like the sound of it. Maybe Fox and I should have insisted on some more counseling, and made it more in-depth. Not that she really gave us the chance.*

Echo tucked his Winchester & Tesla Mark II pocket-sized death ray pistol into the waistband holster in the small of his back, then turned to confront Omega directly.

"Meg, do you approve of YOURSELF?"

"What?!"

"Do you approve of yourself?"

"That's a funny question to ask."

"Funny ha-ha?"

"No, funny strange."

"I'm still asking it."

Omega looked around the room as if searching for something, avoiding Echo's eyes and ignoring his question.

"...Where's your jacket?"

"In the closet."

"I'll get it for you."

Echo's lips tightened as she walked across the room to retrieve his Suit jacket, seeming to pretend his question hadn't been asked at all. *Well...shit. That sure explains a lot. 'Cause when she first started here as a new recruit, she was calm and self-confident. Not egotistical, not Meg. But she at least approved of herself at that point, I'd lay money on it.*

"Here, Ace." Omega held the suit coat, ready for him to slip into it. Echo turned and put his arms into the sleeves as Omega pulled the coat up onto his shoulders. As he adjusted the jacket, the cell phone rang by the bed.

"I've got it," Omega said, jumping at the further diversion. "Alpha One...Good morning, Fox...yeah, he's just adjusting his tie and jacket, so I grabbed it...um, okay...I mean, yes sir...yes sir, I'll tell him. 'Bye."

"What?"

"Fox wants you in his office right away," Omega told Echo.

"Don't you mean, 'wants US in his office'?"

"That's...not what he said." She shrugged. "I, uh, I'm...not sure I should go, Echo. He didn't even like the fact that I answered your phone while you were busy. He was pretty specific he wanted you."

"And you're my partner, so it's 'us.'"

"Not according to..." she gestured at the phone he was slipping into a pocket, "that."

"Aw, he's probably just aggravated about something to do with those damn toys," Echo pointed out. "Don't take it personally."

"Yeah...maybe."

"Well, come on, then," Echo said, heading for his front door. "Let's go find out what's got his nose out of joint. We'll catch an early first lunch or something."

* * *

When Echo and Omega entered Fox's office, Romeo was sitting in one of two chairs across the desk from Fox. India was nowhere to be seen. Fox stood.

"Hello, Echo. Sit down." As Echo sat, Fox saw Omega behind him and frowned, his expression practically scowling. "Since when is your name Echo?" Fox demanded of her.

"Uh...I thought...I mean..." Omega stammered, bewildered and uncertain how to respond. Echo looked from an irritated Fox to an uncomfortable Omega and furrowed his brow.

"Hold on, Fox. I made that assumption, not Meg, and I insisted she come with me. In fact, she tried to decline, but I wouldn't take no for an answer. Meg and I ARE partners."

"Not this time."

"What??"

"I'm putting you and Romeo back together. You're dismissed, Omega." His voice softened, just slightly. "I'm sorry."

Echo stared, narrow-eyed, at Fox, as he heard the soft, distressed catch of breath behind him, and then the office door quietly closed. Fox sighed as he sat back down, and put his fingers to the bridge of his nose, slumping slightly in his chair, seeming less than happy about something. At last Echo spoke.

"You just rearranged Alpha Line teams. Specifically-defined Alpha Line teams."

"I did," Fox replied, raising an irked eyebrow at Echo's tone...but looking unusually tired.

"Without the approval of the Alpha Line department chief...or even notifying him first."

"Had you answered your own damn phone this morning instead of letting your assistant do it, you'd have been notified, and your approval obtained."

"No, that won't wash. I'm waiting, Fox." He kept his voice cool, and dangerously quiet.

"That makes two of us," Romeo said, sounding mildly annoyed. "That was just about a replay of what went down with me an' India five minutes ago. No offense, Echo, man, but the Alpha One and Two teams work pretty damn good as is, Fox. Why go fix what ain't broke?"

"My reasons are my own, gentlemen. For your purposes right now, it suffices to know that India and Omega can't go where I'm sending you two."

"Why not?" Echo demanded.

"Because *Black Suits* has started filming on location here, but it's a closed set. 'Mr. Rogers' and 'Mr. Williamson' can get in. India and Omega can't."

"Shit," Echo grumbled. "Haven't we done this once already?"

"Yes, you have. And it worked well," Fox replied. "We have Mr. Harwood under surveillance in order to identify his informant. Problem is, we're having to resort to friendly alien operatives to do it. It's getting so the agents can't appear in public."

"So tell me one more time why we're doing this again?" Echo wanted to know.

"Because we have to see who the script writers really are. We need to start putting together the pieces of this conspiracy to expose us, and we need to do it fast, before we're completely incapacitated. You two can get in there directly. Also, just so you know, since your last impersonation of these two, we've discovered they hate each other's guts, though it seems to be a recent thing, brought on by some on-set tiff. So play that up, if you can. Here," Fox handed them documents, "these are the scripts and the shooting schedule. The real actors are being held up by agents running interference. Get going."

* * *

"C'mon, Meg, I'm sure it's only a temporary assignment," India reasoned. "I got the same thing, you know. If Fox were permanently reassigning Romeo and Echo, he would've said something to us."

"Maybe. But India, I'm telling you, something was wrong. I was NOT welcome there. The temperature in Fox's office dropped thirty degrees when he saw me. Did that happen to you?"

"...Mm. No, it didn't," India admitted, frowning, then she shrugged. "I haven't got a clue, girlfriend. But if Fox sent the men off to do their thing, what say you and I hit the streets together and see what we can uncover?"

"All right. Let's do it," Omega agreed, firming her jaw. "Seeing as how we're not wanted on THAT mission, we'll just make our own."

"There you go! Let's go, girl!"

* * *

"This is gonna be cool!" Romeo said as the Corvette moved through city streets en route to the shooting location. Echo activated his holographic disguise before responding.

"Our purpose isn't to have fun. Our purpose is to go in, obtain the information, and get out as quickly as possible, while maintaining as low a profile as possible. Remember that, junior," Echo said brusquely, as he executed a left turn.

"Low profile. Got it," Romeo said, as the 'Vette pulled up at the shoot.

As Echo and Romeo climbed out, a voice called, "There you guys are! All right, everyone, we're behind schedule. Let's get a move on, people!"

Suddenly the two Agents were surrounded by makeup artists, dressers, script supervisors, and other movie personnel. Romeo and Echo found themselves having makeup applied, ties adjusted, hair styled, Suits brushed. Echo's jaw tightened, and he tensed, thankful for the solid nature of the holographic projection. Romeo twisted about, trying to watch everything at once. Their eyes met over the heads of the location crew, and Echo could almost hear Romeo thinking, *Low profile. Yeah, right.*

When everyone was finished fussing over Romeo and Echo, the director approached.

"All right, guys, all I need in this scene is for you to come running up, burst through this door, then act confused when you don't see the alien you're expecting."

Romeo shot Echo a meaningful glance.

"Piece o' cake," he told the director, "I'm already confused."

Echo remembered what Fox had told them about the actors despising each other, so he jumped on an opportunity.

"Do you have any other state?" he wondered, voice as snide as he could make it. Romeo blinked, then Echo saw recollection hit.

"Maybe not, but it's still a damn sight better'n knowin' all the answers... whether you really do or not," Romeo declared, scowling.

"Cute, guys, real cute," the disgusted director observed, sarcasm heavy. "We got a film to shoot, so cut the crap for a while, okay? All right, places!"

Romeo and Echo looked at each other as the film crew moved away, out of camera range.

"Shee-it," Romeo murmured softly. "Now what?"

"Go with it." Echo shrugged. "Get ready to break down that door."

"ACTION!" sounded over the area.

Romeo and Echo sprinted for the door. As they approached the door, they braced themselves and lunged forward. The door splintered the instant they contacted it, and both men had to quickly adjust: they had been expecting a real door, not a breakaway. Echo and Romeo stumbled into the set and came to a stop, blinking in the bright lighting at all of the cameras facing them.

"Cut! Print it! BEAUTIFUL!!" The director came over to the two Agents. "That was PERFECT! First take! Okay, guys, why don't you head back to your trailers while we set up for the next scene? NICE work."

Echo nodded as the director headed off, issuing instructions to the grips as he went. Then Echo turned to Romeo.

"Finally."

"What you said."

* * *

"Ooo, hey look, Jeff, it's a coupla Division One agents!" a voice commented from somewhere behind them.

"Hush, Pete, keep your voice down, you idiot!" another voice shushed as the two Agents turned to see who spoke. "You'll blow their cover!"

"Like it ain't blown to hell an' back already," Pete remarked, as the two extras wandered over to the Agents.

"Yeah, but you don't haveta make it worse," Jeff told his friend. He turned to Echo and held out his hand. "Pardon him, gentlemen. He's pretty enough, but he's got polenta for brains."

Echo took the proffered hand in a firm grip, prepared to do more than merely shake, depending on what happened next.

"Hello, gentlemen. Uh, to whom do we have the pleasure...?"

"Jeff Robertson and Peter Harriman," Jeff noted, shaking hands. "We're extras on the set. The New Worlds Talent Agency sent us." The other man winked, then met Echo's gaze with a knowing look.

"Aha," Echo murmured, returning the handshake. "I see now. This is Romeo, of the Alpha Two team, and I'm Echo—Alpha One."

"Ooo, Alpha Line, no less," Pete murmured, grinning. "Well, you look like the stars, so I guess it works all right. What's up?"

"Waitaminit," Romeo muttered. "Echo, who the hell are these two?"

"Remember the L.A. Office?"

"Yeah?"

"These guys are actors from a special talent agency that office set up. Probably the East Coast branch, I'm betting."

"Right," Jeff affirmed.

"So?" Romeo continued. "They know us f'r the real deal, then? No reason t' go tellin' 'em everything."

"Actually, it is," Echo said, keeping his voice low as a couple of grips came by. "They aren't from Earth, Romeo. They're imports. They have a vested interest in helping us keep the Agency under wraps."

"Right, or we'd have to leave, and couldn't work as actors," Jeff explained in a murmur. "My homeworld doesn't even have this sort of entertainment."

"Really? That's...interesting," Romeo said, thoughtful. "I'm not sure I'd like it much, though."

"We don't," Pete said. "That's the point. So you're here about the whole film an' shit? Tryin' to find out what's going on?"

"Exactly," Echo agreed. "Given the resemblance, my partner had the idea that we might get closer to the heart of the plot if we came in as doppelgangers for the movie stars. We already hit up the toymakers, and Fox decided to continue the ruse and sent us here."

"Good idea, but awful risky," Jeff decided. "Then again, not any worse than gettin' recognized on the street, I'm betting."

"Right," Romeo agreed. "Done had that happen a few days back."

"You planning on taking over for 'em?"

"NO," Echo declared, vehement. "The faster we can get the necessary info and get outta here, the better." He glanced around. "And to that end, you two better scram, or it WILL blow our cover. I seriously doubt that Rogers and Williamson do a whole lotta schmoozing with extras all the time."

"Good point. I got some ideas, though, how to help out; I'll get in touch with Juliet in L.A. about it," Jeff said. "C'mon, Pete, let's quit botherin' the stars."

"Shouldn't we, like, get autographs or somethin'?" Pete wondered. "It'd explain why we came over."

"It might get us fired, too, but yeah, I see your point," Jeff agreed, pulling a notepad. "Just scribble something, guys. It'll look legit, 'cause we're not gonna show it to anybody."

Echo and Romeo both jotted *thank you* on the pads the extras produced, and the two alien actors scurried away.

"All right. Now what?" Romeo wondered.

"We need the—" Echo began.

"GUYS!" the director called, waving at the pair. "We need you back on set for the next scene!"

"Shit," Echo grumbled.

* * *

"Okay, guys, here's what I want you to do," the director told Echo and Romeo. "I know there's a whole long dialogue passage for this scene, but we're gonna strike most of it. I think it'll be way more dramatic if we minimize the chit-chat. You're looking for the pertinent clue that'll tell you who the Alien Big Bad is, you're in a hurry because you could get discovered any second, and you're going to spread out and search the room. The actual clue is the note in the second drawer of the desk in the corner, but I want you to start by the door, here on the other side of the set, and work your way over."

"But the script?" Echo wondered.

"Forget the script," the director said with a grin. "Just this once. All I want to hear from the two of you is some monosyllabic ad-libs. Got it?"

"Yeah, we got this," Romeo agreed. "C'mon, m' man, let's get ready t' do this shit."

* * *

"QUIET ON THE SET! Aaand...Action!"

Romeo and Echo, weapons drawn but held in ready position, slipped through the open door into the study set, one after the other, and moved to opposite sides of the door. A couple of quick finger-flips by Echo served to tell Romeo to start on his side and search the premises, while Echo took the other side.

Each man carefully riffled through books and papers on shelves and end tables, opening file folders and leafing through, before replacing everything exactly where it had been. After several moments, Echo glanced over his shoulder and addressed his fellow Agent for the cameras.

"Mm?" he queried. Romeo looked up.

"Uhn-uh," Romeo replied, shaking his head. "You?"

"Nope."

"Go on?"

"Yup."

They resumed their search, as around them, the dead-silent film crew grew excited.

Romeo reached the desk first. He moved the papers around on the desk top, finding nothing...because of course, nothing was there to find.

He started to open the top drawer of the desk, and it began what promised to be a long, loud, eerie creak. Romeo froze, even as Echo looked up momentarily at the noise. Then the younger Agent lifted up slightly as he pulled, and eased the drawer open without it making another sound, searching its contents before closing it equally quietly and opening the next.

Halfway down through the contents, he found the planted note prop, and pulled it out. Romeo's eyes scanned the page, then he glanced at Echo.

"Hey."

Echo looked up from searching a book for hidden compartments.

"What?

"C'mere."

Echo glanced at the open door, then moved to Romeo's side. Romeo held out the note; Echo took it and scanned it briefly.

* * *

Aw shit, Echo thought, fighting back the urge to laugh as he read the note. *You gotta be kidding me.*

It read,

This is the clue right here.
Now you know the murderer was Zaxifras.

He looked up at Romeo, whose wide dark eyes telegraphed a certain desperate stifling of laughter himself.

"That's it," Echo said then, managing to keep a straight face and level voice with a Herculean effort of will. "It's Zaxifras. Let's go."

Echo stuffed the prop in his pocket. Both men turned and ran for the setpiece door.

"CUT!" yelled the excited director, as the rest of the crew whooped and yelled in jubilation. "BRILLIANT! I'd almost think you guys did this all the time!"

* * *

As the two Agents finally headed away from the set, a woman angled toward them. She had a familiar face, and Echo suddenly recognized her: She was the non-Agency reporter who had shown up at the toy manufacturer.

"Shit," he murmured to Romeo, lips barely moving. "Get ready. It's that reporter again, the same one that got past our cordon at the toy-making company."

"I see her," Romeo responded in kind, then raised his voice to a slightly higher than normal volume. "C'mon, asshole, you can't be tellin' me you're gonna go back to your trailer an' run lines all by yourself! Who's gonna feed you the other half of the dialogue, if it ain't me?"

"Get the hell away from me," Echo snarled. "Ah don't need you t' tell me how t' run mah damn lines!"

Echo had hoped the nasty argument would deter the woman, and she did pause for a couple of seconds, then kept on coming anyway. She walked right up to him, simpered a bit, then addressed him.

"Mr. Rogers? Would you have a moment to answer some questions for me? And, uh," she hesitated, blushing, though there was something odd about her flush to Echo's knowledgeable eye, "maybe, um, maybe you could autograph something for me?"

"Ma'am, Ah'm sorry; can't yew see we're busy?" Echo grumbled. "An' this is s'posed t' be a closed set; what's the press doin' here?"

"I got no idea," Romeo complained, "but you're right about this bein' a damn closed set. Miss, you're gonna haveta leave, or we're callin' security."

"Security is already on it, Mr. Rogers, Mr. Williamson," came a voice to the side. To their surprise, Jeff the extra stood there, attired in a police uniform. "Come with me, ma'am."

"But I wanted to talk to Mr. Rogers!" the woman protested, as Jeff took a firm grip on her arm.

"Oh, I just bet you did," Jeff said, practically dragging her away. "Now you behave. Don't make me have to read you your rights..." He glanced over his shoulder. "Gentlemen, if you would, wait right there. I'll be back in a moment to take your statements."

And he was gone, headed past the barricades surrounding the cordoned-off film crew.

"What the hell was that all about?" Romeo wanted to know.

"I got no idea," Echo said. "Which is why we're waitin' right here until Jeff gets back to tell us."

* * *

"You two okay?" Jeff asked in obvious concern, as he returned in the police uniform.

"Yeah, we're fine," Echo murmured. "What the blazes just happened?"

"Well, today I'm playing a beat cop extra, which was kinda lucky for you, Echo," Jeff explained. "You acted like you've seen her before."

"I have. When we went to the toy company a few days ago, she showed up. There weren't supposed to be any real reporters there, but somehow she got through our cordon and got in—all the way to us."

"I'm not surprised. That's a shapeshifter from Altair IV. She also happens to be a huge fan of Rogers, and she snuck in planetside about six weeks back. Showed up out in California first, according to some, uh, mutual friends, if you get me. She's been following Rogers across the country, pestering him. As soon as she got close enough to you for you to sign an autograph...assuming you even tried...she'd be trying to put a lip-lock on you...or worse. And believe me, you'd be surprised how long those arms can become when she shifts. The L.A. Office has already had to brain-bleach Rogers about three times after she got done with him, I was told by VERY reliable sources."

"She's a STALKER?!" Romeo demanded.

"You got it," Jeff said cheerfully. "And at the least a would-be molester, to boot. So far, she's always gotten away. We think she shape-shifts into one or another of the agents who get sicced on her ass, and then just walks out. So I really hated having to let her go just now, but better that than her finding out who you really are. I had to get her away from you two as fast as I could. While we need for you guys to take her into custody, I kinda figured you would want to do it without her blowing your cover here. Not to mention, wanting to gargle with fluoro-antimonic acid for the next week."

"Oh HELL no! You figured right," Echo averred. "Thanks."

"No big deal, man. Your current problem is my problem, too, you know?"

"Oh, we know," Romeo muttered. "'Preciate it, man."

"Yeah," Echo agreed. "We'll get somebody on her ass right away."

"It's all cool." And Jeff sauntered off.

* * *

"Now what?" Romeo wondered, watching the alien actor depart. "I'm startin' to want to get done what we need to do and get the hell outta here. Next thing I know, some Betelgeusian arachnoid is gonna come after ME to play kissy-face."

Echo bit his lip to keep from laughing.

"Well, we need to find out who's coming up with all this shit—or rather, who's taking our reports and converting them into a script."

"Wait—you mean you recognized that scene we just did?"

"Yeah. Came straight from one of Butter's reports. I happened to be working that case too, with X-ray, back in the day."

"Damn, skippy!"

"Exactly."

"Okay, so we want the writer-dude, right?" Romeo asked. Echo nodded. "How we gonna do that? There's, like, a bazillion people runnin' around here..."

"You and Meg been spending a lot of time Christmas shopping together, huh?" Echo shot him an amused glance.

"Some," Romeo replied, startled. "Why?"

"Never mind. All right, then..." Echo pulled the script, and walked over to the nearest film crew member. "Hey, is the writer around today? Ah've got a problem with a couple o' lines...they don't feel natural to me. F'r a wonder, Williamson agrees."

"Yeah, he's here." The lighting technician pointed. "There he is, over there."

"Oh, yeah, thanks. Didn't see him," Echo replied. He wandered back over to Romeo, who cocked an eyebrow. "Let's go see the man about a script."

"After you, 'Mr. Rogers.'"

* * *

As the two Agents approached the writer, he glanced up from his laptop and saw them. Echo watched the writer stiffen, and he realized that they had been identified, not as actors, but as Agents.

"We've been made," he muttered to Romeo. "Come on."

The writer got up, closed his laptop, shoved it under his arm, and worked his way slowly and unobtrusively out of the crowd of people involved in the shoot. Echo and Romeo followed, picking up the pace. When the writer had cleared the populated area nearing the cordons, he broke into a run. The Agents followed suit, pursuing him toward a nearby alley. The writer—who was surprisingly fast—disappeared into the alley, and Romeo and Echo darted after him. But as they reached the alley's opening, a green sports car careened out, nearly running them down. Romeo bolted left, and Echo made a flying leap to the right, landing hard in some discarded packing cartons as he narrowly avoided being run down by the madly-driven car. Romeo ran across the alley and helped Echo to his feet.

"Quick! The Corvette!" Echo exclaimed, and they both sprinted for their nearby vehicle. Echo lunged for the driver's door, as Romeo vaulted onto the polished black hood and slid across, landing on his feet beside the passenger door. They were strapped in and rolling before the green car could get far. When the driver saw he was being pursued, he slammed the accelerator and took off at high speed, cutting the car hard to the right. Echo smoothly dropped the Corvette in behind as the green car made a sharp left.

"Echo!" Romeo pointed as the car abruptly darted into another alley.

"I see it." Echo cut the steering wheel hard. "Time to morph. Hang on, this one'll be rough." His hand slammed down on the dashboard control, triggering the emergency morph, and the 'Vette shifted configuration as Echo pulled back on the steering wheel to send it airborne. In seconds, they pulled ahead of their quarry. Echo rapidly coordinated a complex maneuver sequence consisting of a simultaneous landing, ninety-degree left turn, brake, and de-morph, bringing the 'Vette to a halt across the alley, a substantial roadblock. The green car screeched to a halt, and Romeo and Echo jumped out with blasters drawn. Romeo ran across the Corvette's hood and leaped down beside Echo; together they advanced on the green vehicle. Echo jerked open the drivers'-side door, and he and Romeo quickly brought up their weapons.

The unknown—to them—stunt driver grinned up at them as they heard, "CUT! Print it! And somebody get me George on the cell phone!

We're gonna get an Oscar for these effects! He's brilliant!"

A surprised Echo and Romeo looked around the alley at the cameras mounted on the rooftops—they hadn't had time to look for anything except safety hazards during the chase. Echo nudged Romeo, and ever so slightly jerked his head back toward the Corvette. Romeo nodded his understanding of the surreptitious signal.

"C'mon, m' man, let's get the car outta the way for the next shot," he said aloud.

"Gotcha," Echo said. They got in the Corvette, and Echo maneuvered it out of the alleyway. Once out, the Corvette drove slowly down the street, turned right, and disappeared.

* * *

Several stories overhead, and unseen by most New Yorkers, who tended to look down at the pavement, the morphed vehicle flew quietly...

...Aimed in the general direction of Division One Headquarters in Brooklyn.

* * *

Just then, a limousine pulled up at the film set. The chauffeur emerged, and opened the rear door for two men.

"Let me outta this damn car with that fool. Hey, Larry," the younger, ebony-skinned man called, "we're finally here, man."

"The hell you say. Damn New York traffic," the other man muttered in a deep west Texas drawl. "Rather be tendin' th' ranch than workin' with this jackass idiot anyway. Well, let's get started. The door scene is up first on the schedule..."

"Very funny, guys," the director said. "Your first three scenes today were terrific. Let's just keep going the way you've been doing and it'll be great. Rogers, I didn't know you were a stunt driver."

The two actors stared at each other.

"Do YOU know what th' damn hell he's talkin' about?" Rogers asked.

"Nope," Williamson answered, curt. "Like I ever know what the hell you're doin', loser."

"Shut up. Just shut up. I'm starting to get mighty damn tired of people makin' all these strange assumptions about what I can or can't do. Figure skating, stunt driving...*FIGURE* SKATING?? Hell!"

"Know whatcha mean on THAT one, jerkface. 'Scuse me, I don't EVEN have a redheaded publicist..."

"All right, gentlemen. Enough with the jokes and zings. I already warned you about that. Let's just get set up for the next scene," the director cut off the diatribes.

The two actors shrugged, and headed for their trailers.

Chapter 5

"Well, Meg, looks like WE accomplished something, at least," India told the Lexus' driver with satisfaction.

"Yeah, we've got something to tell Fox and the guys, for sure. Trifle came through for us," Omega replied. "I'm glad we teamed up and went out, now."

"Hey, that little trick you had of scratching under Trifle's chin had a lot to do with it," India grinned. "He chilled out, relaxed, and remembered right off! And I've got as much invested in this as you do. Plus, I wasn't too thrilled with the way you said Fox treated you. It was..."

"Out of character?" Omega finished for her.

"A little, yeah. I mean, I know Fox is the Director, and he has the authority to do what he did, but he's usually a little more...diplomatic. Not to mention, not giving Echo a heads-up. He really blind-sided Echo as much as you?"

"Yup. Echo about dropped his jaw on the floor."

"Wow. I'd have thought Fox would've done that, at least, what with Echo being the department chief and all."

"I know," Omega responded. "Now, maybe he explained to Echo after I left; I dunno. 'Cause like I said, whatever's going on, I was not one of his most favorite people at that moment. Not even on the waiting list, seemed like to me."

"Ouch," India said, grimacing.

"Yeah. Ready to head back?"

"Actually...could we stop by the electronics store on the way?" India had a twinkle in her eye. Omega shot her a knowing glance, lips curling slightly.

"I think we could manage a brief detour."

* * *

Omega entered her quarters and hung her overcoat in the coat closet. As she headed for the kitchen to grab a quick snack before heading back for the Alpha Line room off the Core to write up a report, a muffled voice came distantly through the back door, accompanied by the sounds of...splashing. Lots of splashing.

"Meg? That you?"

"Yeah, Echo."

"Anybody with you?" The squeaking sound of skin sliding on porcelain was succeeded by an even louder splash. "Damn!"

"No..."

"I could sure use a hand, then. Ow! Hell..." he sounded annoyed.

What on Earth? a shocked Omega wondered, listening. *From all that water splashing, it sounds like he's in the BATHTUB! But surely he wouldn't call me in there if he's in the tub...unless he were hurt. And that 'Ow!' sounded as much pained as aggravated. Yeek. Maybe I better go see. No matter WHAT I get an eyeful of.*

She turned for the back door.

* * *

Omega followed the sound of Echo's voice through his apartment until she encountered him, shirt off, face in the bathroom sink...literally. Water was splattered all over the granite vanity top. There were even a couple of substantial puddles splashed on the ceramic-tile floor.

"What's up?" she asked, curious, and he raised his head, water streaming from his nose and chin, all over the vanity and onto the floor.

"Fox sent us...to the damn movie set...undercover..." Echo said, between splashing handfuls of water on his face to rinse off the soapsuds she saw there, "as Williamson and Rogers. Now..."

"Oh, no," Omega anticipated him, "they put makeup on you."

"Yeah. Straight through the solid hologram, dammit. How it did THAT, I dunno. And now I can't SCRUB the damn stuff all off. Shit! In about five more minutes of this, my eyeballs are gonna start bleedin', and my face will fall completely off—still with the damn makeup on it...!"

* * *

"It'll come off, hon. You just gotta do it the right way. Dry off your face and hang on." Omega put a towel in his blindly-groping hands and ran out of the room as Echo blotted his face with the towel. When she came back, she had a couple of bottles of unguents, cotton pads, and swabs, as well as several spare towels. Placing the unguents on the counter by the sink, Omega dried the vanity with the towels, then spread the towels on the floor to soak up the puddles. After that little safety concern was out of the way, she studied his face in detail, taking his chin in her fingers to turn his face into the light. "Yeah, that's what I figured. Looks like water-resistant stuff, especially the eye makeup..."

"Which is irritating as hell." Echo dug a fist into his watering eye; tears streamed down his face as he did. She grabbed his hand and pulled it away.

"Stop rubbing it! You're just making it worse! Take it easy. I've got everything under control, I promise. Wow. Wish I had those lashes." Echo shot Omega a dirty look, eyes still watering profusely, and she grinned. "Let me get a chair for you, otherwise my arms will be what's gonna fall off, trying to reach up so far, for so long. Lean back against the vanity and keep your eyes closed. And DON'T RUB 'EM. I won't be gone a second."

She scampered out, and he obeyed, waiting as patiently as he could, given the discomfort. Moments later she returned, bringing in a dining chair and parking it in front of the sink, facing the wall.

"Here. Sit," she ordered, "close your eyes again, and just relax. Leave it to me."

Echo complied, and Omega got down to work.

"I'm gonna start on your eyes first, since that's what seems to be bothering you the most, so don't blink."

He sat very still, eyes squinted shut, as she moistened a cotton pad with remover and gently wiped his eyelids.

"Try to relax your eyes a little," she murmured, continuing to work. "You got 'em all squinched up, and I can't get down in the creases that makes."

"Okay. Is it working?" Echo asked, eyes still tightly closed, but trying to relax his face as much as he could.

"There we go. Oh, yeah, it's coming right off now. You just have to use the proper stuff."

"How do you stand this shit on your face? Feels like mud," Echo remarked with intense distaste.

“I guess it does take some getting used to,” Omega acknowledged, continuing to work outward from his eyes with fresh cotton pads soaked in makeup remover. “I remember having a similar reaction when I first started wearing makeup as a teenager. But it’s expected, so you get in the habit. And like I told you the other day, I usually don’t wear much. Almost there.”

“Good.”

* * *

“Okay, look at me...” Omega studied Echo’s face a few minutes later, having removed all the makeup she could see. Now she cupped his chin in her fingers again and turned it from side to side in the bathroom’s bright lighting, looking for anything she might have missed, then she dipped a cotton swab in fresh remover. “Look up, keep your eyes open, and hold really, really still. Do. Not. Blink.” He obeyed without question, staring as intently at the ceiling as if it was a killer alien. Delicately, she worked the swab around his lower lashes. “There. Still had a little eyeliner on. Now rinse your face. Cool water. Don’t rub.”

Echo obediently splashed tepid water on his face, then toweled off, blotting carefully as instructed.

“Now,” Omega said, “sit back down.”

“Why?”

“You’ve probably irritated your face trying to scrub all that stuff off. If I finish with a little witch hazel it should help soothe your skin down, and have a little astringent effect too, closing the pores. Go easy on the skin for a day or two, though,” Omega added, as she swabbed his face down. “Absolutely no aftershave.”

“Why?”

“Do you LIKE pouring alcohol in a raw wound? I’ll leave the witch hazel and you can use it for a couple days, in place of the aftershave. Mm, lessee. Oh, and if your eyes still feel irritated, or if they get bloodshot, get a small bottle of saline solution—like contact-lens wearers use—and flush ‘em out with that, really good, once or twice. That should clear any mascara flakes or whatnot. Also—do you have any, like, guy moisturizer? Maybe something you use since it's winter?"

"Like windburn shit?"

"That'll work, yeah. Put just a very thin layer of that on. Your skin is a little dried out from all the washing. Otherwise your face might turn red, maybe even peel. Some Rejuvic would be great, but I don't have any more, do you?"

"No, we used up the last of my stuff a month ago on the 'boo-boos' from taking down that Hatteratt, and I haven't had a chance to go by Medical for another bottle. I'll just use the windburn crap. It'll be all right. I've used it before; it doesn't feel too greasy."

"Okay."

She watched as he fished out the windburn cream from a drawer in his vanity—then turned and offered it to her.

"What, you want me to apply it?" she wondered, surprised.

"I figure you know what you're doing, baby," he murmured, meeting her eyes. "I tried for half an hour to get that damn shit off, and couldn't do it. You had it off in under five minutes. BEFORE my face could fall off."

"All right, then. Gimme it, and sit back down. Was Romeo in the same boat?" she asked as she removed the lid on the small tub of cream, dipped her fingertips in it, and started to work.

"Yeah." The answer was laconic almost to the point of terseness. Echo slid down in the chair until he was in a comfortable slouch, leaned the back of his head against the rounded edge of the vanity, rested his forearms on the chair arms, and simply let her smooth a thin layer of the cream across the planes of his face, rubbing it in gently as she went. She raised an eyebrow, and wondered if he was enjoying the light facial massage. Judging from the way his features started to relax, she suspected so.

Good. I'm glad he likes it. I wonder if he's ever had anybody work on HIM like this before, she thought. *Seems like turn about would be fair play, but maybe he doesn't get as much as he gives,* she decided, before turning her consideration to Romeo's identical predicament.

"Well, India can probably handle whatever Romeo's got on," she decided after a moment. "I'll try to give 'em a call later on and check. There," she said, wiping off her hands on a tissue and replacing the lid on the cream. "Better?"

"Yeah, it is, a lot—thanks."

"Not a problem. Just have some feeling for what we females go through, hmm?" she said, teasing.

"You do this every day?"

"Every day. Not to mention applying the makeup. And the moisturizers and stuff. That's actually one reason you had trouble with it—your skin hadn't been prepped for makeup application, so it got all down in the pores and junk."

"Ugh. You have my sympathy," Echo said, rueful. Omega grinned.

"It's not so bad. Why do you think I don't look my age?"

* * *

Echo studied her youthful-looking, smiling face and nodded his understanding, following her out of the bathroom and into his bedroom. She sat down on the end of his bed, and he sat beside her.

"So what were you up to while I was being tortured?" he asked.

"India and I decided to team up and hit the streets, to see what we could dig up."

"And?"

"Well, according to Trifle, the Antarean felinoid, the same sentient was seen at both the toy company AND the movie set in recent weeks."

"Alien?" Echo pressed.

"Of course." Omega grinned.

"Did you get a description?"

"Better. We got a name."

"Romeo and I got a face. We almost got the body, but we lost 'im in an alley. Let's go see if they match."

"Great! But you might want to put your shirt back on first." Blue eyes twinkled at him in amusement.

Echo raised an eyebrow at her cheek, yanked his shirt off the bed, and ducked back into the bathroom, closing the door.

* * *

While he got ready, Omega sat on the bed, staring thoughtfully off into space, pondering. Finally she volunteerered, "Echo? I saw something today and had an idea, but it's kind of farfetched..."

"Try me," Echo said, exiting the bathroom while tying his tie.

"Granted, we got way too high visibility right now for comfort, and that needs to be...negated. But since we gotta deal with it for the time being, I thought that it would be good if we could somehow make this publicity work to our advantage, especially with the Prime Minister's arrival coming up..."

"Go on."

"Well, I think I know how."

"I'm listening."

"Have you ever been to a science fiction convention?"

* * *

Echo stopped, tie ends in hand, and stared at her.

"IS there one? Now? In the city?"

"Not quite yet. But there will be by the time the Prime Minister arrives. If I remember right, it's called YuleCon, and it's in that hotel with the big atrium over in the financial district. It doesn't last the entire duration of the diplomatic visit, but it might help. And at least we would blend in as is, even the Lambda Andromedans."

"Come on," Echo said, slipping on his holsters and grabbing his jacket. "You can tell Fox."

"No," Omega said flatly.

"What? Why not?" Echo looked puzzled as he shrugged into his jacket.

"Echo, something's up. I'm not high in Fox's favor right now, but I have no idea why. Is he reassigning you and Romeo permanently?" she asked, blunt.

Echo paused, blinking in surprise and a certain amount of carefully-hidden, sudden—and unexpected—trepidation.

"He...didn't say so," Echo recalled. "I assumed it was temporary."

"Okay." Omega nodded in obvious relief. "That's good. Still, if you think the convention is a good idea, let it come from you. If he's on the outs with me, it may go over better from you."

"You sure? It's your idea."

"Doesn't do any good if it isn't used," Omega pointed out. "We're not competing, Echo, we're working together as a team. Who cares which one of us it comes from, as long as it works?"

Echo stood looking down at her, allowing the faintest of smiles to curve his lips, as he considered his partner's willingness to allow him to take credit for her idea, all for the sake of mission success. Then he turned and, putting his hand on her back, said, "Let's go, teammate."

* * *

Fox, with Alpha One and Two in attendance, was conference-calling with the head of the Los Angeles Office, Juliet. Her image was projected on one of the wall screens.

"...So what's the latest?" Fox asked.

"Mm, lessee. We filed the cease and desist on the basis of infringements of copyrights and trademarks, and that's being looked at as we speak," Juliet said. "The *Black Suits* producers are fighting it tooth and nail, but that's to be expected."

"How is that shaping up?"

"Oh, it'll take a while," Juliet said with a wolf-like smile, "but our I.P. lawyers say it's just a matter of time."

"Good," Echo remarked.

"Very," Fox agreed. "What else have you got?"

"Oh, well, the *Black Suits* has put out a casting request for extras. It's basically a cattle call—"

"Cattle call? What's that?" Romeo interrupted.

"An open call for actors," Omega murmured. "Anything and everything. They pretty much herd everybody in, hence the term 'cattle call.'"

Fox pressed his lips together, partially disguising a scowl at Omega interjecting remarks, but his Office chief nodded onscreen.

"Right," Juliet confirmed. "Think a small room with way the hell too many people...who all look alike."

"Oh," Romeo said, nodding. "I get it. Okay, thanks, guys. Sorry for interruptin'."

"No problem," Juliet noted. "Omega, there, seems to be on the ball with it, anyway."

Omega offered the other woman a slight smile, and Juliet returned it.

"So what are we doing about it?" Fox wanted to know, getting the conversation back to its principal focus.

"You know that pool of alien actors we've got? New Worlds Talent Agency?" Juliet queried.

"Yeah?"

"Now, I want you to know, Fox, this was Jeff Robertson's idea; he's one of our offworld acting talents. Anyway, we've got a batch of the East Coast talent pool we're sending in. None of 'em are happy about the possibility of our cover getting blown, because if we get exposed, it'll mean most of 'em have to leave the planet, never mind the entertainment industry—probably nobody knows better than you do, Earth is Galactic Central for filmmaking. So they wanna help, wanna work with us."

"Doing what, exactly?"

"They're gonna be our boots on the ground, and our eyes and ears," Juliet explained. "They keep us apprised of what's going down on the set, and whenever we have something that needs scoping out, we ping them and they do it for us. If we need to slow down the filming, they do that, too—a busted camera, a missing widget, an 'accidentally' damaged costume, a prop gone walkabout—we have it all worked out. That way, you don't have to put your actual people at risk, let alone two of your top Agents, sending 'em back to the set every time you need intel."

"Dammit," Romeo grumbled under his breath, and India elbowed him.

"Hallelujah!" Echo exclaimed simultaneously—NOT under his breath. Juliet laughed.

"Kinda figured," she said in reply, dry humor evident in her tone. "Echo's reputation precedes him, even when the man himself doesn't show."

Omega and Romeo both choked laughter into snorts. India giggled outright. Fox merely rolled his eyes. Echo shot his partner a surreptitious grin, before addressing their superior.

"Fox, this must be the plan those two extras said they had, from the set," Echo pointed out. "The ones Romeo and I put in our report."

"That's right," Juliet affirmed. "I've seen the report, and that's exactly who came up with this."

"Oh, I remember. That'll work," Fox decided. "That'll work nicely. How many do you think you can get on set?"

"We already have a good half a dozen, including Robertson and his friend, and more are auditioning," Juliet noted. "I anticipate at least twenty, total, by the end of the week—maybe more."

"Excellent! And you're sure no one can trace them back to us? After all, they're OUR pool of actors."

"I'm sure. The L.A. Office already had THAT buried deep."

"Good. Anything else?"

"Yeah. We worked with some of your people on that offworld undocumented shapeshifter doing the stalking on Rogers and Echo—because she started it out here first, so we had some experience, and could help out—and we finally located her and took her into custody. She was shipped home, in restraints suited to shapeshifters, on the first flight out of Area 51, earlier today. Rogers has been brain-bleached...again...and now only remembers her as a somewhat eccentric stalker-fan sort. Minus the eye-stalks."

"Outstanding! Anything else?"

"No, that's all we got for now."

"It's a great start, Juliet. Keep up the good work, then, and keep me posted."

"Wilco, Fox."

"Headquarters out."

"L.A. out."

Fox turned to the four Agents in his office. "Now let's hear what you lot have found out..."

* * *

"All right," Fox summarized, after the Alpha teams had debriefed to Fox about their respective excursions, "so we have the connection between the toys and the movie. A Dabanoran going by the name of Michael

Smithers is feeding information to the toy designer, AND developing the script for the movie. The cartoon is a promo spinoff."

"Looks that way," India confirmed.

"Good job, India. Between that information and what Romeo and Echo brought back from the film shoot, we've got our connection," Fox commended.

"Uh, Fox, it was partly Meg's idea," India volunteerered. Fox ignored her and continued.

"I'll have Smithers taken into custody. And Echo, great idea about using the science fiction convention as cover for the diplomatic visit. I'll set that up right away."

"Will you still want Alpha Line to work the diplomatic detail, Fox?" Echo asked him.

"Probably...or at least, those of you who aren't already on assignment. I'll let you know. Call it a day and get some rest for now. Dismissed. And Romeo, goth eyeliner is not an acceptable part of the male Agent attire. We want to blend in, not stand out."

Romeo and India both looked chagrined as India muttered, "Oh, hell, I thought I got it all."

* * *

The four exited Fox's office, and the door closed behind them.

"What gives?" Romeo asked, confused and worried, as they walked across the Core toward the Alpha Line room. "I saw four of us in there, but it looked to me like Fox only saw three."

"You noticed that, huh?" Omega noted, wry. A silent Echo watched Omega, concerned.

"Looks like you were right, girlfriend. I wonder what's wrong?" India pondered.

"I don't know." Omega shrugged and tried to act nonchalant. "I guess I'll find out soon enough."

* * *

Zero Days—Eight Days

Omega was almost ready to report to work the next morning, and was reaching for her Suit jacket, when the cell phone rang.

"Omega here. Oh, hi, Fox..."

She listened for a long time. Halfway through the call, she went white to the lips.

"Yes...but I...well, no! Of course not! Surely you don't think...but... oh...yes...all-all right. I...understand, Fox."

She slowly closed the cell phone, staring at it in shock.

"No," she whispered. "It can't be...after everything, this was the only place I...had left..." Finally she threw her head back, closed her eyes, and fairly howled. "NOOOOOOooo...!" It was a cry of despair.

A despondent Omega sank slowly to her knees, arms dangling in front of her, shoulders bowed, head hanging dejectedly, utterly hopeless. She still unconsciously clutched the cell phone.

* * *

An alarmed Echo, in sock feet and shirt sleeves, cuffs undone, tie loose, slammed through the bedroom door scant seconds later and hit his knees in front of her, grabbing her shoulders.

"What's wrong?! Meg??"

She raised her head and looked at him, so white he thought she would pass out.

"It all makes sense now, Echo. Fox...has confined me to quarters. They think...Echo, they think I'M the mole."

* * *

Echo, alone, stormed into Fox's office, heedless of the other four agents already there.

"Fox, what the hell do you think you're doing? Confining Meg to quarters? What's going on?"

"What he should've done long ago," one of the other agents answered, belligerent, from behind him. "Locking down the traitor in our midst."

Echo spun on his heel, furious.

"What the hell is that supposed to mean?!"

"I'm surprised I have to spell it out for you, of all people," the other agent, codenamed Monkey, replied, contempt in his voice. "You're the one she tried to assassinate only a few months ago."

"Meg wasn't responsible for that. It was—"

"Oh, that's right, I forgot. It was that Snail's fault. Funny how it was she managed to see he got bumped off before she made her move on you. Getting rid of a liability, maybe?" Monkey's sarcastic tone dripped venom.

"Your point?" Echo said through gritted teeth.

"My point is that our little blonde traitor was probably no more anyone's puppet than I am. And even if she was, how do we know she isn't still carrying out orders? She's the only agent who doesn't have an action figure, so she's the only one who can move freely. Isn't that convenient?"

"The only reason there's no Omega action figure is that the toy company decided not to produce it. We've got photos, and the design sculpture is on my desk in my quarters right now," Echo told him.

"Aw, isn't that nice? Yeah, I've already seen 'em. It means NOTHING, Echo. The statue has no FACE. It could be anybody. Who's to say she isn't the one who arranged for production to halt, anyway? She's not in that damn cartoon, either! And...why are you defending her so hard??"

Echo glared at him.

"Maybe she's not just some Snail's toy..."

Echo got right up in the smaller man's face, eyes glittering dangerously.

"...Maybe Echo's got a pretty little—"

Seeing red, Echo grabbed Monkey by the collar, drew back a fist—

"Echo! STOP!" Fox intervened. Echo looked over his shoulder at the Director and slowly lowered his fist—but his other hand still held Monkey by the throat. Fox continued.

"Monkey, that was so far out of line it doesn't warrant consideration. If I EVER hear such an allegation again from your mouth...or anyone else's," he looked at Monkey's other companions in the room, "not only will I LET Echo punch your lights out, I will then PERSONALLY brain-bleach YOU back into INFANCY. They'll have to put a diaper on you and send you to a nursing home when I'm done. Is. That. Clear?"

The four Agents nodded, surly.

"Caution is one thing, gentlemen. Malicious, unfounded slander—

especially against fellow Agents—will NOT be tolerated. Dismissed."

Monkey glared at Echo. Echo let go of the other man's collar, pushing him back slightly, and said, in a low, deadly voice, "Get. Out. ALL of you."

"You aren't the Director yet, Echo," an agent called Yankee noted, voice dripping insolence. "We'll leave when we're ready to leave."

"You're ready to leave," Fox ordered. "Get out now. All four of you. My DEPARTMENT CHIEF stays."

When the other agents had left the office, albeit very slowly and in a sulky, truculent fashion, Echo slammed the door and spun around to Fox.

"Fox, we both know this is ridiculous. Meg isn't the mole. She would no more betray the Agency than I would."

"Maybe not deliberately, Echo, or consciously, but we both know she was programmed once—"

"You KNOW Zz'r'p removed all the programming."

"Echo, Omega herself isn't even certain of that. That was one of the reasons she left last summer. To get away, to ensure she didn't pose a danger to you...or anybody else."

"That's exactly my point!" Echo spread his hands in a kind of plea for understanding. "Fox, when Slug forced Omega to...attack me, she's told me that she was aware of what was happening the whole time. Conscious. She WASN'T behaving OR moving normally."

"What do you mean?"

"Just what I said. In fact, her movements were downright jerky, not the smooth coordination we're used to seeing in her, that I'M used to seeing in her. It was like there was another mind in her body, one that wasn't used to that body—and if you think about it, in a way that's exactly what was happening. Remember, I work with Meg every damn day, in the gym, on the street, on a mission—if anybody knows how she moves, it's me. I HAVE to know, because I have to be able to 'read' her movements to coordinate action with her—especially in a battle scenario."

"That's...true."

"Yeah, it is. And Fox, nothing about her motions in those moments was right, nothing about 'em was normal. I'm TELLING you, as the subject-matter expert, it was NOT NORMAL. And that's at least partly because she was fighting it, Fox. With everything she had. Once I realized that, I understood why her actions looked like they did. She was FIGHTING it. Every move, every muscle flex. Every step of the way. Fighting as hard as she could. It was Slug's damn programming versus her conscious will. And it SHOWED."

"Interesting..."

"Given all that, it means in THIS situation she would have to consciously, DELIBERATELY betray us—it's just not credible. I KNOW her better than that!"

Fox listened carefully, considering, then nodded.

"And how do you expect me to solve this case if you cut off my right arm?" Echo continued. "Omega and I are a TEAM, Fox. Both of us. Together. Not either/or."

"Echo, I know how you feel. If what you say is true, and I know it is, then I don't really believe it either. But, my friend, I've got a situation here. The publicity and exposure have made it nearly impossible to get our job done as an organization. Paranoia is setting in among the agents. It's getting ugly, Echo. You saw that yourself just now, and that wasn't the half of it. I'm not at all happy about it, but I've still got to deal with it. Between the two of us, I'm really doing this to try to protect Omega, not punish her. To minimize her apparent involvement and keep her in the clear until we can find out who's actually doing it."

"Then it isn't working, Fox. She let out a howl fit to wake the dead, and was as white as her shirt when I found her. It may not be punishment, but it damn sure feels like it to her."

"What do you want me to do, Echo?" Fox sighed.

"Give me back my partner."

"Echo," Fox began, frustrated. Then he paused, thinking. He put a hand to his face, rubbing his chin as he looked Echo up and down, considering. "All right, Echo. You've got it. On ONE condition, and one only."

"Name it."

"You do not let Omega out of your sight."

"FOX—"

"Echo, listen to me. Suspicion is rife. Feelings are running high among some of the younger, less-seasoned AGENTS as well as some of the ALIENS. You SAW that, just now. Those four, in particular, are absolutely convinced that Omega is the mole, and—like it or not, and let me note that I didn't—they had some damn logical arguments. Arguments that they're apt to pass on to some of the other agents...if they haven't already. If ANYTHING goes south on a mission she's working, it could turn nasty in a heartbeat. I am NOT asking you to be her jailer. I'm asking you...to be her bodyguard."

* * *

Echo met Fox's eyes for a moment, looking for sincerity. The Agent and the Director had known each other for a very long time, as Fox was one of the Originals, too. Fox knew the Agent in front of him considered him a good friend, and fully expected such sincerity in the circumstances.

And, in the circumstances, Fox knew if that sincerity and support was not forthcoming, there would be hell to pay from this particular Agent...and rightly so. Echo was capable of many things, but he insisted on justice and a strong moral stance. And Fox knew Echo's current partner was much like him...or at least appeared to be.

* * *

So when Echo searched for that expected sincerity in Fox's eyes, he found it, and a considerable amount of concern, even worry, as well...and then nodded in understanding.

"All right, Fox. Deal."

"Get Romeo and India to help, if you need to. Be aware, though, that in order to avoid the appearance of collusion, if I call in backup teams, it's apt to be from the two teams who just created such an unpleasant scene."

"Aw, dammit."

"I know, but you know how my job works—how it HAS to work."

"Yeah, I do," Echo sighed.

"And you'd best get used to it, because you'll have it yourself, one day, zun."

"I know." Another sigh. "But I don't have to like it."

"Good. And I don't, either, just so you know. Now get going."

* * *

When Echo entered Omega's quarters from the back door, he was surprised to find that Romeo and India were there.

"Where's Meg?" Echo demanded as soon as he got well past the back door, glancing around and not seeing his partner. He did note, however, that the bedroom door was closed.

"She's lying down, Echo," India said, confirming his suspicions. He immediately moved toward the bedroom door, but the pair blocked his way. "Give her a few minutes."

"Why?"

"Echo," Romeo began, hesitant, and apparently searching for words, "she be pretty upset by all this shit. And it's a bad time for it to be comin' down..."

"I know," Echo interrupted. "I've been talking to Fox. I need to tell her—"

"Echo, she's ill," India told him.

"Ill?" Echo paused and stared at her in blank astonishment.

"The stress from this was so great, on top of some other things, that she became physically ill," India said.

"We're not completely sure, but we think—we're pretty damn sure—she tossed her breakfast," Romeo explained. "Like, ALL her breakfast."

"And maybe last night's dinner, even," India added, shaking her head.

"Damn, India baby, from what I heard when we got here, didja check t' make sure she had all her toenails? I swear it sounded like they were comin' up. Not t' mention her pancreas an' liver."

India simply offered a tight, mirthless smile.

"What?? She was THAT upset?" Echo exclaimed, stunned.

"Yes. Especially when you left so abruptly," India continued.

"She didn't think—"

"Echo, she didn't know WHAT to think."

"She knows I wouldn't turn on her."

"She didn't think Fox would, either."

"...Let me talk to her, India."

* * *

When Echo entered Omega's bedroom after lightly knocking on the door, he saw her lying face-down on top of the bedspread, her face buried in the pillows, arms tucked underneath them. Her jacket and holsters were laid to one side, on a corner of the bed.

He moved quietly to the bed and sat down beside her. Gently, he tugged at the silver-white braid, trying to tease her. She made no response. He laid a hand tentatively on the middle of her back, splaying his fingers out, applying light pressure, much as he had before beginning her first massage. After a moment for her to get used to the sensation, he began to rub gently, in an effort to soothe.

"Meg?"

"I didn't do it, Echo." Her voice was muffled by the pillows.

"I know."

"Where did you go?"

"To defend your honor, milady." He smiled, and assumed an exaggerated, courtly medieval accent—with a slightly Texas-sounding twist.

"What??"

"I went to talk to Fox and the agents that had accused you."

"Oh. You've been readin' too much Shakespeare again."

"Well, Cervantes, actually."

"Oh. So...does that make me Dulcinea, or Aldonza?"

Echo raised an eyebrow at Omega's deliberate contrast of characters.

"Neither," he said. "It makes you my partner and my friend. Someone I know as well as I know my own face in the mirror, someone I trust with my life, and someone I'll defend...to the death, if I have to." He paused. "And I did, too. With some success. Only not to the death, yet! It's okay, Meg," he continued with a grin, "Fox believes you now, too."

"Then why—"

"Tension is high right now, baby—among the aliens AND the agents. The work isn't getting done. Fox is trying to protect you."

"So I'm stuck here?"

"No. Fox lifted the confinement under one condition."

"What?"

"I pull double duty until this thing blows over: Agent...and your bodyguard."

"Bodyguard?! Don't you mean PRISON guard?"

"No. I mean bodyguard. I saw the paranoia firsthand, and damn, it's bad. It's not really personal, Meg. But they're looking for a scapegoat. And unfortunately, the history of one of Alpha Line's earliest missions left you a likely target. I don't think you're the only one, the only target, I mean... but maybe you're the most obvious. Anyway, you're back on the case. And I have specific orders from Fox not to let you out of my sight." He sat watching her for a few moments, waiting for a response. He got one...but not the one he had expected.

"Echo," she finally rolled onto her back to speak to him face to face, a distressed look in her dispirited blue eyes, "how do you do it? And what am I doing wrong?"

* * *

"You're not doing anything wrong." His expression was puzzled. "What do you mean?"

She sighed and shook her head in mingled disgust and frustration.

"You're ALWAYS so cool. Everything under control. I USED to be like that, but right now...my life suddenly seems like the crisis *du jour*. I don't think I need a bodyguard as much as I need an emergency management coordinator." Omega offered a wry smile, trying to keep it from wobbling too badly.

* * *

Echo grinned back at her. He was pleased to see her sense of humor returning—though he saw the wobbly lips—but his voice when he answered her was serious.

"Well, I'm not one of those, but maybe I can offer some advice..."

"Please do."

"Look, Meg, the first year as an Agent is always rough. I've heard it described a lot of ways, but it boils down in the end to what you're feeling right now. We've all been through it, one way or another. Giving up your past and facing what we face every day is...just damn hard." He shrugged. "And you've had to give up more than most, I think. Then again, you've got a partner who has, too, and trust me, he gets where you're coming from."

He laid a light hand on her shoulder and looked down into a troubled face, letting his eyes express his understanding for only an instant, but HER eyes registered that she saw it, and that was enough for him. She offered him a half-smile in thanks, just before it wobbled too much for her to hold it, and she glanced away, blinking several times.

"Shh, Meg. Hush, now. Don't cry on me." He rubbed her shoulder lightly, comfortingly. "Everything's fine. Everything's gonna be all right, baby. I'm not surprised you feel down, especially at this time of year. Maybe you understand a little bit, now, why I don't much 'do' Christmas any more. I'm not saying you should or shouldn't; that's not a decision I can make for you. It's your call. But hang in there. Like Ari Ho'd'ni would say, 'This too shall pass.' I'm right here beside you, and I promise I'm not going anywhere. We'll get through it. I swear we will."

Omega nodded, suddenly blinking hard again. Echo gave her a moment to gather herself.

"Ready to go to work?" he asked then. "We got a planetary potentate to guard. His ship will be landing in less than an hour, and we need to be at the hotel to meet him. You got this?"

"Yeah, I guess so." She sat up and reached for her jacket and holsters. "Let's go."

* * *

"...Here comes the Prime Minister now," Echo told them quietly, as Romeo, India, and Omega watched the alien entourage approaching on one of the VIP floors in the hotel. "We've effectively commandeered the entire floor, so we shouldn't have any interruptions here. Fox will introduce us. Follow my lead."

"Wilco," Omega murmured, and Romeo and India nodded.

"...I'm very sorry your mate could not attend you on your visit this time," they overheard Fox saying as the party neared them. "I was looking forward to seeing her again, to make up more properly for the unfortunate events of her last visit."

"She was...indisposed...this trip," the Prime Minister of Lambda Andromedae III said, his face coloring a slightly deeper shade of chartreuse than normal. "Perhaps...next time."

"Very good, then. I will look forward to your next visit. For now, allow me to introduce the Agency teams attached to guard your diplomatic visit. We have assigned several teams from our newest and most highly-trained department, Alpha Line, to your cortège. This is Alpha Line's chief, Agent Echo, the senior partner of the Alpha One team."

Echo bowed formally to the three-eyed potentate with bulging cranium and tentacle legs, and in crisp, clear tones, enunciated, "The Agency welcomes you to Earth, Mr. Prime Minister. It's a pleasure to work alongside your entourage."

"Thank you, Agent Echo," the tripedal planetary leader responded. "I, too, look forward to our...collaboration."

Fox moved to Omega.

"This is Agent Echo's partner and executive assistant, and the junior member of Alpha One, Agent Omega."

Omega bowed, and in her most formal tones—which also happened to be her most Southern—declared, "It is an honor to meet you, suh. Ah'm pleased to be assigned to your visit."

The Prime Minister studied her for a moment, curious.

"You are...unusual in speech. There is perhaps a slight hint of that speech in your partner, but otherwise...You are perhaps a somewhat different species of Terran?"

Omega felt her cheeks heat as she blushed, uncertain how to properly respond—she didn't want to contradict the planetary potentate and risk angering or offending him.

Then again, she thought, somewhat bewildered, *I'm really not the same species, quite, no matter what Zebra says. Not any more. But how the hell would I explain THAT?*

Fox scowled slightly, seeming displeased at the interaction, and Omega became even more flustered and uncertain. Echo smoothly filled in for her.

"Actually, Mr. Prime Minister, Agent Omega is of the same species, but a different region of the planet." This time he allowed more of his own native speech patterns to emerge.

"Ah, I see. So it is merely her dialect that is somewhat different," realized the Prime Minister, addressing Echo. "And now yours as well, as you permit it to be heard." The Prime Minister turned back to Omega. "I should find it interesting to converse with you and your partner at some point, Agent Omega. Your speech patterns are...intriguing. I find them... pleasant to the ear." Omega nodded silently, still pink-cheeked. Fox, with brows still knit, continued on.

"This is the second Alpha Line team, Alpha Two, made up of Agents Romeo and India."

India and Romeo bowed also, and, warned by Omega's experience and the expression Fox still wore, murmured a simple, "Honored, Mr. Prime Minister." Neither attempted to determine which of the Prime Minister's six appendages was appropriate to a handshake, nor did Fox—or Echo—provide them an example.

* * *

The Prime Minister studied the agents, recalling their dossiers, with general genetic backgrounds provided: a black male elite soldier, a Caucasian female scientist with alien 'enhancements,' a black female physician with Oriental heritage, and a Caucasian male career Agent with Amerind admixture; as well as dark and fair complexions...and yet, all one species. He recalled what he knew of Earth humans, and realized that before him was essentially a complete representation of *Homo sapiens* in all its variety. He shook his head in bemusement, blinking all three eyes.

"Earth truly has an amazing diversity of beings," he considered. "It is a wonder that things function here as well as they do."

"We try, Mr. Prime Minister," Echo replied. "It does sometimes cause difficulty, but the Agency prizes having a diversified membership. We feel it makes us stronger overall. Personally, I know without a doubt," he added, waving at his Alpha Line colleagues, "it makes our department stronger to have a broad range of personalities, experiences, skill sets, knowledge bases, and abilities, all working together for a common goal."

"I am.. certain it does," the Prime Minister declared, quirking two out of three spiny 'eyebrows' quizzically.

* * *

"Now, Mr. Prime Minister, your suite of rooms has been swept and is secure. I hope they are to your liking," Fox said, turning and waving a hand around the suite as they entered.

"They are acceptable," the Prime Minister said, gesturing permission to his bodyguards, who spread out through the rooms to familiarize themselves.

"And you have been informed of our use of the science fiction convention—which officially starts tomorrow—as cover for your visit?"

"I have."

"Then let us discuss the agenda of your visit. Alpha Line, you are dismissed for the moment."

The four Agents nodded acknowledgment and slipped out.

* * *

"Oh, great," Omega moaned, as soon as they were well out of earshot, down the corridor. "I blew that big time."

"Why?" Romeo asked as they walked. "You can't help the way you sound."

"Kinda like listening to *Gone With The Wind* all the time," Echo teased.

"Especially when you put the two of us together, 'Rhett,'" she shot back, then sobered. "No, it was bad. I was trying to follow Echo's lead, but..." she shook her head. "All I did was call attention to myself. And judging by his expression, that's what Fox saw, too. Thanks for bailing me out, Echo. Sorry you had to," Omega apologized.

* * *

"No problem. You ARE the same species as me, aren't you?" Echo replied, letting the barest hint of mischief lurk in his dark brown eyes; he watched as his companions, one by one, spotted his expression—first Omega, then Romeo, and finally India. Omega raised an eyebrow as he added, "See, I'd really hate to have lied to the Prime Minister."

"Sorry to tell you, Echo," Omega deadpanned with a completely straight face, "but I'm really a polymorphic amphibious anthropoid. My true form is seven and a half feet tall, with red gills, purple scales, flipper-feet, and black feathers. Oh, and I'm a male." She pointed at her mouth, which at that moment was puckered, as if she were trying to blow a bubble, or mimicking a fish. Sure enough, she started smacking her lips together repeatedly, like a goldfish in a bowl, making soft little popping noises. "Gets really complicated when I try to put lipstick on my beak, believe me."

By the time Omega had finished, all three of her fellow agents were laughing uproariously. Romeo and India were doubled over.

"Well, that makes MY job a helluva lot easier," Echo finally fired back, when he could stop laughing at the mental images his partner had conjured long enough to speak.

"Howzzat?" Omega grinned.

"If you're male, then I don't have to send India into the ladies' room to keep an eye on you for Fox. You can just come along with me, and we'll hit the urinals together," he told her, brown eyes gleaming as he waited for the reaction he knew was coming.

He got it.

"Oh!! Well, um," Omega said, blushing and thinking so fast—judging by the way her blue eyes were darting back and forth—that Echo was surprised smoke wasn't coming out of her ears, as Romeo and India went off into fresh gales of laughter. "Well, I can't morph back into my male form without the equipment in my spaceship, which as you can see, isn't handy. And I'd really hate to shake up all the other mens' room occupants, looking like this."

"Not t' mention, 'hitting the urinals' might be exactly th' problem," Romeo pointed out, guffawing.

"You beat me to it, junior," Echo laughed.

"Um, well, yeah, you got a point. The, ah, 'personal plumbing' morphs too, ya know," Omega jumped on the offering. "So maybe we better stick with the original plan."

"Smooth, Meg!" Romeo choked, gleeful.

"You go, girl! Or should that be 'guy'?!" India exclaimed merrily.

Ha! We needed that. Especially Meg. I'm glad she was up to joining in. Echo grinned down at Omega, still chuckling, and put a hand on her shoulder.

"C'mon, y'all, let's go check out the convention."

* * *

The four Agents entered the festively-decorated hotel lobby and surveyed the scene calmly.

"Huh. Kinda looks like the first time I saw the Core," Romeo remarked.

"Except there weren't any Kronons in the Core," Omega agreed. "Or empire stormtroopers. Or Christmas decorations."

"I see three space princesses," India observed.

"There goes a cyborg," Echo said. "Not bad."

"Izzat one 'a those anime moon chicks over there?" Romeo wondered.

"Oooh, the alien queen gives me the creeps," Omega commented. "Somebody spent some time on that one."

"What's with the dude in the fedora and the...damn! How long IS that muffler?" India wondered.

"Ah. The Doctor has arrived. Number Four, by the look," was all Omega said, to India's puzzlement. But then she grinned, and added, "Ever seen *Doctor Who*?"

"Doctor What?"

"No, Who."

"I dunno what you're talking about," India protested.

"Third base," interjected Echo; Omega let out a bark of laughter, and he grinned slightly.

"Hey, Echo, check out the slave princess," Romeo remarked in admiration, as a scantily-clad woman walked past the quartet. India's eyes narrowed; she gave her partner and lover a sharp elbow, and Romeo quickly tore his gaze away. "Hey, I was just checkin' out the costume," he told her.

"Riiight," she said, eyeing him. "Sure you were."

"I ain't chasin' skirts," Romeo protested. "I got my partner already, an' I'm happy with 'er. But please allow me t' have eyes an' a sense of appreciation."

"The hell you say," India grumbled.

"India, babe, look—I can appreciate without wantin' to touch."

"You better not touch, or you won't have anything left to touch WITH."

Omega chuckled.

"Better keep an eye on him, India," she told the other woman, joking. "I can guarantee that won't be the last skimpy costume we encounter."

"Oh joy," Alpha Two said in unison, in exactly the same ironic tone.

* * *

Omega glanced at Echo with a grin, to watch his reaction to their exchange, only to find him studying her instead.

"What is it?" she asked, caught off-guard. "Something wrong? My tie not straight?"

"YOU obviously know your way around a science fiction convention, too," Echo remarked, and Omega caught the inclusive *too*. "I was just trying to picture you in...this environment, back before you joined the Agency."

"I've been to a few, yeah. NASA scientists and astronauts are usually fairly popular at cons. I've been a special guest speaker a number of times."

"'Cons'?" India asked, then frowned. "Sounds like something illegal."

"Short for convention. SF cons have their own lingo. You'll catch on," Omega explained with a chuckle. "Oh, and the safest term these days is SF, guys. Depending on what group you run into, 'sci-fi' is a pejorative, and they will take vociferous offense." She shrugged. "To others it isn't, though, and they will argue that it is SUPPOSED to be called 'sci-fi,' which is sometimes pronounced 'skiffy.' And then there's the whole 'speculative fiction' thing, also sometimes called 'spec-fic.' So just pay attention to what the people around you are saying. But I've never heard anyone complain about the abbreviation, SF."

"Right," India murmured, apparently filing away the information. "SF is the safer term. Got it."

* * *

"Hey, Meg—did you ever show up in costume?" Romeo asked, and India and Echo waited with interest for her answer.

"Oh, yeah. The night of the masquerade just about everybody shows in costume. I didn't do the barbarian stuff, though. I usually showed in either a NASA flight jumpsuit or as a member of the spandex set," Omega answered him.

"Spandex set?" India asked. "More lingo?"

"Yeah. It refers to comic book superheroes. C'mon," Omega said as the others blinked at the mental image, "let's go to the con suite and get a Coke."

* * *

As the four Agents sat around a table together and sipped soft drinks in a corner of the relatively quiet con suite, they began noticing curious glances and whispers as the conventioneers slipped in and out of the room. India went to the door of the room and looked out, then motioned for Omega.

"Uh-oh," India said as Omega walked up, "take a look."

"Oh boy," Omega agreed, "time to get the guys out of here."

"What's up?" Echo asked, standing and walking over.

"No, no, stay back, away from the door," Omega pushed him back, "unless you want to get mobbed. Williamson and Rogers have been 'recognized.' There's at least fifty people in the hall, trying to get up the courage to come in."

"Shit!" Echo exclaimed, annoyed. "This is getting old."

"Come on, Meg," India said. "Let's go scout an escape route."

"Right behind you. We'll be back soon, guys. Hole up here. At least it's a small room," Omega said, and grinned mirthlessly. "You can defend yourselves easier."

"Do we haveta?" Romeo said, disappointed.

Echo just glared at him.

* * *

"Back to the Prime Minister's suite?" Omega guessed, out in the corridor.

"Sounds good. You scope the stairs, I'll check the elevators," India said.

"Done. Meet you back here in ten."

* * *

As soon as the female Agents—translated 'gatekeepers' to the fans—got well out of sight, the hordes began to descend on Romeo and Echo.

"Wow, man, are you guys here to promote the movie?"

"Hear it's gonna be a blockbuster. When's the release date?"

"Is it true George is doing the FX?"

"I thought you two didn't get along very well...?"

"Loved that miniseries you did a few years back..."

"You were great in *ÜberSpies*!!"

Echo tapped Romeo on the shoulder, and they slowly maneuvered their way toward the door. Once into the corridor, however, the situation rapidly became worse—the corridor was wall-to-wall science fiction fans, with more pouring in from every direction as the word spread.

"Oh, no," Romeo murmured, eyes wide.

"Oh, yes," Echo said grimly. Just then, India appeared at the far end of the hallway.

"May I have your attention?!" she called. The hubbub quieted.

"Mr. Rogers and Mr. Williamson have kindly elected to spend part of their holiday break from filming here at YuleCon. They're tired, and need some quiet. All they really want to do is to wander around the...SF con...and watch, for a change. Let's be considerate of them, and MAYBE we can talk them into a panel and an autograph session later."

Applause broke out, and the hallway began to clear. India worked her way through the dispersing crowd.

"Thanks, girl," Romeo murmured, intensely grateful. "That was...way the hell over the top."

"What he said. Where's Meg?" Echo asked.

"Isn't she here?" India responded, glancing at her wrist chronometer. "We were supposed to rendezvous back here five minutes ago."

Echo and Romeo exchanged a glance, and Romeo saw Echo's lips tighten.

"No," Echo said, "we haven't seen her since the two of you left. Where did she go?"

"She went to check out the stairs."

"All right," Echo said. "We need to find her fast. Spread out and start looking."

"On it."

* * *

The three Agents swiftly moved out into the atrium-style lobby and separated, heading in three different directions as they searched for their missing compatriot. Echo ran the stairs quickly but saw no sign of Omega. He stopped off at the Prime Minister's suite to double-check.

"Echo? What are you doing here? And where's Omega?" Fox asked, stepping outside the door so the Prime Minister wouldn't hear.

"That's what I'm trying to find out, Fox. The fans downstairs mistook Romeo and me for the damn actors, and damn near mobbed us. Omega and India went to scout us a quick way out. Meg never came back."

"What about India?"

"She and Romeo are searching, too."

"This isn't good, Echo," Fox said, pulling his cell phone. "I'll bring in backup. We need to find her before anything happens."

"Fox—it isn't gonna be THOSE agents, is it?"

"You know what I told you, Echo."

"Shit. Okay, Fox. I'll keep looking. Maybe I can find her before they get here, and it'll all be moot."

"Stay in touch."

"Always."

* * *

Echo emerged from the stairwell and entered the open lobby just as Romeo and India re-entered from different directions, both alone.

Damn, Echo thought, puzzled and concerned. *Meg, where the hell did you get to?*

As he moved out from under the balcony overhang, Echo saw both Romeo's and India's eyes widen in horror.

"*ECHO!!*" Romeo yelled, and both members of Alpha Two began sprinting toward him. Echo threw a swift glance behind himself, but there was no one there. Romeo tackled him in a flying leap, taking him completely off his feet, and Echo watched over Romeo's shoulder, airborne, as India caught a small, falling object and flung it back up, high into the open air of the huge lobby atrium, then dived for cover. There was a loud electronic shriek, a bright flash, and a strong concussion as Romeo and Echo landed hard in a corridor entrance. Con attendees in transit through the lobby clapped enthusiastically at the 'special effects demo.'

India ran over, followed closely by Fox, who had seen the explosion from the hotel elevator. Echo and Romeo picked themselves up from the floor. Monkey ran up from another corridor, and Sierra appeared moments later from the stairwell.

"What the hell happened?" Fox exclaimed.

"Sounded like a Winchester & Tesla in grenade mode," Echo remarked, and India nodded.

"It was. Somebody tried to drop it on you from somewhere up there," India pointed up into the depths of the high-rise hotel.

Just then, Omega emerged from a door beside the reception desk.

"Thanks!" she called, looking over her shoulder, and waved to an unseen person on the other side of the door. Then she turned and saw the cluster of agents. "Hi, y'all! Sorry I'm late. Did I miss anything?"

The six agents exchanged tense glances as Omega sauntered across the room.

"Yeah, Meg," Romeo remarked, "you could say that. Somebody just tried to kill Echo."

"WHAT?!" Omega ran across the remaining distance toward her partner. "You all right, hon??"

"I'm fine, Meg," Echo said quietly.

Abruptly, Fox moved forward with Monkey and Sierra. The pair of field agents moved in front of Echo, blocking Omega from reaching him. She stepped back in surprise, and as Echo pushed them aside, Fox placed a strong, restraining hand on Omega's shoulder.

"Where have you been?" Fox asked, stern.

"...Lost," Omega remarked, confused. "I took a wrong turn somewhere and got back into the service corridors. Once I got into those, I couldn't figure out how to get back into the real world. Finally I found a maid who led me out." She jerked a thumb back the way she'd come.

Echo's eyes narrowed as he watched Fox's austere, unsmiling face, and Romeo and India exchanged worried glances. Monkey and Sierra stood glaring at Omega as Fox continued interrogating her.

"Where's your Winchester & Tesla?"

"It's...back in my quarters."

"Meg!" India caught her breath. "I thought you ALWAYS carried your Winchester & Tesla."

"I...I HAVE been..." Even more confused, Omega looked around at the faces staring at her, at least half of which were accusing. "But today...I got tired of the thing bumping around in my back...I mean, the kids at the toy store tried using it for a CLIMBING RUNG, of all things...and I prefer my blasters anyway..."

"Meg," Echo told her softly, seeing her confusion and understanding it, "someone just tried to drop a Winchester & Tesla in grenade mode on me."

Omega's breath caught then, and she scanned him quickly to make sure he was all right. Then the significance hit her, and she paled, eyes dilating.

"Oh no. And...and you think *I*..."

"That's one way to get rid of the guard dog, I suppose," Monkey muttered to Sierra.

Omega went white.

"Echo," Romeo observed in a subdued tone, "your jacket's torn. Sorry, man."

"That's okay, hot shot, that's all that got torn, thanks to you and India. Appreciate it." Echo turned to his partner. "C'mon, Meg. Let's run home so I can get another jacket."

Omega blinked, totally confused by this point.

"No. She stays here with me, Echo," Fox said firmly.

"No, Fox." Echo was calm. "My partner goes where I go." He gave Fox a meaningful glance, and after a moment, Fox nodded.

"The woman just tried to kill you! Are you crazy?!" Monkey exclaimed, shocked and angry.

"No, and no," Echo replied, watching Omega throw a pleading look at Romeo and India, who glanced away. "Come on, Meg."

* * *

Back in Echo's quarters, Omega grabbed him by the arm and led him straight through the back door, across her holiday-decorated living area, and into her bedroom. Moving to her dresser, she scooped up an object and held it out to him, open-handed. It was the missing ray gun, and Echo noted that she held it out to him—with the barrel pointed at her own chest.

He noted, too, that the positioning had been deliberate, as she had shifted the weapon in her hands before offering it.

"Here's my Winchester & Tesla, Echo," she said then.

He looked down at the weapon in her hands, drew a deep breath, and let it out slowly. He wrapped his hands around hers, turning them gently so that the weapon pointed away from them both. Only then did he meet her eyes and nod.

"Here. Take it." She offered it to him. He took it from her, looked it over briefly but thoroughly, and handed it back to her.

"Yep. It's your Winchester & Tesla. I recognize the serial numbers. I'm gonna get a fresh jacket. May need a new shirt, too. My sleeve caught in the door latch when Romeo tackled me and knocked me outta the way. Back in a minute."

* * *

The shirt did indeed need replacing. Having completed the wardrobe swap and put the damaged items into the laundry chute, Echo came through his bedroom door still adjusting his tie, and stopped dead when he saw the closed back door.

"Aw, shit." He grimaced to himself, a flash of pain shooting through his being. He moved over to it and tried the latch. It was double-locked; his side AND hers. He unlocked his side, then said quietly, "Voice authorization override: Line-Alpha-One-Echo." There was a soft click, and Echo opened the door.

Omega was lying on the couch staring vacantly at the ceiling; her tie was loosened and her shoes off. Her jacket and dual-wield shoulder holster were also off, hanging on a dining table chair; the Winchester & Tesla, tucked into its proper holster, lay in the chair's seat. She didn't even look at him.

"I thought you'd feel better if I did that," she murmured. "Nobody wants an accused, would-be murderer having free access to his home..."

"You have to feel bad about something before you can feel better. Now get your jacket and your pieces—all three of 'em this time—and let's go. We've got a job to do, partner."

"You didn't bring me back here to stay?"

"No." Echo crouched beside the couch. "C'mon, let's—"

Abruptly, Omega turned to him, grabbing his shoulder.

"Echo, you're the department chief. Confine me to quarters," she demanded, intense.

"WHAT?!"

"Please."

"Why?"

"You'll function better if you don't have to deal with a partner you don't trust..."

"Who the hell says I don't trust you?!"

"But—"

"Meg, we 'read' each other about as well as any team I've EVER seen. I worked with X-ray for YEARS and we didn't read each other as well as you and I do, only about eight or nine months in! We lucked out, you and I—"

"All things considered, Ace, do you still think luck really had anything to do with it? Given the fact that an alien psychopath engineered me to get close to you, to be your perfect partner?"

"In this regard, yes, I do...although if you'd prefer, I can argue the theological aspect, too. You're you, your own unique being, with your own personality, and nothing some alien nutcase did to you has changed, or ever will change, THAT. Your personal will is way too strong for it. And you and I are a LOT alike, in all the ways that count. Look, Meg, it's pretty simple. We're just a REALLY well-matched team, baby. You know me. I know you. I know when you're acting a part, I know when you're bluffing, or when you're just flat lying through your teeth. I also know that you've never lied to ME. EVER. You've omitted some details a couple times for the sake of mission success," he held up a forestalling hand when she opened her mouth to protest, "like the Antarctic mission when you didn't tell me nobody gave you heavyweight clothing—and I understand, and I'd have done the same thing if the positions had been reversed, for the same reasons—but you've never lied to me. So when you tell me you didn't do it, when you say you'd never willingly TRY to hurt me, much less try to kill me...I know, Meg. I know you're telling me the truth. I KNOW. Because I know YOU." She sighed at his words, and he saw her relax slightly, her blue gaze warming in gratitude and affection. He patted her shoulder. "So come on. Let's go."

The warmth and affection vanished, replaced by a kind of bleak desolation.

"I...still think I should stay here."

"Why?"

"Echo, did you SEE the looks the others gave me?" Omega asked in a low voice. "Even Romeo and India..."

"So, did you try to kill me?"

* * *

"What?!" Omega cried, shocked and hurt. "Echo, you just said—"

"I know what I said. Answer the question."

"NO! I'd NEVER willingly try to HURT you—much less...THAT."

"Just like I said. Wording and everything. I told you, Meg—I know you."

"So you know it's true."

"Right. So why act guilty?"

"Huh?"

"Meg, we both know you're innocent. So you're going to hold your head up, go back to the hotel, and find out who DID do it."

Omega searched her partner's eyes for a moment. Echo met her gaze, his own calm and confident. And completely trusting.

"Yes, Rhett," she finally said, voice slightly choked, and VERY Southern. Then she got up to fetch her holsters and jacket.

"How's that?" Echo asked with amusement.

"YOU'RE the one always teasing me about *Gone With The Wind.*

Remember that scene where Rhett makes Scarlett go to the party?" Omega queried as she fastened her shoulder holster. Echo handed her the waistband holster, the Winchester & Tesla already in it, and she tucked it into place.

"Mmm...that the one where everyone thinks she and Wilkes have been—"

"Yeah. Only she was innocent, too." Omega shrugged into her jacket as her partner held it for her. As she adjusted its positioning across her shoulders, he tightened the knot on her tie for her until it nestled comfortably but neatly at the base of her throat.

"There's one big difference, Meg," Echo told her as they headed out.

"What's that?"

"Butler dumped Scarlett at the door and left. I'LL be with you the whole way."

"...Promise?"

Echo's lips twitched in an almost-smile; the earnest expression on his partner's face once more reminded him of a small recent acquaintance. So he held out his hand, little finger extended.

"As a certain toy store moppet recently said to me..." he pitched his voice in a high falsetto, "'Pinky pwomise.'"

Omega burst out laughing.

But she also joined his little finger with her own.

Chapter 6

Alpha Line—or at least, its two available field teams—stood at attention before the Director in the hotel room that the Agency was using as a base of operations in the hotel. Fox was grilling the junior member of Alpha One.

"So you have your Winchester & Tesla now, eh?"

"Yes, sir."

"And Echo saw you retrieve it?"

"Yeah, Fox," Echo interjected. "She took me straight to it and gave it to me. It was on her dresser—right where I've seen her put it before."

"If it's not on me, it's on my dresser," she shrugged.

"And it WAS *HERS*, wasn't it, Echo?" Fox pressed.

"Yeah. Saw the ID number."

"Is it on you now, Omega?"

"Yes, sir." Omega started to reach around to draw it and present it to the Director, then thought better of it when she saw Fox's face. "Uh, Echo, maybe YOU better pull it for me. It's in the mini-holster in the small of my back," she sighed.

"I know. I saw you put it there, remember?" Echo reached under her jacket and withdrew the tiny pistol. "Here, Fox."

Fox examined the weapon carefully, then handed it back to Echo, who passed it to Omega. Omega stared down at the weapon with an odd expression, then slowly re-holstered it. Romeo and India watched silently, then glanced at each other with curious expressions of their own. Echo noted the look, and answered their unspoken question.

"Meg's wishing she could chuck the damn thing in the Hudson right now. From here, no less. As far and as hard as she can fling it."

Fox, Romeo, and India looked startled, as Omega rolled her eyes heavenward, but she didn't deny it. She turned to Fox.

"Shall I...return to quarters, sir?"

Fox looked from Omega's averted, almost downcast gaze to Echo's direct, impassive, almost challenging one, then shook his head.

"No, that won't be necessary. Echo trusts you, and he obviously knows his partner well enough that I trust his judgement. The evidence is all circumstantial anyway. But from now on, STICK TO ECHO. Preferably like glue. You are now his shadow."

Omega nodded wordlessly.

"Omega?" Fox said quietly. "Echo is your alibi; you do understand that?"

"Sure, Fox. Of course he is. Suspects always have alibis, right?"

Fox sighed, and Echo threw him an *I told you so* look.

"Um...can we get back to work now, sirs?" Omega requested quietly. "We've got negotiations to prepare for, and I've got an attempted murderer to find..."

"Well said, Omega," Fox replied. "Dismissed."

Romeo and India stepped out of the room; Echo moved over to Fox. Omega stood stiffly where she was.

"Omega? You can go now," reiterated Fox.

"No, sir. I can't."

Fox and Echo both looked at her, confused.

"I'm a...shadow now, remember? No life of my own..."

Fox nodded comprehension, and Echo's dark eyes flashed silent understanding and sympathy for a moment. Then Echo turned back to Fox.

"Got an agenda worked out with the diplomatic team?"

"Yes," Fox said, pulling a paper. "Here's your copy. I wanted it in electronic format, but Sugar has a thing for jotting it all down by hand, and nobody's had time to key it in yet. He's a damn good negotiator otherwise, so I can't complain. Coordinate with Omega and Alpha Two and make sure everything is under control. Remember the Prime Minister has his own bodyguards, too. Make use of them if necessary. I'll be working with the negotiations team out of the Diplomacy department, but other than final approval, I plan to mostly stay in the background. Come get me if you need something."

"Got it." Echo took the agenda and studied it for a moment. Then he turned to Omega and laid a light hand on her shoulder. "Come on, shadow."

* * *

Zero Days—Seven Days

The next morning, both the diplomatic visit and the science fiction convention got well under way; there had been some scattered panels the previous day, but both scheduling and attendance were light. Today, there were multiple tracks of programming.

The *carte noirs* of the Agents had converted themselves into con badges, and they could move freely through the large con as a consequence. The diplomatic envoy were also provided with similar IDs, and YuleCon and the negotiators smoothly traded off meeting rooms, with the convention attendees being none the wiser...for the most part.

Leaving Omega in the current negotiations room beside Fox, observing, Echo slipped out and headed for the con suite, where drinks and snacks could be found. He was intent on grabbing a soda and possibly something to munch; Alpha Line had spent the night quietly patrolling the hotel and hadn't been back to their quarters, nor yet had time to swing by the hotel restaurant for breakfast.

Looking over the offerings on the counter tables, Echo found individually-wrapped pastries and various soda products in one room.

"Aha. That'll do for breakfast," he decided, snagging five cellophane-wrapped Danishes and dropping them into various warp pockets. "But I'd really love some coffee, and I'd bet Meg would, too. Maybe in the other room..."

The Alpha Line chief moved into the back room of the suite, hoping to find a coffeemaker there.

Instead, he found one of the Lambda Andromedan bodyguards, slumped in a chair in the corner, a mostly-empty two-liter bottle of ginger ale clutched in her hand.

Uh-oh. That doesn't look good, he thought, concerned, and moved to the alien woman's side. *She's either sick, or dru...wait. That's just a bottle of ginger ale. She can't be drunk. There's no alcohol in here; that's all in the green room for the guests of honor.*

He bent over the barely-conscious female and sniffed.

*Damn, she IS drunk. But the smell is like...*Echo blinked. *Like ginger ale.*

Oh, wait a minute. What if the carbonation, to the Lambda Andromedans, is like nitrogen narcosis to human divers? Like, when they get all loopy an' shit?

Echo crouched by the bodyguard's chair and took a tentacular arm in hand, searching for the pulse. Eventually he found it, but it seemed normal to him, based on his decidedly exhaustible knowledge of the particular species' physiology.

But her skin feels warm, he thought. *And she's definitely pretty out of it, but she's not entirely unconscious. She's still responding to external stimuli, a little bit.*

He leaned forward and carefully peeled an eyelid back, producing his cell phone and activating the flashlight app. He swiped it across in front of her eye as he held it open, watching for reaction.

Wow. Rapid eye movement. Yup, this chick is definitely drunk. And probably had no clue this would do it to her; I'm sure if she asked any of the con suite attendants, or the fans, er, fen, they'd have told her it was harmless. So would I, for that matter. And it is...to us. I better see about getting her back to the bodyguards' room, before somebody else finds her.

"Ma'am? Ma'am," he murmured, shaking her gently.

"Mm? Ommini boop?" came the slurred reply in the alien's native tongue.

"Um," Echo began, rapidly trying to dredge up his limited supply of Andromedan; he hadn't had a chance to use one of the Agency's crash courses on the language, and hadn't thought it would be a problem, since the entire contingent was supposed to be able to speak fluent English. *But then, nobody expected one to get drunk out of her gourd on ginger ale, either,* he thought ruefully. Finally he tried, "Boopty floppa gunk? Gakka Agent Echo. Archoo guggle puff."

Either I just told her I'm getting her back to her room, or I just propositioned her, I'm not sure which, Echo thought, trying not to cross his eyes while he waited to see what the woman would do.

"Guggle puff doh," came the answer, and Echo relaxed.

"C'mon, then," he murmured, pulling her to her feet before dragging one boneless arm across his shoulder and putting his arm around what passed for her waist. "Let's get you back to your shift supervisor. Hopefully I can explain what happened without getting you in trouble. I really hope you're not AWOL..."

* * *

It wasn't as easy to get her back as Echo had hoped; the lack of major bones in the limbs of Lambda Andromedans meant that when she went all wobbly-legged on him, he was effectively dragging her. And the species wasn't as light as he could have wished, either—especially beefed-up guards in body armor. But eventually he got her back to the floor reserved for the alien diplomatic team and guard contingent, pretty much unseen by con-goers, who were all in panels at that time of day.

As it turned out, the shift supervisor had been quite worried; Echo's new charge was one of his best guards, and finding out she had gone missing overnight had been troublesome, to say the least. When she hadn't shown up for the start of her shift either, he had become downright worried, even sending out two off-duty guards to try to find her.

So when Echo showed up with her in tow—literally—and explained what had happened and why, the supervisor called in his searchers and promised to ensure that the entire contingent was made aware of the potential effects of the 'harmless'—to humans—carbonated beverages. He also assured Echo that the woman was not in trouble, as she had obviously had no idea the substance would have such an effect.

He took the nearly-asleep bodyguard off Echo's hands—literally—and carried her into the hotel room, as Echo turned back for the con suite to grab a few individual-serving bottles of Coke for his own team.

* * *

Once back in the negotiations area, Echo doled out the approximation of breakfast to Alpha Two, warning them not to share their drinks with the Andromedans along with a brief explanation why, then slipped into the negotiating room to deliver Omega's breakfast. She nodded her thanks and promptly opened both pastry and bottle of Coke, tucking them away with some speed.

Heh, he thought, watching with affectionate amusement. *Somebody was really hungry.*

But he pulled Fox into the corner of the room to give him the snacks.

"What's wrong, Echo? You didn't drag me away from the table for a Danish and a soda."

"No, Boss, it's something potentially more serious. I found one of the Prime Minister's bodyguards in the con suite, drunk...on ginger ale."

"What?!"

"Yeah. I dunno. Near as I can figure, I think maybe the carbonation gives them something akin to divers' nitrogen narcosis or something. That's my theory, anyhow. But I'm not a medical sort, so I dunno for certain; it could be something else entirely. All I know for sure is, she was drunk, she had a two-liter of ginger ale in her mitt, it was mostly gone, and her breath smelled of ginger. No booze breath, just ginger."

"Well, damn..."

"Exactly. I got her back to her room, and her supervisor took over..."

"Is she in trouble?"

"I don't think so. Evidently she's got a pristine record, and I explained that, if she'd asked, she would have been told that it was a harmless drink to quench thirst. She'd have had no way of knowing. Hell, I didn't even know. I'd have said the same thing, if she'd asked."

"Okay. I'll give Zebra a call, see what she knows or can tell me. Maybe there's an antidote. We need to set up a separate 'con suite' for our own group, if that's the case. Or at least for the Lambda Andromedans."

"Yeah, kinda figured."

"All right. That was an important little discovery. My thanks, mayn khaver."

"No problem, Fox. How's Meg doing with watching the negotiations?"

"Not half bad. She whispers—or scribbles—questions to me occasionally, whichever form of communication seems appropriate at the time, and I try to explain. But now she's starting to offer suggestions...and damn, Echo, they're good suggestions."

"Terrific. She's not bothering you, is she?"

"No. She was quiet for the first little bit, just watching and listening. Getting her sea legs, I suppose. When she finally did ask a question, she did it subtly, and waited for a good opportunity to ask me without diverting my attention, or calling the others' attention."

"Well...great. I'm glad to hear it. I, uh, I hope you don't mind, but I'd told her she could ask you the occasional question if she didn't understand something. I figure she needs to get a handle on the diplomacy thing, probably sooner rather than later, and if anyone in the Agency is expert at that, it's you, since you founded the department. Not to mention representing Earth in the Galactic Council for the first few years."

"No, that's fine." Fox smiled slightly at the sincere compliment. "I'd have said you do an excellent job as well, especially given one of your degrees. But since you went to fetch food, it was a moot point anyway. You don't always use that diplomacy degree, at least on an everyday basis, but when you do, you know what you're doing."

"True. Thanks, Boss. I don't use it every day, because I choose not to. I prefer straightforward, honest interactions on a day-to-day basis. I've seen too many of the guys who took the same courses I did, and they turn into schmoozers and used-car salesmen. You know the type."

"Yes, I do, and I understand. You're a WYSIWYG mensch."

"Huh? What's WYSIWYG?"

"It's an acronym. Stands for What You See Is What You Get. And a real mensch into the bargain."

"Oh." Echo felt his face warm slightly at the praise from the older man. "Well, as Meg would say, I try, I guess."

"I know. I think you do damn well, for what it's worth. I still can't think of anyone better suited to introduce Omega to the whole interstellar diplomacy bit, though."

"It hasn't been hard. She's already pretty good—I mean, she gets the idea of negotiation and compromise and junk, and her folks raised her with that whole Southern gentility thing, so she's automatically polite, most of the time even if she's pissed off—and I think she's only gonna get better with experience." Echo paused, and threw a worried glance across the room at his partner. "Provided we can keep her out of trouble long enough."

Fox sighed.

"Come on," he told Echo. "Let's get back to the negotiating table before someone other than Omega starts to ask questions."

"Right."

* * *

"What's this visit all about, anyway, Echo?" India asked him at one point, after they'd escorted the Prime Minister back to his suite for a break, amid comments of "Cool!" and "Great costumes!" from science fiction fans, as well as a few enthusiastic cries of, "YAY, *BLACK SUITS*!"

"The Lambda Andromeda system is looking to start formal trade with Earth," Echo explained. "The agreement will be an addendum to the Sydys Concordat. The governing body of the Concordat is keeping a close eye on the details."

"Why are you sometimes in there during the negotiations?" India asked him. "I know you occasionally leave Omega with me and Romeo because of what's going down and all, but..."

"One of my degrees is in diplomacy and diplomatic relations, and I've done this kinda thing a few times. So I'm just helping Fox and the negotiators out," Echo told her, with a shrug. "Probably you should all come in and get involved at some point, get some experience under your belts. The Division One diplomatic corps can't always be there when the need for negotiation suddenly comes up. That's why I had Omega in there this morning, watching."

"I thought it was because Alpha Two was doing a quick morning sweep," Omega said.

"That, too," Echo agreed. "I figured if you were with Fox, nobody could accuse you of clandestine activities. Besides, I wanted that gray matter of yours taking it in. And Fox says you were, too. I think he was a little impressed at how well you understood. Now," he added, looking around at his team, "I want you ALL to start participating. Not all at once; we still need patrols and stuff. But I want you to have the experience."

"I'm cool with that," Romeo said.

"Me, too," India added. "Let me know when."

"...Let's not and say we did," Omega muttered. "More likely I'd get accused of trying to start a damn interplanetary war, the way things have been goin' lately."

"C'mon, Meg," Romeo nudged her, "it's all right. We'll get the real perp. An' you can DO this. You did, this morning, enough to impress th' boss-man."

"I wouldn't have suggested it otherwise," Echo said. He checked his wrist chronometer. "Whoa. It's gettin' late. Let's grab something to eat while the Prime Minister gets lunch."

* * *

"Oh, hey, George," Echo murmured as they passed a fan with spiky blue hair en route to the hotel restaurant for a bite.

"Hey, hi, Echo," George answered, pausing. Echo stopped, and Omega and Alpha Two paused with him.

"What are you doing here?" Echo wondered.

"Eh, no big deal," George shrugged. "I wanted to come to the con. I'm a big fan of the Doc, and thought maybe I could meet 'im this time."

"Okay, right. Yeah, if you don't get the chance to get an autograph from him, ping me. You know how to reach me."

"Oh? You know him?"

"Little bit, yeah. I can get you in to say hi, anyway."

"Cool! Thanks," George said, grinning. "I might just take you up on that. Goin' to grab lunch?"

"Yeah. Wanna join us?"

"Thanks, but there's a panel coming up I wanna catch. And I'm meeting some other, uh, 'special' friends afterward..."

"Okay, don't let me keep you. See ya around."

"Thanks, Echo. Later!"

As George departed, Omega lightly touched Echo's arm.

"Who was that?" she wondered.

"Him? That was George Leeks," Echo murmured to the other Alpha Line members. "Old friend from Chesharilzi. I think he's Zarnix' cousin, if I remember right."

"Zarnix, like the head of Medical?" India asked.

"Yup," Echo agreed, heading for the restaurant's door. "George is a big science fiction fan—especially of the off-world writers, who about half the time are really writing historical fiction from elsewhere in the galaxy. He gets enthused over the guys who are tryin' to get Earth mentally prepped to join the Galactic Council, I think. That group of 'special friends'? That's gonna be his SF club...not one of whom is from Earth."

"Oh!" Omega said, as they went inside and the maitre d' met them.

* * *

"So," Romeo began, as they waited for their food to arrive in the corner booth, "I guess there's a lot more aliens here than I realized, huh?"

"What, you mean at the con?" Echo wondered, sipping his glass of water.

"Yeah."

"Oh, quite a few, yeah. I wouldn't say a LOT, but enough to where, when they see me with a Lambda Andromedan, they know the Agency is using the con as a cover. It's kinda useful, actually," Echo noted. "Fox told me earlier that a few discreet inquiries had come in, and he'd put out the word that we were using that movie as our cover story. So, when any human civvies ask questions, the aliens just tell 'em this is all a big Hollywood promo push." He shrugged. "We're managing to make it work to our advantage...so far."

"That works, I guess," India decided.

"Yeah, decently enough. At least until people start recognizing individual agents on the street," Echo agreed.

"Damn," Omega murmured.

"Something like, yup," Echo averred.

* * *

Much later, the inadvertently-drunk but now-sober bodyguard, whose name was Dehman, approached her superior, as he watched over the Prime Minister's entourage, who was crossing the lobby as they returned from luncheon.

"Andango blop-boo?" she murmured, submissive and ashamed. The head of security waved a dismissive tentacle.

"Dagoop," he told her, offering a slight smile.

"Ondo?" She blinked, confused. "Dagoop blop-boo?"

"Dagoop. Gopy do Agent Echo archoo giggle puff."

"Oo! Doy ablopa ping."

"Oop da. Um..." The security chief looked around, then pointed at a dark-haired human male in a black Suit. "Dok-dok cho Agent Echo, aglodo bop."

"Ping ping!" Dehman told him, and headed for the indicated human.

* * *

As she walked up behind the handsome human, Dehman smiled and murmured, "Gloppity poop, ping ping, Agent Echo."

The man turned.

"Um, excuse me?"

"Oh!" Dehman said, startled. "Please forgive me. I do not think you are who I thought you were. Agent Echo?"

"No," the man smiled. "I'm Agent Five. Different fandom, I guess."

"Um, perhaps," Dehman offered, confused. "Perhaps you can pass on a message, though?"

"Uh, I can try," the costumed 'Agent Five' agreed. "Depends if I know the guy or not. Cool costume, by the way."

"Er, thank you," Dehman said, as polite as she knew how to be, though she had no idea what the man referenced by 'costume.' "If you would be so kind as to tell Agent Echo thank you for his rescue of me last night, I would appreciate it. I had no idea the beverage was...what is the term...? Ah! I think the word is 'spiked.'"

"Damn," Agent Five noted in disgust. "Somebody tried to spike your drink? It wasn't rohypnol, was it? Did they jump you after? And this Echo guy—he looked after you? Or was he the one who did it?"

"Oh, no, no, he did not do it," Dehman averred. "This I can swear. I remember him looking after me and helping me get back to my room—and he did not come in. He delivered me to my dango, who saw to it that I was properly cared for. As for the rest, I do not understand, and I cannot answer your questions."

"Ooo, I get it. You're not from the US, are you?" Five wondered.

"English isn't your native language."

"No, and no," Dehman answered truthfully. "But I did want to ensure Agent Echo knows I am grateful."

"He knows," came a deep voice behind her.

Dehman spun, just as Five exclaimed, "Oh hey! It's the movie people!"

Behind her stood a tall, dark-haired human Agent, a pale blonde female Agent at his side. Flanking them were two darker-skinned Agents, one male, one female.

"Ah! Agent Echo!" Dehman said in recognition, offering him a wide Lambda Andromedan smile.

* * *

Echo nodded in a friendly, if reserved, fashion at the strange man dressed in the black suit, and he smiled back and wandered off.

"I'm glad to see you feeling better, ma'am," Echo murmured then. "You ARE feeling better, aren't you?"

"Oop da. Gakka Dehman. Gloppity poop, ping ping, Agent Echo," the alien woman said.

Echo cut his eyes to the side, and saw Omega blink in surprise. *Oh boy,* he thought. *Now I gotta try to dredge up some more Lambda Andromedan, or risk an undiplomatic incident. And said undiplomatic incident just might be Meg laughing her head off while Mr. Linguist, here, makes a fool of myself. Plus I have to explain to Dehman that just because someone is wearing a black suit doesn't automatically mean they're an Agent, especially with all the fans dressed like* Black Suits.

He sighed silently, dredging up his Lambda Andromedan and thinking fast.

"Dagoop da lala, Dehman," he tried then. "I'm sorry if I get the syntax wrong. My Andromedan is a little rusty."

"You did fine," Dehman told him, smiling even wider. "Just now, and last night...what I remember of it. Or perhaps it was this morning. Thank you for caring for me. My dango told me what happened, and I appreciate it."

"Not a problem, as I said—at least, as I tried to say," Echo said, returning her smile. "But you and your colleagues should probably stay out of the carbonated sodas. Our Medical staff is trying to ascertain exactly what happened, but it might not be good for you."

"Oh! That is good information. I shall tell everyone," Dehman agreed. "I was told that it was a safe beverage, but obviously it was not—at least, not for me and my people."

"Exactly. Plus, you need to know that, just because they seem to be dressed like us, it doesn't mean that everyone dressed like this," Echo fingered his Suit lapel, "is part of the Agency."

"No?" Dehman murmured, all three eyes widening. "What...?"

"There is an attempt being made to expose us," Omega said, beside him. "They are using a movie, a film, to do it, along with some other things related to it. So some of the people here at this fiction convention are dressed up like us, because they think we are part of that movie."

"We're usin' it for cover," Romeo added.

"Ohhh..." Dehman said in a soft voice, thoughtful. "That man I was just talking to...?"

"Was not one of us," Echo confirmed. "If at all possible, I'd like for you and your contingent to get to know me and my team, so we can recognize each other." He turned. "This is my partner, Omega. Omega, this is Grakkada Dehman, of the Lambda Andromedan Majestic Guard. Grakkada is her rank, let me add, not part of her name."

"Very pleased to meet you," Omega said with a grin. "Call me Omega."

"Indeed," Dehman replied, offering a tentacle. Omega took it and lightly squeezed it, and Dehman smiled. "Call me Dehman, please."

"Omega and I are the Alpha One team, and these two over here are our friends, the Alpha Two team, Romeo and India."

"Ah! Alpha Line! Yes, yes, of course," Dehman affirmed, shaking appendages. "And there is also Director Fox, and the diplomatic team..."

"Right," Echo said. "And while there are occasionally a couple of other partnerships who come in to give us a break now and then," he indicated Alpha One and Two, "I'd much prefer if you got to know us four, and came to us with anything you need. That way, we avoid any potential misunderstandings among the convention fans."

"Aha, I see," Dehman said sagely, and nodded. "Yes, I will pass this on to my dango. In fact, perhaps you could come with me so that I may introduce you all properly...?"

"Sure," Echo agreed, after glancing at the others. "I saw the Prime Minister go through with your people, and Fox was right behind 'em, so they're okay for now. And I think we actually SHOULD spare a few minutes to do this."

"Makes sense to me," Omega agreed.

"Damn straight," Romeo murmured, and India nodded vigorously.

"C'mon, guys, let's go make some new friends," Echo said with a grin, and the four followed the alien woman toward the elevators.

* * *

Half an hour later, as they left the hotel rooms which had been reserved as quarters for the Majestic Guard, Omega glanced around to make sure they were well out of earshot, then commented, "Well, that was the strangest language I've ever heard. At least to this point."

"What do you mean?" Echo wondered, and India and Romeo listened with interest.

"Just that, when you two were talking, I couldn't tell if you were speakin' baby talk or comin' on to each other, Ace," Omega teased, a wide grin on her face. "I mean, really? 'Oop da floppity poop'? An' you're the linguist, too, according to one o' your degrees, with plenty of past evidence supporting..."

India bit her lip, eyes twinkling, and Romeo snorted; Echo flushed.

"I was NOT comin' on to her," he declared in a low tone. "Not every language 'out there' has to sound like Einstein's."

"No, some of 'em sound like birds chirping," Omega agreed. "And others, like somebody forgot the vowels, or is tryin' to swallow the letters. But that one? I was just surprised you could keep a straight face while you were talkin' to her. I had all I could do, and I was just listening."

"Oh. That explains why you kept tucking your head, then," Echo realized.

"Yeah. I didn't think it'd be very diplomatic if they saw me laughin' myself silly," Omega confirmed.

"No, it wouldn't, and you've got enough on your plate right now as it is, without creating a minor diplomatic incident," Echo reminded her in a mild tone.

Omega decided to shut up about the sound of Lambda Andromedan speech patterns.

* * *

Despite her earlier claim of being a male cyborg polymorph, when Echo jokingly suggested Omega join him in a quick trip to the men's room after they met the Majestic Guard—by way of a small payback for the teasing comments about the Lambda Andromedan language—she turned redder than he'd yet seen her manage. So he grinned, left her with Alpha Two, and headed to the restroom alone.

But as he was washing his hands at the sink, he overheard an unpleasantly-familiar voice coming from outside the restroom's doorless dog-leg entryway.

"...And so the way me an' my partner figure it, either the programming is still in effect, or there was never any programming to begin with, and she's the whole brains behind the operation. She's certainly smart enough to do it, from what I've heard."

Echo scowled, as raw fury washed through him. But he had not gotten where he was in the Agency by letting his emotions control him; he calmed himself, dried his hands on a strip quietly torn from a loose roll of paper towels left on the counter—the hotel's convention center janitorial service couldn't quite keep up with the demand from the con—and glanced around the men's restroom, including checking for feet under the stall doors. Then he pulled his cell phone, initiated an app, and used it to scan the room before checking the readout.

Good. I'm the only one in here, for a wonder. I can do what's necessary, if I have to, he decided.

Then he eased over to the entranceway and leaned against the interior wall, positioning himself in shadow where he could watch the interaction in a full-length mirror while himself remaining out of sight—

—But not out of earshot.

* * *

Just outside the men's restroom, Monkey stood with several others in black Suits, earnestly trying to discuss the matter of Omega's presumed guilt with them.

"Dude, you're great!" one of the other agents commented, sounding amused. "I thought Ken was good, but you got him beat!"

"Shush, Joe," another remarked. "You're blowin' the atmosphere. Go with it. So, Agent...Monkey, did you say?"

"Yeah."

"This Omega chick...she's not in the cartoon..."

"She doesn't have an action figure, either," the first agent commented. The three others laughed, but said nothing.

"No. That's part of the genius of it, you see," Monkey explained. "She's the ONLY one who can get out and about without being recognized. SHE goes out, sets up all the shit, comes back to Headquarters, and nobody's the wiser."

"Except you."

"Yeah. Well...us. My partner, a couple other colleagues, and me. Yeah," Monkey agreed.

"What about the bosses? Don't they suspect anything?"

"Fox is on the fence," Monkey said, shaking his head in disgust. "We're workin' on him, though. I think he's starting to see the light. As for Echo, well...Sierra has his own ideas about THAT one."

"Such as?"

"Such as how they're probably lovers, and he's in it with her. See, if anything happens to Fox, he becomes the Director. I'm not sure about that, though. I think she's just got him wrapped around her little finger. Probably what she's doin' to him in the bedroom. And he doesn't even realize she's tryin' to kill him."

"Damn, man." The first agent shook his head in disbelief.

"Exactly! You're hearin' me!" Monkey exclaimed, frustrated. "You get what I'm sayin'!"

"I dunno, dude," the second agent said, skeptical. "Sounds like some weird shit to me." He checked his wrist watch. "Ooo. C'mon, Mike. We got places to be. Guys, c'mon, or we'll miss the special panel."

"Oh, hey, right," Monkey agreed, stepping back. "Hard enough to get around and do our jobs with all the street recognition. I don't wanna make you late for your assignment."

"Catch you later, dude!" Mike remarked, waving as the group of agents departed, headed down the hall toward convention programming.

Monkey waved back as he watched them go. A satisfied smirk spread across his face.

"Bingo," he muttered. "Five more agents converted."

"Is that so?" came a deep voice behind him, as a powerful hand slammed down onto his shoulder.

Monkey flew clear off his feet as he disappeared into the men's restroom.

* * *

As the fans walked away from the men's restroom, en route to the special panel with all of the con's guests of honor, Mike turned to his friend David.

"Damn! Best cosplay I've seen since DragonCon!"

"Ain't it the truth," David agreed, laughing. "I thought my *Black Suits* costume was good...until I saw that guy!"

"Didn't we all!" one of the other fans agreed, also laughing. "I'm betting he was from the film! I cannot WAIT for that movie to come out! I'm so STOKED! I'm gonna get in line for tickets the night before!"

"Hurry up, guys," another said. "We're gonna be late to the panel and have to stand up, if we can even get in. And I really wanna hear Doc Taylor talk about his latest book!"

* * *

Inside the bathroom, Monkey soared through the air and slammed hard against the far wall, sliding down the tiling to the floor. He sat there, stunned, for several moments, then instinctively reached for his blaster, inside the shoulder holster under his jacket.

"Oh HELL no," Echo said, looming over him and grabbing Monkey's wrist before he could reach the blaster. "You are NOT gonna shoot ME!"

Monkey shook his head, trying to clear his vision, and looked up into Echo's furious face.

"Oh. It's you," he said, sullen. "Heard it, huh?"

"Damn straight. What the hell do you think you're doing?!"

"Making sure other agents know just how blinded you've become from your partner's charms," Monkey said, deliberately insolent. "You've lost your perspective, Echo. She's using you."

"The hell you say!" Echo exclaimed, dragging Monkey up from the floor by his shirt front and slamming him against the wall again. Monkey felt his head hit the tile once more, and he saw stars for a brief moment. "First of all, Meg and I are NOT LOVERS! Never have been! She IS the best friend I've got, however, and she's someone I know like the back of my hand. Someone I TRUST! With my LIFE! And I am NOT," he shook the smaller man like a terrier shaking a rat, "GONNA," he slammed Monkey against the wall again, "LET you and your little CLIQUE smear her in the gutter! DO YOU HEAR ME?" An incensed Echo shook Monkey one more time for good measure.

"Yeah," Monkey panted, dizzy. "You're gonna have to convince the Agency of that. All it takes is a few of the agents coming around to our point of view, you know." He jerked a thumb at the restroom entrance. "A few more encounters like that, and it's all over for your precious partner. Other agents will be able to see the truth, even if YOU can't."

* * *

"Oh, like you've done such a great job at that," Echo said, feeling a deadly chill flood him as he glared at the other man. He abruptly let go his two-fisted grip on Monkey's clothing, and the other agent dropped nearly a foot to the floor. Monkey staggered, but landed more or less on his feet.

"Yeah, I have," Monkey declared, still insolent. "You heard 'em."

"I heard a bunch of science fiction fans in costume, laughing at you," Echo asserted, icy calm.

"What?"

"You heard me. You were so eager to win new converts that you didn't even realize you weren't talking to fellow agents, you were talking to fans. They thought you were talking about the *Black Suits* movie."

"No! You're lying!"

"Fine. Suit yourself. Go try to find 'em in the Agency rosters. Meanwhile, I'll be explaining to Fox how you were airing the Agency's dirty laundry...to CIVILIANS."

"Shit!"

Monkey pushed past Echo and ran out of the restroom, in search of the 'agents' to whom he'd just been preaching, as Echo laughed coldly in his wake.

* * *

"...He did WHAT?!" a shocked Fox said, alone with Echo in the hotel room that had been designated for Alpha Line's down time. "Oy vey! That's meshuginah! Tell me you're shittin' me, son."

"Hell, Fox, I wish I was," Echo said, shaking his head. "Near as I could tell, he told 'em just about Meg's whole life story, at least as much as would be available to an agent that wasn't a Director or Department chief. Or partner," he added. "AND out-and-out said that, if I wasn't part of the plot—which of course I'm not, and neither is Meg—then Meg must be controlling me using sex. Hell, she's never even made a pass at me, Fox. And I've never come on to her, either. We're PARTNERS, dammit."

Fox remained silent for long moments, his expression grim, considering the situation. He ran his hand over his jaw, an abstracted gesture, and noted absently that he needed a shave. *That's beside the point, though,* he thought. *This is getting out of hand.*

"I'll have a talk with him, Echo," Fox finally decided, then held up a hand, as Echo started to speak again. "No, that's not all I'll do, I promise you. That was uncalled-for, and now that I know what's going on—whether it's to other agents, or to civilians, it doesn't matter—I WILL see to it that it stops. One way or another. He—and the others—were warned, that day in my office. More, Monkey is going on report, and a permanent black mark is going into his record."

"Good."

"Now, did you brain-bleach the civilians?"

"No, I didn't have to," Echo explained. "They were absolutely convinced that Monkey was doing promo for that rogue film that's causing us so much headache. They think they were getting a sneak peek at the plot, I'm pretty sure."

"Well, that's something, I guess."

* * *

"Yeah." A distracted Echo ran a hand over the back of his neck. Then he tried not to bite his lip over the confession he was about to make. "Listen, Fox...just so you know, I, uh...was a little rough on Monkey. And I don't mean verbally."

Fox looked up, met Echo's eyes, and held them.

"What did you do, son?"

"After the civvies were gone, I grabbed him and yanked him into the bathroom, out of sight, hard enough to throw him across the room. I didn't mean to do that," he admitted. "But I had some adrenaline up by then, so when I jerked him through the doorway, it was more forceful than I'd realized. Then I picked him up," Echo mimicked grabbing Monkey by the shirt front, "and shook him a couple times, kinda for emphasis, before I dropped him—on his feet—on the floor."

* * *

Fox looked Echo up and down. The younger man was in prime physical condition, tall and muscular, with strength commensurate, and the Director suspected that it had likely been not unlike watching a pissed-off Superman apprehend a criminal for harassing Lois.

And Monkey is NOT endearing himself to me, Fox thought in annoyance. *So I rather wish I'd seen it. It's good for him that he was recruited by the Chicago office; if I'd had the handling of it, he'd never have been brought into the Agency. Maybe he'll think next time before shooting off his mouth. But there's one more thing I need to know.*

"Echo, old friend, you didn't throw a punch at him, did you?" Fox asked quietly.

"No, Boss, I swear I didn't. I thought about it—damn, did I think about it—but I didn't. Besides," Echo shook his head, seeming somewhat bemused, "you might think this sounds strange, but...I don't think Meg would have wanted me to."

Now THAT...is telling, Fox thought, raising an eyebrow. *I wonder if he understands it himself. Judging by his expression, I think not. Then again, I've been around the block quite a few more times than he has, yet.* He addressed his department chief. "No, son, I don't think it strange at all. I've seen many things in my long life that WERE strange. That would not be one of them."

"Shall I put myself on report?"

"Oh hell no," Fox said with an amused snort. "I think you showed admirable restraint. You gave him the straight and narrow on the matter, but you got him out of sight first...and you didn't punch his lights out."

"But...throwing him across the room...?"

"You said yourself your adrenaline was up, and it wasn't intentional." Fox shrugged. "Frankly, and this is just between us...if it got his attention, I'm all for it."

"Okay. Thanks, Fox."

"No problem, old friend."

"One more thing...should we tell Meg about it?"

Fox bit his lip at that, and pondered it for long minutes, while Echo waited patiently.

"No, for right now, let's keep this to ourselves," Fox decided. "If anything further comes of it, or if it proves detrimental to Omega's anonymity, then we will. But I think she has enough to deal with right now, without worrying about this, too."

"That was my assessment," Echo said, sounding relieved, "but I wanted your opinion and direction, as well."

"Well, you have it," Fox said, with a slight smile. "Now let's go see what the Prime Minister has gotten into."

"Okay."

* * *

Late that day, the Agents watched as the off-duty Andromedans mingled with the YuleCon attendees. The aliens appeared to be having as good a time as the humans, and most of them gravitated and congregated in one room, from which music filtered.

"What's going on in there?" India asked.

"Filking," Omega replied. "Looks like the offworld diplomats are enjoying themselves," she added, peeking through the door. She turned around to see two pairs of blank eyes staring at her. The third pair gleamed knowingly. She grinned.

"What's filking?" India wondered.

"You could call it, 'folk music for science fiction fans,'" Echo answered, to their surprise. "Sometimes it's stuff people have deliberately written from scratch, sometimes even professional composers. Other times, it's stuff the fans have come up with, either sung to a traditional folk tune, or an outright sendup of a traditional folk tune. A lot of it is pretty damn funny."

"If you're curious, slip in and sit in the back," Omega suggested. "All you're expected to do is listen and not disturb anyone."

India peeped in.

"Oh, no, one of the Andromedans is singing!" she hissed. "I think it's that bodyguard who thanked Echo earlier. Dehman, wasn't it? We've gotta stop her!"

Echo laid a restraining hand on India's shoulder.

"Settle down, India," he murmured. "Everything is fine."

"Don't worry, India," Omega added. "This is a con, remember? Everybody will just think they're very imaginative fans."

"You're right," India verified, as she continued to watch. "She's got a pretty voice, and she's a big hit. Romeo, let's go in and listen for a while. We can keep an eye on things while we're at it."

"You gonna join 'em?" Omega asked Echo, as Alpha Two slipped through the door.

"Thought I might, for a little bit, anyway. I could use a good laugh."

"Oh. Lead on, then. I'm right behind you." Omega's face fell slightly despite herself.

"You don't want to?"

"Never got into filking much. But that's okay. Where you go, I go."

"Then...let's go the con suite and get something to drink."

* * *

While they sipped on Diet Cokes at a table in the corner of the quiet con suite—it was between mealtimes—they discussed the day's negotiations.

"That was a good compromise you came up with this afternoon," Echo told her. "Could've been an impasse otherwise."

"Thanks," Omega responded, then shrugged. "It just seemed to make sense to me. But I'm glad you presented it, not me. NASA typically doesn't do diplomatic negotiations," she said with a crooked grin, "at least not like this, and I'm still trying to watch and absorb it."

"How are YOU doing?" Echo asked meaningfully.

"Okay. For a shadow."

"Out with all of it."

"Huh?"

"Remember, I know you, baby," Echo reminded her, his voice soft but firm. "You've managed to avoid telling me everything before, but that won't wash any more. Tell me the rest."

"Oh." Omega shrugged. "I dunno, Ace. It's just..." She broke off, drawing a deep breath, and Echo suddenly realized she was struggling to verbalize it. He paid close attention, grasping that whatever she managed to get out would be extremely important to her. "Did you notice how Fox managed to come up with a reason to keep me in this position, because YOU trust me, but never actually said he trusted me himself?"

"Damn," Echo murmured, running a hand through his hair. "I was kinda hoping you hadn't noticed that."

"You know me better than that," she pointed out. "You've spent all day saying so. And proving it."

"Yeah, but a fella can hope, can't he?" he said, giving her a lopsided, rueful half-grin. "I'm sorry, baby. I think..." he broke off, considering what he knew of Fox and the situation, then resumed. "I think maybe... Fox DOES trust you, or else you wouldn't be here with me right now...but he's in a position—thanks to the stir these other, more paranoid agents are making—where he's having to walk a fine line, you know? He told me he was having to do stuff to ensure it didn't look like he and I were colluding with you over...whatever the hell it is they think you're trying to do. After all, I'm your partner, and Fox and I have known each other for years, pretty much since the beginning, so..."

"You're kidding," a shocked Omega said, voice flat. "You mean, if he doesn't keep me at a distance, they'll start accusing the two of you, next? The top two Agents in the whole damn place?"

"It's possible, Meg," Echo said, deadly serious. "I'm gonna say it again, baby—you did NOT see it in full action, and I hope you don't have to, but there is some serious craziness going on."

"Well, hell," she murmured.

"Exactly," he agreed.

* * *

Just then, Omega saw a nervous fan come purposefully into the room. Echo had his back partly to the door, trusting his partner to watch it, and she leaned across the table and whispered urgently.

"'Mr. Rogers', you're on."

"Again?!" Echo's face tightened.

"Mr. Rogers, do you have a moment?" the timid fan asked, behind Echo.

"Does that answer your question?" Omega murmured. With an effort obvious solely to Omega, Echo relaxed his face, and only then did he turn to the young woman. When he spoke, his partner understood he was laying on the west Texas accent with a trowel. *Ease up, Ace,* she thought with a hidden grin. *Rogers' dialect isn't THAT thick. At least,* I *don't think so...*

"Yes ma'am, what can Ah do for ya?"

The woman's face lit up. *Then again,* Omega thought, watching, *maybe he nailed it.*

"I...I just wanted to tell you...how much I enjoy your work," the fan said, almost painfully shy. "Are you here for publicity on your new movie?"

"...Thank ya very much; yes, Ah am."

"The guys running around in the chartreuse, three-eyed alien costumes, are they, like, the bad guys? They are sooo cool...!"

"Well now," Omega broke in, rescuing Echo, "you'll just have to see the movie to find out, won't you?" She smiled at the girl.

"Yeah," she responded with another shy smile. "Can I, um, maybe have an autograph?"

Echo looked at Omega, and she read his expression. *I can't leave a paper trail like that...*

"Mm. That might be a problem. How's the hand after that little stunt accident the other day?" Omega said, thinking fast. Echo smoothly followed up by flexing his right hand slowly and wincing.

"Still pretty stiff. That sprain, an' all...Ah don't know..."

"Oh! You're hurt!" the girl exclaimed. "Oh, I'd love to have it, but don't worry about it! I don't want to make your hand worse. But...thanks for talking to me."

"You're welcome."

"'Bye."

Once the fan was out of sight, they both stood.

"Come on," Echo said, glancing around, then heading for the door in a hurry, "let's get the hell out of here before more show up."

"And go where?"

"Up to the Agent Ops room. We can take a break."

"Right behind you, then."

"Just where a shadow's supposed to be."

* * *

As they slipped quietly through the corridors and stairwells toward the room assigned for Division One Agents, Omega shook her head. Echo noticed; he caught her eye, and cocked his head in an unspoken query—*What?*

"Oh," she said. "No big deal. I'm just puzzled how it is that people look at you and Romeo and see Rogers and...whatever the other actor's name is; I forget at the moment."

"Williamson," Echo supplied.

"Yeah, that's it." Omega nodded. "I mean, okay, there's a resemblance, but for instance, Rogers is a good ten or fifteen years older than you, and you can TELL he's older than you. I suppose you might get away with being his kid brother or something, but people think YOU are HIM. Even without the hologram disguise. And Romeo, he's probably easily five or six years younger than Williamson, himself, and the resemblance isn't even as close, *I* don't think. I just don't get it."

"Unfortunately, Meg, most people don't pay that much attention," Echo explained. "They aren't like you and me, or Romeo and India, or Fox. Or ANY field agent, truth to tell. Especially not the top Agents. We NOTICE things, you and me—and the others, too—little details like age and facial features."

"And most people don't? Really?"

"Really. Some are worse than others, a few—very few—are better. If they're real good, sometimes we try to recruit 'em. Since you had your nose to the grindstone trying to become an astronaut, you might not have seen it the way I have, out in the field, doin' this job."

"Wow."

"Based on what I've seen over the years as an Agent, I have this idea that humans have a sort of built-in, hard-coded pattern recognition system in their brains, at least where faces are concerned. Some have better coding, some have worse. So they look at their favorite movie star, and the pattern of the face registers on their subconscious, and gets fed into the system database. Then, if they see somebody whose face kinda fits that pattern, they say, 'Did you know you look like Somebody Famous?' But if the face triggers enough correlations to the pattern, they become convinced that the person IS the Somebody Famous. Whether they are or not. Now, nine times out of ten, that person WILL be the Somebody Famous. But now and again, there just happens to be a strong resemblance. Maybe it's a distant cousin or something. Or maybe the Big Guy Upstairs, as you like to put it," he grinned, "just doesn't like to break molds; I dunno. But that seems to be what's happening with Romeo and me, and Williamson and Rogers."

"It's a pain in the ass, at least in this case," she remarked, then sighed.

"No argument there." Echo paused, hearing the sigh. "You okay, baby?"

"Yeah. Just...tired. It's been...a rough day. Not in the physical sense; just...you know."

"Yeah. I got no argument with that, either."

* * *

Alpha One entered the empty hotel room, and Echo went back to the sink in the bathroom to get a glass of water. Omega sat down on the edge of one of the beds and completely relaxed for the first time since the attack on Echo. Within moments, she slumped sideways onto the pillow, half-asleep.

A few minutes later, she dimly felt her shoes slipped off as her feet were lifted and laid on the bed. Her entire body was lifted and shifted as her Suit jacket was carefully removed.

"It's just me, Meg, relax and go to sleep," she heard Echo whisper, as both of her proto-cyclotron blasters and her Winchester & Tesla were removed from their holsters.

Her tie was loosened next, followed by her trousers belt being unbuckled, and covers were pulled over her. The overhead lights disappeared; the bedside lamp seemed to magically dim itself.

She sighed, vaguely grateful for her partner's consideration, and sank deeper toward oblivion.

The second bed creaked softly with the sounds of another body stretching out, then there was a quiet click as Echo hit the TV remote.

* * *

Unfortunately, housekeeping had left the TV volume on MAX, and Echo heard a little scream from the other bed as Omega was startled awake by the sudden blare of sound. Automatically she went for her empty shoulder holsters as she sat bolt upright in the bed.

"ECHO!" she called instinctively for her partner.

"Damn!" he exclaimed in dismay, stabbing the mute button with a fingertip and leaping off the mattress to move rapidly to the other bed. "Sssh. It's me. It's Echo. I'm right here, baby. It's okay. Relax." He gently pushed her back down to the mattress. "I'm sorry, baby. I didn't mean to give you a coronary; I didn't know the volume was maxxed out. I'll turn it down. Try to get some rest, if you can."

Omega nodded, caught her breath for a moment, and then curled back up under the spread Echo had laid over her earlier. After a few moments, her regular breathing told him she was asleep again, and he returned to the other bed and resumed surfing, with the mute still on.

* * *

Half an hour later, the door lock clicked, and Echo rose swiftly to intercept Romeo and India as they entered, a finger to his lips. He jerked his head toward the sleeping form, and they nodded.

"Good sign," India whispered. "She's been tighter than piano wire ever since that whole mess with the grenade went down."

"Yeah. She's really jumpy though."

"Hell, do ya blame her?" Romeo wanted to know.

"Nope. Just makin' an observation. Try not to startle her, okay?"

"No problem, Echo," India murmured. "We'll be quiet and slow."

"Who's babysitting the Andromedans?"

"Fox called in that other agent team to give us a break," Romeo told him in hushed tones.

"Who?"

"Monkey and Sierra."

"Mmm," Echo responded noncommittally. "How long have we got for a break?"

"Couple-three hours."

"All right. I've got the recliner in the corner next to Meg's bed. Y'all got the other bed. Get some rest, you two."

"I'm so there," Romeo told him, as India dimmed the lamp to nightlight level and turned off the TV.

* * *

Alpha One woke before Alpha Two, and Omega and Echo shoved on shoes, caught up weapons and jackets, and slipped out of the darkened hotel room, leaving Romeo and India still sleeping. Outside in the empty corridor, they studied each other carefully, each straightening the other's tie and jacket in lieu of a mirror, combing each others' hair with dextrous fingers, then they nodded approval to each other and headed across to the Prime Minister's suite. Fox met them at the door.

"All's well here, Echo," he murmured, keeping his voice as low as he could make it, given the time; it was still very early in the morning for the regular con-goers, and several bangs on the ceiling had accompanied a too-loud late arrival of a member of the alien diplomatic contingent, five minutes before—especially when he inadvertently slammed the door to his hotel room. "I have Monkey and Sierra downstairs, keeping up with a few Andromedan party animals. You two check in with them, hand over, and then get ready for the day's activities."

"All right. You get any rest?" Echo wondered.

"Couple hours. I'm good," Fox averred. "Oh, and we're going to get a special 'con suite' set up for our...more UNIQUE...guests; I'll see to that later today, as a top priority. Zebra confirmed your theory, Echo."

"Carb narc?" Echo queried. Omega blinked in puzzlement at that, but Echo didn't notice, and didn't elaborate.

"More or less, yes."

"Is it as dangerous as nitrogen narcosis is to humans?"

"Not quite. But it still doesn't do Lambda Andromedan physiologies any good."

"Mm. Okay. Still on schedule?"

"A little ahead, actually, thanks to Omega's compromise."

"Wait," Omega said, startled. "Mine? But, but...Echo presented it... how did...?"

* * *

Fox smiled.

"I'm not Director because I'm stupid, my dear. It did take me some time to convince myself it was your idea and not your partner's; you do think a lot alike. But a good idea is a good idea. And yours was good." He paused, then sighed. "I am not against you, Omega, even though from your perspective, it might appear so. And for that, I am sorry. My gut says to trust you, and truthfully, I do. But the situation is such that I'm being forced into..." Fox shook his head. "My head is having to overrule my gut here. So

I'm trying to protect you...and Echo...AND me, from a possible lynch mob of our own people, if anything should go south."

"Lynch mob?!" Omega managed to keep her voice low—only with patent effort.

"I believe it," Echo noted. "Especially based on what I saw that day in your office, Fox."

"The problem is, Omega, recent history is against you," Fox tried to explain. "I'm sure Echo has told you this. It makes you a likely target with agents looking for a scapegoat to this whole PR nightmare."

"Yeah, he and I have talked about it a little," Omega confirmed. "Okay, we've talked about it a lot. But...so...you really DO trust me...?" It was wistful, though both men suspected she had not intended for it to be, and behind Omega, Echo winced. Fox met his eyes and bit his lip for a moment before answering Omega.

"If it helps any, yes, I do," the Director confessed.

"Yeah, it helps."

"Good. But this conversation never happened, all right? Plausible deniability."

"Oh, okay, yeah," Omega murmured, nodding. "I get it. Didn't hear nothin'."

"Good girl," Fox said, and grinned. "Just keep up what you're doing. We'll figure this out. So, as Echo would say, 'You're doing great, baby.'"

Omega laughed.

It was the first such laugh Fox had heard from her since the whole debacle had started, and he decided it sounded good. *There's a certain relief in there, too,* he realized. *Which is more than good; it sounds as if she sorely needed the morale boost. Maybe it really DID help to have this little talk, then. Ah well, back to work.*

"So now—I think we are prepared to start our day in about," Fox checked his wrist chronometer, "about an hour."

"Good," Echo said. "We'll be ready."

Chapter 7

Zero Days—Eight Days

Downstairs, Echo and Omega looked around for Monkey and Sierra, but were unable to find them. They did, however, find the last two Lambda Andromedans that were still up and about, and escorted them back to the Andromedan sector of the hotel. By that time, Romeo and India were awake and about, and joined the search for Monkey and Sierra.

"Damn, skippy," Romeo remarked to India, "we're spendin' as much time keepin' up with each other as we do the Andromedans." Omega winced, and Echo shot Romeo a stern look before he and Omega headed off to continue the search in a different area of the hotel.

When Echo finally spotted the two missing agents, they were in a lobby alcove, intent on a being across the festive holiday-decorated lobby from them. He tapped Omega on the shoulder, getting her attention, then jerked his head in the direction of Sierra and Monkey. She nodded acknowledgement, and they strode toward the two agents.

"What are you two doing?" Echo asked quietly behind them, as he and Omega walked up, silent as ninjas.

"What?!" Monkey jumped, startled. "Oh, it's you two. We've got an undocumented alien over there." Monkey pointed at the creature beside one of the lobby sofas. "I don't even recognize what species it is."

* * *

Omega shot an amused glance at Echo, and caught the gleam in his eye; he understood, too.

"You're kidding, right?" she asked the two agents, chuckling. "You two haven't ever been to a con, have you?" Calmly she strode across the lobby toward the alien creature.

* * *

"Dammit, what the hell does she think she's doing?!" Sierra exclaimed. "She'll blow the bust!"

"It's probably what the little bimbo wants! And she even has the nerve to talk about conning people! See, Echo?? I told you! C'mon, Sierra!" A determined Monkey started forward.

A strong hand came down hard on each man's shoulder, clamping tight, refusing to let go...and refusing to let them move.

"WATCH the LADY," Echo murmured in a quiet, perilous tone, with deliberate, meaningful emphasis. "You might actually learn something."

Had either bothered to glance back, they would have seen, firsthand, Echo's 'Yellowstone look'—and might have thought twice before continuing in their actions.

The three watched as Omega walked right up to the alien, apparently striking up a conversation. After a few moments, she began running her fingertips across the alien's face and nodding.

"DAMN, what a slut! What's she doing? Coming on to it?" Monkey muttered in deep disgust. Echo's hand tightened on his shoulder until the other agent squirmed in discomfort.

"I SAID, watch. I DIDN'T say, talk." His voice was cold as Antarctic ice, a substance with which Alpha One was all too familiar.

Just then, the alien put both hands to its face and lifted. To Monkey's shock, the alien's head came completely off, and it deposited its cranium in Omega's hands.

* * *

Omega lifted the head and placed it over her own, as the alien's body turned in greeting two friends, revealing a very human head protruding between the shoulders of the 'alien' body. Omega adjusted the full-head mask, and turned toward the three agents, waving.

"So much for your 'unauthorized offworlder,'" Echo told the two agents with a deep disgust of his own. "You two idiots nearly caused an interplanetary incident over a COSTUME. As for your other remarks...I have a VERY long memory, 'gentlemen.' And I use the term loosely."

"Echo, wait! Look!!" Sierra cried.

* * *

Omega was just removing the mask when she heard a voice call,

"Look! It's the lady from the movie!"

She turned to see a group of 'aliens'—Kronons with ridged foreheads, in full battle armor—walking up to her, and she grinned, recognizing their costumes from a certain classic TV series; she promptly spat out a gutteral greeting in their 'native language.' They nodded solemnly in reply, though a few broke character and grinned at her fluency and willingness to play along.

"What are you bunch of wimps doing out here?" she joked. "Isn't it a bit late for you lot to be up and about? I thought your nanny would have put you to bed, hours ago!"

"Nanny?! Late?? When it is not yet mid-morning? Woman, you have just issued a challenge!" the leader bellowed. "Are you prepared to do battle?"

"Try me." She was still grinning. "But do so with honor. I am...'unarmed.'"

The 'Kronon' leader cocked his head, then gestured to a follower, who promptly and without hesitation, tossed Omega his gleaming, curved, highly-stylized blade. Omega caught the blade nimbly, and raised it to the ready position; curious con onlookers gathered around, excited to watch a live-action 'battle.'

The Kronon contingent murmured approvals as Omega stepped forward and ceremonially locked blades with their leader. Then he abruptly stepped back and brought his own blade around in a glittering arc.

* * *

Sierra went for his blaster when he saw the con attendee swing his blade at Omega, but Echo slammed him into the wall.

"You damn fool! Haven't you figured this out yet?!" he growled. Glancing over his shoulder, he barked, "Monkey! DROP IT! Dammit, you idiot, these are CIVILIANS IN COSTUME!! They're PLAYING!"

Monkey stopped, startled, lowering his blaster, and the three watched from the shadows as Omega continued the mock battle, her laughter echoing across the lobby amid the clang of clashing weapons.

* * *

Omega dropped to the floor as the blade slashed by, and caught the Kronon behind the knee with her foot, toppling him to the carpeted floor; the move was intended expressly to take his feet out from under him without hurting him, and it succeeded admirably. Leaping up, she swung her own blade at the prone leader, who parried hard, flipping her over his head, then sprang to his feet. Omega landed on her own feet, her back to her opponent, and fluidly twisted at the waist, extending her blade to block the blow that came from behind. She swiftly followed the block with a roundhouse kick, disarming her opponent, before spinning into a low tornado kick and once more taking his feet from under him.

"Are you ready to die today?" she growled playfully as she swung her blade in for the 'kill,' halting it several inches from the man's exposed throat. "Good! But I give you your life, in honor of the season. Merry Christmas!"

Applause broke out among the con attendees who had surrounded the scene of battle. Omega returned the borrowed blade, and helped the Kronon leader stand. Upon regaining his feet, the disguised human bowed low over her hand in a courtly fashion.

"You are indeed worthy of one of us, milady," he said. "Would you do me the honor?"

"I am indeed honored," Omega bowed formally, "but I fear duty will not allow me to avail myself of your noble offer. I have...obligations to, ah, the film, you know."

"Ah, yes. The *Black Suits*! I look forward to it. Another time, perhaps." The Kronon contingent moved off, and the fans dispersed. When the crowd had thinned, Omega saw Echo, flanked by Monkey and Sierra, at the back of the pack, watching. Echo's lips curled in the slightest of smiles, but Monkey and Sierra looked sullen.

"How'd I do, Coach?" Omega asked Echo with a grin as she wandered over, and he nodded, returning the expression.

"I can't say as I recall teaching you that particular form of combat, but your moves were really good," he told her.

"You'd be amazed what you can pick up at a science fiction convention," she remarked with a smile, and Monkey and Sierra listened carefully, frowning. "Are these two on the curve yet?"

"Yeah, they are now, I think," Echo told her, looking sternly at the two misguided agents. "But not until nearly starting a firefight when they saw that 'alien attack.'"

"You're kidding!" Omega's jaw dropped open. "The blades weren't sharp. We never even took the guards off. They could've been thrown out otherwise. Standard con procedure."

"Yeah, yeah. We caught on," Monkey grumbled as Romeo and India walked up to them.

"Hey, pretty lady! That was some cool stage show!" Romeo grinned.

"And the great thing is, everybody thinks I'm a stunt woman in that movie," Omega grinned back. "I get a workout, and nobody gets brain-bleached."

* * *

Echo saw Monkey and Sierra glance at each other, and his eyes blazed for a moment.

"Alpha Line is back on duty," he told them brusquely. "You two can report back to Headquarters."

A curious Omega watched the two men as they left.

"What was that all about?" she asked Echo. "There was more going on there than met the eye."

"They're the ones accusing you of being the mole. Along with Tare and Yankee, according to reports," he answered her, brusque and still annoyed.

"Oh," Omega said, all sign of levity vanishing. "I guess I just provided them some fresh ammo." She sighed, and gave Romeo a lopsided attempt at a grin; none of them missed the fact that it didn't reach her eyes. "Have I got the *Charlie Brown Christmas* disorder going on these days, or what?" Omega meandered across the lobby to watch Monkey and Sierra drive away, being careful to stay in Echo's line of sight.

"What did that mean?" India asked Romeo, watching her go.

"I'm not completely sure, but I think she's talkin' 'bout a line from the cartoon," Romeo guessed.

"What line?" Echo followed up.

"'Everything I touch gets ruined.'"

"Damn," Echo whispered, watching his dejected partner, across the lobby.

* * *

"Lloyd," Fox murmured, just outside the convention's hospitality suite, also known as a con suite, "I need some help."

"Sure, Fox, whatcha need?" the native-born Kydeenian immigrant wondered.

"Well, we've discovered that the Lambda Andromedans don't handle carbonated soft drinks very well, so we thought we'd set up a 'con suite' of our own. But you've got experience in these 'con suites' and I don't. So..." Fox shrugged. "I did manage to get together a list of the items that they prefer, along with the condition in which they seem to prefer it, but..."

"Lemme see."

Fox handed him a small scrap of paper.

"Mm. Okay, yeah, that'll work. I can do that, and use what we got, and nobody will even be the wiser. In fact, they'll be glad to have me do it, the way I'm figuring to do it. You got a room I can use?"

"Sure do. Come with me..."

* * *

"And so you're sure it won't be a problem?" Fox pressed.

"Are you kidding, Fox?" Lloyd said. "Look at this list you gave me: stale coffee, spoiled milk, moldy bread, chip dip that's been out too long, crusty mustard...this is the stuff the regular con suite would be throwing out anyway, because it would make humans sick. It'll be the proverbial piece of kharkun for me to 'throw it out' by bringing it over here for your visitors to use."

"All right, then let's do it," Fox ordered. "Send me any bills you incur for it, and I'll see you get reimbursed."

"Consider it done," Lloyd replied with a grin. "I'll have it set up inside an hour."

"Fantastic."

* * *

True to his word, by the top of the hour, Lloyd had a very special convention hospitality suite set up for the alien embassage. Once the room itself was ready, with the tables set up and decked with disposable tablecloths, he went back to the regular con suite and fished out all of the items that needed to be thrown out anyway.

"Hey, Lloyd, whatcha doin'?" one of the other con suite workers asked, as he loaded the foodstuffs into an empty cardboard box.

"Eh, this stuff has been sittin' around too long, and it's not fit to eat," Lloyd told her, thinking, *Not for humans, anyway.* "So I'm gonna throw it out. But I thought I'd take it to the dumpster out back, so it doesn't start smelling up our trash cans."

"Ooo, good thought," the other con worker said. "Thanks!"

"No problem. While I'm gone, if you want to get together anything else like that to be thrown out, I'll take care of it."

"All over it!"

* * *

"Hey! Hey, Rob! C'mere!" one of the convention attendees, clad in an olive drab t-shirt and jeans, called, as he hurried up to his buddy.

"What's up, Steve?" Rob, in eyeglasses, a black t-shirt, and jeans, replied. A billed, camouflage-print military cap was shoved down on his dark hair.

"Anything in the con suite?"

"Nah, I missed lunch 'cause of the gaming, so the Mongol hordes have eaten everything. Pickings are pretty bare, and they haven't put anything else out yet."

"C'mon with me, then," Steve said, grabbing Rob's arm. "I know a secret." He dragged Rob toward the elevator.

"What kinda secret? Steve, I'm starved. I just wanna wait for 'em to put out some fresh chips and dip in the con suite. If I'm lucky, they'll put out a loaf of bread and some sandwich makings, or at least some peanut butter and jelly."

"That's what I'm tryin' to tell you, buddy. They got a secret con suite, an' it's up a couple floors."

"Really?"

"Yeah. I saw Lloyd setting it up. He was bringing stuff from the back and taking it up there."

They passed another man in a t-shirt and khaki kilt, who waved at the pair.

"What's up, guys?" the man in the kilt wondered. "I just got out of my last panel for a while, and was gonna pop by the con suite and grab a soda."

"No, no, no. Come with us, John," Rob murmured. "Secret food stash."

"Really? I'm there."

The trio entered the elevator together, and Steve punched the button for an upper floor.

* * *

Two of the guys in three-eyed alien costumes from the *Black Suits* movie were leaving the secondary con suite as the three hungry con-goers arrived. Peeking inside, they saw no one around, but there was a considerable array of foodstuffs, including a large carafe of coffee on a hot plate.

"Caffeine! Nectar of the gods!" John exclaimed, making a beeline for the pot.

"Good idea," Rob decided. "I was up all night gaming. I could stand a bit of awake-juice."

"I can go with it, too," Steve agreed.

The three grabbed styrofoam cups and poured their coffee, black. John raised his in a mock-toast.

"Bottoms up," he said, and chugged the hot beverage in a few quick swallows. "Eugh," he muttered, coming up for air. "That was not the freshest coffee. Had an odd taste to it, too."

By this time, Steve had taken a big gulp of coffee himself, but Rob was scanning the food offerings, cup in hand but not yet touched.

"Ugh, he's right," Steve agreed, and took another gulp. "Well, Rob, they got bread and some other shit. Let's make sandwiches."

"Okay. John, you want something to eat?"

"Nah, I'm gonna have another cup of coffee, then maybe go out for something to eat. I'm tired of con food and hotel restaurant food. I did see where there was a Brazilian churrascaria about three blocks over. I'm for some meat!" John poured himself another cup of coffee and downed it. "Later, guys."

John dropped the styrofoam cup into the trash and headed out of the room. Rob grabbed some bread, peanut butter, and strawberry jam, and commenced making a PBJ. He took a big bite and began to chew.

"That...tastes really...odd," he remarked, as Steve continued to drink his coffee. Rob turned the sandwich over and looked at it. "EWWW!" he exclaimed. "The bread's COVERED in MOLD! That's DISGUSTING!"

Rob grabbed his coffee and downed several big swallows to try to flush out the moldy taste, before calling a halt to that, as well.

"Oh SHIT!" he exclaimed. "Are they tryin' to POISON us?! Steve! Stop drinkin' that, fast!"

"Why?" Steve wondered. "So it's stale, and tastes a little off. You can't really spoil coffee."

"You idiot! The reason it tastes odd is because it's mixed with PRUNE JUICE! Urrk," Rob added at the end, one hand grabbing his mouth, the other his stomach. "Ohh, I'm gonna be sick..."

"PRUNE juice?!" Steve blurted. "You're shitting me!"

Rob ran for the bathroom...just as Steve's gut delivered an alarming kind of screeching growl. Steve paled.

"Oh boy," he murmured, even as the sounds of projectile vomiting came from the bathroom. "Speaking of shitting me...Rob, you better be throwing up in the sink, 'cause I got dibs on the toilet..."

And Steve ran for the bathroom as well.

* * *

Moments later, Lloyd led Fox to the new 'special' con suite, accompanied by Alpha One.

"Here's your spread for the Lambda Androme—" Lloyd began, just as several really disgusting sounds, accompanied by even worse smells, emerged from the partly-closed bathroom door of the hotel room they were using for hospitality.

The three Agents and one friendly alien eased over to the door and pushed it open.

Inside were two very ill fans. One leaned over the sink, throwing up violently into it, and splattering the entire vanity surrounding with vomitus. The other had his jeans around his ankles and sat sideways on the toilet, alternating between throwing up into the tub and having explosive diarrhea in the toilet. Neither man so much as looked up at the intrusion.

"Shit," murmured Omega.

"There goes that talent for descriptive commentary again, baby," Echo noted in an undertone.

"They must have got hold of the special cocktail I mixed up for your guests," Lloyd remarked.

"What in God's name was in it?" Fox wondered, shocked.

"Coffee, prune juice, senna, ayahuasca, and di-phenyl disacodyl," Lloyd answered. "It's really popular at some of the offworld spas on my planet."

"Three laxatives—one a galactic pharmaceutical—a peristalsis initiator, and an emetic," Omega observed, stepping back as another round of vomiting started, splattering the bathroom. "All in one drink. No wonder."

"I'd better call India and have her see to these two," Fox decided, pulling his cell phone. "Then we can brain bleach 'em and..."

"And somebody's gotta clean up the bathroom," Echo observed. "And Fox? Just so you know, Alpha Line doesn't do toilets."

"Or sinks. Or tubs," Omega added.

"Or floors," Echo appended, as the three Agents and one alien stepped even farther back, out of the way of splatter.

"I'll call maid service," Lloyd said with a sigh.

* * *

It took some doing, but eventually India—with some assistance from Omega—was able to neutralize the effects of the alien cocktail on the humans' digestive tracts. Fox himself brain-bleached the two men and sent them off, slightly weak but otherwise none the worse for wear.

Meanwhile, Lloyd called hotel housekeeping, explaining that a couple of convention attendees had had a brief bout of intestinal illness while visiting one of the hospitality suites, and bathroom cleaning was needed.

Omega flushed the toilet several times, then turned on the shower to help rinse the tub, while Echo turned on the sink tap.

Then the Agents left, getting out of sight—and earshot—before the maids showed up to clean the place.

* * *

The rest of the day proved relatively uneventful, a fact which all the Agents appreciated, but for which Omega was especially grateful. Negotiations were going smoothly, and Alpha Line even ventured a few more small suggestions which were received favorably, though they mostly came from Echo, and occasionally from Romeo or India; a determined Omega kept quiet, for the most part, despite her partner's gentle urging. The agenda was now well ahead of schedule.

Late in the afternoon according to local Earth time, the Prime Minister requested a break in the negotiations, principally, it seemed, to give himself and his curious entourage the opportunity to explore the science fiction convention in more detail. Romeo was particularly enthusiastic over this good fortune, and spent a fair amount of time in the gaming rooms with Tortok, an Andromedan bodyguard with whom he'd struck up a tentative friendship, as well as with several other Andromedans, mostly military, fascinated by the gaming. Romeo, an ex-Navy SEAL, had a lot in common with the group, and Echo was pleased to see the bonding that was occurring, deciding it could only help interstellar relations.

India was correspondingly fascinated by the dealers' rooms and art show, mulling over the possible acquisition of various eclectic items she found intriguing, as she kept up with the serious collectors in the alien diplomatic cadre. Periodically, she would drag Romeo away from whatever role-playing game he was involved in to show him some new art piece.

Echo and Omega found the whole tableau entertaining as they floated between the various groups, maintaining an overall presence.

"Why do I think I'm looking at two new con fans?" Omega said once, as Romeo and India came through with yet another package.

Mm-hmm," Echo replied, hiding a grin from Alpha Two, though not from his partner. "Hope their Lexus can hold it all."

"Don't they have a warp seat too?"

"Warp trunk, really. That model Lexus has a decently sized back seat already. Still, those things have limits. We may be helping 'em get it all home."

"Yeah, Romeo better tell her to—OHMIGOSH!!"

"What??" Echo was instantly on alert at Omega's exclamation.

"Oh, sorry! Sorry! It's all right, stand down, everything's fine...oh, wow, was it him? Really??"

"Him who?" Echo asked curiously, still not entirely at ease.

"I think...hey, let's just kind of...stroll down this way a minute..."

Echo patiently followed his partner down the corridor and around the corner.

"Mind telling me what's going on?"

"Yeessss!" Omega whispered, looking into one of the meeting rooms as a speaker was being introduced. Grabbing Echo's arm, she stood on tiptoe and murmured in his ear, "Echo! Do you know who that is??"

Echo studied the man's face, and raised an eyebrow. "It's—"

"Yes! It IS! He is my all-time FAVORITE science fiction author! I was reading his warp drive series when I was still at NASA! I never did think the screen adaptation they did a few years ago did it justice..."

"I take it you'd like to listen to him?"

"Of COURSE I would! But..." Omega watched an Andromedan diplomat wander by, and finished, "we have more important things to do."

Echo consulted the schedule posted by the meeting room door. "I think we could spare you for an hour. It's not like I won't know where you are."

* * *

"No. Just...no." Omega shook her head firmly. "Not after what's happened. I'm your shadow, remember? And we can't BOTH be out of touch for an hour with the entire Andromedan envoy wandering the hotel." A thought occurred to her. "Or...maybe you'd like to get rid of your shadow for a while? I'll go find India and give you a break."

"No, it's all right. I'm fine."

"Come on, Echo, you haven't had a real break from babysitting me in a couple of days. You're gonna be sick of my face. We'll go find India, and I'll hang with her for a while. Then you can shake loose, and spend some time to yourself."

"You've been spending too much time around ROMEO, doing all that Christmas shopping, not me."

"Why do you say that?"

"You're starting to sound like him." Echo shot her a glance, his lips curving slightly, while Omega mentally replayed her statement.

"Oh," she said with a grin, "is that a bad thing?"

"Depends on how many of his expressions start to crop up in your everyday vocabulary."

"Aha. I'll try to remember that. Anyway, how about it?"

"If that's...what you want."

"Not necessarily," an uncertain Omega answered him, hearing the hesitation in his voice, as they walked back toward the art show. "I'm just trying to be considerate, Echo."

"Meg, if I couldn't stand to be around you for extended periods of time, I'd have asked for another partner a long time ago. Besides, I thought we were pals."

"Oh...okay. Well...good. Yeah, we are. Thanks," she murmured, grateful. Echo nodded, and Omega thought for a moment. "Then what say we see where the majority of the Andromedans are and find out what's up?"

"That should be easy. There they go." Echo pointed as the Prime Minister led virtually his entire entourage into the corridor Echo and Omega had just vacated. "And it looks like you're going to get your wish," he added as they entered the author panel.

"All right! Do you mind?" Omega asked, enthusiastic.

"No. I like his books too. Besides, it gives me a chance to say hi."

"Say hi?! Oh DAMN! Ace, you DON'T mean..."

"Yup."

* * *

As the writing panel ended, Echo sent a text message to Alpha Two to meet the Andromedan prime minister and his company outside the room, then he and Omega waited until the room cleared out. The author threw a couple of his books into a backpack, then reached for the pack zipper. Looking up, he stopped what he was doing as a smile spread across his face.

"Echo! Why am Ah not surprised?" the author exclaimed in a pronounced Southern accent. He came around the head table and made a beeline for the Agent, who stood to meet him. "Ah take it you're here for the negotiations?"

"What negotiations?" Echo replied, taking the man's outstretched hand. "My partner here just wanted to hear your talk."

Instead of shaking hands, the author drew Echo into a brief male hug.

"The hell you say," he replied. "When Ah see a bunch o' Division One Agents wandering around a science fiction convention with a bunch o' Lambda Andromedans—INCLUDING the damn system's prime minister, no less—Ah know something's goin' on, an' it AIN'T science fiction."

"You're imagining things, Travis."

"No, Ah'm not! Ah'm bettin' money with th' Erikian in the dealer's room that you got a trade negotiation underway." The author eyed Echo. "Now you tell me which of us owes money to who."

* * *

Omega eased to her feet and watched as Echo's brown eyes twinkled.

"Let's just say you'll be going home with some extra spending money, then, Travis," he commented, and the author grinned.

"All right! There's a nice steak dinner when Ah get home! Now, you said this pretty lady here was your partner? But Ah thought Romeo was your partner..."

"Yeah, he was, but he went and got himself involved with a cute little former ER physician. He and India, the former ER doctor, comprise the Alpha Two team these days; they're wandering around here, too. Travis, I'd like you to meet my partner, the junior member of Alpha One, Agent Omega. Meg, this is Dr. Travis S. Taylor, polymath, government consultant, popular science and science fiction author...and former inhabitant of what you'd know as Tau Ceti f, better known to him as Kirakalla."

"Pleased ta meetcha, Agent Omega," Taylor said, grabbing her proffered hand and shaking. "You must be pretty damn good, if you got Echo for your partner."

"Oh, I dunno. I try," Omega said, feeling her cheeks heat.

"She's damn good, all right, Travis," Echo vouched. "This lady mopped up on that hypercube puzzle you developed for us."

"She did, huh? What was her time?"

"Try nineteen and a half minutes."

"DAMN!" Taylor exclaimed. "That is some fine work, Omega! Hey, Ah heard scuttlebutt about a new department formin', this 'Alpha Line' thing. Ah guess y'all are it, huh?"

"Yes, Dr. Taylor, we are," Omega said softly. "We have six teams currently, with more in the application pipeline. I was sort of the prototype new recruit for the department. Echo is the department head, and I'm his assistant."

"Assistant department chief, huh? Not too shabby."

"No, no, just assistant," Omega corrected. "I'm not nearly experienced enough to make that kinda rank. Think more, um, executive assistant. I haven't been with the Agency a year yet. Only about, uh," her eyes defocused for a moment, and she waggled fingers absently as she mentally tallied, "maybe eight and a half, nine months?"

"It wouldn't surprise me, though," Echo noted. "If we can get over a few hurdles through the holidays, I can see Meg moving up through the ranks at a pretty fast rate. She's kinda like you, Travis—she's a polymath, too. And she was an astronaut with NASA when we recruited her."

"'Zat so? That's pretty interestin'. How did THAT happen?" Taylor wondered. "Leavin' NASA and joinin' the Agency?"

"Um, it's a really long story," Omega murmured. "And we don't wanna keep you from your next panel..."

"Aw, that's okay. Ah got a good-sized break before my next panel. Ah was goin' up to th' green room to grab a 'bheer' anyway. Why don't y'all come along, an' we'll sit down and chat for a few? Echo an' Ah can get caught up, an' Omega here can tell me her long story an' we can start gettin' to know each other."

Uncertain how much of said long story was acceptable, Omega glanced at Echo, deferring to him.

* * *

Echo saw the glance, interpreted it, and responded for her.

"Sure, Travis, that'll be fine. Officially, we're on duty, but I keep a couple of DeTox tabs on me for things like this. So Meg, you and I can knock back a beer with your favorite author, here, and you can tell him your life story. It's a damn interesting one, too, Travis. Though," he shot a sympathetic look at his partner, "not all of it was particularly pleasant to live through."

"No," Omega murmured, glancing down. Taylor caught the subtle exchange, and immediately changed gears.

"Hey, look," he said, voice soft, "if it's something you're not comfortable talkin' about, you don't have to tell me jack-shit. It's just," he shrugged, "Echo an' Ah go back a ways—Ah met 'im when Ah processed in from Kirakalla, an' he helped me out of a little bind—an' Ah thought Ah'd like t' get t' know his partner."

"It's okay," Omega said, looking up with an overly bright smile. "It's Agency record, anyway. If Echo says it's all right to tell, then hey. I'll tell."

Echo watched Omega's face and thought, *Maybe I better have a Diet Coke and let Meg have both of the DeTox tabs. She might need several beers, if she really intends to tell him the whole big ball of...shit. Especially after the discoveries back around Halloween. And then I'll have to get her un-buzzed after.*

* * *

The green room, a sort of private con suite on a concierge floor reserved for the convention's guests of honor, was several floors up, and the trio knew it would be empty at that hour of the day; the other honored guests were either in panels of their own, or getting a very late lunch or a somewhat early dinner in the hotel restaurant. So they headed for the banks of elevators.

Echo mostly kept silent, watching and listening, as they commandeered an express elevator for the three of them, and Omega launched into the whole story of Slug's machinations as soon as the elevator door closed on them, somehow managing to cram the whole tale into the elevator ride up to the green room.

Once in the green room, Taylor and Omega both got chilled longnecks from the refrigerator and popped the caps. Echo got a Diet Coke, and they all sat down in a cluster of armchairs in a corner. Then Omega finished by telling the author-slash-scientist the latest sequence of events, involving the Agency's potential exposure and the accusations against her as the chief conspirator.

"...Wow, that really was—IS—some serious shit," Taylor finally murmured, processing the story. "You okay after all that? Especially given what's goin' on right now, with th' accusations an' all?" He took a swig from the bottle—his second, just started—while watching her in some concern.

Omega shrugged, then took a pull from her own bottle. It was her third, and it was halfway gone—yet she showed no obvious signs of inebriation. Taylor eyed the bottle in her hand, then shot a quick glance at Echo, who also shrugged, then frowned slightly.

"I suppose," she replied. "It isn't like I actually have a lotta choice, you know? The only place I really belong now is the Agency, although it took me a while to figure that out. And as long as I'm here, I might as well do some good. And that's best served right where I am, I think. At least I've got Echo to help point me in the proper direction when I flounder."

"You are one damn tough badass lady, Omega. Ah'm glad to meet ya. To tell the truth," Taylor admitted, "until you told me your whole story, Ah was gonna tell you that you reminded me of somebody. There's this lady Ah've written a couple books with..."

"Oh, yeah, I know of her," Omega said, nodding. "She's my cousin, so there probably is a little bit of family resemblance there."

"Cousin?!" Echo exclaimed in surprise. "I didn't think you had any family left, Meg!"

"Well, she's not close kin, Ace, not at all. To be honest, I forgot about her until Dr. Taylor mentioned her," Omega confessed, scrunching her face.

"It was...lemme think...I think her mama's grandmother and my great-great-grandfather were...brother and sister? Or was it...No, I think that's right. So that'd be...what? Oh, that cousin stuff just gets me all mixed up. Third cousin, once removed? Something like that."

"Not close, though," Taylor said. "You're right about that."

"Did you ever meet her, Meg?" Echo wondered.

"Only once, at a convention," Omega said, then shrugged. "But she wasn't a writer yet. She's a good bit older than me, too. And, well...I don't actually know her. I doubt she'd even remember me. Let alone consider me blood."

"Yeah," Taylor noted. "Just 'cause you share a little bit o' genetics doesn't automatically make y'all family."

"Nope," Omega agreed.

"So it isn't like you really DO have any family left," Echo realized.

"Not really. And now that I'm supposed to be...whatever kinda story Fox put out about me when I disappeared from the outside world, I can't go tell her, 'Hey cuz, it's your long-lost relative!'" Omega pointed out. "It's okay, though. I still have a kind of family inside the Agency. Provided the current PR debacle doesn't destroy that, too."

"Not if I can help it," Echo said, firm.

"Hey, if Ah can help out some way, just yell," Taylor volunteered. "Ah know where th' maglev tube station is under Marshall Space Flight Center. Ah can be here in a couple hours, if y'all ever need me."

"Thanks, guys, both of you. I appreciate it. Okay, enough about my sordid past," Omega said, with that too-bright smile again. "Tell me about you, and how you got to be an author, and stuff. Oh, and why you have such a strong Southern accent! You sound like me!"

Taylor glanced at Echo, his blue eyes revealing some concern at Omega's facial expression; Echo let his own dark eyes mirror that concern.

"Well, lessee," Taylor said. "Ah sound like you 'cause the part of mah planet Ah come from pretty much sounds like this already. When Ah arrived, they took one listen to me, and sent me off to Huntsville, Alabama with mah family..."

* * *

"So you liked that series, huh?" Taylor said, some time later.

"Yeah, I did," Omega admitted. "I liked the whole space connection, and NASA and the Air Force, and all that. It's kinda what I wanted to do in real life. What I almost did do—and then I landed here."

"And damned if we've been able to manage an off-planet mission yet, so Meg can get her wings with the Agency," Echo interjected. "But it'll come, in time."

"I know," she said, offering him a kind of tired smile. "I'm being patient."

"Well, how's about a little something to reward that patience?" Taylor suggested. "Ah got something here that's kinda special, a little bit of a collector's item, and Ah was wonderin' what to do with it. Ah'd been thinkin' about maybe donatin' it to the con's charity auction, but Ah'm bettin' it just found a better home."

"What's that, Travis?" Echo wondered, as Taylor picked up his backpack, hefting the heavy bag into his lap before rummaging in it, finally coming up with a book.

"This is an advance review copy of the next book in that series," Taylor said, waving it in the air. "One step removed from a galley proof, an' easier to handle, 'cause it's bound. The book ain't gonna be released for another three or four months. How 'bout Ah autograph it and give it to Meg, here?"

Omega just gasped in surprise.

"Hey, baby!" Echo exclaimed, grinning. "Score!"

"Yeah! Thank you, Dr. Taylor," Omega murmured, as the author jotted a note on the title page, then signed it. "You didn't have to do that!"

"Sure Ah did," he said, handing it to her with a grin. "Y'all agents did, and do, take good care o' me an' my family. Besides, you been through hell an' back, hon. This is just a small thank you by comparison."

"No it isn't," she murmured, accepting it and peeping at the inscription. "It's weeks, even months, of hard work. Oh wow."

"What's it say, Meg, baby?" Echo wanted to know, leaning over her shoulder to look.

The inscription read,

To Omega, one of the baddest of the badasses.
Thanks for hanging in there for us "imports."
~Travis S. Taylor

"And on that note, Ah do gotta get to my next panel now," Taylor said, tossing his empty beer bottle into the recycling bin in the corner. "Hope Ah'll see y'all around the con, though."

"You will," Echo averred. "And we need to get back to work, too."

They rose, and Alpha One discarded spent drinks containers. Omega popped the pills that Echo offered, and the three meandered companionably back toward the elevators.

* * *

"You played WHAT?!" India demanded, as Alpha Two stood in the commons area of the convention center.

"You heard me, babe," Romeo said, turning. "Now c'mon. I wanna see if I can find it in the dealer's room, maybe get a copy of it, so we can find out how bad this whole pile o' shit really is."

"I'm right behind you, hon," India said, turning for the dealer's room. "Let's go."

* * *

"Oh, yeah, I'm familiar with it," the huckster told them. Her Earth name was Aaishah Jones, and she was from Kaceerlon, the fourth moon of a gas giant orbiting HD 156411 in Earth's southern sky. "And madder than hell about it."

"Huh?" Romeo said. "Why are YOU mad about it?"

"'Cause if they expose you, they expose us, and don't think I don't remember the anti-alien paranoia during the Klydonian invasion," Aaishah pointed out. "Half your species, and all o' your military, had about as soon shoot us all on sight, near as I could figure."

"Too many bad sci-fi movies," India murmured. "Um, I mean SF movies."

"Well, there is that," Aaishah noted, flashing her white teeth in a grin. "But I still ain't carryin' any of the *Black Suits* merchandise, just on principle. It might put a few extra bucks in my pocket, but I don't see any reason to help the bastards." She sighed. "Still, I get what you're tryin' to do. Gimme a few minutes to scope out which dealers got it, and I'll see about setting you up with a deal. The Agency oughta reimburse you for it, but like I said, it's the principle of the thing. If I can do 'em outta a couple bucks of profit, hell yes! Wait here."

And Aaishah headed off to see if any of the other dealers carried *Black Suits* toys.

* * *

She came back about ten minutes later.

"I got one for ya, right here," she said, handing the couple a long, flat package. "Figured I could get one for wholesale if not better, an' I'm giving it to you."

"How much was it?" India wondered, pulling out her wallet.

"No, no, sweetie, you don't understand. I mean I'm GIVING it to you," Aaishah told the Agent, holding out the box. "Free of charge. Consider it my contribution to the cause. I want you to have all the info you need to take this mess down and stomp it into the mud, down past the light of day."

"Oh...well, THANK you," India murmured in gratitude, accepting the package. "We're already working on that, but Romeo thought this might have some stuff in it that'd help."

"It just might," Aaishah agreed.

"Do YOU know anything that might help?" Romeo asked the dealer.

"You know, sugar, I been rackin' my brains tryin' to think of something—anything," Aaishah said, frowning. "I don't really know nuthin'. But the word has it on the street that y'all done pissed off somebody important, somewhere. I dunno where, or when, or nothin' like that. But you got your work cut out."

"Damn," India murmured.

* * *

Later that day, Alpha Line met up in order to get coordinated.

"Is your Lexus filled up yet?" Echo asked India, a twinkle in his brown eyes.

"Let's just say we'd better not have to give anybody a lift," India replied with a grin, and Omega laughed.

"How 'bout you, Romeo?" Omega asked. "Gaming go well?"

"Slammin'!" Romeo replied enthusiastically. "Did encounter one thing you guys might be interested in, though."

"What's that, tiger?" Echo asked.

"The *Black Suits* roleplaying game. I played a round or two to investigate."

"Surprise, surprise. Yeah. Shoulda thought of that," Omega murmured. "There's probably a video game out, too."

"Not yet, but it's comin', accordin' to the other players," Romeo noted.

"Damn," Echo grumbled.

"Yeah," Omega agreed. "We ought to be able to pick up a copy in the dealers' room, and check it out."

"Been there, done that," said India. "It's one of the things filling up the trunk...and back seat...of the Lexus—thanks to a friendly dealer from Kaceerlon, who actually arranged to GIVE us a copy. We can check it out further back at Headquarters if we need to. She also said that the word on the street was that, whoever was after us, it was somebody powerful that the Agency pissed off."

"Oh really, now?" Echo said, raising an eyebrow. "That's interesting."

"It is," Omega said, thoughtful.

"What did you two do?" Romeo wondered.

"We killed two birds with one stone," Echo told them, "and kept an eye on the Prime Minister while Meg got a chance to talk to her favorite science fiction author."

"Who??" Romeo asked, and Omega pulled a certain not-yet-released trade paperback from her warp pocket to show him the inscription. "Day-um, girl! Taylor?? You got to talk to HIM?!"

A happy Omega nodded.

"For at least an hour, in between his panels. He likes Guns 'n' Roses a lot," she confided with a grin. "He's a pretty cool guy."

"Think you could get me an intro?"

"I don't think you actually need one," Omega told him. "This guy here," she elbowed an amused Echo, "was kind enough to provide me the opportunity in the first place. Turns out he's an old pal of Echo's from the Tau Ceti system. And he already knew that you had been Echo's partner, Romeo, so you can probably just introduce yourself. There he goes now..."

A well-built man, apparently human, athletic, cleanshaven with pale skin, dishwater blond hair and a slightly ginger complexion, a bit under six feet in height, emerged from a programming room, a familiar backpack slung over one shoulder. He glanced up and spotted Echo and Omega, grinned, waved, and headed off down the corridor. Romeo's head swiveled around, watching, and he began edging away from his companions.

"Uh, 'scuse me, guys, uh, I gotta...oh, man!...I'll meet up with ya later!" And Romeo was off.

* * *

"Well, what say we three go to the regular con suite and get some snacks?" Echo suggested, when Romeo had disappeared around the corner. "I can't say when we'll get our next meal, all things considered, and I dunno about you two, but I'm kinda hungry."

"Me, too," Omega agreed.

"Me three," India averred.

"Me four," came a voice behind them.

They turned, and a grinning Fox stood there.

"Not only am I rather peckish," the Agency Director noted, "and could use something that isn't stale, soured, or moldy, I rather want to see this 'con suite' to ensure that we have ours laid out properly."

"I'd have thought the little misunderstanding earlier would have put paid to any concerns on that account," Echo said, as the group headed for the con suite.

"Mostly, but I did want to tag up with Lloyd," Fox said.

"What, the guy that runs the regular con suite?" Omega wondered, as they got in the elevator. Echo hit the floor button, and the fen that rushed for the elevator came to a dead stop when the solemn gazes of four powerful Agents turned on them. The elevator doors closed, and the four were left alone, as it moved upward.

"The same," Fox said then, with a nod. "The other person who was with us when the whole, ah, cross-species cocktail confusion went down. Since we found out that the Lambda Andromedans prefer their food a bit, er..."

"Fermented," Omega offered.

"I'd have said half-rotten," Echo decided.

"Pathogenic," India declared.

"...I was just going to say 'off,'" Fox concurred, "but damned if I don't think Omega hit on a more diplomatic term than any of us." He shrugged. "Anyway, since Lloyd's home planet has an active trade with the Lambda Andromedan system, he's familiar with their preferences—"

"Wait, wait, wait," India interrupted. "You mean the guy running the convention's, um, hospitality room is what we called 'em at medical conferences..."

"Yeah, same difference," Omega affirmed.

"...Is an extraterrestrial?" India continued.

"Precisely correct, India," Fox agreed. "And he's helping us with ours, too, by pulling the rejected foodstuffs—the stale, moldy, crusty, or otherwise-out-too-long stuff that the regular con suite would ordinarily throw out—and bringing them to OUR con suite, under the guise OF throwing it out."

"Hey, waste not," Echo said with a rueful chuckle. "If our guests can stomach it, more power to 'em."

"Agreed," Fox said. "But I'm still glad to get away from the smell for a while."

"No wonder," Omega observed, as they entered the civilian con suite. "Ooo, speaking of, smells like they just finished a nice batch of curry."

"We did," Lloyd said, coming out of the back room. "Hi, Fox! How's... erhm, the stuff going?"

"Perfectly," Fox told him, looking around. "I just wanted to see what the other side looked...and smelled...like, and maybe get something to eat."

"I'll bet," Lloyd laughed. "Listen, the curry isn't supposed to come out yet, but c'mon back and I'll get you guys some, before it gets released for the Mongol hordes. You want it over rice...?"

* * *

"Hey, Ed, come here a sec," one of the YuleCon convention chairs called to her guest liaison.

"Yeah, Brandy? What's up?" Ed Smith replied, detouring from his intended route to the con suite and veering over to the Ops Room door. Ed was a stocky, strong brunet of about average height, in his mid-forties, though he looked younger. His eyeglasses gave him an intellectual appearance, and his goatee a rather dashing look.

"Have you seen Doc Taylor in the last, oh, half an hour?"

"No; I left him in his last panel with Howard and Sarah and ran to the con suite to grab something to eat. I didn't get lunch or breakfast either, and I was starved. I got there just before they cleared out the food, as it was. Then I had to run back to my room for a minute."

"How long ago was that?"

Ed glanced at his wristwatch.

"I dunno. Maybe an hour and a half, an hour forty-five?"

"Mm," Brandy said, thinking.

"What's up?"

"That big panel he's moderating this evening? We got a no-go from one of the guests. I have no idea where they went, but John apparently picked up a touch of food poisoning when he went out to dinner with that group last night, and he can't get outta his bathroom, let alone leave the hotel room."

"Shit!"

"Pretty much, from what I understand. Some puking, too."

"Ooo, that was cold, Brandy!" They laughed.

"Well, you started it! Anyway, I need you to find Travis and give him a heads-up that John won't be there. I know he kinda had a loose plan for how the discussion was supposed to go, so I need to know, like, ASAP, if I need to grab a substitute from the rest of our pool of guests. I've only got about two and a half, three hours, before that panel starts, and I'll need to juggle some stuff in the schedule to find a substitute."

"Oh! All right, I'm on it. I'll track him down, tell him what happened, and get back with you in the next..." Ed glanced at his watch again, "if it takes me an hour, I'll be surprised."

"Good man! Thanks!"

And Ed headed off, to track down YuleCon's Author Guest of Honor, Travis S. Taylor.

* * *

"Okay, he wasn't in the con suite; he wasn't in the green room," Ed muttered to himself, twenty minutes later, rushing through the hotel. "He wasn't in the dealer's room or art show. He wasn't in his hotel room. He's not in the hotel restaurant OR the bar." He shook his head. "I ain't got a clue where the hell he is!"

He abruptly stopped dead in the lobby, and three fen promptly ran into him from behind. Quick apologies were exchanged all around, and the fans moved on, as Ed stood where he was and pondered where to look next.

"Maybe he's sitting in on somebody else's panel," he decided. "I'll just stick my head in the back of all the programming rooms and check."

He headed off to the convention center area to look.

* * *

Ed started at one end of the row of programming rooms and systematically worked his way down and around the corner. He eased open each door, nodded at the moderator as he slipped inside, then stood silently in the back, looking for a certain familiar dishwater-blond head with ginger highlights. Upon failing to spot it, he nodded to the moderator again, and slipped out, heading to the next room.

He got to the corner of the L-shaped convention center and went around it, checking the last room that he knew had active programming. There were two more rooms past that, carved out of a ballroom, but no panels were scheduled in them for that time of day. Consequently, Ed fully expected them to be locked.

"Still," he considered, "I oughta go check. It'd be just the sorta thing for him to drag some fans off for a long technical discussion, if somebody left one 'a the doors ajar. And it ain't like I don't have the keys, anyway."

So he headed down the broad corridor toward the nearest door.

* * *

But when he reached it, he could indeed hear voices coming from inside. Ed took hold of the door knob, but it was firmly locked.

Reaching into his pocket, he fished out the special key ring for the hotel, selected one of the master keys, and stuck it in the lock. Pushing the door open, he stepped inside, prepared to tell Travis that he was needed and to quit hiding out with a brew—

—And stopped dead, gaping.

The two rooms had been merged into the full ballroom; the tables for the panelists had been rearranged to form a long central table, and around that table, and at several chairs along the periphery, sat an entire phalanx of people in costume, from black Suits to chartreuse, betentacled, three-eyed aliens.

"Who are you and what are you doing here? You're not supposed to be here! These rooms are supposed to be closed to all convention members when not in use! Are you with that film or something?" Ed demanded to know.

One of the people wearing black Suits, a strapping, middle-aged blond man, pushed back from the table and stood up, moving toward Ed, who stood his ground despite the fact that the man was intimidating as hell...and easily a head taller than Ed, who was not especially short.

"May I help you?" the man asked, in a soft, cultured, European accent.

"Um, you haven't seen Dr. Travis Taylor, have you?"

"No, we have not. Is there anything else we can do to assist you?

"You can help me by getting outta here before I have to call Security," Ed said, stern. "I don't care who the hell you are, or if you're from Hollywood or what! This facility is supposed to have been contracted exclusively for YuleCon's use this weekend! And I'm on the con comm, and I've never seen any of you before in my life! If you're practicing for the masquerade competition, you'll just have to practice someplace else! Now, c'mon, get moving!"

The man in the black Suit glanced back at the others.

"I believe we shall have to do just that," he said, reaching into his jacket pockets with both hands. Behind him, the others all produced some sort of odd-looking wraparound sunglasses, putting them on and staring at him in silence; the aliens just looked odd to Smith, with their three-eyed spectacles. The man slipped on his own pair of glasses, then waved a cell phone in Ed's face. There was a multicolored flash of light...

* * *

Ed found himself back in the broad corridor of the convention center, wondering how he'd managed to nod off while standing up. He looked around; the current hour's panels had not yet ended, but he'd checked all of them, and Dr. Taylor was not there. Nothing was left except the two ballroom segments.

"But they should be locked. Still," he considered, "I oughta go check. It'd be just the sorta thing for him to drag some fans off for a long technical discussion, if somebody left one 'a the doors ajar. And it ain't like I don't have the keys, anyway."

So he headed down the broad corridor toward the nearest door.

* * *

But when he reached it, he could indeed hear voices coming from inside. Ed took hold of the door knob, but it was firmly locked.

Reaching into his pocket, he fished out the special key ring for the hotel, selected one of the master keys, and stuck it in the lock. Pushing the door open, he stepped inside, prepared to tell Travis that he was needed and to quit hiding out with a brew—

—And stopped dead, gaping.

The two rooms had been merged into the full ballroom; the tables for the panelists had been rearranged to form a long central table, and around that table, and at several chairs along the periphery, sat an entire phalanx of people in costume, from black Suits to chartreuse, betentacled, three-eyed aliens.

"Who are you and what are you doing here? You're not supposed to be here! These rooms are supposed to be closed to all convention members when not in use! Are you with that film or something?" Ed demanded to know.

One of the guys in an alien costume, dressed in rather more opulent clothing than the other alien costumes, turned to a strapping, middle-aged blond male in a black Suit.

"Did we not just do this?" the guy in the alien costume wondered.

Ed watched in amazement as everyone donned odd-looking wraparound sunglasses, in despite of the fact that the room had no windows. The blond man rose and hurried toward him, pulling a smart phone from his pocket.

There was a multicolored flash of light...

* * *

Sugar pulled his actual smart phone from one pocket as he dropped his brain bleacher into another. He activated it with a couple of swipes, then waited for the other party to answer.

"Yes, Echo, this is Sugar. We have a little problem here. Yes, someone with the convention has come looking for Dr. Taylor, and he has a key to the room. Of course I brain-bleached him...for the second time just now. Can you gather up your Alpha Line team and send them out, find Taylor, and bring him down here as soon as possible? I think if the man could actually be sent off with Taylor, we'd be good. But he is systematic, and keeps coming back here to search. Yes, he would be...but that's up to you lot. My team and I have a treaty to negotiate. Of course, if the Director wants to help you look, that is his business. But if this 'Ed' person—according to his con badge—shows up many more times, it is going to look like a Keystone Kops routine down here. Yes? Excellent; thank you, my friend."

Sugar looked up at the Prime Minister and his entourage.

"My apologies about that, all. Alpha Line has gone to find Taylor, and they'll bring him down to the man in the hall. That should solve our problem."

"Let us hope so," the Prime Minister noted, seeming peeved. "We have had interruptions enough aplenty."

* * *

Ed found himself back in the broad corridor of the convention center, wondering why he felt so very strange, almost light-headed. He hoped he wasn't coming down with con crud, the ubiquitous, influenza-like disease that so often plagued such large groups of people.

He looked around; the current hour's panels had not yet ended, but he'd checked all of them for Dr. Taylor. Nothing was left except the two ballroom segments.

"But they should be locked. Still," he considered, "I oughta go check. It'd be just the sorta thing for Doc Taylor to drag some fans off for a long technical discussion, if somebody left one 'a the doors ajar. And it ain't like I don't have the keys, anyway."

So he headed down the broad corridor toward the nearest door.

* * *

But when he reached it, he could indeed hear voices coming from inside. Ed took hold of the door knob, but it was firmly locked.

Reaching into his pocket, he fished out the special key ring for the hotel, selected one of the master keys, and stuck it in the lock. Pushing the door open, he stepped inside, prepared to tell Travis that he was needed and to quit hiding out with a brew—

—And stopped dead, gaping.

The two rooms had been merged into the full ballroom; the tables for the panelists had been rearranged to form a long central table, and around that table, and at several chairs along the periphery, sat an entire phalanx of people in costume, from black Suits to chartreuse, betentacled, three-eyed aliens.

"Who are you and what are you doing here? You're not supposed to be—wait a minute..." Ed swayed, dizzy.

"Again?" said the important-looking alien. "Perhaps you should take him farther away this time."

Ed watched in amazement as everyone donned odd-looking wraparound sunglasses, in despite of the fact that the room had no windows. A tall blond man rose and hurried toward him, pulling a smart phone from his pocket.

There was a multicolored flash of light...

* * *

Back in the ballroom, Sugar, the head of the Agency's Diplomacy department, sat back down, mildly annoyed. He pulled his actual smart phone, activated it, and waited for the other party to answer.

"Echo? Yes, it's Sugar again. Yes, that's the third time now. We REALLY need for you lot to find Dr. Taylor and bring him down here before I have to brain-bleach this man into nappies or some such thing. No, I don't know how they work! I'm a diplomatic negotiator, not a neuro-engineer!"

"Perhaps," Tortok suggested, "we should make the annoying human disappear permanently? It would solve a great many problems at the moment."

"NO!" Sugar exclaimed. "Echo! Did you hear that? Yes! You and Omega have GOT TO FIND TAYLOR! No, I don't know WHAT the deuced man wants, I just know he's looking for Taylor! No, I don't even know Taylor. Look, just find him as soon as you can, and get him down here, preferably five minutes ago. Yes, thank you!"

A distracted Sugar raked his hand through his short pale locks, and pondered what to do next. He looked up to see the Prime Minister scowling.

Just then, a key rattled in the door's lock, and the door opened.

"Who are you and what are you doing here?" Ed Smith demanded to know.

"Oh, damn it all to hell and back," Sugar grumbled, rising and putting on his goggle-glasses.

* * *

"No, no, no, Ace! I KNOW it was him! I swear, I saw him come down this way!" Omega declared, grabbing her partner's arm and towing him down a hotel corridor. "I think he went into one of the party rooms!"

"We gotta find him fast," Echo said, as Fox followed along. "I gathered the Lambda Andromedans were getting more than a little annoyed by the constant interruptions. But somehow, I think the convention would be kinda upset if one of their guest liaisons went missing...permanently."

"Farkakt!" Fox exclaimed behind them. "That wouldn't do us any favors with the Galactic Council, either!" He pulled his cell phone. "India? Have you found Romeo yet? Good. What about Taylor? Damn. Keep looking! We have a situation!" He ended the call and slipped the phone back into a pocket.

"No, it's okay, Fox, I'm sure I saw him go in here!" Omega banged on the door with her fist, and it was jerked open seconds later. The soft buzz of at least a dozen voices emerged from the depths of the suite.

"What the hell?!" the occupant demanded. "The party doesn't start until tonight, guys!"

"We're lookin' for Travis Taylor," Omega said, dropping into her deepest Southern dialect. "There's an emergency, an' we need 'im, right away!"

"Meg? That you?" Taylor's voice emanated from somewhere in the depths of the hotel room, and abruptly he appeared in the entryway, sporting a longneck in one hand. "It IS you! Wow, ALL o' y'all! What's up?"

Echo reached out and took the beer bottle from Taylor's hand, shoving it at the room's occupant. Then he took him by one arm and hurried him out of the room and down the hall.

"We have a situation," Echo murmured, using Fox's terminology. "We'll tell you on the way, but we need to get you downstairs to the con 'five minutes ago.'"

"Dammit," Taylor complained, "couldn't Ah have finished mah bheer?"

"NO!" all three Agents chorused.

"Okay, okay, Ah'm goin'," Taylor said, holding up his hands.

* * *

They spotted a bemused Smith standing near the dog-leg, where the various programming rooms wrapped around the interior corner of the building, and Omega gently pushed Taylor's shoulder.

"There. Go. GO!" she told him, and Taylor set off at a jog across the expansive area, just as Smith turned back for a certain ballroom door.

"Ed! ED! Hey, dude!" Taylor called, waving, and Smith looked up.

"THERE you are! Finally!" Alpha One and the Director could barely hear Smith say, from their position partly hidden behind some large potted plants. "Listen, I gotta get some information from ya, or better yet, get you back to Brandy so she can ask ya some questions. I told her an hour, but I'm runnin' late—I'm more'n twenty minutes past when I said I'd have you. No idea where the time went..."

"Whew," Omega murmured, as they watched the pair wander off toward the Ops Room. "At least he's in one piece. I wonder how many times they had to brain-bleach him?"

"I'll let you know," Fox said, chuckling. "I need to get back to the negotiations anyway. Now that I 've gotten a look at this 'con suite' I think we're in good shape where that's concerned. And thank you for the company while we ate."

"That was good curry," Omega agreed.

"Yeah. You need us to do anything special at the moment, Fox?" Echo wondered. "Now that we've discharged our little emergency?"

"No, just keep doing what you're doing," Fox told his department chief, as he headed across the convention center. "That should cover things."

* * *

Fifteen minutes later, after rendezvousing with Alpha Two in an upstairs corridor, Echo put his cell phone back into one of his many odd pockets, and looked up into three pairs of expectant eyes. He grinned tightly.

"At least six," he told Omega, India, and Romeo. "Fox said Sugar lost count at some point, and just stood by the door with goggle-glasses and brain bleacher at the ready, waiting for Smith to come back in." He pursed his lips, then raised his eyebrows. "And that, my friends, is why some agents—no matter how smart they may be at other things—do NOT go out into the field."

Omega put her fingers to the bridge of her nose. She snorted softly, then began to giggle.

"Oh, maaaan!" Romeo said, eyes wide in amusement, and he snorted as well, then let out a snicker. That set India off, and she started laughing.

Finally, when he met Omega's twinkling azure gaze, the whole thing hit home for Echo too. He snorted three times in a desperate effort not to laugh, before giving in and laughing anyway.

Omega, watching him, howled with renewed mirth, and all four Agents doubled up in the hall, laughing until the tears flowed.

* * *

"What's on the schedule next, Echo?" India asked as the Alpha Line Agents patrolled the convention, having finally managed to get control of their laughter—though both Romeo and Omega were prone to sudden, unexpected snorts of amusement, which tended to set the others off into residual chuckles. Echo pulled out a sheaf of papers and studied them.

"Hm...Seems there's a dance tonight," he noted.

"That would be standard." Omega nodded. "Andromedans going?"

"Yep. Guess we will be, too, then." Echo's voice was slightly quieter than usual, but no one noticed.

"Starts at midnight, right?" Omega verified.

"Right again," Echo replied.

"Then it'll probably last all night, or most of it. We four might want to catch a nap between now and then," Omega remarked.

"Good idea," Echo said. "There should also be a set of clothes for each of us waiting in the Agent Ops room by now. We can shower and change while we're at it. But I'd rather not have to bring Monkey and Sierra back over here after everything that's happened."

"No problem, Echo," India told him. "Alpha Two can keep an eye on things for a while. That will give you and Meg a couple hours to rest and take turns freshening up in the bathroom, then we can trade off."

"What she said," Romeo agreed. "Then maybe we can all go get some dinner."

"Done," Echo told them, and they split up.

* * *

At the dance a couple of hours later, a rested, refreshed and properly fed Alpha Line sat at a table near the back of the room, where they could effectively view the event without being particularly noticeable themselves.

"Nice layout," Omega decided, looking around the ballroom. "Cool decorations, too."

"Yeah," Echo agreed. "Interesting, imaginative mix of science fiction and Christmas stuff."

"Exactly."

"Look, there goes Tortok with that little Andromedan babe," Romeo observed. "Told 'im he oughta go ahead 'n ask her out. Look at 'em go!"

"Is that some sort of Andromedan dance?" India wondered, intrigued.

"Why don't y'all go get 'em to teach you?" Omega encouraged. "Looks like fun."

"Shall we?" Romeo looked at India.

"Why, thank you, 'Mr. Williamson.' I'd love to dance with a celebrity," India teased, and they headed for the dance floor.

Omega and Echo watched them in silence for a few minutes, sharing their amusement through several glances at each other. Then one of the costumed 'aliens' from the group of Kronons with whom Omega had done battle came up to the table and bowed low.

"Worthy lady, might I have the honor of this dance?"

Echo saw Omega's eyes widen slightly, the pupils dilating, and her body language closed. Watching her carefully to make certain he was doing what she wanted, he spoke to the man on her behalf.

"She, uh...had a nasty migraine earlier. She's still a little weak. Maybe later..."

Omega merely nodded slowly in agreement, taking her cue from Echo's story, wincing and rubbing her temple.

Oh, I'm sorry," the man said, dropping character, distressed over her apparent malaise. "Now I get why you're sitting in the back of the room!"

"In a dark corner, too," Echo added, building the case for her 'migraine' as he went. "The light, you know."

"Yeah. I just, um, didn't wanna miss the band." Omega shrugged.

"I've got those earplugs right here, if you need 'em," Echo offered, leaning back to reach into a trousers pocket. He did, in fact, have earplugs; they were one of several small, standard items he kept on his person in the event they were needed. *But in this case,* he thought, *they'd just be a prop. A useful one, in the circumstances, but still.*

"No, it's okay," Omega demurred. "The sound isn't what's bothering me right now, and it's dim back here, like you said."

"Is there anything I can do?" the other man asked, concerned. "Some aspirin or acetaminophen, maybe? Ibuprofen? I have some, back in my room. I can run get it in just a couple minutes..."

"No...no, thank you," Omega shot him a wan smile. "I, uh, I already took something for it. Prescription, you know; I shouldn't mix it with something else. I'll be okay...in time."

"All right, if you're sure. Take it easy, then. Hope I'll see you tomorrow." The Kronon wandered off, and Omega gave Echo a grateful glance.

"Thanks for the quick thinking, and for playing along," she murmured. "I'm just...not in the mood for dancing with a stranger after everything that's happened. It could be anybody doing this...and they'd really love to split us up to pull something else."

Echo nodded in agreement. *And approval, too, when I get right down to it,* Echo thought, pleased. *Meg really has a good grasp of situational concerns. I couldn't ask for a better partner. We have GOT to find out who's doing this, AND who's framing her for it, dammit!*

India and Romeo returned just then, and Omega smiled at them.

"Was it fun?" she asked the pair.

"Yeah!" both agents enthused, and Romeo continued, "You two ever danced together?"

"No," Echo replied briefly, and Omega turned to him.

"Why do I suddenly think Romeo's got a bee in his bonnet about something?"

"Because he does," Echo replied knowingly. *Because he does this to me every chance he can get. Because he thinks he can fix something that's broken, without ever knowing what it is that broke, or how or why,* the senior agent thought, annoyed.

"Why don't you two hit the dance floor, have some fun?" Romeo urged. "You dance, Meg?"

"It's been a while, but yes, I can dance. Ballroom dance, in fact."

"Wow. I didn't know you could do that," India remarked. India and Romeo smiled at each other, then at Omega, who grinned back somewhat shyly.

"Like I said, it's been a while. NASA doesn't throw too many dances."

"How about you, Echo?" India wondered.

* * *

"I've...been known to," Echo said, throwing an odd, vaguely hurt look at Romeo.

Romeo suddenly remembered what he knew of the reason why Echo no longer danced. Simultaneously he realized that this was something that Echo really did NOT want to do, even with Omega, and he shut his mouth quickly. The damage had been done, however. India pressed on.

"So?! What are you two waiting for??"

* * *

"I don't think Meg is...comfortable dancing with anyone right now," Echo told India, glancing at his partner. *Maybe that'll be a good enough excuse,* he thought. *Besides, it diverts attention from me.*

"Actually," Omega told him quietly, "you're probably the only person in the room—with the possible exception of Romeo, assuming India would let him go—" she shot a wan smile at the female Agent, "that I WOULD feel comfortable dancing with...under the circumstances. 'Shadow dancing,' you know," she joked.

Damn. That didn't work. Echo sat silently, scanning the room. *If I ignore it, it'll go away,* he thought. *Works with most other things. Maybe it'll work here, too.*

"Well?" India pressed, ignoring Romeo's elbow nudging her side. "Like I said, what are you waiting for?"

* * *

"Let him alone, India," Omega told her, watching Echo's averted face. "If he doesn't want to dance, he doesn't have to."

"But Meg, it would be..."

"Maybe I'm not who Echo would rather be dancing with," Omega said perceptively, and both men glanced at her, startled. Then Echo looked at Romeo, a question in his gaze, and Romeo subtly shook his head. Omega noticed the exchange, watching without seeming to do so. "Um, I think I'm...gonna go over to the con suite and get something to drink," Omega said then, standing abruptly. "Any of y'all want anything?"

The others shook their heads, and she exited the ballroom before anyone could react.

She didn't come back.

* * *

A worried Echo finally found her leaning over the rail on one of the balconies overlooking the atrium-style lobby, directly over the ballroom, where she could hear the music but remain relatively unseen.

"What happened to my shadow?" he asked quietly, as he walked up beside her.

"Shadows fade away at night," she said without looking at him, deliberately enigmatic. Then she sighed. "Choices. Do I stick with my alibi, or do I get him off the hook? I figured if I wasn't there, Romeo and India would let you alone."

"You wanted to dance."

"Yeah, I kinda did. I like to dance," she admitted, "and I don't get much chance any more. Not in a long time, anyway. Dad taught me when I was a girl. But it's okay, Echo. There's more to you than you want to talk about, even than you've shown me, and that's all right. I respect that privacy. But there's something I want you to know."

"What?"

"Remember back when I first got sucked into the Agency? You told me if I ever needed to talk, you were a good listener..."

"Yeah?"

"Well, I'm a good listener, too."

* * *

Romeo and India were keeping an eye on the Andromedans in the ballroom while Echo searched for Omega, when a movement near the door caught Romeo's eye. He poked India.

"Look! It's Echo and Meg. He found her."

"Oh, thank God," India murmured, deeply relieved. "I just knew something else was gonna go down that would get blamed on her, before Echo could find her."

Echo handed a note to the deejay—the band having performed their last set while he hunted for his partner—as he and Omega took a position on the dance floor.

"Wha—they gonna dance...?" Romeo wondered, surprised. "I woulda thought..."

* * *

Echo turned to his partner. "Do you waltz?"

"And cha-cha, and salsa, and tango, and foxtrot..."

"I get the idea. A waltz will do for now." He took her right hand in his left, and slipped his right hand around to the small of her back as she laid her left hand lightly on his shoulder. "You ready?" he asked.

"I'm ready," Omega replied, leaning toward him slightly as she shifted onto the balls of her feet. "Pity I don't have those high heels I wore the other day. They're easier to dance in..."

"Mm. They'd kill your feet by the end of the night. Nervous?" Echo grinned. "There's a bazillion people watching."

"No," Omega told him, lifting her chin and meeting his eyes. "For once, I'm not a rookie at something." Then she laughed as the music began. It was *The Blue Danube*, the Strauss waltz from *2001: A Space Odyssey.* "Nice choice."

"I thought it was appropriate," Echo told her as he stepped toward her and they swept out onto the dance floor.

* * *

"WOW," an impressed India remarked, amber eyes widening as she watched the Alpha One team spin across the room. "They DO know how to dance. They could be professionals."

"Yeah," Romeo agreed. "We're not the only ones who think so. Everybody's givin' 'em room. Wup—they're clearin' th' dance floor, just to watch 'em!"

"They work as well together on the dance floor as they do in the field," India observed. "Romeo, can't you just imagine Echo in a tux and Meg in a long gown?"

"Oh, yeah! What color dress?" Romeo joined in.

"Mmm...depends. I could see a black beaded sheath..."

"Slit up to there," Romeo agreed. "With a low back. Yeah. Astaire an' Rogers."

"I think Echo's more of a leading man in the looks department than Astaire was, to tell the truth. But you know," India mused, "with their Southern accents..."

"Hmm. You thinkin' Rhett an' Scarlett?"

"You bet. They joke enough about it anyway. Think about a full-skirted ball gown the same shade of blue as Meg's eyes," India told him with a dreamy smile, amber eyes soft. "And Echo in a cutaway..."

"Whoah, lady." Romeo let out a low, soft whistle.

The music drew to its end, and applause broke out as India and Romeo watched Omega drop into a deep, formal curtsy to her partner. Echo bowed low in response, and offered his arm, escorting her back to the table.

"Hey, it's Fred an' Ginger," Romeo teased as they walked up.

"You guys are really good," India told them. "Romeo and I should've been asking you for lessons instead of the Andromedans."

"You enjoyed it?" Omega asked them, smiling, blue eyes alight. They nodded. "Me, too. Thanks, Echo," she said softly.

"You're welcome," Echo told her laconically, with an inscrutable face. But there was an enigmatic spark in the depths of the brown eyes.

Chapter 8

Zero Days—Five Days

At dawn, a weary Alpha Line escorted the even wearier Andromedans back to their floor of the hotel.

"My feet are killing me," India complained after they'd discharged their wards.

"After dancing all night with Romeo, what did you expect?" Echo asked, mildly amused, but too tired to show it. After quite a few additional dances with Omega—an activity to which he'd grown unaccustomed in the last couple of years—he had to admit to himself that his feet were not entirely happy either. *Nor my back, nor my glutes, hamstrings or quads. Not that anyone else needs to know that fact,* he thought. *Training specificity, I suppose. Maybe I oughta do a little more hoofing after all. It wasn't SO bad. I mean, it didn't really remind me as much as I thought it would. You never know when I'm gonna need to do it for some diplomatic thing...and Meg fit right up against my body, and followed my lead perfectly.* The remembrance of her body nestled so close to his, moving in flawless cadence together, caused him to smile to himself, and a wave of warmth washed over him. *Just like in everything else we do; we sorta go together. She makes a...really good...partner...*His mental voice tapered off, as unexpected recognition dawned. *Aw, damn. Tell me I didn't just do this.* He dared one quick look at his partner, and felt something in his gut stir, and something else in his chest quiver. *Hell. I did.*

"I know, but..." India sighed and broke off.

"Come on, India," Omega soothed, "I've got a trick or two that'll help. Let's go back to the Agent Ops room for a minute." She turned to the two men. "Y'all okay with that?"

Romeo nodded agreement. So did Echo...with an addendum.

"Stick with India," Echo told his partner quietly. Omega sighed and nodded.

"Come on, India," Omega said, wry. "The Shadow knows...how to get you going again." The two women moved off, and Romeo and Echo turned, headed for the meeting rooms.

* * *

"Uh, Echo..." Romeo began, hesitant, as they walked, "I'm sorry, man."

"Hmm?" Echo seemed preoccupied.

"I'm really sorry 'bout the dancin' thing last night. I jus' kinda wasn't really thinkin' it through," Romeo apologized.

"Oh. That."

"Did Meg twist your arm, too?"

"No. She just likes to dance." Echo's face wore a distant look. Romeo watched him closely.

"Echo? You all right?"

Echo shook himself out of his musings to answer.

"Fine, hot shot. Why wouldn't I be?" He looked around at the meeting room area. "You wait here and greet the Prime Minister's party. I'll be back after I've swept the area."

"Gotcha," Romeo responded amiably, and settled down to wait.

Some time later, a surprised Romeo spotted Echo on one of the balconies overlooking the lobby, directly over the ballroom, lost in thought.

* * *

"...And the email invitations ought to be going out today," Omega told them, some time later. "I set the batches for automatic send. But I wanted to go ahead and tell y'all. And I, um...I invited the Prime Minister and his entourage."

At that, she shot an anxious glance at Echo, who returned it calmly, seeming unperturbed by the revelation; so she settled down about the matter.

"Aaall riiight!" Romeo exclaimed enthusiastically. "Damn, skippy! Now that's what I call a plan, girl!"

"Good!" Omega smiled. "Then I can count on y'all being at the party?"

* * *

"You know it!" Romeo answered for them all, and India and Echo both shot him annoyed glances. Romeo was oblivious to their irked expressions, but Omega saw them, and the anticipatory light in her eyes died.

"Well...um..." Omega changed the subject abruptly, "how are the negotiations going?"

Romeo blinked at the sudden diversion of topic, and Echo responded.

"Pretty well, Meg. I think we're way ahead of schedule."

* * *

"Good! Maybe we can get it all done and the Prime Minister headed home before the countdown winds down. We've only got three more days, and YuleCon basically ends tonight anyway," Omega remarked, satisfied. "Tomorrow's events are just windups."

"So tonight's the costume competition?" India asked.

"Right," Echo replied.

"You comin' in costume, Meg?" Romeo asked enthusiastically.

"No."

"Aw, c'mon. It'd be fun," Romeo egged her on.

"No, Romeo. I don't feel like calling any MORE attention to myself."

"But Romeo's right, Meg. It would be fascinating to see that side of your personality," India agreed.

"Yeah, c'mon, don'tcha have somethin' in the closet you c'n pull out from a past convention or somethin'?" Romeo pressed on. "I can run ya over to Headquarters to pick it up..."

The blue eyes narrowed in annoyance, then all but began to glow, as Alpha Two kept urging. Echo saw the warning signs of the Celtic temperament coming to the fore, and shot quelling looks at their companions—doing everything except drawing a finger across his throat—but they pressed on eagerly, curious to see his partner in yet another new light.

"C'mon, Meg, why don't you?" India asked, smiling.

"Yeah! Show us the foxy super-lady under that Suit. Betcha got a big 'S' on," Romeo teased.

"LET ME *ALONE*!" Omega erupted. "I'm NOT doing it, and that's final! Even if Fox had approved it—which he HASN'T—I don't feel 'foxy,' and I SURE as hell don't feel very 'super'! So just shut the hell up about it!"

She glanced at Echo, jerked her head in a *come on!* motion, then stalked off around the corner and out of sight.

Echo shrugged, gave Romeo and India stern looks by way of instructing them to stop pressuring his partner—*Or me, for that matter,* he amended mentally—and headed after Omega at speed.

* * *

Echo managed to get his partner to settle down, but Omega wasn't in the mood to go back to the negotiations just yet. So Alpha One was patrolling the hotel in the convention area when they heard a voice behind them call, "Megan? Megan, is that you?"

Omega stiffened slightly. Her gaze locked on the corridor in front of her.

"Ignore him, Meg," Echo murmured, sotto voce, not moving his head and barely moving his lips. "He only thinks it might be you. If you don't respond or react, he'll go away."

"Not this guy," she replied in like manner. "Trust me."

"You don't know that. Just do what I say, and—"

"MEGAN MCALLISTER! I know it's you, woman! Stop and TALK to me, dammit!"

Echo blinked, then halted in concern. *Damn,* he thought, *Meg's in enough hot water from the accusations; she does NOT need somebody yelling her birth name all across a science fiction convention.* He glanced at his partner, who was looking up at him with a knowing gaze.

"Told you. I know this guy. Now what?" she asked. Echo shrugged.

Let's go see what he wants," he decided. "Better that than having him chase us all around the con, yelling your birth name. We've always got brain bleachers handy, if it comes to that."

Omega winced; Echo noticed, but they were out of options.

The pair turned, and Echo saw an older man, roughly retirement age by Echo's judgement, with salt and pepper dark hair, a beard that was more salt than pepper, and glasses. He was somewhat shorter than average, stocky, and limped along at surprising speed with a cane. The man's gaze was fixed on his partner.

"MEGAN!" he exclaimed with a huge smile, hurrying up and enveloping Omega in a bear hug. "I KNEW it was you! What the HELL is going on, woman? You're supposed to be dead! What happened?!"

Omega sighed.

"Larry, this is Agent Echo. Echo, this is an old friend and colleague from Marshall Space Flight Center in Huntsville, Alabama, 'Uncle Lar,' aka Larry Bauer."

"Pleased," Echo murmured, grasping the other man's proffered hand and shaking. "You and Meg actual kin?"

"Likewise, and no, not unless you count me as being kin to half of fandom. That's just my fen nickname. Agent, huh? Echo, you said?" Bauer gazed at the other man, a thoughtful expression in his eyes. "You wouldn't be Doc Taylor's friend, would you? He's got some old friend I've never met that he only calls 'Echo.' And I notice you and Megan are dressed just alike..."

Echo grabbed Bauer and Omega, one hand on each upper arm.

"This way," he said, urging them down the corridor. "We can't be talking about all this in the hallway where anybody can overhear."

* * *

Safely ensconced in an unused meeting room behind a closed and locked door with a chair wedged against it—both members of Alpha One had learned after the Ed Smith debacle—the three sat down on stacking chairs. Echo turned his backward and straddled it, resting his forearms on the back.

"Well, this is a wonderful surprise," a delighted Bauer said, smiling widely. "We all thought you were dead, girl, killed in West Texas by a cougar or the like, this past spring."

"In a way, I was," Omega explained, "only this guy here," she patted Echo's forearm with affection, "was the 'cougar.' It's a...long story."

"Let's hear it!"

Omega sighed.

* * *

"...Aw, damn, girl," Bauer murmured, when Omega, aided by Echo, had finished an abbreviated—but not abridged—version of the story... again. "That's just hard shit."

"Yeah, it has been," Echo agreed. "I'm doing my best to help grease the skids, but it still doesn't help the pain...or the memories."

Omega just shrugged, staring at the pattern of the carpet.

"So you must be Taylor's old friend," Bauer mused, looking at Echo.

"I know him, yes," Echo admitted. "I just introduced Meg, here, to him yesterday, I think it was—I've kinda lost track of days, what with the security detail and all. I take it you know Travis, too."

"Yeah. Worked a couple projects with him. I, uh, I know who he is...or maybe I should say WHAT he is."

Omega's head shot up.

"You do?" she wondered, sounding surprised.

"Sure," Bauer said, with a mischievous grin. "Just because I was working console for missions when you and I worked together, doesn't mean it was ALL I did. Remember how I told you I used to work in the basement of MSFC's headquarters building?"

"Yeah?"

"That's where the maglev station is for Huntsville, baby," Echo explained, heart suddenly lightening.

Thank God, he thought in some relief. *It's obvious they're old friends just watching 'em talk, especially if they 'sat console' together, as Meg calls it. If this man already knows about the Agency, has even worked with it, then we don't need to brain-bleach him, and that means Omega has an old friend available to talk to, if she ever needs it. Fantastic! I was dreading figuring out how to brain-bleach him without upsetting her any more than she already is. She's got enough on her plate to deal with, without that. But if he hadn't already worked with us, I'd have had to, BECAUSE she has enough on her plate to deal with.*

"Baby, huh?" Bauer said, picking up on the expression swiftly. "You two an item, in addition to being partners? You make a handsome couple, and I can tell, you're sure close enough..."

Echo blinked in surprise; he hadn't thought of how the familiar mode of address might sound to someone who didn't know them as Alpha One.

"No, no," Omega said, a wan smile gracing her face, and Echo decided she hadn't quite recovered from explaining her history to the second person inside twenty-four hours. "Yeah, we're...close friends, but it, uh, it isn't like that. No, 'baby' is kind of a nickname Echo's got for me. It's a reference to 'baby Agent,' because I'm a rookie."

"No, you're not," Echo countered. "I've told you, Fox, and tons of departmental applicants before. You left your rookie status behind you months ago, back when Fox formally inaugurated Alpha Line. You're just working on additional experience. I started off teasing you, and then got in the habit of calling you that." He shot a surreptitious glance at Bauer, who was watching him with a skeptical expression. *Well, shit,* he thought, hiding his annoyance, and returned his attention to Omega. "It doesn't apply any more, not really."

"If you say so, Ace."

"I say so...baby." Echo grinned.

"So I guess 'Ace' is YOUR nickname for HIM?" Bauer wondered.

"Exactly," they said in unison, and all three laughed. "It's 'cause he is one damn fine pilot," Omega elaborated.

"Well, then I'm pleased to meet you, Echo—hope you don't mind if I call you just Echo."

"Not at all. You're friends with Travis AND with Meg, so we had to meet sooner or later."

"Look," Bauer offered, "I get the problem with your current situation—a mole in the Agency and all, and it sounds like whoever it is, they're here at the con! I wanna help. So I'll keep my eyes open, and if I see anything suspicious, I should—what? Find somebody in a black Suit?"

"No!" Omega exclaimed. "There's some fen who are here in similar costume, because of the movie and the cartoon."

"Yeah, we're having some...interesting...incidents, because of that," Echo agreed.

"Oh, right! So...do I come find one of you? What if you're not around?"

"C'mon with us," Echo decided. "We got some more people you need to meet."

* * *

"Not bad," Fox decided, as Omega escorted Bauer back to the science fiction convention, the pair chatting the whole way. "We have a definite ally there. And it doesn't hurt at all that he's in Omega's corner."

"No, it doesn't," Echo agreed.

"Hadn't you better get after her, Echo? You're still her alibi in the Agency, even if she is with her friend. And once she leaves him at the convention, she'll be by herself."

"Good point, Fox." Echo hastened off.

"There go three really good people," India murmured, watching.

"It's t' be expected," Romeo declared. "Good people tend t' hang with good people, ya know?"

"Indeed I do, Romeo, indeed I do," Fox said with a meaningful glance at Alpha Two, and turned for the negotiating room.

* * *

The negotiations were not going well this day. The Andromedan Prime Minister was balking on a fine point, and no amount of wheedling or compromise would persuade him to back down. Even the Alpha Line Agents had joined in after Alpha One returned from seeing Bauer back to the con, but the Prime Minister would not be moved.

"So much for your idea of getting him off-planet soon," Echo murmured in his partner's ear as they sat side by side in two chairs near the negotiating table.

"Yeah, looks like it," Omega leaned over and said under her breath. "Uh, look, Echo, can I—can WE—step outside for a second?"

Echo glanced at her, then caught Fox's eye and jerked his head toward the door. Fox nodded, and Echo and Omega stood.

"Back in a few," Omega told Romeo and India quietly as they went by.

* * *

Outside in the breezeway, a concerned Echo asked, "What's up?"

"Nothing, really," Omega told him. "I just needed to get out of there for a couple o' minutes. I'm...kinda in a mood today, I guess. I'm sorry. I know this negotiation is important, but sitting around arguing over nitpicks just seems stupid to me. I was getting frustrated and figured I'd better TAKE a break before SOMETHING broke."

"Smart move, then." Echo nodded, secretly relieved that nothing worse was involved, then admitted, "Truth is, I agree with you. Let's go by the con suite and get some caffeine."

"All right. Echo, can I ask you something?" Omega said as they walked.

* * *

"Shoot."

"You don't want anything to do with my party, do you?"

"It's like I told you a while back, Meg...I just...don't do Christmas."

"Echo?"

"Hm?"

"After all that's happened...is everything okay? With us. With YOU..."

Echo shot her a swift, interrogative glance, searching her face for clues regarding what had brought on that particular line of inquiry. They turned the corner and entered the con suite.

"Sure, we're fine," he told her. "Why?"

"You've been unusually quiet...and, and distant...this morning."

This time the glance he gave her was more than a little startled.

What does she know, he wondered, worried, *and how long has she known it? And how much did I give away before I finally figured it out my own damn self?* But he recovered quickly and shrugged.

"Eh. No big deal. Getting tired of babysitting, I guess."

"Oh!" Omega blushed scarlet, but Echo was making a business of getting a cup of coffee—thereby hiding his own discomfiture—and didn't notice.

* * *

When Alpha One returned to the conference room, Echo sat down in his previous chair near the negotiating table, but Omega hung back by the door. Catching Fox's eye, she motioned him over and then stepped outside with him.

After a moment, Fox looked through the door and summoned Romeo. Romeo exited the room, and a few minutes later, Fox came back in alone.

When Romeo and Omega didn't return in a reasonable amount of time, Echo signaled the Director over to a distant corner of the room.

"What happened to Romeo and Meg?" he murmured, perturbed.

"Romeo will be back shortly. He's taking Omega back to Headquarters."

"What?!" An offended and highly irked Echo had to make an effort to control his voice. "Fox, I thought we had an agreement!"

"I thought so too, Echo. But Omega told me you were tired of babysitting her, and asked to be relieved—for the remainder of YuleCon."

Echo blinked in surprise; of everything he had considered as a possibility, that hadn't even been in the list. But he instantly comprehended it, and knew exactly what had happened. Then he ran an agitated hand through his dark hair.

"Aw, damn, Fox—I meant the Andromedans, not Meg," Echo muttered, chagrined. "I've been a little...preoccupied today. She must've misunderstood."

Fox nodded, then surveyed his senior agent with a considering gaze. He nodded again, as if to himself. Echo promptly blanked his expression, realizing his supervisor had just read far more than he'd intended him to see.

* * *

"Been thinking about Chase?" Fox asked quietly, having accurately read the slight nuances of expression his department chief had not meant for him to observe.

"...Partly." Echo's eyes were now hooded.

"Hm. Yes, I see your point. They're nothing alike, you know." A perceptive Fox eyed his department chief.

"No. No, they're not."

"Which explains, at least in part, why one is here and one...isn't. In the big picture, I mean."

"Yeah. I suppose you're right about that."

"What are you going to do, old friend?"

"...Nothing." Echo returned his attention to the negotiating table.

"Going through it once already proved enough for you?" Fox raised a dubious eyebrow.

"More than."

Fox hesitated in his response, pondering his department chief, his history and his personality. Finally Fox offered one more suggestion from his wealth of experience.

"You might want to reconsider that decision, you know, zun. Don't close doors that don't have to be closed, or you may find that, later, you want them open again...only to discover they've been locked from the other side."

* * *

They were silent for a moment, watching the negotiations, while Echo mulled over Fox's statement—and remembered a certain double-locked back door, and the pain and distress it had generated—on BOTH sides. He hid the wince produced by that thought, and filed away the advice, to muse on it later in more depth.

"Want me to have Romeo bring Omega back?" Fox asked then. Echo took a deep, considering breath, reviewing what he knew of his partner's current mental state, then sighed.

"No. Much as I'd prefer to have her here with me, after everything that's happened, she probably needs the break anyway. She'll be out of harm's way at home. I'll talk to her later and tell her that she misunderstood me."

Fox raised a skeptical eyebrow.

"Good luck with that," was all he said.

* * *

Later that night, Alpha Two and fifty percent of Alpha One watched the masquerade competition, in which several Lambda Andromedans had entered for fun. But the empty chair beside Echo reminded them all—rather painfully and pointedly—of their missing companion. After all the costumes had been presented for the intial judging, there was a break while the judges deliberated, and most of the audience stood up, stretched, and started to move about. Dr. Taylor came up to the small group just then.

"Hey, y'all," the alien author greeted them. "Good to see ya again,

Romeo."

"Hey, m' man," Romeo said with a welcoming smile, "I want you t' meet my partner. Dr. Taylor, this is India. India, Dr. Travis Taylor, the author I was tellin' you 'bout."

"Pleased to meet you, Doctor," India smiled, and shook Taylor's proffered hand. "I've heard a good bit about you, especially in the last, oh, twenty-four hours."

"Likewise, and likewise," Taylor said with a smile. "Ah have it on good authority you're a doctor yourself, only a different kind. More of a patch-'em-up sort. Or maybe that should be put 'em back together."

"I am, that; and it's a little bit of all of it," India admitted. "It comes in handy with this bunch, sometimes."

"Ah bet!" Taylor's smile grew into a grin. "Hey, Echo. How's...things... goin'?"

"A little rough around the edges, Travis, but they're still going. Slower than we'd like, but that's the way it works sometimes."

"Damn, ain't like Ah never heard THAT before, myself. Well, better slow than backwards, Ah guess. Where's Omega? Ah wanted to talk to her about that theory of hers..."

"She, uh, went back to Headquarters," Romeo rescued Echo from having to answer.

"Back to Headquarters? Everything okay?" Taylor wondered, perturbed by the answer. "Nothin' else has happened, has it?"

"No," Echo said, trying not to sigh. "Everybody's just tired and stressed, is all. A little misunderstanding. She thought she was giving me a break from watching her back, so she went home."

"Aw, dammit. Ah'm sorry, buddy. Don't take offense, but you kinda look like you're missin' an arm or something, with her gone."

Everybody's seen it BUT me, Echo thought, hiding annoyance and dismay. *She's got to have known, then. Dammit.* He paused. *Well, at least she's not pressuring me about anything. She's not even acting on it. Maybe... maybe she DOESN'T know.* He addressed the other male.

"Well, I suppose there's a reason for the term, 'right-hand man,'" Echo agreed, shrugging.

"Or in this case, right-hand woman." Taylor grinned. "Saw y'all dancin' together last night. That was some smooth moves you two had! Pity they didn't have a dance competition. You'd 'a walked away with the prize, even over the Andromedan couple doin' the hoochy-coochy."

"Thanks, I guess," Echo said, trying to return Taylor's grin and failing. Taylor laughed.

"Okay, Ah get that message, loud an' clear, buddy," he said. "Drop the subject, huh?"

"Please."

"Roger that. Well, tell her Ah said hi when you get back to HQ, all right? An' Ah wanna talk to her about her idea whenever we can get synched up to do it. Nothin' important, no rush. It's just been in my head since we talked."

"All right. Wilco, Travis."

"Be seein' y'all, then."

If anything, the trio missed their companion even worse after Taylor left. They watched in subdued mirth as Tortok and his girlfriend walked away with top honors, but they departed the costume competition as soon as it was over, quietly shadowing the Prime Minister's entourage as it made the rounds of the post-competition parties.

* * *

Back at Headquarters, Omega wandered aimlessly around her decorated, dimly-lit apartment. Periodically she checked the clock, then the convention schedule and the negotiations agenda, keeping up as best she could with what should be going on with her partner and colleagues.

Finally she threw in the towel and went to bed early.

But she didn't sleep.

* * *

Zero Days—Four Days

The next morning, Larry Bauer was waiting in the convention center. As soon as he saw Echo and Fox enter the commons area, he made a beeline for them.

"'Mornin', there," he greeted the pair. "Wow, you look kinda down, there, Echo. Where's Meg?"

"Uh, she had to go back to Headquarters for something," Echo made excuse, ignoring the speculative glance Fox gave him. "Do you need to talk to her about anything? I can run fetch her if I need to..."

"No, I can tell the two of you just as easily. I was only hoping to say hi to her again before the con ended."

"I'll make sure to pass on the message," Echo agreed.

"You have something for us?" Fox wondered.

"Yeah. It's not much, but it might be useful, I dunno. Whatever it is that's goin' down, it's gonna happen on Christmas Eve."

Echo and Fox exchanged a meaningful look.

"Remember what Meg said in your office, when we first decoded the tree signal?" Echo reminded the Director.

"I surely do," Fox said, nodding. "Looks like she nailed it. Christmas Eve is our target date."

"Wish we knew for what," Echo grumbled.

"I can't tell you that, but I CAN tell you it's gonna be here, at the hotel," Bauer added.

"Where did you get your information, Mr. Bauer?" Fox asked.

"I overheard a kinda suspicious conversation in the men's room this morning. They were making arrangements to meet in the lobby that evening, and at least one of the guys in there—they were both in stalls—and, well, one of 'em wasn't speaking English...nor any other Earth language I ever heard," Bauer asserted. "It sorta sounded like one of the Kedor languages, but I'm not even an Earth linguist, so I dunno. The other guy was mostly speaking English, but it was with a strong accent. They didn't know I was even in the bathroom, 'cause I was already in a stall when they came in, and I kept it that way. Put my feet up on the sides of the stall door, and stayed quiet. They came in separately, let me note; one came in, then about two or three minutes later, the other one."

"Kedor?" Echo wondered. "The English speaker, I mean. Was his accent Kedor?"

"Echo IS a linguist," Fox pointed out to Bauer. "That's what he specialized in at university. That, and diplomacy."

"Oh. Well, I couldn't tell you for sure," Bauer admitted. "Sorry about that. I kinda have a hard time sorting out accents. I can identify regional dialects, no problem. But this one...all I know for certain is that it wasn't any Earth-based accent I've ever heard. And I've heard a few. And it wasn't any offworld accent I've heard, either. But I'm sorta limited in those, just what y'all sent down to Huntsville, while I was working the station."

"That's good though, good intel. So we have something going down on Christmas Eve at this hotel, that's being timed, and being done by offworlders," Echo strung it all together.

"AND we have an attempt to expose us, by someone who's pissed at us, and is also offworld," Fox added.

"Do you suppose they're connected, or coincidental?" Bauer wondered.

"I was about to ask the same thing," Echo noted.

"I don't know," Fox admitted. "But one thing I've learned: Never discount an apparent coincidence."

* * *

The next morning Omega dropped by the break room off the Core to meet Irokin and ask him for a favor. Happily the squat—but hardly small—Hypothenemoid, waving at least half of his limbs and both prehensile antennae in the air, agreed to help obtain some of the supplies for Omega's party. Omega, bereft of her companion and alibi, promptly hurried straight back to her quarters to begin the preparations, glad to get away from quite a few staring, accusatory eyes in the Core.

She was in the kitchen baking cookies, and had just put a fresh batch in the oven, when she turned...and caught an unlooked-for kitchen towel in the face.

"Hold still. You've got a big blotch of cocoa smudged on your nose," the familiar, deep voice said. Omega stood passively while Echo wiped away the offending spice on the bridge of her nose. "There. Now you don't look like you've been playing in your food." He grinned.

"How long have you been standing there?" she wondered, taking off the silicone oven mitts and laying them aside on the counter.

"Only a couple of minutes. I knocked at the back door, but I guess you were concentrating on your cooking, 'cause you didn't hear me. Besides, you had a hot cookie sheet in your hands, and I didn't want to risk startling you. A burn from one of those things is almost as bad as leaning on the hull of a spacecraft that's just re-entered."

"Which we both know about. How are the negotiations going?" Omega started removing the hot cookies to a cooling rack. Echo swiped one, juggling it from hand to hand as it cooled, and took a bite as he replied.

"Mmm. That's REALLY good. You are a damn fine cook, woman."

"Thanks. So are you, ya know. But cookies are best while they're hot, I always think. You know—when they're still soft, almost gooey. That's how I like 'em."

"Yeah, me too. You're better at this sorta stuff, though. I'm not much into baking, unless I just gotta."

"Meh. I like to bake." She shrugged. "You're really good at casseroles and stews and stuff, though. Whenever you make a pot pie, or one of those cottage pie things, I think I'm gonna drool myself to death."

"Hah! Thanks. I've had a lotta practice, I guess."

"So about the negotiations..."

"Right. The negotiations are still stalled. The Prime Minister has postponed further discussions until after Christmas, in deference to our holidays."

"Damn it."

"Yeah. Your friend Larry confirmed for us that something's going down right at Christmas, too. What, we still don't know. And he says hi."

"Really? Well...good, but oh shit. And hi back, I guess."

Echo chuckled. It sounded somewhat rueful, to Omega's knowledgeable ear.

"I assume the 'good' was because he brought us info, and the 'oh shit' was because there was info to be brought?" he confirmed.

"Yeah."

"Oh, and by the way, the Prime Minister sends his acceptance of your invitation, and says he's looking forward to it."

"Oh, okay. That's nice...I think. Can't say as I've ever entertained a planetary leader in my home before."

"Always a first time for everything," Echo remarked with amusement. "Especially in this job."

"I guess. How did the rest of the con go?"

"All right, I suppose. Tortok and his girlfriend won the masquerade last night."

Omega snorted in amusement.

"I guess it's a good thing the judges didn't ask to see how the 'costumes' were constructed," she chuckled. She wiped off the cookie sheet and sprayed it with cooking oil, then used a scoop and started dropping blobs of cookie dough onto it at regular intervals, dipping into a big mixing bowl of dough at her elbow.

"Yep. Oh, and Travis said to tell you hi, too."

"Oh? Me specifically?"

"Yeah, you specifically. I gathered he was hoping to sit down with you after the masquerade, over a 'bheer' or three in the green room, and talk over that idea you proposed to him the other day."

"Aha, you said it like he does, this time!"

"Yeah, it's a fen thing, in some circles."

"All right, I see. Yeah, I'm up for that at some point."

Echo, done with the fresh cookie, pointed at the dough blobs on the sheet.

"That got eggs in it?"

"No, these don't."

"Good." He swiped a blob and popped the entire thing in his mouth. Omega paused dropping dough onto the cookie sheet to stare at him in astonishment, then started laughing. "Wha?" he got out around a mouthful of dough.

"You're a thirty-four-year-old department chief, but I swear, Ace, sometimes you're only five."

Echo just grinned, his mouth too full for rebuttal. After a moment he managed, "Tol' ya you're a goo' cook."

"Yeah, yeah, an' I'll save the mixing bowl for you to lick, too. So I guess Dr. Taylor—uh, Travis, he told me to call him Travis an' I keep forgetting—I guess he's headed back to Alabama now though, isn't he?"

"Yeah, but I got his email. Had it for years. Occasionally we pop a line to each other. I'll give it to you, and you and he can discuss your theory. Sounded like a good idea to me, and I gather it did to him, too. If we need to, we can run down to Huntsville on the maglev and meet him for lunch or something, and you can talk face to face."

"Okay. I'll ping him after the holidays, then." She paused, and pulled a face. "Provided I'm still an active Agent after the holidays."

Echo winced.

"...Sounds like a plan."

* * *

Echo waited until Omega had the next batch of cookies ready for the oven, then he untied her chef's apron, tossed it on the counter next to the oven mitts, and drew her into the living area of her quarters.

"C'mon. We need to talk."

"About what?"

"Babysitting." Echo pushed her down near one end of the couch and sat down near the other end, facing her. She shrugged.

"There's nothing to talk about, Echo. You got tired of having me underfoot, so I cleared out, and gave you some breathing space. It's gotta be stressful, having a suspect for a partner."

"Meg, I was talking about the Lambda Andromedans, not you."

"Uh-huh." She looked at him skeptically. "I didn't see anybody coming back to get me."

"Fox and I seriously discussed it, and I started to do just that, but then I thought maybe YOU could use the time off. It's MORE stressful to BE the suspect."

Omega closed her eyes, sighed painfully, and stood.

"Look, Echo, I know I'm a liability right now. And everybody thinks that...that I'M the mole, that I'm the one that tried to...to kill you. Again. Like Slug's damn machinations weren't enough. Given all that, I wouldn't be surprised if you agreed with 'em after all. So don't feel like you have to..." she shook her head, hands in the air, looking for the right words, apparently unaware of the misery etched on her pale face, "spare my feelings."

"I'm not. And I know you didn't. I TOLD you. I KNOW."

Dispirited blue eyes looked back at him.

"Look, just go get some rest." Omega nodded in the direction of the back door. "The whole convention thing was long and exhausting, and none of us really got more than a couple hours' sleep at a go. At least last night I was in my own bed; you weren't. And I'm already cooking, so I'll take care of dinner tonight. I promise it won't be poisoned." She gave him a weak attempt at a smile and vanished back into the kitchen.

Echo looked after her for a moment, troubled, then quietly withdrew into his own apartment.

* * *

Zero Days—Three Days

The next few days were quiet, relatively speaking. While negotiations were ongoing at the hotel, the relative dearth of hotel occupants as the holiday rapidly approached meant security wasn't needed quite so much, and Fox deemed that Alpha One and Two deserved time off anyway, after several days of continuous operation with only a few hours of rest. So he brought in some agents from the Security department, and gave the in-house Alpha Line teams a couple of days' down time.

Omega chose to stay in her quarters; the one time that Echo managed to convince her to go to the gym with him, even he noticed the stares and whispers that followed in her wake. So he didn't push her to do more.

She spent most of their days off in the kitchen, cooking up delectable things for her party. Echo fully approved, because he got the benefit of her culinary experiments, usually for every meal, and sometimes in between.

* * *

Zero Days—One Day

"Echooo!" Omega let her anxious voice float through the back door, amid spicy, enticing aromas. "It's almost time for the party!"

She got no response.

"Echo?" Omega came to the back door. Echo, in black jeans and v-neck pullover sweater, sat in the recliner in his living area, finishing *A Christmas Carol*. He looked up.

"...You're really NOT coming, are you?" she said in a low voice, heart sinking.

Echo just gazed at her, calm but unmoving.

"Is it because you think I tried..."

"NO. I told you—how many times?—I know you didn't." He waved a dismissive hand. "So stop that."

"Then why not?"

"I've already told you that, too...I don't do Christmas."

"Didn't you used to?"

Echo hesitated, then finally admitted, "Yes."

"Why did you stop?"

"Let it go, Meg." Echo looked back down at his book.

Omega knelt beside his chair, holding the chair arm and looking up at him.

"Maybe I should be saying that to you," she said perceptively. "Echo, whatever...or whoever...you lost," she continued softly, as he looked startled, "please, could you put it aside, just for tonight, and come over? Even if it's only for a few minutes. I want you to be there. I NEED you to be there. It's...important to me. I'm sorry. I don't mean to twist your arm, or pressure you, but...you're my partner. I'm closer to you than anybody else in this whole damn place. Without you, this will just be a collection of acquaintances, near-strangers...AND a few outright ENEMIES."

"There's Romeo and India."

"That's true. IF they come. Big if, 'cause India doesn't really want to. But it's not the same, and you know it."

* * *

Echo looked down at her for a long moment, as she looked up at him, silently pleading. Something inside him abruptly wrenched at the imploring look in those blue eyes.

She needs me, he realized. *I dunno why, or what's up, but she really needs me to be there. For her. Every bit as much as she needed me to watch her back, if not more.*

With that thought, he made his decision...which was not the decision he wanted, but the only one he felt right making. He rolled his own eyes to the ceiling, stood, and headed for his bedroom without another word.

"...Where are you going?" Omega asked him in apprehension. He paused and glanced back.

"To put on my Suit. I can't go to a party that the Prime Minister will be attending while wearing jeans."

Omega's eyes lit up like stars.

Echo turned back for his bedroom, a certain sense of calm satisfaction washing through his being.

* * *

When Echo walked through the back door a little while later, he was astounded: Omega's comfortable apartment had been transformed into a sophisticated, celebratory holiday environ. Elegant holly and evergreen centerpieces now decorated the dining table and coffee table, both of which were laden with food. A huge punchbowl stood at one end of the dining table, a bubbling, luminescent green brew inside, and a selection of wine bottles sat nearby on the kitchen bar. More evergreen garland decorated door and archway; poinsettias, pink, white, and red, clustered in odd corners. A sprig of mistletoe hung from the ceiling near the end of the couch. The Christmas tree twinkled cheerfully in its corner. Subdued lighting and soft Christmas music set the mood.

Omega herself was in her usual Suit, but instead of her standard lace-up menswear shoes, the stiletto pumps had emerged again. Sparkling stones dropped from her ears and glittered in her upswept silver braid. A diamond tie tack, most likely her father's, twinkled on her black silk tie. Her makeup kit had come out again, he noticed, and her smoky blue eyes appeared to glow, her cheeks flushed with the barest hint of color; her lips were full and soft. She looked from a battered sheet of paper in her hands to the room, unaware of his scrutiny, periodically murmuring, "Got it..." to herself.

"Got what?"

"Oh! I didn't realize you were standing there, hon. Got wha-huh? Oh, wait, I get it." Omega looked up and grinned, waving the tattered paper. "This is my 'countdown checklist.' I was just running down it, making sure I got everything."

"Never guess you're ex-NASA," Echo deadpanned. "Done this a few times, huh?"

"A few," she acknowledged, the smile dimming slightly.

"Anything I can do to help?"

* * *

"Mmm...let's see." She returned her attention to the list, scanning down it. "No. It's pretty much under control, I think. Oh, but you can dig out the corkscrew in the kitchen and open a couple of those wine bottles for me while I finish this, if you wouldn't mind. I've got some chocolate stout hidden in the back of the cabinet for you and me to drink later—after the party—if you want to. Romeo and India should be here any time now. At least, I hope so. India was almost as hard to convince as you were."

"Why?"

"She was an ER doctor, Echo. She associates the holidays with accidents and death."

"Oh. Yeah, I think Romeo said something about that, now you mention it."

Omega continued to do the final checks as Echo opened the wine bottles. Then he brought over two glasses of Zinfandel.

"Here," he said, handing one to her. "You look like you could use this."

"Shows that bad, huh?" she asked, taking the glass and looking up at him with a hint of anxiety.

"No." He looked down at her with a slight smile. "But you're talking to someone who can glance at you in a firefight and know what you're about to do."

Omega chuckled.

"You can read me just as well in non-combat situations, then. Thanks." She sipped the wine and tried to relax.

* * *

"Non-combat? Depends on your point of view," Echo remarked,

laconic. "YOU call that a countdown checklist, *I* call it a battle management plan." He was rewarded by a peal of laughter.

"Then c'mon over here a minute, partner, and let's have a toast before the battle starts," Omega remarked with a grin, holding up her glass as she settled down on the arm of the couch. "To partners."

"To partners," Echo murmured, and they clinked their glasses together before sipping from them. Omega sipped again, then stood, putting a light hand on his arm.

"Meg, before I forget, I saw the drip coffeemaker pulled out, but no coffee made. Did you mean to..." Echo began. He never finished the sentence.

"OH!" she exclaimed, shoving her wineglass into his hand as she rushed by him into the kitchen. "I always forget SOMEthing. 'Preciate the reminder."

Just then, a knock sounded at the door. "I've got it," Echo called.

"Thanks..." came wafting from the kitchen.

* * *

Romeo and India stood at the door as Echo opened it while trying to hold both wineglasses in one hand.

"Two-fisted drinker there, huh, Echo?" Romeo deadpanned, as they entered.

"One of 'em's mine," Omega volunteered, taking it from Echo on her way to greet them. "Thanks for coming, y'all," she said softly, giving all three Agents a warm smile. "My...family...is all here. Except for Fox, and he'll be here as soon as he can shake loose from work. Now the guests can arrive."

* * *

Shortly thereafter, the party was in full swing. Really more of a holiday open house, Omega's apartment was soon crammed, not only with Agents, but aliens from all over the galaxy as well—ambassadors, envoys, and staff. It proved to be a welcome release from the stress all of the agents had been under, and the Agency turned out in force. A few of the more suspicious types, however, carried pocket analyzers and other gadgets to check the food safety—with varying degrees of subtlety—before indulging. Omega sighed and shrugged in resignation, then headed across the room.

"Echo," Omega came up to him and murmured, "you might want to close the back door, if you don't want the party to overflow into your apartment."

"Mm. Good point. I forgot all about it. Thanks." Echo discreetly wandered over and through the door, checked for strays, then came back, casually closing the door behind him. As he re-entered Omega's quarters, he saw Monkey and Sierra watching him with suggestive leers. He returned the look with a cool stare.

* * *

While Echo was thus occupied, Omega surveyed the room with the eye of a practiced hostess, and her attention was caught by a translucent, vaguely humanoid alien that had taken up a location beside the Christmas tree. As the tree lights twinkled, multicolored luminescent areas within the alien glowed in response. Fascinated, Omega began to drift over. A hand came down lightly on her shoulder.

"Let 'em alone. They're talking," Echo said quietly.

"Talking?! But...that's a Christmas tree!"

"The Photoid doesn't know that. He thinks she's cute."

"You mean...there's an alien hitting on my Christmas tree??"

"Yep."

"Oh, for the love o'..." Omega rolled her eyes upward, then paused for a split-second, looking up. "Echo..."

"I think I'm going to get a cup of coffee. Want some?" Echo said, heading for the kitchen. Omega grinned lopsidedly at his unexpected exit.

"No thanks," she called after him. "I left my wineglass around here somewhere..."

"I'll bring you another."

"Just half a glass."

Echo responded with a thumbs-up as he disappeared into the kitchen, and Omega considered for a moment.

I've been wondering for a while now, she thought. *I mean, one minute he seems like it, the next minute, he doesn't. All things considered, I wouldn't blame him if he didn't. Still and all, I guess I need to know, one way or the other. And how he reacts to this ought to tell me all I wanna know. I just hope I'm ready for what I get.* Then she moved over to Romeo and India.

"Guys," she said with a grin, "listen up. I need a little help. It's not a big deal, just a little Christmas prank, but so far, the strategy looks like having all the subtlety of a 3-D chess match..." Her voice dropped to a low murmur, and Omega jerked her head back over her shoulder. Romeo and India scanned the ceiling, and grins spread slowly across their faces.

"Hah!" Romeo exclaimed, and India and Omega both shushed him.

"So can I count on you?" Omega asked, smiling mischievously.

"You know it, girl!" Romeo responded enthusiastically, as India nodded vigorously. "I can't wait to see his face!"

"Ssh. Here he comes," India murmured. "And I just love that double dark chocolate torte, Meg. Where'd you get it?" she continued in a normal voice.

"I made it," Omega replied as Echo walked over with a cup of coffee and a glass of wine. "Spent all day yesterday, the day before, AND most of today in the kitchen."

"Yeah, I was telling Meg—was it yesterday afternoon? last night? whenever—that she is one helluva good cook," Echo agreed, and Omega smiled.

"Thanks, Ace; but like I said, you are, too. I'm just more into baking than you are. But I don't have that much time to do it."

"Good thing, too. I'd never fit into my Suit if we both baked all the damn time. Here, take this, before I spill something." He handed her the wineglass.

"You want the recipe, India?" Omega took the glass Echo offered. One hand freed, he leaned over to the coffee table and snagged a shortbread cookie from the plate there, taking a bite.

"Ab-so-lutely!" Romeo answered for India.

"All right. Remind me, and I'll give it to you tomorrow."

Just then, Omega heard a cry of "Jacuzzi!!" She spun.

"Oh, no!" The others turned at her exclamation.

Three Sluuites, small intelligent salamanders from Sluu in the Kepler-969 system, splashed and played in the punchbowl, and Omega groaned.

"Nubuv, what do y'all think you're doing?!"

"Ease up, pretty lady. Ain't no big deal. Sluuites do this at every party," Romeo explained. "They just havin' a good time."

"Yeah," Echo agreed. "Just because they wander around in the odd corners here at Headquarters all the time and eat the dust and random bits for us—"

"And we all forget they're even here, half the time," India interjected.

"—Don't forget, they're amphibious," Echo tag-teamed. "And evidently most varieties of human punch are pretty similar to their oceans back home."

"But..." Omega scanned the room, and saw that indeed, no one was even reacting to the situation. She shrugged and beat a hasty retreat into the kitchen to check on the food.

* * *

Popping some hors d'oeuvres—prepared earlier in the week—into the microwave to heat quickly, Omega turned and ran into a hypognathous Lacertilian in orthodontia, who was staring in total fascination at the microwave while sipping from a coffee cup.

"Now what?" Omega mumbled to herself.

The Lacertilian began beeping, and the translator around its neck said, "Pardon me, what is this device?"

"It's a microwave oven," Omega responded. "It cooks food fast."

"Oven...this is a device for preparing consumables?"

"Um, yeah, that's what I just said."

"So this device is functional as well as beautiful..."

"Beautiful??" Omega queried, startled.

"Oh, yes," the alien replied through the translator. "The scintillating colors, the flickering lights...so soothing. MUCH nicer than the...what was it Gertrude called it?...lava lamp..."

"You can see the microwaves?!"

"Of course. Can you not?"

"Oo-kaay, um, no, I can't...well, would you do me a favor? When the lights stop flashing, would you take out the tray that's inside and put it on the table out there?"

"I would be happy to, for the privilege of watching this lovely display."

"Knock yourself out," Omega muttered, well under her breath, as she left the room.

* * *

As Omega emerged from the kitchen, she saw India motioning across the room, where Romeo had engaged Echo in conversation at the end of the couch. Omega's eyes twinkled, and she headed over. But before she could reach them, Echo held up an index finger to Romeo in a *hold it* gesture, and moved toward the front door, greeting the Prime Minister as he entered with his retinue. Romeo looked at Omega and shrugged. She grinned and nodded.

"Gotcha," she whispered to Romeo, as she dropped a light kiss on his lips on her way to join Echo with the Prime Minister. "One down." Romeo looked startled, and India grinned. On the other side of the room, Tare and Yankee, observing the byplay as they indulged in the excellent wines, exchanged meaningful glances.

"Welcome, Mr. Prime Minister," Omega said formally, bowing. "Agent Echo and I welcome you and your entourage to Agency Headquarters over our holiday season. Please, make yourselves at home."

"Thank you, Agent Omega, Agent Echo," the Prime Minister responded ceremonially. "Your gracious hospitality is accepted with alacrity." His group moved deeper into the apartment.

"Well done," Echo remarked quietly to his partner.

"Thanks," Omega said with a warm smile. "But, Echo...what's happened to the evergreen garlands? Look at all the bare patches..."

"The guests have been snacking," Echo replied simply, shrugging.

"Snacking? On the decorations??"

"Of course."

"Waitaminit! There was tinsel roping over the front door, too!" She looked at Echo, who gazed back, taciturn. "Let me guess: more snacks?"

"More snacks."

"Hope it gives 'em a..." she grumbled under her breath.

"How's that?" Echo asked, suddenly working to keep a straight face.

"Nothing," Omega answered in a normal tone. "C'mon, let's go mingle. Looks like you need some more coffee anyway. Here, I'll get it for you."

When Omega returned with the coffee, India had struck up a conversation with Echo over by the coffee table. Looking around, Echo saw his partner moving through the crowded room with two full, steaming coffee mugs and quickly moved to help her. Behind him, India snapped her fingers in an exaggerated *drat!* gesture, and Omega bit her lip to keep from laughing.

"Here, let me get that from you before you spill it," Echo said, taking one of the hot mugs.

"Thanks," Omega said. "Should be the way you like it."

"You oughta know by now," he responded companionably.

"Yeah. We drink enough of it."

"Listen, I'm going to run back to my quarters..."

"Oh. Okay. Thanks for coming." A disappointed Omega's voice sounded flat, even to her own ears. To help counter it, she manufactured a smile and slapped it on.

"No, it's okay, I'll be right back," Echo reassured her. "India wanted to borrow a book of mine."

"Oh." Omega moved toward India as Echo headed for the back door. "'Borrowing a book,' huh?"

* * *

"Yeah," India grinned. "It's one I wanted to read anyway, so..." Unexpectedly, India felt herself bear-hugged as Omega kissed her cheek.

"Two down!" Omega grinned, and India started laughing. "Go on, girlfriend, go find Romeo and get him to refill your drink."

She gave India a playful nudge, and India hugged her in return, then moved off to find her partner—in the Agency, and in life.

* * *

Just then, Omega noticed several of the Andromedan negotiators, who were downing quantities of the carbonated drinks.

"Echo," she murmured as he returned from handing India the book, "some of the Lambda Andromedans appear to be getting smashed rather rapidly. But they haven't touched the alcohol."

"Mm-hm," he answered softly. "Might want to stash the ginger ale and sodas. Carbonation—carbonic acid an' shit—is to the Lambda Andromedans what alcohol is to us, as near as I can figure. Well, actually, it's worse—more like nitrogen narcosis, according to Zebra, it's just not, you know, potentially deadly. And they don't appear to be used to it. We don't need the Prime Minister's entire team drunk."

"Oh, great. NOW he tells me..."

As Omega headed back to the kitchen for the thousandth time, she noticed that Fox had arrived—alone; Zebra was on shift at the medlab and had sent her sincere regrets—and that Romeo and India had buttonholed him. Fox looked up, saw Omega, and winked at her, his hazel eyes twinkling with mischief. Omega grinned back, realizing they'd recruited him to her cause, and continued on her way.

Once back in the kitchen, Omega frantically gathered up all of the carbonated beverages she could find and stashed them in the backs of cabinets and cupboards, as far out of sight as possible. Then she looped the dining area, trying to remove as many two-liter bottles as she could unobtrusively grab. Carrying them into the kitchen, Omega secreted them in the back of the pantry. Then she made another pot of coffee to combat carbonation hangover.

* * *

"Evening, Echo," Fox greeted the agent, walking across the room to meet him by the black leather couch. "Mazel tov. Merry Christmas and happy holidays."

"The same to you, Fox," Echo responded. "Happy Hannukah."

"Thank you, zun. Quite a party you and your partner have going here."

"I'm just along for the ride. Meg deserves all the credit."

"She really gets into the holidays, eh?" Fox asked.

Echo nodded.

"Making it rough on you?" Fox continued.

"I'm...getting my arm twisted a little bit." Echo shrugged.

"You don't have to let her, you know, Echo."

Echo just looked at Fox stoically, without answering.

Mm-hm, Fox thought. *That's what I expected. But I'll bet she hasn't got a clue. I wonder if I should provide that clue. I need to think about this.*

"So how's the bodyguarding going?" Fox asked then, deciding to shift the subject.

"Fine," Echo responded, seeming glad of the change of topic. "Meg understands which way the wind lies, and she's sticking to me like glue when we're out, especially after the attack on me—which makes keeping an eye on her pretty much a no-brainer. It upset her kinda bad, if I'm interpreting things right. Anyway, I think she's still trying to convince you—and maybe me, juding by certain comments—that she's innocent." Echo paused, then added, "But since we got back from the convention, she's pretty much holed up in her quarters, and I don't blame her. Whenever she walks through one of the public areas in Headquarters, there's this wave of silence that follows her, accompanied by glares and stares, and then whispers in her wake. It even makes ME self-conscious, and I'm pretty unflappable."

"Mm. Not good. How about the Prime Minister?"

"Right over there. Meg invited him and his entire entourage. And they came. The whole damn lot of 'em."

Fox looked in the direction Echo indicated and nodded, pleased.

"Good. Nice touch. She's doing pretty well at this whole diplomatic thing, even if she is a rookie at it."

"No, no. She's no rookie—not any more." Echo shook his head. "She hasn't been in a long time. A little inexperienced still, but not a rookie."

"I know, Echo," Fox mollified his department chief. "I didn't mean rookie agent, just rookie diplomat. She's got the whole Agent thing down, long since. And if recent days are any indication of her diplomatic abilities, she'll make a damn fine partner for you, when I send you out to do first contacts."

"Thank you," a familiar, feminine voice suddenly interjected from just behind Echo. "After recent events, that makes me feel a lot better. I've been working hard."

* * *

Echo turned, to see Omega standing extremely close to him, looking up with a smile. In fact, she was so close that he could feel the slight heat radiating from her body, and catch a whiff of the subtle, private-edition perfume she wore...just as he'd been able to do when they'd danced. *Heavenly Bodies,* he remembered it was called. *And damn, does it fit.*

He glanced at Fox, only to watch in astonishment as Fox faded back, a twinkle in his hazel eyes. Scanning the room rapidly, Echo saw Romeo and India standing near the Christmas tree, arms folded, grinning in something like triumph as they watched. Sierra and Monkey scowled from across the room, and the Prime Minister watched with curiosity. Echo looked back at Omega, who had moved in front of him, laying both palms flat on his chest. She leaned in even closer, looking up past his head at the ceiling, and smiled.

"You're a hard man to outmaneuver, Echo."

A bemused Echo followed her gaze upward, where the mistletoe hung directly overhead. He blinked, startled, having forgotten all about that particular bit of ornamentation. He felt her hands slide up his chest toward his shoulders, hands slipping behind his neck, fingers stroking gently, just once; and he looked back down at her, into sparkling blue eyes.

"Meg??" he murmured, fully grasping just what was coming next, and wondering how to respond to it, not really wanting to have to consider it. *Aw shit,* he thought in dismay.

Omega pushed up on tiptoes and leaned in, smiling softly. Echo's gaze became riveted to twin shining sapphires, as soft, full lips moved toward his.

"Merry Christ...mas...Echo..."

A slurping sound suddenly came from behind Echo, and he saw Omega's focus move past his face as her eyes went wide and her jaw dropped slightly, in shock.

Looking back up, he was just in time to see a long, amphibian-like tongue adhere to the sprig of mistletoe and retract, pulling the entire mass of plant material down. The soft sound of munching wafted over his right shoulder. Moments later, a loud belch emerged from the same direction as a pine-scented fragrance floated through the air, and Echo had to bite his lip to keep from laughing at Omega's bemused, startled, and mildly repulsed expression.

"Forgot to tell you—Grendels consider mistletoe a delicacy," he deadpanned.

As his gaze swept the room again, he noticed Fox struggling to keep a straight face, as Romeo, disgusted, handed over a ten-spot, and India was openly laughing. Monkey and Sierra looked surprised. The Prime Minister appeared puzzled.

Omega pushed away from his chest, still staring up in surprise. Finally she folded her arms, rested her cheek on one hand in a classic Jack Benny pose, and addressed the room in general.

"Why doesn't anyone ever tell me these things beforehand?"

Then she shrugged, took Echo's coffee mug, said, "Here. I'll refill that for you," and headed for the kitchen.

* * *

Well, I guess that answers THAT question, she decided as she walked into the kitchen. *It didn't go anything like what I expected, and in the end I didn't succeed, but I guess I got my answer, anyway. The expression on his face...I'm probably the only being in the room who could see the tremendous relief in Echo's eyes when he realized the Grendel ate the mistletoe. He's good—most people don't see squat if he doesn't want 'em to, not even Fox—but he's let me get to know him a LOT better than that. I dunno if even he knows how well I can read him now. Of course, I dunno how much of that is because I'm not exactly normal, either.*

She sighed, then shrugged to herself, as she rinsed out Echo's coffee mug at the sink and prepared to refill it. Then, discovering the coffeemaker carafe almost empty, she poured out the last few drops and set about making a fresh pot; the pod brewer had been set aside in favor of quantity tonight.

Not that it matters, really. I mean, let's face it—I'm an alien construct.

The base model is human, sure, but I suppose it's been a long time since I could legitimately lay claim to the title, 'human.' Zebra disagrees, but I've caught some of Zarnix's looks, and I don't think he does. Which means my serious romantic prospects are...pretty limited. Which, she thought with a shrug, *is probably the way it should be, I guess.*

And of all the guys in the place, after all the water under the bridge, Echo is the one guy here least likely to be interested. I mean, after all, I was designed to be his assassin, and he SAW ME IN ACTION, trying to kill him, even if we did manage to circumvent that bit. So he's NEVER gonna look at me like THAT. Ever.

But, at least for now, we're still a team, and that's what counts, I guess. Of course, if I can't clear my name, it's all moot anyhow.

* * *

She was pouring the fresh coffee when unfamilar hands caught her waist, and she jumped, startled. The scent of alcohol drifted over her shoulder as Yankee's unusually-hoarse voice said suggestively, "Well, well, look what I caught. Pity the Grendel ate the mistletoe."

Omega glanced over her shoulder, and Yankee turned her to face him.

"Yankee, are you okay?" Omega asked him, concerned at the sight of his flushed face and feverish eyes.

"Sure," he told her. "Just a bug. Of the viral sort. Cold medicine's workin' fine. I'll run by the medlab tomorrow for some antivirals. Now how 'bout a kiss for Christmas?"

"Okay," she said quietly, politely, realizing he had mixed alcohol with the cold medication and probably wouldn't remember a thing tomorrow except a vicious headache. She lightly brushed her lips against his cheek.

"Damn you!" Yankee exclaimed, irritated. "You can do better than that. You've had plenty of practice. I've seen the practice you've already had just tonight."

"What??" Omega exclaimed, startled. "But I've only—"

Unexpectedly, she found herself on the receiving end of an unwanted embrace, as an intoxicated Yankee attempted to force a kiss on her, pinning her against the kitchen counter and catching her head in one hand.

* * *

Just then, Echo appeared in the kitchen door, looking for his coffee. Taking in the scene, his eyes widened, then narrowed in grim anger as he recognized Yankee, read Omega's body language, and realized what was happening. He started forward to rescue his partner.

Omega, however, needed no rescuing. Before Echo got well into the room, he saw her calmly raise the steaming coffee mug to Yankee's waist level, then deliberately tip it forward. The front of Yankee's wool Suit trousers absorbed every drop of the hot liquid, and he jumped back with a yelped expletive. Immediately, Omega put several feet of distance between them.

Echo backed off, thoroughly enjoying the scene.

* * *

"Oh, Yankee, I'm so sorry, how clumsy of me," Omega said solicitously, as he continued to curse. "I had completely forgotten I was holding that. What a shame. Now you'll have to go home and change."

"Bitch!" Yankee shot her a hard glare and, swaying alarmingly, sidestepped Echo on his way out.

A furious Echo grabbed his arm as he passed, and spun the drunken man to face him.

"What did you say?" he murmured, tone deadly.

Yankee stared at Echo for a long moment, his addled brain slowly processing the menace in the other man's stance and facial expression, as well as the fact that Echo was several inches taller and correspondingly broader.

"Nothin'," he muttered, shaking Echo's hand off his arm, and staggered out.

* * *

Echo promptly moved over to his partner.

"You all right?"

"Yeah..."

"Interesting defensive tactic." Echo glanced at the floor. "And not even a mess to clean up. Nice job."

"Thanks...I think," Omega responded doubtfully as she put the mug in the dishwasher, got a clean one from the cabinet, and filled it from the freshly-made pot. "Here. Sorry about the delay."

"Understandable, under the circumstances." Echo shook his head, disgusted.

"Whatever possessed him to do that? I know he was on cold medicine AND drinking, but...he acted like he thought I was...some sort of..." She shrugged. "'Tramp' is the word my momma would have used."

"He did," Echo told her quietly.

"What?! Are you serious?"

"Yeah, I'm afraid so. Been several nasty remarks. Agents' imaginations are running wild, with everything that's been going on. I was hoping you wouldn't find out."

* * *

Omega closed her eyes and tilted her head back in pained disbelief.

"Let me get this straight: Those people out there think I'm a traitor...an attempted murderer...and a slut. That about got it covered?"

Echo didn't answer, and Omega moved to the kitchen door to look out. Echo walked over to stand beside her and look over her shoulder.

Her own gaze took in the Sluuites in the punchbowl, the drunken Andromedan diplomat guzzling ginger ale straight out of the bottle Omega hadn't been able to tactfully take from him, the half-eaten holly garlands, the Photoid still 'conversing' with the Christmas tree, the empty mistletoe hook in the ceiling.

Just then, Sierra picked up a meatball from the platter on the table, pulled a photometric chemical analyzer, and scanned it.

* * *

Echo sensed, rather than saw, his partner stiffen, and he looked down, concerned. Catching Omega's glance, Echo could have sworn her blue eyes flashed sparks. Her cheeks had flushed a dusky red. *Shit. If I've got a 'supervolcano stare,'* he thought, *then that must be Meg's supernova burn.*

"That's it," Omega's low voice was suddenly full of fury. "I...have... HAD it." She spun on her heel and headed for the front door.

Taken aback, Echo watched her for a moment, then headed after her, catching up as she opened the door.

"Meg—where are you going?"

"OUT."

"What about the party?"

"What about it? *I* have no control over it at this point. Or over much else, for that matter."

"You're the HOSTESS, Meg."

She sighed, acknowledging responsibility.

"Look, fill in for me, would you? I'll be back shortly."

"No, Meg, I don't do—"

"DAMMIT, Echo, then ask India to!" The door slammed behind her.

He stood for a moment looking blankly at the door, only inches from his face, then turned slowly and went over to India and Romeo, still by the tree.

* * *

"Echo, my man, she almost had you tonight!" Romeo grinned at his ex-partner. Echo ignored him and turned to India.

"India, Meg asked if you'd fill in for her as hostess for a few minutes."

"Sure. What's up?"

"She...left. I think she's upset because it's not going the way she planned. And a drunk Yankee trying to paw her in the kitchen just now sure didn't help. Aw, hell, he wasn't just trying; he had his hands all over her. AND he was forcing a kiss on her."

"Shit!" Romeo exclaimed in a low tone, scowling. "Th' pretty lady okay? Do we need t' go take care o' Yankee, you an' me, f'r messin' with her?"

"No, she had it under control. An entire mug of freshly-brewed hot coffee on the crotch sent him home in a hurry. Walking funny, but in a hurry. The fact that his wool trousers soaked up every drop didn't help the funny walk, either."

"Good for her!" Romeo said, stifling a laugh.

"Yeah. But discovering just what some of the more suspicious agents think of her moral fiber didn't do her mental state much good."

"Oh. Damn," India said softly. "I get it. Yeah, I'll take over here for a while. Echo, you better go catch up with her, see if you can calm her down."

"I...don't think that's a good idea," Echo told her. "I don't seem to be at the top of Meg's list at the moment."

"What makes you think that?"

"Oh, maybe the fact that a minute ago she cussed me out and slammed the door in my face."

"What? MEG?!" Romeo exclaimed.

"OUR Meg??" India echoed. "I've NEVER—"

"*I* have—just now."

"Echo, look, just go and find her," India told him. "I've got my hands full here, and you'd stand a way better chance of finding her than Romeo."

Echo shrugged and headed for the door.

* * *

Echo had been everywhere he could think of that she might be: the roof—her favorite stargazing refuge and the first place he'd checked; the library; the gym; even the chapel. But Omega was nowhere to be found. Stopping back by the party, which was still in full swing, Echo shot Romeo and India a questioning glance from across the room. They shook their heads in the negative, and he slipped back out.

As a last resort, he headed to the Core. He could log onto the Agency network from a laptop in the Alpha Line room and locate her by sensor if he had to. But as he walked into the bustling, open room and his eyes habitually swept it, he saw a familiar platinum blonde head leaning over one of the catwalk rails, high up near the galactic map on the ceiling.

Aha, Echo realized. *I should've thought of that. She's been walking through the map.*

Omega saw him at the same time, and straightened up, but didn't move from the spot as he headed for the lift. When he finally stood beside her, Echo reached out to lay a concerned hand on her shoulder.

"Meg—"

"So when were you going to tell me, Echo?" Her azure eyes blazed. He withdrew his hand.

"Tell you...?"

"What the rest of the Agency thinks of me. What my reputation—the only thing I had left—has devolved into."

Echo sighed, and looked away, over the Core.

"I was hoping I wouldn't have to," he admitted. "I thought maybe we could get this resolved and you cleared before you found out. It's NOT everybody, Meg. Most of us know better, because we know YOU. It's just a few..."

"So you let me go merrily along, totally oblivious, without warning me, giving Yankee and—who all else?—plenty of stuff to misunderstand. Dear Lord, tonight ALONE..." She turned her back on her partner and walked away. As she disappeared through the doorway at the end of the corridor, she coolly remarked over her shoulder, "Maybe you SHOULD'VE let Fox confine me to quarters, Echo. Or done it yourself like I asked. At least I wouldn't be tying the blasted knot in my own damn noose."

* * *

Omega reappeared at the party, and India said, "THERE you are! Did Echo find you?"

"...Yes."

"Where is he?"

Omega just shrugged. Fox walked up and saved her from having to answer.

"Omega, there you are. The Prime Minister has been looking for you. Where have you been?"

"I, um...got a little too hot," Omega made excuse. "So I stepped out for a few minutes...to cool off." India eyed her knowingly. An aloof Omega returned the look.

"Ah," Fox responded, raising an eyebrow that was just as knowing as India's gaze. "It IS a bit crowded in here. And it almost certainly isn't like any party you've ever thrown before. But I really must congratulate you. You've pulled off the best such gathering I've ever seen under Agency auspices. Certainly the most fun. And much needed right now." Fox smiled, then leaned forward in a conspiratorial fashion. "And I think you might ALMOST have had Echo going, for a minute there." He winked at her, a meaningful look in his eye, and Omega understood he was trying to tell her something, but she didn't know how to translate the message. Besides, her mind was fixed on another comment he had made.

"Best...Fox, you're joking, right?" Omega asked in consternation, glancing around the room.

"No, he is not," the Prime Minister said, gliding up. "I see we have found the elusive master hostess. You Terrans have most unusual holiday activities. This...'mistletoe' tradition...quite interesting." Fox grinned, and Omega realized he must have explained the history to the alien being. "I should like to compliment you, Agent Omega, before I and my cortège depart for the evening. I have never encountered such festivity...or such HOSPITALITY...under this roof."

Echo slipped in through the back door in time to hear the Prime Minister's last pronouncement, and to register the quick flash of confusion on Omega's face before she resumed a smooth, sophisticated veneer.

"Thank you, Mr. Prime Minister," Omega said, bowing slightly. "I'm honored that you could attend my little celebration. May the rest of your visit to our planet go...MORE smoothly."

The Prime Minister nodded an acknowledgment, signaled for his bodyguards, and the group departed. Fox escorted them out, carefully herding the less-sober members of the group.

Echo walked up to the other three Alpha Line agents. A reserved Omega scanned him dispassionately from head to toe.

"Excuse me while I go check on the food," she said then. She turned and walked away. Romeo, Echo, and India stood looking after her blankly as she left the room; Echo managed to hide the wince of rejection produced by his partner's reaction.

"Ow," Romeo responded finally, staring at Echo. "That was cold."

"That's not like Meg," India agreed. "Even if the party really were a disaster—which it isn't...even if she and Echo had had a knock-down, drag-out argument—which you didn't..." India looked at Echo for confirmation, and he nodded, "she wouldn't react like this."

Echo nodded again, shoving the hurt away into a corner of his mind. *After all, she's been through hell over this shit already, and I guess maybe Fox and I SHOULD have told her everything, after all. I just...wanted to protect her from any more of the crap.* He sighed silently. *Still, something's goin' on with her. Something she hasn't told me. Turn about's fair play, I suppose.*

"There's something more than we're aware of going on under that blonde braid tonight," he decided aloud, pondering what it could be.

* * *

"An' she ain't lettin' anybody inside to find out what," Romeo finished.

"Well, I can understand that," Echo said absently, watching Omega bring out a tray of hot hors d'oeuvres across the room. Romeo shot a glance at India.

"He should know," he whispered.

* * *

"Well, that helped—sort of," Omega said enigmatically after the last guest had departed, and she began trying to tidy up the nearly-deserted room, gathering up napkins, paper cups, shredded tinsel, and the like, and throwing them in the trash. Echo pitched in silently, beginning triage on the few remaining leftovers, tossing what was unrecoverable and refrigerating the rest.

"Good party, Meg," India said, as she and Romeo prepared to leave. "I'm glad I came."

"Thanks. I'm glad you came, too." Omega smiled, unable to keep a certain wistfulness from the expression. "I...always have a party on December 23rd, if I can. It's...a little tradition I started a few years back. Glad Y'ALL enjoyed it..."

"'S cool. Lookin' forward to the next one," Romeo said enthusiastically.

"Me, too," India admitted.

Omega looked around the disaster area of a room and muttered to herself, "I'm not."

"...See you tomorrow," Romeo continued.

"Good night, y'all. Merry Christmas," she managed to get out, and decided it sounded actually pretty normal, despite the presence of what felt like the asteroid Ceres in her throat.

"Merry Christmas!" came the dual response, and Alpha Two was gone.

* * *

Echo, still in the kitchen, heard the front door close, followed by a long, tired sigh, and the apartment grew quiet for the first time in many hours. He dispensed with the last of the party food, and headed for the living area, turning out the kitchen light.

The only light in the silent living area now came from the Christmas tree, and Omega knelt beneath it, head bowed, looking down at something in her hands. Echo walked noiselessly up behind her, and glanced over her shoulder to see what she was holding.

It was a small, framed portrait of Megan McAllister's family. Echo had never seen it before, but the family resemblance was unmistakable. A much younger Meg sat between a blonde woman and a dark-haired man, obviously her parents. Beside them was a tiny, roly-poly, white-haired woman, evidently Meg's grandmother. In the background was a beautifully decorated Christmas tree, not at all unlike the one Omega sat beneath now; Echo even recognized quite a few of the older, heirloom ornaments.

Three family members then...and three 'family' members now, Echo realized. *Well, plus Fox. But she's not comfortable including him any more, I don't think; not after the way he's had to distance himself.*

"Meg?" he said softly, bending over her.

She jumped slightly, startled, and hid the photograph against her breast.

"Oh! Echo. I had...forgotten anyone else was still here..." Her voice was slightly husky, and her cheek glimmered wetly. Echo sat down on the floor beside her, folding his legs and adopting a cross-legged position, facing her.

"Meg, TALK to me," he urged gently, holding out both hands. "I'm not a telepath."

She opened her mouth to speak, but nothing came out, and abruptly she bowed her head, then shook it in the negative.

"Meg, c'mon, baby. I'm sorry you're mad, but I really was trying to protect you. Even Fox agreed at the time, 'cause I asked him for his recommendation. I wanna protect you, wanna help you, but I can't if I don't know what's wrong. TELL me."

Still she was silent, staring into the depths of the tree, and he could sense her internal struggle.

"Meg..."

"...It was tonight, Echo. Twelve years ago tonight." Her voice was hoarse, almost choked, and Echo suddenly realized that she wasn't being stubborn, wasn't angry—she was simply having trouble forcing out the words. Omega handed him the photograph. "Here. This is the last family portrait we ever had made."

He sat listening, looking from the photo to Omega, as she rocked back into a sitting position and wrapped her arms around her knees.

"Ever been to Huntsville, Alabama?" she asked him. "To visit Travis, maybe?"

"No. Friendship with Travis notwithstanding; he keeps inviting me down for a visit, but I never manage to make it."

She nodded acknowledgement of his answer, and began to explain.

"Huntsville is mountainous on the east, but flattens out as you head west. Tail end of the Appalachian chain, basically. There's a big ridge on the east called Monte Sano Mountain; a lotta people like to live up there 'cause it's a good thousand feet above the rest of the city, it's cooler in summer, and the views are pretty. The top is fairly flat, 'cause it's got a caprock, but some of the sides are pretty steep." She glanced at him to see if he was listening; he nodded immediately, and she went on.

"...I was on console at the Payload Control Center at Marshall Space Flight Center, twelve years ago, working an early, experimental space plane flight. It was Mission Number...well, it doesn't really matter which one. Not any more. And twelve years ago tonight, they all went to a Christmas party a family friend threw, up on the mountain."

Aw shit, Echo thought, dismayed, as he realized what was coming. *I get it now. Tonight. Slug did away with 'em, twelve years ago TONIGHT. And this year, for the first time, she knows what really happened. She knows Slug murdered 'em.*

"The payload was stowed around, oh, two a.m., the deorbit burn was about an hour and a half later, and the payload ops director released the cadre after that. I'd been on console for pushing twenty-three straight hours to get the payload stowed properly, so I went back to my apartment and grabbed a couple hours' sleep." She chuckled humorlessly, an odd note in the laughter, and Echo's eyes narrowed in concern as he listened. "Workin' Division One days even back then. Then I loaded the presents into my car, watched the landing, and headed for Mom and Dad's."

She stopped, suddenly fighting to maintain control, and Echo watched her with ever-deepening concern. Eventually Omega continued.

"I arrived at home bright and early on a gorgeous Christmas Eve morning, but they weren't there. Instead, the police were there, looking for the next of kin. They'd found the car at the foot of the mountain, two hours before."

"Damn."

"Yeah. More, the distance the car had traveled in the air after leaving the road indicated it was being driven WAY the hell faster than Daddy ever drove. And way faster than ANYBODY should have been ABLE to go, on that stretch of road. It didn't make sense, but the police report chalked it up to driver error." She sighed for a moment. "I'll never know for absolute certain how he did it now, but the way I think it happened...I think Slug used his saucer to grab their car in a tractor beam. I think he simply dragged them up into the air, and then turned off the tractor beam and dropped 'em." She smeared her hand across her face. "I keep imagining Momma and Grandmomma screaming..." Her weary voice faded away.

The room was still for a long moment.

"What did you do then?" Echo finally murmured. "After the police told you, I mean."

"...I don't really remember." Blue eyes looked deep into the past. "I went...I lost it for a little while. I think I busted up some of Mom's everyday crockery, and a cheap florist's vase, but I couldn't tell you for sure."

"So that's why you always throw a party on December 23rd," he realized. "And why it was so important that it went well."

"Yeah. Sorry I've been...difficult the last few days. But that's also why it was so important to have you, Romeo, and India here." She shrugged. "I don't feel so alone...at least until the guests leave. Every year I think, 'Surely this time it'll be easier.' It never is. But somehow, this year..."

"Was harder than ever?"

"Yeah. A lot."

"What are you going to do now? The party's over..."

"What I've always done. Get through it."

"How?"

"I don't know." Omega shrugged again. "Channel surf. Read some library books. Maybe go up on the roof and do some stargazing. I generally... don't sleep."

Echo was silent for a while, watching the tree lights twinkle. Then he turned to her.

"You know, I'm not tired at all," he declared. "In fact, I'm wide awake. Would you mind some company up on the roof?"

Chapter 9

Zero Days—Zero Days

"Well," Omega said softly as she sat in the dark, "I didn't expect to be spending my first Christmas Eve in the Agency on a stakeout..."

Echo, in the driver's seat of the matte-cloaked Corvette hidden in the dark alley of the financial district, replied somewhat brusquely, though his tone was not harsh.

"Comes with the territory. Deal with it."

"I am. It's not a problem, really. I've worked spacecraft missions over holidays before. I guess I just hadn't thought about it, that's all."

"What had you planned on?"

"I thought I'd go to the chapel service." Omega glanced out the window, then unbuckled the seat belt, moved the seat all the way forward, and reclined the back. She folded her long legs up into the seat, then twisted around. Echo watched her contortions, perplexed.

"...Meg, WHAT the hell are you doing?"

Omega stretched her legs out on the seat back and crossed her ankles. She leaned back against the dash, letting her head rest on its top. Folding her arms, she stared straight up through the windshield, into the night sky.

"...Oh," Echo said with a grin. "I should've known."

"Yeah."

"Once a stargazer, always a stargazer."

"I suppose."

"Hey, I been meaning to ask...you all right?" Echo asked then, with some concern.

"What do you mean?" The response was guarded.

"You coming down with a cold?"

"Nooo...oh, I sound funny."

"Yeah. You sound all stuffed up."

"Mm. Last night was a bit rough on the mucous membranes, shall we say. I'm a little stuffy—okay, maybe a lot stuffy. Eyes are swollen some, too. Thanks for the company, though. It helped."

"You cried some more after I went to bed." It was a statement.

Omega shrugged by way of response.

"Should I have stayed longer?" he asked, still concerned.

"Nah. No sense in both of us going without sleep." She was matter-of-fact. "An' it ain't like I haven't done it before."

Alpha One was quiet for a while, Echo watching the hotel entrance and Omega dividing her attention between the entrance and the sky.

"I take it your family always went to church on Christmas Eve?" Echo asked her then.

"Actually, no. Christmas Eve and Christmas morning were important family times. But...on Christmas Eve, Dad always got his Bible and read the Christmas story..."

"Aha. A special family tradition."

"Yeah..."

"So now you go to church to hear it instead?"

"Uh-huh. Never seems right if *I* read it, somehow. I guess it's the male voice thing. You know, the pitch and the resonance. I've never missed a Christmas Eve service before...at least, not since the year after they died." She sighed unconsciously.

Echo momentarily turned his attention from the stakeout to study his partner. Her face, beneath the windshield, was softly illuminated by moonlight and the distant street lights, and he could read her expression easily. It spoke of a bleak aloneness to which Echo could relate, of important things missing on this night that had once been so meaningful to her.

And I can understand that, all too well, he thought. *Sometimes friends can help...and sometimes, no matter how much we want to, we can't.*

He returned his attention to scanning the area around the Corvette.

* * *

In the silence, Omega heard Echo's low voice as he quoted from memory.

"Now when Jesus was born in Bethlehem of Judea, in the days of

Herod the king, behold, there came wise men from the east to Jerusalem, saying, 'Where is he that is born King of the Jews? For we have seen his star in the east, and are come to worship him...'"

She pushed up in surprise and a certain amount of delight, and watched his face as he spoke, the whole time never taking his eyes off their surveillance.

* * *

A little while later, the inside of the Corvette was quiet once more. Omega still looked out the windshield, but her face had lost the loneliness. Her eyes glimmered suspiciously in the moonlight. Her lips curved up slightly. Eventually she whispered, "Echo?"

"Hmm?"

"Thank you. That was one of the nicest Christmas gifts you could have given me."

Echo only nodded, pleased.

Then something caught his attention across the street, by the hotel, and he sat up straighter, trying to ascertain what was happening. Without looking at Omega, he reached out and tapped her on the knee, then drew a series of circles in the air with his index finger. She immediately sat up and began twisting back around in the seat.

"We got something?" Omega asked, back to normal as the action picked up.

"Yeah. Hand me the cell phone."

"Here." She placed it in his outstretched hand. Still without looking, Echo activated it on the speed dial and held it to his ear.

"Fox? Whatever it is, it's coming down now. Meg and I are going in."

* * *

The Alpha One team slipped into a rear door of the hotel, unnoticed by those they trailed. Echo and Omega functioned together like a well-maintained machine as they silently reconnoitered empty corridors. Verbal communication had long since become unnecessary, replaced by body language, eye contact, and their special codes. Omega occasionally thought she and Echo could exchange more information in a glance than some people could in an entire conversation.

Now Echo looked at her and nodded ahead of them. *The lobby.*

The lobby? Omega furrowed her brow. *Isn't that a little open?*

This time of night, Echo glanced at his wrist chronometer, then at her, *it won't matter. It should be deserted.*

Good point. She raised an eyebrow; her eyes narrowed in thought, and she nodded, then cocked that same eyebrow. *Suppose they're meeting someone?*

Could be. He shrugged, nodding.

After you, then. She swept one hand out and down the hall in a fluid gesture.

My turn, huh? He grinned tightly.

She shrugged, grinned. Then she pointed at the outline of his shadow on the floor and put her hand to her chest. *Hey, I'm your shadow, remember? Shadows follow.*

*All right...*Echo rolled his eyes upward.

Omega patted him noiselessly on the back in a companionable fashion as he stepped forward, then she dropped in behind him.

The next time Echo glanced around to check on her, Omega caught his eye and, frowning, jerked her head several times in the direction of the lobby, then back over her shoulder. *Who are we after, anyway? What did you see in the street?*

You didn't see? Echo gave her a puzzled look.

No. She shook her head once, feeling sheepish. He stared at her, considering, then nodded.

Oh, I get it. Pointing to his own eyes, he cupped his hand in front of them. *Eyes swollen? Can't see well?*

Yeah. She nodded, pulling a wry face, then shrugged. *'Fraid so. Sorry.*

All right. He brushed his fingers in the air. *No big deal.*

She raised her eyebrow again. *So who is it?*

Not now. Echo shook his head, touched his wrist chronometer and jerked his thumb away. *I'll tell you later.* He flipped his index finger forward, pointing. *C'mon.*

* * *

As Alpha One approached the lobby, they slowed, becoming even more cautious. They slipped up to the rear entrance, Echo on the right, Omega on the left, and peered out.

The lighting in the large area had been dimmed; this late at night, the hotel presumed no one would be about. Festive garlands and wreaths bedecked the lobby, and a large Christmas tree stood to one side, in the hotel atrium, its lights twinkling gaily in the low illumination. The reception desk was unmanned, but a light showed around the edge of the door behind it. *Probably playing cards,* Omega thought with a hidden grin, remembering her little escapade behind that door.

Just then, Omega heard the barest hiss from Echo. She glanced at him, and followed his gaze out into the lobby, where the Prime Minister now appeared, wandering—alone—across the open area.

* * *

"What the hell..." Echo breathed.

"Where are his bodyguards?" Omega asked under her breath.

"That's what I'd like to know. As well as what he thinks he's doing down here in the first place. Fox gave him a strict warning to stay holed up tonight, given the countdown in the Plaza."

"He seems to be...just looking at the decorations. But he already saw those during YuleCon."

"Uh-oh..." Echo caught a movement out of the corner of his eye.

* * *

"'Uh-oh'? What?" Omega quickly scanned the room, but saw nothing. She rubbed her eyes, checked the room again. "Damn stupid eyes."

Damn eyes, damn Slug, damn murdering alien psychopaths, damn anniversaries, she thought the addendum, but did not say.

* * *

But Echo's eyes flicked rapidly around the decorated lobby, analyzing swiftly, then he turned to his partner and drew his primary blaster.

"Meg, listen carefully, baby: No matter WHAT happens, see to it that the projectile gets to Fox for analysis." His voice was urgent.

"Projectile? What? Echo, what's going down?!"

"Stay here."

Echo was already stepping forward when he hesitated, and turned back for a moment. His left arm went around his partner's shoulders, and he pulled her tight against his side for a split-second, pressing his lips into the silvery hair and breathing in her scent one more time, then he released her.

"I'm sorry, baby. Goodbye, Meg." He was sprinting across the lobby by the time she could react.

* * *

Echo saw the glint of light on metal to his left, out of the corner of his eye.

He put on a burst of speed, and lunged in front of the Prime Minister just as a silent muzzle flash appeared where the metal glint had been.

Echo's body lurched backward as white-hot, searing pain tore through his abdomen. The parquet flooring rushed upward.

The last thing he heard was Omega's voice screaming, "*ECHO!!*"

* * *

Omega set a speed record crossing the lobby, laying down her own cover fire with both of her blasters as she went. She tackled the unhurt Prime Minister, shoving him down behind a couch and out of sight, as hotel employees, drawn by the noise, emerged from service corridors.

"Stay here!" she ordered the potentate, brought her blaster up over the back of the couch, and cautiously raised her head, surveying the area. Seeing the hotel staff, she yelled, "Take cover! This is the FBI! We have an assassin on site!" There were a couple of startled, frightened exclamations, but the staff quickly disappeared into the same back rooms and service corridors from which they'd emerged.

There was no sign of life across the lobby where the shot had originated, and Omega vaulted the couch and ran to Echo, sprawled awkwardly on the floor, a pool of blood already beginning to form beneath him.

"No...no...dear Lord, not that, not tonight, not ever," she whispered as she knelt beside him, holstered her weapons, and felt for a pulse. She glanced upward, and mouthed, "Thank you."

Omega opened Echo's jacket and inhaled sharply. The entire left side of his white shirt was stained red. Omega fought back recollections of recently rereading *Catch-22* as she fumbled with the buttons on his shirt. Finally, in frustration, she simply grabbed the lightweight material and tore, then gasped at the large, ugly entrance wound in the upper left quadrant of his belly.

Where the hell is India when I really need her? Omega wondered, then carefully slipped her hand underneath her partner, unwilling to try to lift him yet, and felt gently for an exit wound. There was none.

"...See to it that the projectile gets to Fox...Goodbye, Meg..."

"No. Echo, in the name of heaven, what have you done??" Omega whipped out her cell phone. "Fox, priority code Alpha-One-Black! Echo is down. Do you copy?!"

"We read you, Omega. Status?"

"Assassination attempt. Echo took the shot intended for the Prime Minister."

"Bad?"

"Dear God in heaven, Fox..." Omega whispered fervently into the phone, her voice shaking despite herself.

"Where were you, Omega?"

"What??"

"Where were you when it happened?"

Omega felt herself pale slightly as she realized the question's significance.

"Standing in the damn lobby's rear entrance where Echo left me, FOLLOWING HIS INSTRUCTIONS, Fox." Her voice was calm, but firm. "I've been with Echo all day. Per YOUR instructions."

"But not for a period last night during the party."

"...No," she admitted. "Not last night during the party."

There was a lull in the conversation. Finally Fox broke it.

"Do what you can for him, Omega. Romeo and India are already rolling. They'll be there soon."

"Fox, I don't think Echo can wait that long."

"Omega, what are you—"

"Fox, have the medics standing by with a ballistics team in the vehicle hangar."

"What about the Prime Minister?"

"Fox..." Her eyes closed, her head tilted back and her blood-covered hands extended toward the ceiling, in a blind, mute plea to Heaven. Then, as she looked down, miraculously she saw the Prime Minister's own personal bodyguards running to escort him back to his suite. She tried to smile as she saluted Tortok.

"Under control, Fox. His bodyguards finally showed. I'm on my way. Send a cleanup crew. Tell 'em to be prepared for a lotta blood."

"Omega—"

She clicked the cell phone off, and worked frantically.

First Omega removed Echo's tie, then her own. She eased off his jacket and shoulder holster with an effort, then pulled her pocket knife and simply cut off his shirt. It required some strategic maneuvering to remove the waistband holster containing his Winchester & Tesla death ray pistol without moving him too much, nestled as it was in the small of his back, but Omega managed it by dint of getting down on her elbows in the puddle of his blood, to worm her hand underneath her partner. Then she slipped his jacket back on his torso as best she could—his skin was cold and clammy from blood loss and shock.

Omega folded the bloodstained, shredded shirt into a pad for the wound, and fixed it securely in place with both ties wrapped around his torso. Then, unsatisfied with the cover provided by his Suit jacket alone, she removed her own jacket and laid it over him. She slung his dual-wield holster across her right shoulder, on top of her extra firearm, and stuck his death ray holster into her own trousers waistband, beside her own backup piece.

His shoes came off next, and Omega dug a pen out of a jacket pocket. She ran the retracted tip the length of Echo's right sole and watched his foot flex, then repeated the process on his left foot, with the same results. *Good. No spinal involvement—yet. But I got no way of telling where the projectile has lodged. I guess I'll just have to risk it and hope nothing will happen. If I don't act fast, it isn't gonna matter anyway.*

Echo moaned.

"Echo?"

"Nnn..."

"Echo, can you hear me?"

"Nn...hnn..."

"Do you know who I am?"

"Ommm..."

"Yes. Do you know where you are?"

"Mmmiiinn..."

"Yes, the Prime Minister's safe. I'm getting you to help, Echo. Hang on." Gently, Omega lifted Echo's upper body, resting his head carefully against her left shoulder. She slipped her right arm under his knees, planted her feet, and arched her back.

"Echo? This will hurt some. I'll try to be as gentle as I can."

"Can't..." Echo whispered, slightly more coherent.

"Can too. Just watch me."

Omega hyperventilated for a moment, clenched her jaws tightly shut, then slowly, painfully, straightened her legs, forcing her way upright, Echo's body in her arms. He groaned involuntarily and loudly as his body cleared the floor, his lips whitening, and she winced in sympathy.

"St-stay with muh-me, Echo."

"'M...here..."

Omega stood still until she was certain she could handle his weight, then stumbled toward the door as fast as she could manage.

THIS is going to be a painful ride for Echo, she thought with a grimace, but speed was essential. She could already feel a wet spot against her own belly where his blood was soaking through the pad of his shirt, her jacket, and her own shirt. *Oh, Lord God help me, he's bleeding to death in my arms.*

Outside, Omega called to their vehicle, "Echo-Two, Alpha-One-Omega passenger unlock." This activated the Corvette's voice recognition system, and the car's passsenger door popped open. *Thank the good Lord for THAT new gadget on the 'Vette,* she thought. *I'd never have gotten him in otherwise.*

Kicking the door wide open, she placed Echo gently into the passenger seat, still reclined from her stargazing. She grabbed their overcoats from the back seat and spread them across his cold, shocky form, strapping him in securely. Then she closed the passenger door, ran to the driver's side and got in, starting the ignition in the same move.

"Echo? Are you with me?"

No answer.

"Echo?" Omega reached across the console and took his hand. Her Southern dialect thickened as fear gripped her. "Hon', if ya hear me, squeeze mah fingers."

Light pressure grasped her fingertips.

"Good. Echo, I...I'm not...It wasn't...I DIDN'T—"

Fingers tightened on hers again.

"...Know..." His voice was a barely-audible whisper.

Omega choked, and her hand clasped his in intense gratitude for a moment, thankful that, whatever happened—even if he didn't survive, Echo would know, would leave this world knowing that his partner had not been the one to harm him, but the one trying desperately to save him.

Then she disengaged her hand gently and put the car in gear, moving out at high speed, burning rubber. Once into the deserted streets, she turned back to her gravely-injured partner.

"Echo, I'm gonna morph..."

Echo's head nodded the merest fraction of an inch, and Omega entered the command on the console keyboard. Almost instantaneously the acceleration kicked in as the Corvette became a rocket. She pulled back gently on the steering wheel, and it went airborne.

"Nnghh..." came from the passenger seat. Omega reached over and took his hand again, squeezing it lightly.

"I'm sorry," she murmured.

Gentle pressure on her fingers told her he understood, but she was troubled; Echo's grip was growing weaker.

* * *

Omega piloted the Corvette at top speed above and through the icy city streets as the glow of a Christmas pre-dawn lightened the sky ahead of them.

She looked over at Echo, put a hand out, and felt the makeshift bandage through the coverings. Her fingertips came away sticky-wet. She rested her hand lightly on his stomach and prayed.

Lord God, the poets call Christmas the season of miracles. We could sure use one about now. I can't lose another family member. Not right at Christmas again. Not him. Above all, not him. Not now, not ever. Please... help me. Help US.

* * *

Echo was unconscious again when Omega put their car into a hard ninety-degree turn and skidded to a stop in the vehicle hangar at Headquarters. Fox was there, accompanied by an emergency team with an antigrav gurney. The medics gently removed Echo's limp, unmoving form, and Fox hurried around to help Omega out of the car.

"Is he..."

"I don't know, Fox. I was too busy driving."

"You're covered in blood. Are YOU—"

"No." Omega shook her head. "It's his. It's all his. I would've..." She choked for a moment. "I wish it WAS mine."

* * *

Fox looked her over, taking in her pale, worried face and disheveled appearance—an almost frightened appearance, if an Alpha Line Agent could ever be said to show fear, and Omega was without doubt an Alpha Line Agent, trained by no less than the youngest—and some said the toughest—of the Originals. It was not an appellation that even Fox, an Original himself, would dispute.

The Director of the Division One Agency merely nodded, and put a fatherly arm around her, uncaring of the bloodstains. The medics were already disappearing through the hangar door with Echo.

"It doesn't strike me as that long since we were doing this sort of thing in Australia," Fox observed.

"No, you're right. I was thinking about that at the hotel. But this... might be worse."

"Do you want to go to the medlab?" he asked her.

"Um...why don't I meet you there in a few minutes? You can beep me on the cell phone if...if you need me..."

"Omega, where..."

"Ask Father Papa."

"Ah. Right. Go, dear."

"I'm gone. See you in five. Take care of him while I'm gone, Fox," she said, blue eyes wide. "I can't...I CAN'T...not again, I just can't..."

"I know," Fox told her, understanding as much of the unspoken communication as the spoken. "I will."

* * *

When a pale, disheveled Omega appeared alone in the chapel entrance in the middle of the Christmas morning service, four blasters slung between both arms, two pistols protruding from the small of her back, jacketless, tieless, and thoroughly bloodsmeared, all eyes turned to focus on her, and a horrified buzz filled the room. Omega saw Madrid, from the weapons lab, look up in shock and sympathy; Monkey and Sierra leaned toward each other and whispered, as did Tare and Yankee. Faces in the congregation seemed to Omega to be evenly divided between concern and accusation.

The chaplain, Father Papa—whose codename was generally considered singularly apropos—stopped his message at sight of her, and held out a compassionate hand.

"Agent Omega? Is it Echo?" He gestured at his own torso, denoting her bloodstained clothing. She nodded, but said nothing. "Would you like us to pray?"

She still said nothing, and her impassive expression never changed. She had forgotten all about the morning holiday service, but she didn't let that stop her. Without hesitation, she walked down the aisle and knelt at the rail. The older man tenderly laid his hand on the somewhat unkempt silver-blonde braid, and motioned for those assembled to bow their heads.

* * *

A few moments later Omega's cell phone beeped, and all heads came up. She activated it, listened for several seconds, uttered a wordless, vaguely horrified exclamation, leaped up and ran from the sanctuary.

The old chaplain looked after her with a benign gaze, then spread his arms to his flock.

"Let us continue to pray for our fellow agents."

* * *

Omega slammed through the waiting-room door, blue eyes wide. "Fox?!"

"Sshh," he hushed her, "he's going into surgery now. Ballistics is standing by. He's lost a lot of blood, though..."

"No joke..." She looked down at her clothes.

"We're low on Echo's blood type, Omega, and there isn't time to clone enough...the medics say you're compatible, and..."

Omega unbuttoned her sleeve and rolled it up.

"Point the way," she said.

* * *

When Romeo and India got back from securing the crime scene, Omega was sitting next to Fox in the waiting room, her bloodstained sleeve still rolled up, with a small compression bandage inside the elbow. Fox met them at the door and jerked a thumb over his shoulder.

"She's chilled to the bone, light-headed, exhausted, and running on adrenaline. We had to take as much blood as it was safe for her to give...and a little bit past it. Take her home, get her cleaned up, and see that she eats. I'll let you know as soon as there's anything to hear."

India immediately went over to Omega and knelt in front of her.

"C'mon, girlfriend, let's go get cleaned up."

"No."

India looked up at Romeo.

"Pretty lady, you need—" he began.

"I said no."

Fox came to stand over her, at his most intimidating...which was to say, few beings in the galaxy stood up to him when he wore that expression.

"Young woman, you are a sight. You have also given a damn lot of blood. You need food, a hot shower, and clean clothes. Am I going to have to give you a direct order?"

"Yes. And good luck with that." The response was completely *UN*intimidated.

Fox, India, and Romeo stared blankly at each other, at a loss. Evidently Echo hadn't cornered the market in stubbornness on the Alpha One team.

"Meg," India tried a different tack, "the doctors can't take any more blood from you until you've eaten something and built your reserves back. If Echo needs another transfusion..."

"If he does, they'll clone it," came the calm response. "They only needed blood from me because he'd lost too much, and didn't have time to clone it."

"Um, well, I dunno if they mentioned it or not, but the stem cell manipulator is offline right now, for upgrades."

"You're kidding," Fox exclaimed. "There should be two."

"There are. One broke down, and Maintenance discovered they needed upgrading, before the replacement parts would work. So, since it's the holiday season, Maintenance in their infinite wisdom decided nobody would need it, so they took 'em both offline to work on."

"Aw, farkakt," Fox grumbled. "So we MIGHT have to take more from Omega."

"It depends on how surgery goes. But it's possible." India turned to Omega. "Which is why somebody REALLY needs to do what's needed to build up her reserves."

Omega blinked at that, and they saw her resolve waver. Then she looked India in the face with a wry expression.

"Are you sure you were an ER physician and not a shrink?" she asked, every bit as sardonic as Echo could be.

"Omega, go home, take a hot shower, and eat. Then take a nap if you can. That's an order," Fox commanded, but gently. "If you just can't sleep, then—and ONLY then—are you permitted to come back here without my express notification. I'll be here, and I'll see he's well taken care of. I have no intention of leaving. You have my word."

"If YOU have no intention of—"

"*I* didn't just give near-superhuman levels of blood. Damn, woman.

You shouldn't be upright."

Omega sat in determined stubbornness for a few more moments, then acquiesced. She got to her feet, swaying slightly with exhaustion, and India and Romeo steadied her as they led her to the door. Once there, she turned.

"Fox?"

"As soon as I hear anything, Omega. I swear."

She nodded, and they led her out.

* * *

India helped Omega get cleaned up while Romeo whipped up a Christmas breakfast of pancakes, bacon and eggs in Omega's kitchen. The scent of chicory coffee wafted over all.

"Come an' get it," he called to the two women in the bedroom.

Omega came out, bundled in her long black terry robe against the chills, hair still in a towel, and India followed. Omega looked at the food-laden table and sighed. The sound so perfectly expressed utter fatigue, without need of words, that her friends looked shocked.

"No offense, but do I have to eat?" she finally managed.

"Yes," Romeo and India both said firmly, sounding not too far removed from a Greek chorus.

Omega sighed again, and turned to stare at the dark Christmas tree. There seemed to be more packages under it than she remembered; after a moment, she shook her head, dismissing the random thought. She picked up the family portrait Echo had seen from the nearby shelf, and stared down at it.

* * *

Romeo came over and stood beside her, glancing at the picture. Then he studied his friend's bleak face.

"It's happenin' again, isn't it?"

"Yes." She waved her hand over the photo. "I couldn't do anything for them twelve years ago, when it happened then. Now I have a new 'family.' And twelve years and twenty-four hours later, it's happening all over again. I keep trying to think if there was anything more I should've done last night...something to STOP it. But I didn't see what Echo saw, and once we started moving, there wasn't really time for him to TELL me..." Omega shook her head. "So much for Christmas. I think I can understand now why Echo doesn't do it any more." She choked. "I only hope...he gets a chance... not to do it any more."

Omega reached up and plucked an ornament from the tree, laid it on the side table nearby, and reached for another.

"Stop." India laid a hand over Omega's. "The actual date isn't what's important. MY parents taught me Christmas was about love, and caring... and FAITH. Have faith, Meg. Echo's tough. And...we heard about the prayer request in the chapel service—Madrid called us to ask what happened. It's gonna be okay, hon. We'll celebrate Christmas when this is all over. ALL of us."

Omega looked deep into India's eyes, seeing the sincerity and confidence there.

"Thanks, 'Sis,'" she murmured. India smiled and hugged her.

"Group hug," Romeo said softly, and joined in.

* * *

The first thing Echo saw when his eyes flickered open was a hazy vision of a fair face surrounded by a silver halo. A soothing voice called his name from a distance.

"Echo?"

"Mmm?" he responded.

"Echo, wake up," the voice urged gently.

Under the influence of that urging, Echo fought his way back to full consciousness, and the angelic vision resolved itself instead into a familiar, smiling face.

"Meg?" he whispered through pale lips.

"I'm right here. We all are," Omega said, rubbing his near forearm very gently. "How do you feel?"

"'Bout like Ah've been stepped on by a horse." Echo closed his eyes for a moment, considering his description. "From Caltor," he amended, looking back up at her. Several snorts sounded in the room; Omega just looked puzzled.

"Caltor?" Omega wondered, glancing over her shoulder, just as he allowed heavy eyelids to slide shut again.

"Yes, Omega," Fox's voice sounded from somewhere. "They're about the same size and mass as an American bison."

"Oh, shit!" Omega exclaimed. "Damn, Ace!"

"Coulda been worse," Echo decided, blinking slowly and finally giving in to the temptation to let them stay closed. "It coulda kicked." He paused, feeling the massive ache in his torso. "On second thought, maybe it did..."

Subdued laughter sounded in the room.

"He's going to be fine now," Omega declared with a grin in her voice.

At that, Echo opened his eyes again and looked back up at Omega, studying her face. It was white and drawn, as if she had been in pain; dark circles hugged close under her lower lashes.

"Why...are you so pale...and tired?" For the life of him, he could barely get his voice above a whisper. It was annoying.

"You can tell?" Omega responded, seeming surprised. He nodded once. Romeo moved to the bedside and pointed at the IV stand.

"Echo, can you see the blood transfusion?"

Echo turned his head slightly, until he could see a deep-red IV bag on the stand from the corner of his eye. It was joined by a clear bag of saline; the resulting color of the tube entering his arm was a dark pink.

"Yeah, junior," he murmured.

"That's Meg drippin' into your arm there."

Echo's glance shot back to Omega.

"That's why—?"

She nodded as Fox and India came forward. A doctor hovered nearby.

"The stem cell manipulators were offline for maintenance and repair, Echo, which means they couldn't clone blood for you. So the doctors took as much blood as they dared, and your partner let 'em have every drop they asked for," Fox noted. "Then offered more."

"Damn, baby..." Echo whispered. "Save SOME for yourself, there."

Omega ran a distracted hand through her hair, which was pulled back in a clasp, low on her neck, but not braided.

"Hon," she murmured, Southern dialect thick, "if you'd seen how much blood you left on the lobby floor...Ah didn't think Ah was gonna get you back here in time. An' you were bleedin' the whole way. Ah...Ah just..."

"Ssh. I get it," he mumbled. "'S okay now."

"We're, uh, we're gonna have to clean the upholstery in the Corvette," she added.

"Not to worry, Omega," Fox interjected. "I got that under way while Alpha Two was force-feeding you."

"Um, okay..."

"Echo, how much do you remember?" Fox asked. Echo thought for only a second.

"I remember getting shot," he said with conviction. They all smiled.

"What else?"

"...I remember Meg's scream..."

"I did?" she said, startled.

"Yeah. I remember lying on the lobby floor...then in the Corvette..."

"Echo, how did you GET to the Corvette? I meant to ask Omega..." Fox looked at him consideringly. Echo's eyes narrowed in thought, as he sorted through the fuzzy memories.

"Meg, am I remembering right...you didn't really..."

"Yes. You're remembering correctly," she answered briefly.

"You picked me up and CARRIED me to the car??"

* * *

Omega nodded as the others gaped at her.

"There wasn't anything else to do. There was no one to help, and no time to wait for anyone. You were bleeding to death."

"That's true, judging by the blood I saw in the lobby," India interjected her medical confirmation.

"But Meg," Romeo protested, "Echo's almost a head taller than you. He must outweigh you by—"

"Time out, y'all," Omega interrupted, forming a T with her hands, referee-style. "I'm a Division One Agent, remember? In Alpha Line at that. I'm not helpless, and I'm not exactly frail and petite. I'm not really a small woman at all, but neither am I as big as you menfolk. A few months ago—right before I left on my little 'sabbatical,' actually—it occurred to me that

I might eventually have to carry somebody bigger than me off the field of battle, as it were. And Echo's the tallest and broadest of us, at least so far; so I figured if I could handle his weight, I could handle the rest of y'all. Consequently, handling him was my target goal. So, with Echo's help, I started adding some specific powerlifting exercises to my gym workouts."

"But, back at Halloween..." Fox began.

"Right. Back at Halloween when the Glu'g'ik dumped him in the Outback, I hadn't quite worked up to it, so I had to drag him into the airskimmer. After that, I REALLY buckled down in my workouts. Now I can more than handle Echo's weight—in the gym. But the reality check was the weight distribution. A human body in my arms is a very different thing from, say, an Olympic bar across my shoulders. But the training program worked, and I managed it. Sorry the ride was a little rough, hon."

"So that's what that was all about," Echo mused. "All that gym work. You wanted to be able to carry my ass off the 'field of battle.' Having established in the Outback that you needed the ability."

"Yeah, pretty much. Thanks, Coach," Omega teased.

"Hmm," India murmured, wrinkling her forehead and sizing Romeo up. "That's...a good thought. Think we could work out together some?"

"Sure," Omega told her, "but you'd do better to ask Echo when he's back on his feet. Maybe we should add it into the Alpha Line required training, for just that reason."

"I think that is an excellent consideration, yung froy," Fox decided. "And you are the training lead, so I would recommend you do it. Echo?"

Echo's head bobbed slowly in agreement.

"Okay, I will. And no, I didn't break form lifting you," Omega said, turning and answering Echo's unspoken question, which she could see in his eyes. "Of course," she admitted, wry, "adrenaline helps a whole lot..."

Fox, India, and Romeo shook their heads, faint grins of admiration on their faces. Fox laid a commending hand on her shoulder, rubbing lightly, briefly. Omega glanced up at him for a moment, reading her superior's approving—even supportive—expression, then dropped her gaze. Echo merely watched his partner with dark brown eyes, resting.

"Enough," Omega said quietly, withdrawing into herself. "I did what I had to do. Next subject."

Echo caught her eye, and she leaned over him as he murmured, "The projectile?"

Omega looked back up at Fox, deferring to him, and he replied.

"We're still waiting for the ballistics report, Echo. I'll let you know."

Echo nodded and closed his eyes again. Omega studied his pale, drawn face, laid a compassionate hand soothingly on his, letting her thumb gently—if invisibly—rub the back of his hand, telegraphing her affection as well as offering comfort, and looked up at the others.

"I think Echo's had enough for now, y'all. Let's get out of here and let him rest." The others nodded and turned to go.

As Omega started to leave, however, she felt her fingers gripped and held. She glanced down at Echo, but his eyes were closed and he appeared to be asleep.

"Meg? You comin'?" Romeo asked from the door. Omega looked from Echo's face to the Agents by the door.

"Y'all go ahead. I think...I'll give the medics a break and stay here a little while in case my partner needs anything." The doctor—it happened to be Whiskey's shift—nodded in acknowledgment and gratitude, and left. India, however, stepped back into the room.

* * *

"Meg, you need to eat some more and rest, yourself. You've donated more blood for Echo in less than 48 hours from that first batch. And you never did take that nap Fox ordered, nor yet gone off duty for the night—ANY night. You're pushin' it, girl. Hard. Keep this up, and something's gonna break."

No one saw Echo's eyelids flicker at India's comment. With an effort, he managed to part them far enough to peer out through his lashes, watching without seeming to do so.

"India, I'll be fine. I was available and compatible. I bounce back fast." Omega's face held an ironic expression. "One of the few advantages to having an alien perp supercharge your body. Remember, there's spandex under the Suit," she joked. But Echo caught the bleak look that flashed across her face.

"Well...just promise me you'll stretch out in the chair in the corner and get some rest, then. I'll have a nurse bring in a tray for you in about an hour. And you need to EAT IT."

"Is this what it's like to have a bossy sister?" Omega grinned and gave India a hug. "All right, I promise—I'll eat, and then I'll kick back over here in the corner in the recliner and try to crash, okay?"

"Okay."

"See y'all later."

* * *

As the door closed behind them, Omega moved back to Echo's bedside. She waited several minutes, until she was certain no one would double back, then she brushed the back of his hand with her fingers.

"All right, they're gone. What's up?"

Echo opened his eyes slowly and looked up at her. *Better keep this short,* she thought, studying the tired lines around his eyes. *He really is exhausted, but he won't stop until he's told me whatever he needs to.* She bent over him and smoothed his rumpled hair back from his face with gentle fingers, and he blinked his thanks.

"Meg," Echo's voice was weak and faint, and she had to lean close to hear, "I saw the assassins. Got a glimpse out on the street, then again in the lobby. And just before I hit the floor, I saw them clearly. Faces, Meg."

"Let me go get Fox—" Omega was already turning for the door.

"No!" Echo caught her fingers in his and refused to let go.

"Why?"

"Because I saw black Suits and a high-tech weapon. Meg, they were agents."

* * *

Omega was stretched out in the recliner in the corner of Echo's darkened hospital room, mulling over his revelation and trying to rest after having managed to choke down most of the food on the tray she had been brought. *Not that the food was bad,* she thought. *That's one of the nicer things about this place—it doesn't serve standard hospital food! I've just got way too much going on to be hungry right now.*

Close by, Echo slept deeply, as his body recovered from the gunshot trauma and blood loss. The Agency's chief doctors—Zebra AND Zarnix—had reassured Omega that, with the alien medical technology being used, Echo should be up and about very soon.

In the meanwhile, Omega had to decide how to handle the information to which she alone was privy.

If the assassination attempt WAS an Agency operation, she thought, *who were the assassins? Who authorized it? And who can I trust? Was it possible Fox authorized it? And...I hate to think it, but where were Romeo and India when I needed them? Why weren't they part of our surveillance operation?* Omega was in a quandary. The only person she knew without doubt that she could trust was lying there in the room with her, unable to get out of bed.

And then another thought hit her, dispelling any thought of sleep or taking rest. For if the assassination was indeed some sort of rogue agent op—or an illegally-but-formally authorized Agency operation—and the assassins realized Echo had identified them...there would be hell to pay. Omega moved the chair into an upright position, on alert.

There were two possibilities, as far as she could see. One was the potential for another attempt on Echo's life. But she was here, and she always had at least her Winchester & Tesla on her body. *Well...almost always,* she amended, remembering the one time she had left it behind. *Never again.* Echo should be safe for the moment. *Looks like the bodyguarding duty has reversed,* she thought, irony heavy.

The other possibility was far more insidious: One contingent of agents already thought SHE was a traitor. What if the assassins tried to discredit BOTH of them in the Agency? Omega didn't have a clue how to combat that.

She sighed quietly, then grinned ruefully in the darkness, remembering a conversation from a couple of weeks back.

"Where's that emergency management coordinator when I need him?" she muttered to herself with a wry chuckle.

"I don't know. Will I do?" said a low voice in the dark.

"Echo? I thought you were asleep."

"I was. I'm not now."

* * *

Omega got up and moved to the bed. Echo felt the lightest of touches brush the bare skin of his ribcage—for the time being, the medics had chosen to leave his upper torso bare, to provide easier wound access—as she slid her hand under the sheet to check the bandage. *So soft it doesn't even tickle,* he thought. *She can be tough or tender, depending on what's needed. Damn. I picked an all-around champ in her.*

"Good," she murmured. "It's dry. Did I wake you?"

"No. Woke up on my own."

"Are you in pain?"

"No."

"Would you admit it if you were?"

"Probably not."

"I didn't think so. You're stubborn, Echo."

"Yes, I am. But so are you."

* * *

"How are you feeling?" she asked, laying her palm against his cheek, and ignoring his addendum. To her relief, his skin felt comfortably cool. *Not hot, but not ice-cold either, like he was in the car. He's not feverish, and his vitals are getting back to normal,* she thought, satisfied.

"Okay, considering," he answered, turning his face into her hand slightly, and she decided he was acknowledging her care in an appreciative—but energy-conserving—fashion. "I thought you promised India you'd rest."

"Yeah, well...I promised I'd try. I tried."

* * *

"Past tense," he noted, seeing the sober, worried, almost anxious expression she wore, despite the extremely low lighting. *And probably doesn't realize I can see,* he thought—Omega had turned off the room lights some time earlier, only allowing a sliver of light from the hallway to spill past the door, which the nurse had left ajar. *Maybe I can do something about that. Get her to lighten up a little.*

"Yeah, past tense," she confirmed. "I got to thinking..."

"I knew I smelled something burning. Probably what woke me."

She dropped her head, her face disappearing into shadow. There was a long silence. Then her smiling voice came out of the darkness.

"If you don't watch it, I really will finish the job the assassins did on you."

Bingo, he thought with a grin.

* * *

She just caught the faint white flash of his teeth as he grinned in the darkened room.

"So you were thinking..." he prodded.

"Yeah. If we've got some agent or agents running around—rogue or otherwise—trying to kill the Prime Minister, and they realize you got a good look at them, they may try to finish you off."

"Yeah. I thought of that."

"And you still went to sleep?!"

"Of course."

"HOW??"

* * *

"Meg, for one thing, I was SHOT," Echo pointed out. "The body doesn't give you very many options after something like that. For another, my partner was here the whole time. And I trust her. You know, she's pretty damn good. Always gets it right. I think you know her."

Omega didn't say anything else for a while, and she kept her head bowed and face averted, leaving it in shadow. So Echo listened carefully, hearing slightly irregular breathing coming from his partner, and he fully comprehended that—given everything in which they'd been embroiled of late—she was struggling with her emotions. He waited patiently to see what her reaction would be. Eventually, and in a more or less normal tone, she simply said, "Thanks."

There we go, baby. Good job. You got things under control. Echo remained silent, watching her in the dark, and giving her plenty of time to collect herself. After a moment, she continued.

"Are you still awake?"

"Yeah. Just thinking. Keep going."

"Another thing I thought of, then. There's already been an attempt to label me a traitor. What if the assassins try to do the same to you?"

"Hm. That's a wrinkle I hadn't considered. But there have already been some snide remarks aimed at me, almost as much as at you, and to my face, no less, so..." He drew a deep breath. "It's certainly possible."

"Damn. You didn't tell me that, either."

"Meh. No big wup. It ranged from, 'You're too stupid to realize what your partner is doing,' to, 'You're in it with her,' and everything in between." He carefully avoided mentioning the remarks in which her supposed mode of influence had occurred in the bedroom; despite how he felt about her, he didn't care for the innuendoes, and knew it would only upset her again. "I didn't put much stock in it at the time. What they were doing to you seemed a lot worse, to me. That was what I was concentrating on. But maybe I shoulda paid more attention, after all."

"Echo, how far do you think this goes?"

"I don't know yet."

"Could Fox...?"

"I...don't know. I hope not."

"Romeo and India?"

Echo stirred restlessly, anxious despite himself as Omega vocalized his own concerns, then involuntarily grunted in pain at the movement.

"Oh, Echo, I'm sorry. I should let you rest. I'm asking too many questions."

"That's what an astronomer does. Or any scientist. Ask questions."

"Yeah, but I'm not an astronomer anymore. I'm an Agent."

"Well...I don't think I'd have phrased it quite like that," he deadpanned. "And you'll never NOT be an astronomer. It's a part of you."

"I suppose so. But you still need to rest now. Maybe we'll find out something when the ballistics report comes back."

"Not yet. Let's talk a minute..."

* * *

Fox found Echo asleep and Omega alert and standing guard when he came into Echo's hospital room the next morning with the ballistics report. He slipped over to Omega, seated in the recliner in the corner.

"How's he doing?" Fox asked in a low tone.

"Fine," Omega replied in a hushed, slightly rough voice. "He had a good night. Woke up a couple times, so we um, chatted for a bit, but then he went right off to sleep again. No pain—at least not that he would admit—and he slept well."

"Good. I've got news I think he'll want to hear." Fox waved the report. "Ballistics had some very interesting things to say about the piece of evidence Echo brought us the hard way."

"Hm. You've got me intrigued."

"Hell, I'm intrigued," Fox responded. "But we'll wait for Echo to wake up. Did YOU have a good night?"

Now that's a tricky question. "Well...I didn't get much sleep, if that's what you mean."

"Why? Echo's out of danger."

That's what YOU think. Fox, I could really use your help. I wish..."No. I just...had a lot on my mind."

Fox studied her face, then nodded in understanding.

"Your family?"

"...Yes."

"Are you okay? Your voice sounds rather..."

"Well, I'm beginning to think this scratchy throat is a little more than a scratchy throat. Like I need the flu." Omega was disgusted.

"Shall I get one of the medics?"

"No, I'll talk to one after we go over the ballistics report. I just have to be careful not to get too close to Echo. His resistance is probably in the sub-basement right now. Oh NO, and he's got several pints of me in him!"

"Don't worry. We've got the technology to filter out pathogens on a small scale like this. They'll have done it routinely to your blood before giving it to your partner. Echo's fine," Fox reassured her.

"Small scale?" she asked, curious.

"Yes, one or two people. We're working on adapting it to large-scale techniques, then we'll take it public."

"That's great. The Red Cross will love it."

"That's the idea, yes."

A slight movement in the bed told them Echo was waking. Omega waved Fox toward the bed.

"Go ahead," she told the Director. "I'll sit over here and try not to contaminate anything." Fox moved to the bedside, and Omega watched closely.

"Good morning, Echo."

"Mmh. Morning, Fox...where's Meg?"

"Not far," Omega said from the chair in the corner. "Fox has news for us."

"Ballistics is in," Fox said, holding up the report. "Check this out, Echo. First off, the projectile was made of titanium. Damn near killed you, but a native of the Lambda Andromedae system would metabolize it, absorbing it into the damaged tissue. In effect, the projectile would massively accelerate healing of the very wound it created, closing the wound in minutes."

"How fortunate for the Prime Minister," Echo mused.

"Isn't it though?" agreed Fox.

"So the only one in real danger was...Echo?" Omega asked, and Fox nodded.

"And that's not all. Ballistics recognized the rifling pattern on the projectile. It's one they've seen before, from a weapon routinely confiscated about three or four years ago—remember, Echo, when we were doing the sweeps after the murder over on the Upper West Side, near the planetarium? Right before the invasion?"

"Yeah. So it was a weapon in Agency possession?" Echo asked.

"STILL IS a weapon in Agency possession. It's right where it's supposed to be—but it HAS been fired recently. This was an Agency inside job."

"Did YOU order it, Fox?" Echo asked, blunt.

Omega went on high alert, hand surreptitiously in her jacket pocket, whence nestled her Winchester & Tesla, it having proven uncomfortable in her back while lying in the recliner.

Damn! The man has guts, even after having said guts nearly blown out, she thought, and watched as Fox looked Echo directly in the eyes.

"Of course not, Echo."

Echo studied Fox intently for a moment, searching his eyes, then nodded, apparently satisfied with what he saw there.

"Sorry, Fox. I had to ask."

"I know."

Omega relaxed as Echo shot her a blatant *stand down* look. Slightly startled, Fox turned and glanced back at Omega, then nodded, and she knew he had just realized that she had been covertly covering him. She slid her hand out of her pocket and stood.

"Fox, I'm going to check with that medic now," Omega said, and he nodded. Then Fox turned back to Echo as she left the room.

* * *

Fox watched his injured department chief for a moment, pondering what had just happened, and comprehended that, even with one injured and the other growing ill, the Alpha One team was formidable. *After all, between them, they just managed to get the drop on ME,* he considered. *And I wouldn't put it past Echo to have his own weapon in there, under the covers someplace. Although he might have just trusted to Omega to handle that, I suppose. And in the circumstances, I understand why. But that presupposes foreknowledge...hm. This warrants additional discussion.*

"You act as if you already knew it was an agent," he finally offered.

"I did. I saw the Suits AND the weapon." Echo nodded, studying the pattern in the counterpane in a contemplative fashion.

"Did you see faces? Can you ID the agents?" Fox asked, jumping on the admission.

"Yes, I think so. You're not going to like this."

"Let me guess. Monkey and company?"

"You got it. I notice you didn't suggest Meg." Echo sounded satisfied.

"No, never again. Not after what she went through to keep you alive."

* * *

"Good..." Echo pondered Fox's statement, wondering precisely what had happened while he was unconscious. Fox's next comment brought him out of his musings.

"But why would they be stupid enough to use the one weapon guaranteed NOT to kill the Prime Minister?" Fox demanded.

"That is awfully coincidental, isn't it? Tell me, Fox, did you happen to check who the gun was originally confiscated FROM?"

"Matter of fact, I did, and it was the Prime Minister's. Only he wasn't Prime Minister then. But neither did he have permission to bring it planet-side."

"Uh-huh. I thought so. Why didn't he have permission, though? I'd have thought a planetary leader..."

"He never bothered to ask." Fox shrugged.

"Aha. Okay. So the confiscation was a formality brought on by lack of appropriate paperwork?"

"Right. What does that have to do with anything, though?"

"I'm not sure yet. I'm still working on motivation, and I'm sure that'll factor in. Thing is, Fox, I think the Prime Minister set up the hit on HIMSELF."

"But why?"

"That's what we're going to find out. I've got a plan. When Meg gets back in here, we'll need her to—"

"Hold on, Echo. You might want to re-work your plan. Omega's coming down with the Harrnakian flu. Nasty stuff's been going around all of Headquarters."

"What?! But...she never gets—"

"I know, Echo. She's tough. Like someone else I know. But even artificially-enhanced immune systems can be compromised after severe exposure. She's not some comic book super-heroine, after all. I heard about the little 'incident' at the party, in the kitchen with Yankee; he came in to Medical the next day and was diagnosed with the very strain...in addition to some interesting, if superficial, burns to a sensitive area...so there's her exposure to the shit..."

"Oh. Well, uh, yeah. Are you gonna take personnel action?"

"Without more evidence I really can't, not unless Omega files a complaint, which from all I heard, is unlikely, knowing her. Plus, the involved personnel were all off-duty, which significantly restricts my ability to act, anyway. But he isn't gonna try THAT again, I can guarantee. When Zebra found out the reason for the slight burns, she reamed him a new one. That said, I CAN ream him another one. And probably will, if the whole thing isn't overcome by subsequent events...which it sounds like it might be."

"Good. So...keep going. Yankee swapped germs with her..."

"Right. Then, twenty-four hours later, the woman was literally running around, soaking wet, no coat, no jacket, in sub-freezing temperatures, carrying well more than her own body weight. It wasn't as bad as the hypothermia on the Antarctic mission, granted, but damn. Then she promptly and without hesitation gave away a significant percentage of her own body fluids. Twice."

"She didn't sleep the night before, either—wait a minute. How the hell did she get WET??" Echo was mentally replaying the list Fox had just enumerated, startled.

"Echo, do you really know just how much blood you lost? She had so much blood on her from carrying you, I thought for a minute she was injured, too. Her shirt was fairly plastered to her body."

"No jacket? What happened to it?"

"What's the first rule for a patient in shock?"

Echo's eyes narrowed in understanding.

"Her shirt?" he asked grimly. "Wait, you said it was stuck to her..."

"Right. She kept the shirt. But she told me she was beginning to wonder if she might have to cannibalize it for the bandage, as well. And it was blood-soaked anyway. You might also want to know that it took every wile that Alpha Two and I could muster to get her out of the medlab, cleaned up, and fed. And I'm pretty sure she hasn't slept since you arrived in the medlab."

"Damn, Fox!"

"Exactly, zun. I think..." The Director shrugged. "I think, in some measure, she feels responsible, that she should have done something to stop it. But I'm not sure, and I haven't had a chance to sit down with her for a debrief..."

A knock came at the door just then, and fractions of a second later, it opened. Omega stuck her head through it; her face was partially covered with a surgical mask she held in place with one hand.

"You have the flu, I take it?" Fox asked.

"Yes. Dammit." Her voice was hoarse. "Zebra says I probably caught it from, uh, from somebody at the party the other night."

"Most likely," Fox agreed, nodding. "Are you...going to do anything about that?"

"You know?" Omega looked startled.

"Let's just say I heard some things through the grapevine. Do you want me to take action?"

"Nah, not this time," Omega decided. "I think I got the message across to him pretty well. If he tries that shit again, though..."

"Understood." Fox nodded. "I'll also tell Zebra to expect more significant damage, should he try it again."

"Good idea."

"How you feeling?" Echo asked his partner softly, changing the subject. Omega turned her head to look at him.

"I should be asking you that."

"I'm fine—or, well, I will be. How are you?"

"You want the truth or you want me to lie and say I'm doin' good?"

"That bad, huh?" Echo grimaced in sympathy.

"I'm up to the gills in antivirals, now that the medics are done with me. I'll be okay in a couple of hours. But I think you need a new bodyguard for a while. The last thing you need right now is to get this stuff—trust me on that."

* * *

"I really don't think you have to worry, Omega," Fox told her once more. "Echo will have full-spectrum anti-pathogenics in the IV, even without the filtration process. It's standard Agency medical procedure. Hindsight being what it is, I probably should have ordered the medics to shoot you full as well, before I made you leave the medlab that first time.

I'm...sorry about that."

Omega waved a dismissive hand.

"No big deal. You're absolutely sure he won't get it?" she verified, pointing at Echo in the bed.

Both men nodded. Omega slipped through the door and moved to the recliner in the corner. Sinking down into it and leaning back, she put up the footrest and closed her eyes. The two men watched as all the energy seemed to drain from her.

"Fox, maybe you need to get another hospital bed in here," Echo said. His voice was sardonic, but there was concern in his eyes. "Looks like Alpha One is down for the count."

Omega shook her head slowly, eyes shut.

"No. Echo's bodyguard is still on duty. Just give me a few minutes." She opened her eyes then, and stared at the ceiling. "And some hot coffee would be nice..." She shivered and closed her eyes again.

* * *

Fox and Echo exchanged a significant glance. Fox moved to Omega and lightly touched her forehead. Turning to Echo, he mouthed the word, *Hot.* Echo nodded.

"Omega?" a sympathetic Fox said. "I'll go get you something to drink."

"No, no," Omega said, pushing the recliner upright with an effort. "The Director shouldn't wait on the junior agent. If you'll stay with Echo for a minute and play bodyguard, I'll get it myself." She left the room.

"She's as stubborn as I am," Echo remarked, looking after her.

"And that's going some," Fox shot back. Echo grinned.

"Now, about this plan..." Echo said.

Chapter 10

Omega approached the busy entrance to the Medical Department with a disposable cup of steaming coffee, negotiating the moving crowd of aliens and agents with care, so as not to spill her scalding beverage. She paused just outside the door and took a sip, then sighed, in a combination of bone-weariness and pleasure at the feel of the soothing hot drink on her raw throat.

Nudging open the door with an elbow, she was abruptly confronted by a grim-faced Fox, flanked by Romeo and India. Fox pressed her gently back into the corridor, his hand against her shoulder.

“I’m sorry, Omega,” he said, very quiet.

“What? I don’t—” Omega tried to push past the trio, who moved together to block her path. “Look, guys, I just want to see Echo. Let me—”

Other beings in the corridor slowed down, shocked, as they recognized what was happening. A small audience formed.

“I’m sorry, honey,” India said then, voice gentle. “I know you want to see him. But it’s...too late.”

“No. What...what are you saying, India?” Omega’s face had gone very pale.

“Echo...Echo’s gone, Meg,” Romeo said softly, choking slightly on the words.

Omega went white to the lips. Romeo caught her as she swayed dizzily. The coffee cup crashed to the floor, its contents splattering the nearest wall before puddling on the floor and cooling.

“Gone? You mean—? But...but he...he was fine when I left...I just went down to the break room to get a cup of...”

Fox took her gently by the shoulders.

“It happened suddenly, Omega; the projectile did a lot of damage. All at once, he just...well. There was a bleeder that the medics missed tying off. By the time they realized...it was...too late. One minute he seemed fine, the next...he was gone.”

"No," Omega whispered, then stronger, "NO! Let ME see! He's not...he's NOT..." She stared in disbelief at the three grief-stricken faces watching her in mute sympathy. "Oh, dear God. He can't be. He CAN'T... not ECHO..."

Just then, a gurney was wheeled through the door by a medtech. A body bag lay on it.

"Damn," Fox grumbled. "What timing. Get him out of here," he harshly commanded the orderly.

"NO!!" Omega cried, throwing out an imperative hand. "STOP! I want to see...for myself..."

Fox, India, and Romeo exchanged glances, then Fox nodded. India moved to the gurney and pulled apart the special velcro at one end of the bag.

Omega's breath caught in a single sob, quickly stifled, as Echo's ashen face was revealed. She reached out a tentative hand and ran a testing fingertip across his cheek. The dead-white face of her partner lay like cold stone beneath her touch.

"He...he IS..." Her voice was little more than a whisper. "Oh, dear God. Noooo..." She buried her face in her hands. "Echooo..." she keened softly.

"Come with me, Omega," Fox said quietly, motioning the orderly to continue. The cluster of shocked observers that had formed began to disperse, whispering to one another. "There's a little...tradition...we have when we...lose a partner."

* * *

Omega walked blindly into the Core, guided only by Fox's hand on her shoulder. The stark head-to-toe black of her attire was relieved solely by the whiteness of her face. Around their feet, the soft lighting between the floor tiles fell dark; the wall lighting, too, diminished. A halo of blackness followed their progress across the large room.

As the other Core denizens saw her black shirt, noted how the floor lighting ceased, and comprehended the significance, the huge room fell silent.

"Oh, no. No...not ECHO," she heard someone gasp.

"Did SHE—" someone else remarked, bitter.

"She tried it once before, didn't she?"

"Lay off, dammit. Echo trusted her. So do I."

As they neared the ramp to Fox's office, Omega raised her head, and her eyes started to blaze with a fierce light. Suddenly, at the top of the ramp, she wheeled to face Fox. Omega's sharp, angry, agonized tone cut through the dead air of the Core.

"Call them in, Fox. I demand the right to face my partner's murderers."

Fox nodded and turned to his assistants, Lima and Bravo, who had come to meet the pair.

"Call in Monkey, Sierra, Tare, and Yankee. Have them report to my office immediately. And make sure to put Security on standby. I want a full, armed guard contingent prepped and ready for criminal escort." A shocked buzz filled the huge concourse as Fox and Omega entered his office and closed the door.

* * *

As the four summoned Agents filed into Fox's office, they found an arrangement inside like a tribunal. Four empty chairs sat before Fox's desk. Behind the desk were two more chairs—Fox and Omega filled them. Wordlessly, Fox gestured to the empty chairs. The four men sat.

Behind them, the door into the Core was left...wide open. A curious, anxious cluster of beings formed around the base of the ramp to listen, not daring to go farther...especially with the cadre of highly-armed security agents now standing guard at the top.

Fox and Omega said absolutely nothing, but continued to gaze sternly at the four agents. Omega's eyes were disconcertingly, almost feverishly, bright in her pale face. At last, when the silent tension in the room had reached explosive levels, Omega spoke one word. One single, furious, agony-filled word.

"*WHY?*" she demanded.

The four shifted uncomfortably, looking at each other, at the walls, anywhere to avoid that accusing blue gaze.

"Why what?" Yankee asked, in a lame attempt to seem ingenuous.

"DON'T GIVE ME THAT!!" Fox snapped, furious. "You were SEEN. Echo talked before he—"

"Not to mention the ballistics report," Omega added tersely, interrupting before Fox could finish his sentence—before he could say the word *died.*

The quartet grew even more uncomfortable.

"Echo...got in the way," Monkey offered finally.

Omega's voice when she responded was low, dangerous.

"Got...in...the...WAY? My partner is DEAD, and all you can say is, 'He got in the WAY'?" She rose from the chair, eyes blazing. "Got in the way of WHAT?! Your damned rogue assassination attempt?! At least ECHO was being a credit to the Suit he wore!! AND YOU DARE LABEL *ME* A TRAITOR!!" Omega stood in the middle of the floor now, the dominant presence in the room, despite her smaller stature.

"Rogue?! Hold on! Wait just a damn minute," Yankee's partner Tare interjected, flinching before the Fury in front of him. "Tell her, Fox."

"Tell her WHAT?" Fox replied harshly.

"About the orders."

"What orders?"

"The for-your-eyes-only orders you gave the four of us," Yankee filled in. "The orders for the Prime Minister's assassination on the basis of planetary security."

Omega turned to stare hard at Fox.

"I issued no such orders," Fox replied firmly.

"But Fox," Monkey said, pulling out a paper and handing it to Omega, "here they are. We followed them to the letter."

Omega scanned the page, then handed it to Fox, standing over him, grim.

"Explain," she ordered the Director. "And fast."

Fox glanced over the paper Omega gave him, then met her stone-cold eyes. Without breaking eye contact, he thumbed the intercom.

"Bravo? Would you and Lima please bring up the log of need-to-know, for-your-eyes-only orders, and display the fifty most recent entries on wall screen number three?"

Fox turned to face the five agents before him, as the requested information was displayed. He pointed without a word, and all eyes turned to the screen, studying it intently—especially a certain intense sapphire gaze. The four seated agents gasped; a confident Omega merely nodded. Then she wheeled to face the four.

"The last such order was issued more than one month prior to my first arrival at Division One Headquarters—nearly a year ago, gentlemen. The entry log is automatic and tamper-proof. Your orders are forgeries. Care to explain how they come to be in your possession?"

The four stared at her, flabbergasted. Then Monkey volunteered an answer in a weak voice.

"They were...delivered electronically...over a, a secure link...according to protocol. Sierra was the designated recipient and...and distributor," he managed to get out. Sierra stiffened. "You...you mean we...and now Echo is...?"

Sick at heart, Omega turned away and leaned one hand against the wall, head and shoulders bowed in sorrow and deep grief, as Fox set Bravo and Lima on the task of tracing the forgery transmission.

"God help us," Tare whispered. "We killed a fellow agent for nothing."

"And the four of you are hereby under arrest, according to Galactic Penal Code section 2, paragraph 12." Fox walked to the door of his office. "Security, please come in and escort Agents Monkey, Sierra, Tare, and Yankee to confinement until their hearing. Treat them as galactic criminals. Initiate standard interrogation. Oh, and contact the Arcturan embassy to assist in the interrogation."

As five heavily-armed Security agents in black body armor led the four pale, corrupt agents away, Omega sank back into her chair beside the Director. Fox closed the door to his office and looked at her, concerned.

"That's taken care of. Rest a little while now, tekhter. You're burning up."

A weary, saddened Omega shook her head as her grief-stricken gaze followed the four disgraced agents' progress through the Core, under armed guard, via Fox's bay window.

"No, Fox. You know I can't do that yet. There's one last thing I have to do...something Echo wanted..."

* * *

"Fox," India protested in his office after Omega left, "she's not up to this. She's too ill..."

"I know, India. But she says the illness will work to her advantage. She's determined to go through with it. And you know what that means."

"Yeah. She'll do it if it kills her," muttered India. "No wonder you assigned her to the partner you did."

"I thought it made perfect sense," Fox agreed.

* * *

"Hello, Mr. Prime Minister."

Omega's cold voice in the emptiness of the hotel room startled the alien, who had been sitting at the desk, studying the transcripts of the negotiations to that point. He spun, to see a platinum blonde Agent dressed head to toe in solid black, even to her shirt. He blinked all three eyes in surprise.

"How did you get in—?" he demanded to know.

"Surprised? You shouldn't be. I'm Agent Omega—the sole remaining member of the Agency's Alpha One team. The last of the first..."

"Yes, I recognize you," the Prime Minister said, offering the Lambda Andromedan equivalent of a smile, though it was a little wobbly, and he knew it; there was something very, very odd about this Agent's demeanor, and it unnerved the planetary potentate—as did the head-to-toe black clothing she now wore. "You threw the party. And you were here the night of the assassination attempt. You and your partner saved my life."

"Oh, come now, Mr. Prime Minister. Surely you don't take me for a complete fool. I'm fully aware of the metabolic effects of titanium on Lambda Andromedan physiology. Funny thing is," she continued, walking—almost swaggering—across the room toward him, "it doesn't have QUITE the same effect on humans. That's why I watched my partner carried in a body bag to the Agency morgue a little while ago." She smiled—a chilling, inappropriate expression, eyes unsettlingly bright in her pale face. "Do you know something else? Particle beams have the same effects on Lambda Andromedans as titanium does on humans."

She suddenly pulled a proto-cyclotron blaster and pointed it at the

Prime Minister. All three of the Minister's eyes widened in shock. She laughed then; it sounded like ice shattering, brittle and tinkling and sharp.

"But...but you're a Pan-Galactic Agent..."

"So were the men you conned into trying to 'assassinate' you. Don't try to deny it," Omega added as the alien opened his mouth to protest. "We have the orders you faked, and with some effort we were able to trace the transmission of those 'orders'—straight back to you. So I claimed my right as the surviving partner...to 'bring you in.' Yeah, we'll see if THAT happens." A grim Omega chuckled, then moved even closer. "Do you know what the penalty is on Earth for a conspiracy ending in murder? Do you know what the GALACTIC penalty is?" She laughed again, that same brittle, sharp sound of black mirth.

"But I...but..." the Prime Minister glanced in desperation around the empty bedroom, searching for someone, someTHING, he could wield against this terrifying, emotionless Agent. *Are you INSANE?!* he wondered, badly frightened. *You LAUGH when discussing your partner's death? Tortok! Where are you??*

"Never a bodyguard around when you need one, is there?" Omega smiled again, a cold, deadly smile, her eyes glittering blue ice. "And too many around just when you DON'T want them. Oh, no. You're not getting off THIS time. Not from me. Never again." She took a step toward the alien, and he backed away.

"Why are you so...so...implacable..." A sudden thought struck the Prime Minister as he remembered Echo and Omega, nearly inseparable each time he had seen them, as well as the aborted mistletoe prank at the party, the explanation of which Fox had provided. "Partners...dear Maker... were you also mates?!"

Omega calmly backed the alien into a corner.

"If it's any business of yours. And what do you care? You surely didn't care when you set up the entire hit. I swear, on the dead body of my partner Echo, soon you won't care about anything at all."

* * *

Echo's eyes blinked in surprise at the exchange between Omega and the Prime Minister.

"That...was an...interesting improvisation..." he remarked, mildly perturbed, as he lay propped up on the gurney watching events unfold on a viewscreen down in the morgue. *What...exactly...does she know, or suspect? That's...what? Twice, now, she's alluded to it? Three times? And more importantly,* he decided, *how does SHE feel about it?*

"It was brilliant," India replied, watching the viewscreen with him. "She didn't actually say yea or nay. So it leaves the Prime Minister guessing as to your real relationship. The closer he thinks you were—well, ARE, given you're sitting here, not dead—the more dangerous she becomes."

"Damn, that girl can act," Romeo said, beside India. "I didn't have any idea she was capable of this kind of...of..."

"Menace?" supplied Fox. "Utterly implacable, heartless rage?"

"Yeah. All o' that. Wonder where she's gettin' it from."

Echo studied the familiar face on the screen, the face belonging to the woman who had become the center of his world. It was unaccustomedly cold, hard, with an edge of pain in the depths of the sapphire eyes. He felt his own face become drawn with sympathetic pain as he watched, and he winced despite himself.

"Motivation? Oh, that's easy," he noted. "I know exactly where she's pulling from. Partly, anyway. And it's anything but heartless."

"Where, then?" India shot a glance at him, then frowned at his expression. "Echo, are you all right?"

"Yeah, I'm fine."

"You don't look like it. You look like you're in a lot of pain."

"Nah. I just..." Echo shook his head, and waved a hand at the viewscreen. "We've talked, Meg and me. I get what she's feeling right now."

"Oh. Kind of empathizing the emotional pain?" India asked.

"Yeah, I guess."

"So what's driving her?" Fox wondered.

"You know how we're pretty sure that Meg's family was murdered by the same alien that enhanced, manipulated and programmed her..."

"Yeah. Slug," Romeo replied.

"Well, this is the woman finally getting to confront the alien that killed her family twelve years ago this week. Right at this instant, the Prime Minister is a substitute for Slug." Echo's voice was quiet.

"And it probably only adds to the effect that the Prime Minister just nearly had killed a member of her current 'family,'" India added.

The Agents were silent, watching the tableau on screen.

"In that case, I hope she stays in control," Fox said then.

"She will," Echo said, his confidence unshakeable. Suddenly a movement in the shadows behind Omega caught his eye. "Switch to angle seven!"

The view changed, and the four in the morgue saw one of the Minister's bodyguards slip into the room.

"Oh, hell," Fox exclaimed, "the other agents let one get by." He reached for his cell phone.

"Ease up, Fox," Echo said, waving him off. "Meg just realized he's there."

"How do you know?"

"I can tell."

* * *

Agent Omega? the voice sounded unexpectedly in her head.

Ambassador Zz'r'p? That you? You 'sound'...different.

No, Agent. I am Tt'l'k, the ambassador's new assistant. I am here with your colleagues, outside the Prime Minister's suite. I have just arrived.

Tt'l'k, nice to meet you. But I've got a situation here...

I am aware of that, the telepathic voice told her. *Especially behind you.*

What?! Omega suddenly realized that the flu had reduced her alertness, and that there was indeed someone sneaking up behind her. *Thanks, Tt'l'k. I'm on it now.*

You are welcome, Agent. Given your illness, I thought it might be a timely warning.

Thanks, and yeah. What do you need, then?

I have been interrogating the rogue agents, and have discovered something YOU need, Tt'l'k informed her, *and quickly.*

Shoot. Oooh, bad pun.

Terran humor. Omega sensed Tt'l'k's mental shrug. *Sierra is not an Agent, Omega. The original Sierra is dead.*

*Oh, no...*Omega was grieved.

This creature captured and killed him about three or four months ago, and downloaded Sierra's memories in order to take his place. Then he began subverting Sierra's partner and friends, in order to set them up for the assassination attempt.

But how is that possible? Omega asked.

He is a cyborg polymorph from the Omega Centauri cluster, Tt'l'k explained.

Lemme guess. His true form is seven and a half feet tall, with gills, purple scales, and black feathers. Omega was bleakly amused.

I...do not understand...

Never mind. Terran humor. Anything else?

He has previously been apprehended by the Agency, and holds a grudge against them. Prior to Sierra's murder, he met privately with the Prime Minister on Lambda Andromedae IV, not III, in order to coordinate the infiltration.

That's interesting...

HE is the one who attempted to kill Agent Echo in the hotel with a grenade to frame you. And he passed Agency inside information to a Dabanoran called...Michael Smithers? He received his instructions via ultraviolet-light codes in Rockefeller Plaza.

Damn. I remember that! Romeo and I were there! So that's what the coded messages were about. Very interesting. Huh. Talking Christmas trees. Seems to be a theme this year.

Again, I...do not understand.

I'll explain later. Thanks, Tt'l'k. Gotta go now. Company's coming.

Good luck, Agent. I will see that the Director is informed.

* * *

Omega's every nerve ending was now on alert as she sensed the bodyguard's approach, but her expression never changed. She waved the blaster inches away from the Prime Minister's face as she continued her carefully-worded tirade.

"Why? Why did you want to have us involved in an assassination attempt? It would have completely discredited the organization...destroyed it..." She mulled over Tt'l'k's information, as well as the other puzzle pieces.

'*...The word on the street was that...it was somebody powerful that the Agency pissed off,*' she recalled. Suddenly the pieces fell into place like the hypercube puzzle.

"You WANTED the Agency discredited! You WANTED us out of the picture! YOU'RE responsible for the toys, the cartoons, the movie! Aren't you?!" Omega shook the Prime Minister like a terrier shaking a rat.

The bodyguard leaped. And in one fluid move, Omega shoved the Prime Minister back hard against the wall and executed a high spinning kick, catching poor Tortok in the head. He flew, unconscious, across the room, where he knocked over a chair and lay still.

* * *

"Ingenious!" Fox exclaimed. "I think Omega just put all of the puzzle pieces together for us!"

"LOOK!" India exclaimed, as Tortok jumped Omega.

Echo's body tensed automatically, ready, regardless of his still-weakened condition, to go into battle beside his partner. As she executed the kick in perfect form to powerful result, he clenched his fist, smiled slightly, and murmured under his breath, "Attagirl!"

But then he instinctively sat up, despite the protest in his wounded belly, and reached out to catch her.

* * *

Omega staggered badly on the landing, nearly falling as congestion and fever from the flu threw off her equilibrium. She recovered quickly, and shoved the blaster's muzzle up under what passed for the Prime Minister's chin. Then she struggled to still her spinning head, and continued.

"Tell me why?!" Her voice was threatening. "Why did my...why did Echo...have to die? Why destroy the Agency? Tell me, and maybe I'll only turn you in, instead of..." the muzzle pressed harder.

"Retribution," the Prime Minister finally answered then, fairly spitting out the word. His own voice was stone-cold. "Several years ago, the Agency confiscated all of my luggage. That is where the projectile weapon that killed your mate came from. That is why they confiscated it—it seems I had neglected to file some idiotic permit. As if a planetary leader, who had received death threats from a madman, needed to bother with such trivialities!"

"Wait—luggage?! A man is dead and an organization on the verge of destruction because of lost luggage??" Omega demanded, not sure whether to laugh or rage.

"MY mate was in my luggage! She almost DIED! She has STILL not fully recovered! YOU should understand such matters now." The Prime Minister stared into Omega's eyes, his own triple gaze callous and cruel. "I determined then that I would not stop until the organization that had caused her such distress was destroyed. I decided that the best way of doing so was a two-pronged attack. First, I would expose the Agency via the planet's own vaunted marketing and entertainment media. Second, I would discredit them in the eyes of other planetary entities, especially the Sydys Concordat and the Pan-Galactic Council. My entire political career since that time has been with this sole purpose. And I have succeeded," the Prime Minister gloated. "Your organization is exposed, your agents no longer free to act, your personnel have been involved in an assassination attempt, and your mate was murdered by one of his own."

Omega withdrew the blaster and quickly stepped back to the center of the room.

"Don't worry on my account. No mate of mine is dead," she said, activating her cell phone. "Although another fellow agent is. Fox, did you get all that?"

* * *

"Down to the nuances of expression, Omega." Fox grinned, speaking into his phone, which he had placed in speaker mode and laid on the table beside the viewscreen, so the others could hear.

"Good. Send in the other agents, then," Omega said, and they watched her glance around the room on the viewing screen.

"On their way. Good job."

"Thanks," Omega replied.

"You had me a little worried, the way you were waving that blaster around, tekhter," Fox commented, not bothering to hide his affection as he watched the cleanup crew file into the room and take the Prime Minister into custody. He had decided that, after the last couple of weeks or so, Omega could stand to hear it, anyway, so that she would understand how much her Agency Director appreciated her. "I mean, I know you know what you're doing, but I also know you were madder than hell at what they did to Echo, so..." He shrugged. "Accidents happen. And oy, how you were brandishing that thing, yung froy!"

"You mean this thing?" The four in the morgue watched on the monitor as Omega turned and threw the blaster, hard, against the decorative marble wall. It shattered into hundreds of plastic shards, flying about the room. "I knew that trip to the toy store wouldn't be wasted," Omega remarked with a tired smirk.

* * *

"All right, we've made a clean sweep," Fox stated, satisfied.

They were back in Echo's hospital room, and the OFFICIAL word had spread swiftly that Echo was, in fact, alive and doing well, thanks in large measure to the heroic efforts of his partner—whose exploits, in the doing, were deliberately included in that word. Echo was, at that moment, sitting in one of the visitor chairs—the recliner, to be specific, though his tall, powerful frame was now clad in a medlab jumpsuit—conversing with Fox and Alpha Two. Meanwhile, Fox filled them in on what he and Omega had arranged after putting the three rogue agents plus one impostor into custody. Fox and Romeo had pulled all the visitor chairs out from the wall and arranged them to create a conversation circle, thus ensuring Echo would stay put and rest, rather than over-exert.

"All of the agents involved are accounted for, and the fake Sierra and the Prime Minister are in custody. We'll handle them...appropriately." Fox's expression was foreboding. "We broadcast the recorded confession to the

Earth-based aliens, the Sydys Concordat signatories, and the PGLEIA governing body. None of which are happy, I might add. I fully expect either a swift 'no-confidence' vote in the Lambda Andromedae system's government, or PGLEIA will levy sanctions—whichever comes first. Possibly both. What's left?"

"Where's Meg?" Echo asked.

"Right here," a hoarse whisper said behind him, near the door. He turned in surprise and stared at his partner, as a dizzy Omega entered the room and wobbled up to him, stumbling twice; she shrugged, obviously exhausted. "Lotta emoting doesn't seem to do a sore throat much good. And my head keeps tryin' to go into low Earth orbit without the rest of me. Fox, tell Security thanks for the ride over to the hotel and back, please. No way in hell was I gonna drive like this."

"Wilco, Omega. And I'm glad you had the wisdom to request the assistance."

"Do you feel as bad as you look?" Echo wondered, worried. Omega grinned ruefully.

"Echo, you really have a way with a compliment, buddy mine." She watched as he winced, then she grinned again. "Yeah, I feel like I look—lousy. But it's good to see you up and around, metaphorically speaking, anyway. How are you?"

"Pretty decent, for a dead man." Echo returned her grin.

"Now that's another thing. No offense to Agency tradition, but can I get out of this morbid black shirt now? I feel like the Ghost of Christmas Yet To Come." The others laughed. She sighed, amending, "And I hope I never have to do this again."

The room grew grave at the addendum.

"Yes, Omega, you can. And you did a damn good job. The *Black Suits* movie should've cast you," Fox commended her. "And Echo, it was an excellent idea. It broke everything wide open, especially with your partner on point for it." Echo nodded his thanks. "And your acting job wasn't half bad, either. Most convincing un-stiff stiff I've seen lately."

"Well, the solid hologram disguise helped," Echo averred.

Fox and Echo both grinned. It was Omega's turn to wince, and Echo, spotting the expression, sobered immediately.

"Hey, India, lemme ask you," Omega whispered as she aimed for the door, apparently intent on going back to her quarters to change shirts. "When are the blasted antivirals gonna kick in?"

"You mean they haven't yet? What did they give you?" India asked, surprised. Omega turned back toward her, brows knit.

"Mmm...what was the name of that...imflox-something or other."

"Imfloxidine?"

"That sounds like it."

"It should kick in any time now. I'm surprised it hasn't already. But let me warn you, when it does, you'll get really lightheaded—"

"Oooo. Too late. We have liftoff. The Shuttle has cleared the tower..." Omega nosed over across the hospital bed and simply lay there, unmoving. "I...don't think I'm goin' anywhere for about five or ten minutes..."

"Probably the best place for you," Echo remarked, grinning at Omega's metaphor as he stood stiffly and moved to her side. "Romeo, Fox, help me get her properly into the bed, guys. She's gonna slide off the side into the floor, like that."

"Don' hurt yourself," a groggy Omega murmured as the three men lifted her and laid her, still face down, on the bed—lengthwise, instead of partway across it. "...'At belly wound o' yours still not..."

"That's why I asked Romeo and Fox to help. They did the majority of the lifting, and I just aimed you," Echo said quietly, as he removed her jacket and shoes, coaxed her to roll over, and loosened her tie. India spread a blanket over her. "Meg? You comfortable now? Meg?"

Omega didn't answer. After a few moments, a soft snore managed to escape her congested respiratory system, and the others smiled.

"She's gone," Romeo observed.

"Oh, hell yeah. And needs it, by all accounts. How long will she be out of it?" Echo asked India.

"Not long. Maybe an hour, if that much. This is a new drug we just got from a treaty. It marshals the body's entire resources to combat the virus. Everything else except vital systems kind of goes on standby. When she comes back around, she'll be fine. Still tired, most likely, especially considering the hours she's been keeping, but she'll be okay."

"Does somebody need to watch her?" Echo wondered.

"Umm...it probably wouldn't hurt," India decided. "Just so she doesn't fall in case she tries to get up. I doubt she will, 'cause she looks to be down for the count, but I've heard of cases where the patients did."

"All right," Echo concluded. "In that case, would you please run by her quarters and bring her a white shirt? That way, she can change as soon as she wakes up. If I know her—"

"And you do," Fox interrupted.

"—Meg will want that as soon as she comes to."

"Okeydoke," an amiable India agreed. "Back shortly."

* * *

"There you lot are," Fox said with a smile as Echo and Omega entered his office several days later. "Back to normal?" Romeo and India, already seated, nodded greetings.

"Normal? Around here? What's that?" Omega joked with a grin. "I'm just glad the medication didn't choose one of my Oscar-winning performances to kick in."

"Flu all gone?" Fox pressed.

"Yup. That antiviral stuff kicked its ass. I feel pretty decent."

"Echo? How about you, zun?" Fox followed up.

"I'm fine. Docs still got me on light duty, but I'm okay."

"Good," Fox replied, pleased yet concerned, "but take it EASY. That belly wound won't take a lot for a while, no matter how much you'd like it to." Echo nodded. "Has Omega been taking good care of you?"

"Trying to, Fox," Omega said, shooting her partner a mildly frustrated glance. "When he'll let me."

"Baby, barrel-jumping on ice skates notwithstanding, you're not a helicopter," Echo pointed out. "Ease up on all the hovering."

"I am not hovering!"

"Echo," India interrupted, as Echo frowned and opened his mouth to reply. "Zebra and I gave Meg special instructions to keep a VERY close eye on you. We talked it over with Zarnix, and all three of us decided you were at risk for herniation if you weren't really careful, until you finished healing up. So we told Meg to stay on your case to ensure you didn't pick up anything heavier than about two pounds, or strain yourself trying to do something, until Medical gave the go-ahead. She's only doing what we asked."

"Oh," Echo said, face falling slightly. "So she has specific instructions to hover."

"Pretty much, yeah," India said, shooting Omega a grin. Omega scowled.

"I'm not hovering," she grumbled. "Just because you don't know when to lie down and rest, keep wanting to get back in the weight room, forget to take your pain meds, and I keep up with all of it for you, doesn't make it hovering. I didn't hear you complaining when I baked that fresh batch of shortbread...because you ASKED."

India's eyebrows rose in alarm at that enumeration. Everyone in the room saw it. Fox, concerned, sat forward and opened his mouth to speak, when Echo cut him off.

"Okay, okay, I get the picture," Echo offered, voice quiet. "I'm a lousy patient."

"No, just an inattentive one," Omega replied earnestly, expression lightening a bit as her partner capitulated. "I'm not coddling you, Echo, I swear. I haven't said one thing about your always wanting to walk down to the deli for lunch, just to get out and move around—because the walking is gonna be good for you. But you're HEALING, Ace! You need to rest once we get BACK from that lunch! And you can't stay up until all hours reading, even if you don't feel sleepy. AND you can't go forgetting your meds, because then you start hurting and you tense up, and that makes it hurt worse, and you go into a downward spiral. And yes, I CAN see when you start hurting! You gotta give yourself time for your gut to heal up properly."

"She's right, Echo," India agreed. "I know you're tough, and probably hate the pain meds, 'cause they ARE strong..."

"They make me feel all looped," Echo noted with distaste. "Like I got cotton for brains or something."

"I know...but you'll heal a lot faster if you'll follow the protocol on the meds," India pointed out. "If you have trouble remembering to take 'em, 'cause it's not part of your routine, I get that. Especially if the meds themselves are throwing off your memory, which they probably are, by making you fuzzy-headed. But let Meg help you with that; it's why we gave her the assignment, instead of sending in a nurse-practitioner every day." India shrugged. "We thought you'd appreciate that more than some stranger coming in to see about you, and she agreed."

"Oh..." Echo bit his lip, then threw an apologetic glance at his partner.

"Accepted," Omega murmured, answering what he hadn't verbalized. "And I'm sorry if it seemed like I was nagging you; I'll work on a little better bedside manner. But you scared me a couple times there, Ace. Like that time you were reading and fell asleep in the recliner, and went way past time for your next dose of pain medications. Stupid me assumed that, because you were asleep, you'd already TAKEN the stuff..."

"Oh, yeah. And then I woke up all stiff, forgot myself, and tried to stand up..."

"I was in my study, emailing with Travis over that concept we're working on. I heard you yell, and a couple loud thuds, and I didn't know WHAT you'd done to yourself," she pointed out.

"What DID 'e do?" Romeo wondered, worried.

"Nothing much, actually," Echo explained. "As soon as I tried to sit forward and stand up, the gunshot pitched holy hell. I don't remember yelling, but Meg swears up and down I did, so I believe her. It hurt enough, I probably did, just on instinct. But I was letting the footrest down at the same time, so I guess one of the thuds was when I let go of the handle to catch my guts in case they fell out, and the footrest dropped. And the other thud was me, halfway outta the damn chair from momentum before falling back into it when I couldn't straighten up, 'cause my center of mass was still over my ass, so..."

"Speaking of ass, I hauled mine across my apartment and into his den at maximum speed, to find him sprawled across his recliner, one leg hooked over the chair arm, head hanging off the other side, clutching his stomach with both hands," Omega said. "I just KNEW he'd managed to tear things open all over again. But there wasn't any blood, so I made him pull up his shirt so I could check things. I didn't see any fresh bruising, so..."

"...She turned into an inquisitor," Echo tag-teamed, "except I was still gasping from the pain, and couldn't say a damn thing. I think it took me five minutes before I could say a word."

"Well, that should have taught you several things," India declared, chuckling. "One, you fell asleep because your body needed the rest. Two, if you took your prescriptions on time, it wouldn't have hurt so bad. Oh, you probably would have had some twinges—and will, for a while—but you'd have made it upright and vertical."

"I get it," Echo murmured. "And Meg DID bring my next dose and make me take it right off, then she stayed there, sittin' on the couch, until it had kicked in. She even brought me a Diet Coke, so I didn't have to get up and get it myself until things stopped hurting so much."

"Good. She's doing her job."

"I try," Omega murmured with a sigh. "Lord knows, I don't want anything else to happen to him. What happened Christmas Eve Night was plenty enough for a good long while."

Fox watched as Echo shot her a pained, almost ashamed glance, then dropped his gaze to the floor. The Director chewed his lip for a moment in thought before deciding to act.

"All right, then," Fox broke in, preventing any more complaints from arising. "Enough of all that. Omega, keep up the good work; Echo, LET her keep up the good work. That's an order, Alpha Line Chief."

"Yes sir," Alpha One said in unison.

"Good. Now, we've got this whole mess wrapped up except for one small detail, and I need some ideas."

"We still have the problem of a little publicity." A grim Echo gazed at Fox.

"Right."

"Is the film still in production?" Omega wondered.

"No, it's not, and that's a good piece of news," Fox affirmed. "The Legal department at our Los Angeles Office managed to lay a court order on their collective asses for trademark infringement, just like I expected, and the judge agreed. The film has been killed, the cartoon canceled, and the toys taken out of production and pulled from store shelves. We've also managed to invoke a recall, so most of the toys that had already been sold have also been returned and are being destroyed. More, the Agency has managed to get in and out with all of the film footage, remaining inventory, prototypes and all—including the footage of Echo and Romeo, which we absolutely HAD to have in hand. So that's clear. Your advance planning worked like a charm, Echo. That brainstorming you and Omega did while you were still in the medlab was masterful. Once I had the Alpha One plan in hand, I activated it while Omega was still en route to confront the Prime Minister."

"That's some serious good news," India decided.

"Yeah, it is," Echo agreed. "And I'm glad it worked."

"Me, too," Omega averred.

"I was ready for it t' get over with, too," Romeo allowed.

"But we still have the problem of all the people who remember it," Echo pointed out. "And that's pretty much everybody in the country who's a kid, has kids, is a film buff, in the film industry, is a science fiction fan..."

"Way too many to individually brain-bleach," Omega observed.

"Right," said Fox. "But we still need to figure out how to handle it."

The office fell still as its occupants drifted into thought.

"What we need is a massive brain bleach, somehow," India murmured, and Echo raised an eyebrow. "Can we assume that this hasn't gotten outside North America yet?"

"All indications are," Fox said, nodding, "that it hasn't yet gotten out of the States—maybe part of Canada. There was some film scuttlebutt in Europe and the Far East, but nothing of any real danger to us, because the details hadn't been released internationally yet."

"Well, that helps," India commented.

"Yes," Fox affirmed, "but we're still looking at probably three hundred and fifty million people, at least."

* * *

"What's today's Earth date?" Echo's eyes narrowed. "I lost a couple days there..."

"It's late on December 29th, Echo," Fox answered him. Echo was quiet for a moment, thinking, as his colleagues watched him.

"Did we ever establish that the brain bleacher transmits on a video broadcast?" he wondered, after a few seconds.

"Yes," Fox replied, "quite well, actually, in all forms of video media, at least for human wavelength ranges."

Echo looked up—into Omega's intense blue gaze.

"Yes," she told him thoughtfully, "I think it will work."

"Dick should be able to help us," Echo told her. "He's an alien himself—he's from Kref, in the 55 Cancri system—so he has a vested interest."

"Really?" Omega murmured, raising an eyebrow. "But he's not dead?"

"Nah. He still runs his production company. But he had to fake it, or everybody woulda figured out something was weird."

"Aha. No wonder he never seemed to really age..."

"You ever think it's spooky watchin' them talk an' junk?" Romeo nudged India and muttered. "Like, they know what the other one's thinkin' before he thinks it?"

"Hey, guys," India waved at Echo and Omega, "maybe you two have a telepathic thing going there, but would you mind filling in the rest of us?"

Echo and Omega looked at them in surprise for a moment, then Echo explained.

"The ball. Times Square. New Year's Eve."

* * *

"All right, Romeo, 'whassup, bro'?" Omega asked her fellow Agent with a smile, as they strolled through a snowy Central Park the next day.

"Aw, I thought maybe I oughta give you a heads-up 'bout your partner, Meg," Romeo replied. He didn't return her smile.

"About Echo?" Omega clarified, looking at Romeo's concerned face. "Oh no. Is something wrong? His wound..."

"Naw, girl, nothin' like that."

"Good." Omega drew a relieved breath. "I was afraid India had asked you to warn me...never mind. What, then?"

"Look. I know he's told ya all about his past before the Agency, right?"

"Yeah, he has. Showed me all the files and everything. Even gave me the password, so I have access."

"Good. Has he told you about leaving the Agency and then comin' back?"

"Well...I know he did...but I don't know why. That wasn't...well, it was in the records, but it didn't have a lotta detail." She shrugged. "I coulda asked, I suppose. I didn't wanna pry, though. I figured he'd tell me when he was ready."

"Uh-huh." Romeo sighed. "Thought so."

"Romeo...what's up? Is there a problem?"

"Well, there was this lady named Chase. I don't remember her last name; it's been a couple years back now. It 'uz kinda like how India an' I met; things went south on a mission, an' this Chase helped 'im out. They hit it off, an'...well, he left in order to try to go an'..." Romeo shrugged. "Make a life with 'er, I think. I hadda go handle some shit onna West Coast while all this was goin' down—we were shorthanded after the invasion, so Fox hadda split us up temporarily—so I don't really know all th' details. But it was over Christmas an' New Years, I remember that much."

"So...he left, to try to develop a relationship with her," Omega pondered, "but...he came back?"

"Right."

"Without her?"

"Yeah."

"What happened?"

"I dunno," Romeo answered with a shrug. "Echo won't talk about it. But I could tell, when he got back, he was hurtin'. Not like just anybody coulda seen it, though. You gotta really know the man, you get what I'm sayin'? YOU'D have seen it. An' I saw it. But India prob'ly wouldn't have, so much."

"Yeah, I understand. You and I have partnered with him, so we'd know him better. And he'd be more likely to let his guard down a little around us."

"Exactly. Fox knows everything, I'm pretty sure, but he ain't talkin' either. An' then Echo got all weird while YOU were gone, tryin' t' get your head together after that whole mess with Slug—which none of us blamed ya for doin', just so's you know. We kinda figured you needed space to figure things out; we were just worried you wouldn't come back. Especially Echo, I'm pretty sure. Me 'n' India...well, t' be honest, we didn't think you WERE comin' back. We 'uz glad t' be wrong, though."

"Me, too. And to be honest, Romeo, I didn't expect to come back, either," Omega admitted. "But...I think this is kinda where I belong, now. It's the only place I really feel like I fit in, you know? I mean, what with the genetic engineering and restructuring and stuff..."

"Yeah, I getcha. An' that's cool with us. Me 'n India both like havin' you for a friend, girl. So anyways, back to Echo's thang. I did a little checkin' into stuff, kinda on th' sly ya know, 'cause I, um, I care 'bout Echo too, an'...an' I don't wanna see 'im hurt. An' it turns out some major serious shit came down while you were gone."

"WHAT went down, Romeo?"

"They found Chase...dead in her apartment, 'longside her new husband," Romeo murmured.

"New husband? DEAD?! Both of 'em?"

"Yeah. It was after Echo came back 'fore she got married; I managed to verify that. They'd only been married 'bout a year when they 'uz killed. I think her gettin' serious with th' other dude was maybe what made him come back; Echo ain't th' homewrecker type."

"No, I didn't figure..." Omega felt washed out to sea, trying to take in and sort through all that Romeo was telling her.

"I think it hurt 'im pretty bad, though. An' then she MARRIES th' other guy...an' then they both turn up dead. Best I could tell without stickin' my nose in so far it was gonna get cut off, Fox thinks Slug took care of Chase same as he took care o' your family, and some o' the witnesses, like Tango. Part of the manipulations to set you up to assassinate Echo, and cause Echo as much pain as possible 'til you did."

"Damn the thing! I hope it rots in hell for the pain it's caused us!"

"Yeah, you're preachin' to th' choir, girl. Like I said, though, I don't know all the details. Some of it, I've hadda kinda read b'tween the lines, 'specially right after he came back and we started workin' together again.

So I c'n tell ya, f'r instance, that she liked these funky pink an' white flowers—India says they're called stargazer lilies—an' Echo used to get 'em all th' time for her while they were seein' each other. I dunno as he's all that romantically inclined a dude as to get flowers, but he's not stupid, an' he knows ladies like their flowers."

"So...he must have been pretty serious about her, huh?"

"Yeah, I'd say so. He took SOMEthin' awful hard, 'long about the time you left, an' I told India when I found out Chase was dead, I thought that was it."

"What else?"

"Um...she liked to dance. They used to go dancin' a lot. He'd sometimes go dancin' before that—there's a dance club in the Agency—but after he came back, he never went any more. An' while I kept tryin' ta get him to go, at least until the convention, well..."

Abruptly it all fell into place in Omega's mind. Shocked, she put her gloved hands to her face.

"Oh, no, Romeo...oh, poor Echo...no wonder he didn't want to dance... or come to the party...or...and my idiotic game with the mistletoe probably seemed like I was...taunting him..."

"That's why I wanted to tell you." Romeo nodded. "I thought it was a fun game, 'til I saw the look on 'is face when you finally cornered 'im."

"Yeah...I saw that, too."

"Figured you did," Romeo said with a nod. "I saw you kinda back off a little bit, there, just b'fore the Grendel pulled down the mistletoe an' ate it."

"Chase, huh?" Omega mused quietly.

* * *

"Yeah. She was another 'pretty lady.'" Romeo sighed and shook his head, feeling for his ex-partner. *It must suck,* he thought, *t' love somebody like that, only t' find out they don't love you back. I dunno what I'd do if it turned out India didn't give a rip.*

"You met her?" Omega asked.

"Nah. Jus' saw some pictures." Romeo shrugged. "Echo had her picture pulled up on his tablet once, 'bout a week after he came back to the

Agency..."

"What did she...look...?"

"Couple years older'n you, I think. Brunette. Petite."

"My opposite, huh? Well, at least he's not getting reminded of her every time he turns around..." Omega wore an odd expression.

"Prob'ly jus' because Slug didn't think about it," Romeo said, sarcastic.

"Yeah. Listen...thanks, Romeo. I'll...try to be a little more considerate of my partner."

"No problem, Meg. Family oughta look out f'r each other." Romeo hugged her, and they wandered on.

* * *

"Uh...Echo?"

A subdued Omega, clad in off-duty black jeans and turtleneck pullover, knocked at the back door later that evening. Echo looked up from an Erikian technical journal, saw her solemn expression, and immediately laid the journal on the side table, lowering the footrest on his recliner and sitting up with a slight grimace as the belly wound tugged.

"Come on in, Meg. What's wrong?"

Omega slowly moved to the side of his chair, jammed her hands deep into her pockets, and stared at the floor intently. Echo drew his brows together in puzzled concern at her reluctant, almost ashamed, attitude.

"I...don't even know where to start," she murmured. "I mean, if you'd wanted me to know, you could've told me..."

"Told you what?"

* * *

"Romeo and I just got back from a walk in the park. We had a little... conversation," Omega offered, trying to figure out how to get started. She hadn't met her partner's eyes, but that didn't mean she wasn't watching him. So she saw when realization struck; saw, too, the flicker of pain, almost of betrayal, that flashed momentarily through golden-brown depths.

"Oh. He told you about Chase." Echo looked away.

"Yeah. What he knew, anyway."

Silence.

Anguished, Omega dropped her own gaze even farther and watched her partner with averted vision, and Echo said...nothing. He didn't even look at her.

Ow, she thought, feeling more and more hurt and rejected. *I thought there was pretty much nothing we couldn't talk about, he and I. Looks like maybe I was wrong. Bad enough to know I never had a chance—his heart was given before we ever even met. Worse to realize he doesn't even want to reminisce to me about her.*

"Do...you mind my knowing?" she finally wondered aloud.

"Does it matter?"

"Yes, Echo. It matters a lot. To me, if to no one else. I'm...trying to apologize. I'm just...not quite sure how."

* * *

"Apologize?" A surprised Echo finally looked back at Omega as she stood beside him. "For what?"

"Well...you know what they say about hindsight being 20/20. Since Romeo and I talked, I've been thinking about recent events and...and how they must've felt from your perspective, and..." Omega still had not met Echo's eyes. "I told you only a few days ago that I'd never deliberately hurt you. I was talking about physically, but...it goes for all senses of the word. Only...I DID hurt you. It wasn't deliberate; it was just ignorance of the situation. But I still hurt you." Now she looked down at him steadily. "I didn't know, Echo. I'm sorry. I don't know...what else to say." She shrugged. "I'm so sorry."

Echo gestured slightly with his left hand, and she obeyed the unspoken request, kneeling beside his chair.

"It's all right, Meg. Things have been...busy...lately. And no, I don't think I mind your knowing. We've been partners a while."

"Echo, you don't have to answer this, but was this your first Christmas, after..."

"No. Second. It's been close on two years now, since it all fell apart with her. Well, it's the first since she was killed, yeah." Echo stared thoughtfully at his hands until he felt a light touch on his forearm. He looked up into understanding blue eyes.

"I know," she murmured. "Believe me, I know."

Echo studied Omega's face for a long moment. Then he pointed at the other armchair, across from him.

"Have a seat, partner," he told her quietly. "Feel like a little heart to heart chat?"

"I...could do that, yeah," Omega said, moving to the chair and sitting down.

* * *

Alpha One and Alpha Two sat in the office of the Earth's Oldest Teenager, who not coincidentally happened to be from the fourth planet of the 55 Cancri star system, known to Earth astronomers as Harriott, but to its inhabitants as Kref.

"Truth is, Echo," Dick was saying, "I've been following the situation pretty closely, and wondering how the Agency was gonna handle it. You came to the right place. I'll be happy to help any way I can. I just have to stay...invisible...for obvious reasons."

"Good. We'll provide the equipment and the agents to install and remove it. You provide us an opportunity to do so."

"Done."

"We'll also provide you and your...protégé...with special goggle glasses and a scripted message," Omega added, "for you to read once the ball drops."

"No problem," Dick replied. "Say, this is pretty massive. You sure this will work?"

"Yes," Omega answered.

"You ever done anything this big before?"

"No," Echo replied.

"But you're still sure."

"Yes," Alpha One replied in unison.

"What about you guys?" Dick asked, turning. "Romeo? India?" They nodded.

"We think it'll work too," Romeo added. "But it's their baby." He jerked a thumb at Echo and Omega. "We're givin' support and backup on this one."

"All right, Alpha One's the boss, then," Dick responded. "When do you want access?"

"As late as possible," Echo said, "to avoid accidental detection. Preferably sometime early New Year's Eve."

"Mmm," Dick considered. "Okay, I can manage that. Who will install the equipment? You and Omega?"

"Half-right," Echo said. "Meg will work with India."

Omega sat up straighter, and India said, "Whaat?!"

"This is news to me," Omega murmured. "What gives?"

"You know Romeo and I bear too much resemblance to those actors to appear in public right now, Meg. Besides, the damn medics won't let me handle it yet."

"Yeah, that's true," Omega considered. "Okay, India, let's do it."

* * *

On the morning of New Year's Eve, two female workers clad in black coveralls and toting canvas duffel bags showed up at One Times Square, and took the elevator to the top floor of the mostly-uninhabited building. Exiting onto a desolate, empty floor, they headed for the stairwell to the roof.

Once there, they mingled with the crew already working on ensuring the ball was in proper order for that night's festivities. The Caucasian blonde and the Afro-Asian with the striking amber eyes searched the small rooftop, finally spotting the work crew's overseer; they made an immediate beeline for him.

"Hoy," the blonde murmured in a strong Bronx accent, holding out the special credentials Dick had provided. "Moy name's Pansy Smit'. Dis heah's moy coworkah, Joann Moyphy. Da loyghting company sent us t' check out da boall loyghts, replace any LEDs what ain't woykin' no moah."

"Good," the foreman said, glancing quickly over their identification and approving it. "Call me Jerry. Yeah, we need ya. Evah since we started keepin' da damn ball up heah yeah-round, we pretty much gotta replace out a few o' da lights, ev'ry yeah. Da wind an' weathah give it a real beatin'." He pointed. "Youse got yer gear? Youse'll need to get intah harness. It's a long ways to fall, an' youse'll make a big splat if ya do. Da networks an' advertisers won't like dat much. An' da sanitation workahs what gotta clean it up before tonight'll like it even less."

"Right heah," Joann said, patting her duffel. "Along with th' extra LEDs an' shit. Even got a coupla th' crystals in heah, in case somethin' breaks. Wheah is it?"

The foreman pointed up.

High overhead loomed the huge, lighted year sign, on a special permanent scaffolding over the topmost jumbotron screen. Some twenty feet above that was the bottom of the ball itself.

"We already got it raised partway f'r da drop; youse shoulda come earlier dis mornin', before sunup," he noted. "Ya SHOULDA bin here yesterday. Th' scaffolding's ovah deah. Get at it, den."

* * *

"Shit, Meg," India muttered, as they worked their way around to the far side of the ball, high over the rooftop. "I didn't know we'd be THIS high up."

"Chill, India, everything's fine," Omega offered in a soft voice. "You got your harness rig tied off properly, right? Like I showed you?"

"Yeah. But I'm not too thrilled about this. It feels like the pit fell out of my stomach, my knees won't lock out, and my legs feel like jello."

"Quit lookin' down," Omega murmured. "Focus on what's in front of you."

"What's in front of me is a bunch of skyscrapers with a great big open space between me and them," India grumbled, fishing tools off her belt and handing them to Omega, who—hidden from the workers below by the mass of the ball itself—had carefully removed several LED modules with attached crystals in order to get at the computer equipment in its heart.

"Then look in here with me," Omega suggested, throwing her companion a sympathetic grin. "I didn't know you were afraid of heights. Neither did Echo, or I'm sure he'd have found someone else to do this with me."

"I'm not, normally," India pointed out, reaching through the opening in the ball to help Omega position the Cerebellar Holographic Mnemonic Re-Encoding Induction device that was now inside it. "But I'm not used to being up this high without a net, either."

"Wait. Since when did you perform on a trapeze?" Omega's eyes twinkled.

"Is this where I say, 'I'm a doctor, Meg, not an aerial act'?"

Omega snorted. Loudly. It sounded to India a lot like one of Echo's hastily-stifled guffaws.

"No," India continued, still eyeing her companion, "I just thought the thing'd be on the rooftop, not already flying high."

"Aw, I'm sorry! I thought Echo told you," Omega said then, contrite. "He and I talked it over, and we thought it would be better to wait until it WASN'T on the roof any more. That way, nobody could be lookin' over our shoulders while we worked."

"Oh. Well, shit. Gimme that high wire." India and Omega looked at each other, then started laughing. "Don't worry about it, girlfriend. I'll live. Long as I don't slip."

* * *

"Just focus on the work. That's what always helps me," Omega said, still chuckling. Satisfied with the position of the industrial-sized brain bleacher, she began inserting screws into its support brackets, attaching it to one of the struts that held the LED panels.

"By the way, for somebody with as strong a natural Southern accent as you've got, and not to be from around here, you nailed that Bronx accent!" India murmured with a grin. "I've only heard it that thick before from somebody who grew up there."

"Echo drilled me on it for a couple hours last night," Omega admitted, trading power screwdriver for wire strippers. "Get a couple of those wire splice covers ready, would ya?"

"Huh? Echo? But he's only a little bit less Southern-sounding than you are," India protested, as she fished in her toolkit belt for the desired covers.

"Yeah, but he's been here for pushing a couple decades," Omega pointed out, twisting wires together. "And he's a linguist—that's what one of his degrees is in, and he's really good at it. Just because that's his normal dialect doesn't mean he can't adopt another if he needs to."

"Well, I guess he's been around plenty long enough to pick it up, if he pays attention—and I know he does."

"Exactly."

"I forgot to ask, do we have to come back tomorrow and get this damn thing out?" India wondered, while Omega began hooking the brain bleacher into the computerized lighting system.

"No, you're off the hook for that one. We both are. Once this thing has done its job, Fox is gonna send a couple regular agents back to take it out. It'll probably happen late tomorrow, though he said he might have 'em do it in the wee small hours tonight, once Times Square clears out."

"Then why are WE doin' it in the first place?"

"'Cause it's absolutely essential that it works," Omega explained. "Gimme one'a those covers now. No, we only got this one shot at it, and it has to work right the first, last, and only time. So Alpha Line gets the job. And since we only got the two field teams available right now, what with Four, Five, and Six being on assignment—"

"You guys really need to train Alpha Three to do something besides code-breaking."

"We already are. But they're probably still not gonna be in the field much, 'cause code experts," Omega said with a grunt, stretching as deep into the ball as her arm would reach, to make one of the connections. "But right now, we've only got One and Two available for this, at least until we can test more and get 'em trained. You know what the bad thing is?"

"What?"

"We'd only just gotten done running Monkey, Tare, and Yankee, among others, through the tests, back before Thanksgiving. Well, Sierra too, but we're pretty sure now that it wasn't the real Sierra by that time. Which means, I guess, we need to change the testing, or maybe just thoroughly brain-bleach the polymorph. Anyway, they all passed—they all qualified for Alpha Line."

"Shit."

"Yeah. They looked like good candidates then. Now Echo's not sure he wants 'em, even if they wind up acquitted of all charges...which doesn't look likely anyway. They kinda failed that whole personality and security thing, you know?"

"No joke. I'm not sure I'd wanna work with 'em, after the way they treated you. I can imagine how you and Echo must feel." India shook her head. "I mean, if it turned out we gotta, we gotta, but...wow."

"Yeah. Since Echo put me in charge of the testing and training, this whole mess has started me thinking about adding in some additional qualifying tests....something that would show up personality quirks, psych profiles, ethics, stuff like that. Stuff that is kinda head games, but that would point out the people with the wrong attitudes to be in Alpha Line. They might make perfectly good regular agents, just not for Alpha Line."

"Good idea."

"Echo thought so, too, when I told him."

* * *

"Listen, um...you know that Romeo and I believed in you the whole way through, right? I mean...the setup they did on you at the hotel, it looked bad, and..." India glanced down, and promptly wished she hadn't, as she was powerfully reminded of the many stories of open air between her feet and the street. "Uh. What I'm trying to say is, it threw us off, and we weren't as supportive just then as we shoulda been...and we know it. And... we're sorry. BOTH of us."

Omega shrugged.

"It's okay. I never blamed you. Either of you. It looked...bad. And I knew it. Did it hurt? Yeah. But the whole thing hurt, hon. Not just y'all. You saw how Fox was, too. For a while there, I was even doubting Echo's support. Not that he ever gave me reason to," Omega admitted. "I just figured...well, now I'm thinking that somebody swapped out some hotel signs to ENSURE I got lost in the hotel, so somebody could drop the grenade on Echo while I wasn't there to defend myself. Or him."

"Oo. Good point."

"But no matter how hard I tried to push him away, thinking he'd feel safer, less stressed, whatever, Echo flat refused to BE pushed away..."

"Well, that's...just Echo. He's loyal to the people he knows and trusts, Meg, and he knows and trusts you. I think you're easily the closest friend he's got, maybe that he's ever had, Romeo thinks. He's not gonna back down on that—ever. And you know it as well as I do, probably better."

"Yeah." Omega smiled to herself. "Yeah, I do."

"Seriously though, Meg, by the time you and Echo got back from Headquarters after the grenade incident, Romeo and I had talked it all out, how it was purely circumstantial, and how easy it would be to set you up to look guilty in that particular event, and...well. We didn't know that the backup that Fox was bringing in included the guy setting you up."

"He kinda had to, way I understood it, or get threatened with a charge of collusion. And then there WOULD have been a mess, because they'd probably have charged Echo too, and then who was gonna run the Agency? Which," Omega added, "was a possibility that Echo and I both—independently—considered, at various points. A power play, to wrest control of the Agency away from Fox and Echo, and put it in someone else's hands. Probably somebody that the Prime Mininster of Lambda Andromedae hand-picked, at that."

"Yeah, I can see it. Anyway, back to something more immediate: so why are YOU AND ME the ones doin' this job again?"

* * *

"Oh. Right. So, Zebra and Zarnix pitched a royal fit as soon as Echo even suggested doing this job himself, so soon after getting shot, and right now everybody recognizes him and Romeo anyway—or they think they do, mistaking 'em for the two actors. So you and I got the job, girl. Hold on a sec. Lemme just get this...There! I think that got it. Now I gotta check..." Omega hoisted herself as far as she could get into the opening in the ball, heedless of feet dangling in space.

"Damn, girl! Be careful! I know we got harnesses and all, but shit!"

"I'm okay," Omega's voice sounded as if she were in a barrel—which she was, in a way, India decided; the ball wasn't solid, but the majority of the sphere was certainly enclosed. "Yeah, that has it taken care of. Now, let's get the LEDs swapped out, the panels back on, and get the hell down from here."

"Suits me fine!"

* * *

Times Square saw a preponderance of New Year's celebrants dressed in black Suits that year. As the ball fell, a significant number of revelers extracted special wraparound sunglasses from pockets and put them on, approaching midnight notwithstanding. But since they were decked out to look like the stereotypical New Years party-favor glasses, no one really noticed.

The Alpha One and Alpha Two teams sat rowed up on Romeo's couch in front of his wide-screen flat television, goggle glasses on and ready. As Dick's protégé—who also happened to be his younger brother—counted down to midnight, Omega and India leaned forward, anxiety obvious. Romeo and Echo each laid a calming hand on their respective partners' shoulders.

As the Times Square ball touched down, a brilliant, scintillating, multicolored light flared, saturating the TV's picture for a long moment.

"*YES!!*" Romeo exclaimed, punching a fist into the air, as Dick's brother began the voice-over that the Agency's Special Operations department had prepared. Omega and India turned and fist-bumped each other in relief. Echo, satisfied, merely removed his goggle glasses and tucked them away.

"Happy New Year!" Romeo said, standing and breaking out the bottle of champagne chilling nearby. Popping the cork, he filled four flutes on the table, and handed them around.

"To th' Agency," he toasted, raising his glass. "To a job well done."

"To anonymity," Echo said.

"To good friends and a unique 'family,'" India said, smiling at Omega.

"To TRUST," Omega said fervently, glancing at Echo, and the others nodded in agreement. Then they lightly touched their glasses together and sipped from them.

Setting their two glasses on the table, Romeo drew India up from the couch, and then pointed up. All eyes turned to the mistletoe on the ceiling as Romeo said, “Gotcha!” and planted a big one on India. Omega laughed, realizing where Romeo had gotten the idea.

“At least there aren’t any Grendels here tonight,” she declared, still laughing.

Echo sat back and watched Omega’s laughter in silence, and she caught his thoughtful glance out of the corner of her eye, sobering immediately.

“You okay?” Omega asked her partner gently, under her breath.

“Some reason I shouldn’t be?” Echo responded in the same tone. Omega jerked her chin slightly at Alpha Two.

“Thought you might be feeling a little...alone?”

Echo shook his head and met his partner’s concerned gaze, the hint of a warm smile in his own.

“You’re never alone if you’ve got...‘family,’ Meg,” he told her quietly. Then he rubbed her shoulder lightly, and eased his arm along the back of the couch behind her, not quite touching her.

But to Omega, it still felt rather like an affectionate hug.

Chapter 11

Based on information gleaned in his telepathic interrogation, Tt'l'k led them to the hidden burial site, far out in the national forests of rural northeastern Minnesota, not far from the northern shore of Lake Superior. Monkey—with a security guard contingent—as well as Fox, Alpha One and Alpha Two watched as Special Operations teams exhumed the body of the real Agent Sierra.

"Dumb question, Echo?" Omega whispered to her partner.

"From you? I doubt it. Go ahead."

"How will we know it's really Sierra? No fingerprints..."

"Mmm...dental records, probably. And DNA."

"Oh. Yeah; shoulda thought of that."

"Why? You're an astronomer, not a coroner," Echo remarked with some amusement. "If I wanna know about dead bodies, I'll talk to a coroner. If I wanna know about wormholes and spacetime, I'll come to you."

"Yeah, but—"

"Sshh," India hushed them in a low voice. "Look."

An anguished Monkey, in black Suit and black Shirt, moved over to the body of his partner as soon as Special Operations DNA-verified its identity to Fox. Monkey knelt beside it.

"Damn, buddy," Monkey told the partly-decayed corpse softly, "this just can't be for real. Somebody, please tell me this isn't happening. Hell, five YEARS together—my closest pal. And the damn cyborg FOOLED ME!! Aw, shit, Sierra...if I'd only gone with ya on that fishing trip..." His voice broke, and he wept.

As the various other agent teams—from Alpha Line, from Security, from Special Operations—listened, deeply moved, hands rested lightly on shoulders; acknowledging looks were exchanged. Romeo put an appreciative arm around India's shoulders. Echo glanced down at his side, brown eyes warm, then started in surprise and concern—his own partner wasn't there. Fox nudged him, and pointed. Beside Fox, Tt'l'k nodded approval.

Omega stood silently behind Monkey.

Leaning forward, she touched him lightly on the shoulder. His bowed head raised slightly, but he didn't turn around or look back.

"It wouldn't have done any good, Monkey." Her voice was soft, consoling. "Don't beat yourself up over it. We'd probably only be recovering both of you right now if you had."

"At least he wouldn't have been alone when..."

"He wasn't, Monkey. He wasn't. None of us are...unless we choose to be."

* * *

"Are we expected at the funeral?" Omega asked as Echo piloted the morphed Corvette back to New York.

They had chosen that mode of travel over the faster maglev tube the rest of the recovery team took, the two of them having discussed it beforehand and decided upon a more private transport system. It was also more comfortable than the T-Bird, Omega had pointed out, because the well-padded Corvette seats adjusted, and the cockpit did not require oxygen masks. And it was more intimate and familiar than the larger airskimmer, if lacking the range and speed. But the Chicago Office was not a great detour off the direct flight between the recovery site and Headquarters, and well-placed for a fill-up, thus fueling would not be an issue. They were in no particular rush, their assignment for the day being to bear witness to the recovery; so they had settled on the 'Vette as their method of transport.

"Yeah. Well, I am," Echo amended. "Department chief and all. You don't have to go if you don't want to."

"What, you don't want your shadow?" she teased.

"I didn't mean that, and you know it." He grinned. "My partner is welcome with me anywhere—but she might wanna change into that purple male form before following me SOME places." They laughed.

"Yeah, doggone it, I gotta remember where I parked my ship," she chuckled. "Shall I buzz Fox and get the details on the service?"

"No, I can tell you those. Funeral's the day after tomorrow; that gives 'em time to do the autopsy. 26:00 hours Division time, at the Crypt."

"The Crypt?"

"Yeah. A vault in Arlington National Cemetery. Um, well, under it, really."

"Let me guess," Omega said softly. "Beneath the Tomb of the Unknowns?"

"Yeah."

"Appropriate," she remarked.

"Uh-huh. And respected. And most importantly, undisturbed."

* * *

"Yeah. Still, I think I'd prefer—"

"I know...deep space," Echo told her, and she shot a surprised glance at him. "Fox...showed me your will some time back."

"Oh."

"My turn—do you mind my knowing?" he asked her.

"No. You're the one the will requests to take me out there...when the time comes."

"IF." He gave her a sharp look. "IF the time comes."

"If," she agreed, amenable. She decided not to point out the inevitability of death for everyone, not after all they'd gone through so recently. Besides, something else was on her mind. "Echo, when did you say Sierra's funeral was?"

"Day after tomorrow. 26:00 Division time."

Omega converted to Earth time mentally, then paled.

"Oh, blast it," she whispered. "It WOULD be."

"What's wrong?" Echo shot her a concerned glance.

"Guess what happened twelve years ago, day after tomorrow?"

"Aw, dammit," Echo said gently. "Don't tell me. Your mom's funeral? Your dad's?"

"Try Mom, Dad, AND Grandmomma," Omega murmured. "One big sorta joint service."

"Well, shit."

"Yeah. It's gonna be one more damn long day."

"You wanna stay at home? You can, you know. You don't have to go."

"I might. But then I'll be there all by myself...with the ghosts..."

"Damn."

"Yeah. I dunno. Anyway, I think I almost have to go, otherwise it'll look like I'm holding grudges or something. I'm not entirely sure I'm not, but..."

"Well, I don't think anybody would blame you. But yeah, for the department chief's assistant, I guess you're right."

"So I have to figure out how to get through it." Omega sighed.

"I'll be right there, baby." Echo reached out and took her near hand in his, holding it lightly. "You know that. If you need a shoulder, you got it."

"I know. Thanks, Ace." She squeezed his fingers in gratitude.

"Always, Meg. Always."

* * *

The chapel at the Crypt was full. Monkey sat on the front pew, in Agency mourning attire. Omega sat in the second pew between the Agency Director and her partner, the Alpha Line department chief.

Six black-Suited pallbearers, Tare and Yankee among them, carried in the white casket. Father Papa and Rabbi Yod moved to the pulpit together. Omega leaned over to Fox.

"Why are the father and the rabbi both up there?" she whispered.

"Sierra was what's sometimes called a Messianic Jew," Fox told her quietly. "A Jewish Christian."

"Oh. I bet that made for some interesting conversations at times. How did the rabbi and the padre feel about that?"

"Oy gevalt. It bothered 'em...at first. But they get along pretty damn well, all things considered, so it all came out in the wash eventually. There's a lotta respect for each other there. Like Echo told the Prime Minister, we prize diversity. Granted, there's diversity, and then there's diversity. But given half a chance, we do our best. And I'd like to think that our best is awfully damn good."

Omega nodded as the solemn service began.

* * *

As the poignant service progressed, Echo sat quietly, his practiced stoicism in place. His partner struggled a bit, however, and he watched out of the corner of his eye as Omega blinked profusely for a while, then began biting her lip, in an effort to remain in control. When he saw her surreptitiously wipe blood from her lip, he leaned over her.

"Ease up, Meg. Let it go if you need to, baby. There's no shame in crying at a thing like this. Better that than biting through your lip."

"No, Echo, it's not. Not now. Not today. Trust me on that one." Despite her best efforts, a lone tear spilled over.

"Here, then." He reached inside his jacket and unobtrusively produced a small square of folded black silk, handing the handkerchief to her. "After you told me about today's date, I came prepared, just in case. I got three more, stuffed in various pockets, and a whole brand-new package of 'em in a warp pocket. And," he added, "it isn't like it's gonna show blood stains, either. I chose the black ones specifically for...whatever."

"Thanks."

* * *

Romeo and India were near the back of the chapel. As the funeral progressed, India sat calmly, unemotionally; Romeo fidgeted.

"Romeo, settle down," India murmured to her antsy partner.

"Easy for you to say," Romeo muttered. "You been encounterin' dead people almost every day for years. I mean, if they're too far gone when they get to ya, that's just what happens. But damn, India, Monkey's PARTNER is dead. An' I already lost my best friend in the SEALs."

"Aww! Is THAT the problem?" India turned to look at him and gave him a gentle smile. "Romeo, that's sweet."

"Um, yeah. Well, shit, girl," Romeo managed to get out, and laid his arm along the back of the pew behind her.

* * *

The coffin was carefully placed into its chamber in the Crypt; the vault was sealed. Father Papa and Rabbi Yod pronounced the benediction together. Guards escorted Monkey, Tare, and Yankee out of the chapel, returning them to confinement. Sierra had been laid to rest.

The gathered agents stood quietly, and a soft, respectful buzz of voices filled the room. Echo turned to look for Romeo and India, and Omega slipped by him unseen, vanishing in the crowd. Echo held up a hand to signal Alpha Two, and Romeo and India, spotting it, headed toward him.

"Well, that's over," he remarked as they walked up.

"Yeah," India answered.

"Shit, you guys are cold," Romeo remarked in annoyance, and Echo and India gazed at him calmly.

"Not really, Romeo," India said. "I don't know about Echo, but if I let it get to me, I wouldn't be able to function as a physician."

"India's right," Fox said over Echo's shoulder. "Take a big mental step back, Romeo; get some distance. You were a Navy SEAL. You should know precisely what we mean. If you let it affect you to the point that it incapacitates you, you're no good to the organization, your team, your partner—or yourself."

Romeo glanced at Echo, who raised his eyebrows in confirmation, and Romeo nodded.

"All right," Romeo acknowledged quietly. "Distance."

"Where's Meg?" India asked then.

"Huh." Echo glanced around. "She must've snuck out."

"Was she all right?" Fox asked, concerned. "She seemed awfully tense to me."

"Let's just say this wasn't the first funeral she's had to attend on this date," Echo offered. The others thought for a moment, then nodded in realization; Romeo, India and Fox all grimaced before Echo continued. "From what she told me, they did kind of a mass funeral for her whole family—"

"Which musta been a hella marathon service f'r her t' get through," Romeo observed, and the others nodded.

"Probably still better than stretching it out over several days," India decided.

"Yeah. But today's the anniversary of it," Echo added. "I think she'd have been fine if the dates had been different. Just too many memories there. She'll be okay. Probably needed some time alone."

"Echo? Got a message for you," Charlie, a field agent who had recently applied for Alpha Line, said as he walked up. He handed Echo a folded note, looking him in the eye, then he nodded to the others and moved off. Echo opened the note, read it, and looked up.

"Gotta go, guys." He headed for the side door.

"Echo? What's up?" Fox called after him. Echo doubled back and handed him the note. Fox opened it and read,

Echo—Im gonna be okay but Im going home now Ill wait by the side door for five minutes then leave

Both men found the total lack of punctuation telling. More, a single drop of liquid had run the letters together. Fox passed the note to Romeo and India.

"Looks like somebody else needs to learn the value of distance," the Director observed.

"She knows it," Echo told them, already en route for the side door. "She knew it way the hell before we co-opted her, or she wouldn't have been an astronaut. But today...she just needs a little help getting there."

* * *

Several days later, the Agency hearing room bore more than a slight resemblance to a formal courtroom, for good reason—three Agents were being charged with two counts of attempted murder, one count of assault with intent to kill, one count of sedition, and one count of conspiracy to destroy the Agency.

Fox sat in the judge's bench, flanked by several members of the Pan-Galactic Tribunal, while Monkey, Tare, and Yankee sat in the dock, arguing in their own behalf. Xerxes, from the Headquarters Legal department, acted as prosecutor. Romeo, India, Echo and Omega sat together in the packed gallery, watching.

As the trial progressed, some agents were called as witnesses. These included both Echo and Omega, who between them, related the details of the failed assassination attempt calmly and precisely.

Echo was also called back to relate how he had caught Monkey discussing the Agency's situation—and Omega's complete personal history—with uncleared civilians, as well as the fact that Monkey believed the civilians to be fellow agents, whom he was attempting to influence in a seditious fashion—and without bothering to double-check their identities.

Omega, in turn, was called back to relate the details of her confrontation with the accused in Fox's office, and this was augmented with computer records, video, ballistics evidence, and the hard copies of the forged orders.

Significantly, none of the accused attempted to cross-examine either member of Alpha One.

The video of Omega's confrontation with the Lambda Andromedan Prime Minister further elaborated on the situation, as did Tt'l'k's testimony of his telepathic interrogation of the fake Sierra, and the coroner's autopsy report.

The Sierra imposter itself—as well as the former Andromedan Prime Minister; a swift vote of 'no confidence' had occurred on the Lambda Andromedan homeworld, and he and his entire cadre of officials were unceremoniously recalled and ousted—had been handed over to PGLEIA for trial and sentencing, as they were not from Division One, but elsewhere in the galaxy, thus raising the murder and conspiracy charges to that higher level.

The defendants, to their credit, were able to demonstrate that the dummy orders, coming as they did through the phony Sierra, had arrived in such a way as to appear genuine. However, the prosecution proved that, had the three agents taken responsible steps to verify the rather extreme orders, rather than automatically accepting them from Sierra at face value, they would likely have seen through them as forgeries...and identified the infiltrator much earlier, into the bargain.

The defense and prosecution rested. The members of the seated Council looked at each other, nodding; one leaned forward and handed Fox a formal, folded note on special stationery. The Director opened it and read it, then looked out at the courtroom, thoughtful. Fox was silent for a long, pregnant moment.

"Will the accused please approach the bench?" he said at last. The men rose quietly and walked forward.

"The verdict of this galactic tribunal is official, and unanimous," Fox declaimed, voice and demeanor ice-cold. "All three defendants are found guilty of all charges. Are you aware, gentlemen, that complete and full mnemonic re-encoding is the penalty for—"

"Fox, no!! Please don't!"

All eyes in the hearing room swiveled toward the voice's origin, and Echo watched, startled, as Omega left his side and moved forward, hand raised in a plea.

"Fox, may I approach the bench?" she asked. "I know it's unorthodox, but..."

"Permission granted, Omega. Give me one good reason why I shouldn't inflict the maximum penalty," a stern Fox responded, waving the defendants back to their seats. "You have every reason to want it. They've agitated against you, tried to ruin your reputation in every possible way, and very nearly killed Echo. Twice."

"That's true, Fox. But almost everyone here knows my history with the Agency, so y'all know that the latter can also be said of me. You gave ME the benefit of the doubt. AND a second chance. Have these agents been manipulated any less than I was?"

"Omega, it just doesn't compare," Fox pointed out, flabbergasted. "You were mentally and physically...violated."

A sympathetic murmur filled the room as a flash of anguish crossed Omega's face. *All because of me,* Echo thought, a wave of guilt washing through him. *My partner, my best friend, the woman I care so much about, was tortured by my old enemy, just to get back at me.* He dropped his gaze to the floor and closed his eyes in pain. He opened them again when he heard her clear, steady voice.

"Haven't we had our faith in our organization, even in each other, violated? Fox, we've just passed through a series of holidays—Hanukkah; Christmas; Kwanzaa, which I know some of our agents celebrate; New Year's; and even Twelfth Night. I'm not Jewish myself, but I've had Jewish friends, and I've celebrated that holiday with them—celebrated all of 'em, in various ways, over the years. Now, it seems to me..." Omega's eyes grew thoughtful, "that these holidays we've just observed—every one of 'em—are all about...starting over. Rebirth. Rebuilding. Forgiving. And if anyone on Earth should know how to let go of the past, it's the Agency. But we shouldn't just IGNORE it. Letting go doesn't simply make it disappear."

Alpha Line watched as a light of comprehension dawned on Omega's face, and they knew she was thinking of her own history. Echo studied her intently, listening closely, pondering her words...and their possible import in his own life.

"We have to start USING it, the past," she continued. "Remembering the past, but not living there...planning tomorrow, but living TODAY, walking toward tomorrow one step at a time...making ourselves stronger by learning from our experiences. It's that old saw about, 'Those who do not learn from history are condemned to repeat it.' It may be old, and it may be trite, but that doesn't make it any less true. We—individually and corporately—need to LEARN from this whole mess. THEY need to learn. And if you force them to forget...then they never WILL learn. WE... never will learn." Omega caught herself, looked around the hushed room, blushed, and sighed.

"Well, that's my big, melodramatic soapbox speech. It's one I didn't know I was gonna make until about five seconds before I made it. Not worth much, maybe. But there's somebody else here whose opinion should be taken into account, Fox, someone who was...violated...by this incident more than any other agent." Omega looked directly at her partner, who sat up straight, startled. "They nearly killed YOU, Echo."

"Omega makes an excellent point," Fox acknowledged. "Echo, do you wish to make a statement before this tribunal?"

* * *

The three accused men stared in horrified, dumbstruck silence as they remembered Echo's anger—his utter, implacable fury—at their treatment of Omega.

'I have a long memory...' he had said to them all.

"It's been nice knowin' ya, guys," Monkey breathed, and the other two nodded.

* * *

Echo sat silently, looking at Omega, intensely aware of the mass scrutiny as all eyes in the room focused on them, and only them.

You want me to do this? He cocked an eyebrow.

Yes. Omega gazed at him steadily. Then she shook her head, shrugged, and jerked her chin at him slightly. *But it doesn't matter what I want. It's your decision.*

Echo considered the entire sequence of events for a long, expectant moment in the dead-silent gallery, then rose to his feet.

"Fox. Permission to approach the bench?"

"Granted."

Omega started past him to resume her seat, but Echo put out a hand and stopped her, then moved to stand beside her, resting his hand on her shoulder for a moment in a subtle show of unity before letting it fall to his side. He glanced down at her, then faced Fox and spoke formally, ensuring his voice carried throughout the courtroom.

"Agent Omega has spoken fairly and compassionately, sir. But that's the nature of this Southern lady Alpha Line has come to know, to respect... and to trust." Romeo and India nodded in firm agreement from the gallery, as did two other Alpha Line teams newly returned from assignment, and Omega gave Echo a grateful smile. "The Agents whose actions are under review today are skilled agents, guilty perhaps of inexperience, misplaced trust, lack of discipline, and overzealousness. But all those things can be changed, just as protocol in the organization will have to be changed in order to prevent future incidents like this. Who knows better than those who have learned the hard way?" Echo turned to face the defendants.

"A lot of water went under the bridge between us these last few weeks. I won't lie before this assembly and say that any of it was especially pleasant. But I will say that, given the circumstances, I agree with my partner. You deserve as much of a second chance as she got." Echo turned back to the Director.

"Alpha One respectfully requests clemency, Fox."

Echo glanced back down at his partner, who met his eyes with a warm gaze, almost but not quite smiling. But they said nothing, and they turned together and, with comfortably matching strides, went back to their seats beside Romeo and India in the gallery, amid a low murmur of voices. Omega looked up at Echo, a question in the blue eyes, as the gallery fell silent once more.

"I don't know," he answered that unspoken question quietly. "It's up to Fox now."

* * *

Fox sat, deep in thought, for several long minutes, as the silence extended until the courtroom's atmosphere became strained. Then he raised his head.

"In light of this plea for clemency, expressed so strongly by both members of the Alpha One partnership—especially given that both were expressly targeted in this conspiracy—it is my judgment that these disgraced agents shall be reinstated in the Agency," he declared. "They shall, however, be placed on indefinite probation and reassigned to a new team which will be formed under Agency auspices, and will be responsible in future for ensuring the Agency is protected against any further such... violations. This new team, as part of the Agency's first line of defense, shall fall under the auspices of Alpha Line, shall be designated the Firewall Team, to be eventually comprised of partnerships Alpha Seven and Eight—once Monkey has been assigned a new partner, from experienced ranks—and shall be overseen by the joint leadership of Alpha One. Alpha Line Department Chief Echo, is this acceptable to you?"

Echo stood, shoulders squared.

"It is, Fox."

"Alpha Line Training Lead Omega, do you accept this assignment?"

Omega stood beside her partner.

"I do, Fox."

"Good. Echo, Omega, let me say in my official capacity as your Director, that I do not expect you to go easy on them. In fact, I will be very disappointed if you do so. I want to see these three agents learn the real meaning of humility, compassion, and service. Self-confidence is one thing; misplaced ego is another altogether. Wisdom, discretion, healthy skepticism —all of these are qualities that these agents need to develop. What I DON'T want to see are more gossip, vice, and malicious slander. Make them what they need to be—Agents worthy of Alpha Line, worthy of Division One—whatever it takes."

Fox watched as Omega and Echo nodded solemn acknowledgement before resuming their seats. Then he turned to the tribunal members of the Pan-Galactic Council.

"Does the Council approve of this ruling?"

An Ergisol, a seven-foot-tall insectoid with a chitinous iridescent green exoskeleton who resembled nothing so much as a giant June bug, rose to its rear feet from its seat with the rest of the Council members, and began clicking its mandibles. The translator around its neck rendered its speech.

"I am Scak Nitida of the Ruling Clan of Ergis, and I head this Council tribunal, convened at Agent Fox's request, as witnesses to this judgement. We have been in private communication during the entire proceedings, thanks to the assistance of Ambassador Zz'r'p of Arcturus VII and his protégé, Attaché Tt'l'k. And I can say without reservation that we are unanimous in our pleasure at seeing such justice—and such mercy—meted out in the Division One government. The Council approves. You may proceed."

"Thank you, Lord Scak and Council members," Fox murmured, nodding.

He paused for a moment, still musing his ruling and the unexpected turn the whole matter had taken, then drew a deep breath, sighed, and looked out over the silent courtroom.

"This hearing is now adjourned." He rapped his gavel on its block.

* * *

The room exploded in a babel of voices as the Agency reacted to the ruling. Echo looked down at Omega with an unreadable expression in his dark eyes as they both stood.

"You can be...unexpected...at times," he told her.

"'Good. Predictable is a killer,' as someone once said to me." Omega shrugged. "Was I wrong? They DID almost kill you..."

"No. I wouldn't have agreed with you otherwise."

* * *

Monkey, released from custody, walked up to them just then, a mixture of emotions on his face making it hard to read the man as he turned to Omega.

A mildly surprised Echo instantly went on full alert, edging slightly nearer Omega, glad for his larger stature; he may have argued for clemency, but he still wasn't sure just how much he trusted the three agents. If it came to an outright attack on Meg, Echo had a certain physical superiority over the smaller male, and he would use it to best advantage. And Echo would not hold back.

Not this time, dammit, he thought, angry and determined. *Meg's had enough shit dumped on her for a lifetime. If he lays one finger on her, he's a dead man, even if I get brain-bleached for it.*

He watched closely as Monkey met her eyes for a long moment, then dropped his gaze in deep shame, flushing and staring at the floor.

"I, uh...I guess I need to offer you a huge apology," Monkey told Omega. "Especially after you saved my ass—um, our collective asses—just now. BOTH of you. The gentleman AND the lady. And I *DON'T* use those terms loosely."

He gave Echo a meaningful glance, reminding him of his own words in Fox's office, so many days before. Echo relaxed slightly, seeing the sincerity in the other man's gaze...finally. Omega shook her head.

"Don't worry about it," she told Monkey. "I never really blamed you for thinking I was the mole. Given everything that went down last summer, it made a certain amount of sense. To be honest, it's still a mystery to me why this guy here—" she jerked her thumb at Echo, who stood close enough to almost brush her shoulder with his chest, thereby ensuring Monkey was fully aware of his presence, "is even willing to work with me, much less trust me as a partner."

"You don't get it??" Monkey said in astonishment.

Echo stiffened, waiting for Monkey's next statement, remembering the nasty innuendoes the man had leveled at Alpha One in the last several weeks. So what Monkey said next came as a slight surprise.

"When you have a partner who ALWAYS comes through, no matter what's set against 'em, well, you don't let 'em go. Not for anything." Monkey looked at a startled Omega with open admiration. "I'm...gonna miss Sierra. Something awful, to tell the truth. But...I hope I'm lucky enough to get somebody like you for a new partner. Uh...you wouldn't... um, happen to know where I could find somebody...like that...?"

Omega raised one knowing eyebrow and cocked her head to one side, considering her response. Echo froze, taken aback, as he realized what Monkey was really asking.

That sonuvabitch! he thought, not sure whether to be angry or just annoyed. *After all that just went down, with Omega AND me dragging his fat ass outta the damn fire, the little bastard turns right around and is already going after MY partner. And I'd lay odds it ISN'T just to be PARTNERS. But...it isn't my call to make, either, dammit. I doubt she will, after everything that's happened...at least, I hope not...but you never know. Meg's just fulla surprises these days.*

So he waited quietly for his partner's answer. A calm Omega looked up at Echo, and met his eyes with a soft, and somehow reassuring, sapphire gaze as she spoke.

* * *

"No. No, Monkey, I don't," she said, firm but gentle. "All the Agents I know are quite...satisfied...with their current partnerships." The brown eyes meeting her gaze flashed golden for a brief moment, and she let the corners of her lips quirk upward, just a little, before she looked back at the lone agent. "But I might know a couple people in Houston that'd probably fit the bill, once we've managed to train somebody..."

A soft, soundless exhalation from the man at her shoulder feathered warm against her neck, tickling her ear, and Omega suddenly comprehended that Echo had been holding his breath, waiting for her answer. *More,* she thought, gratified, *he's relieved. He WANTS me at his side.* A wash of warmth went through her.

Monkey grinned ruefully in full comprehension of her delicate rejection, then turned to Echo.

* * *

"And, Echo," Monkey added, deliberately oblique, "with regard to our previous...um, conversation..." the smaller man pulled a wry face, "as one man to another, well...given all that? Dude, you're a fool if you don't."

An impassive Echo stared down at him, remembering the other man's implication that Echo and Omega were more than 'merely' partners. But he made no response.

"Hey, um, listen, take care..." Monkey cut his eyes surreptitiously at Omega, thereby invoking the addendum, *of her.*

"That cuts both ways," Echo replied then, and Monkey frowned for a moment, apparently puzzled by the remark. Then he shot a quick, understanding glance at the area of Echo's belly where he'd been shot, and Echo nodded once. A thoughtful Monkey pursed his lips, considering; then he too nodded, saluted them both, and moved off through the crowd.

"What was that last bit all about?" a curious Omega asked after Monkey's departure.

"Nothing important. Monkey was offering me his...opinions. For whatever they're worth. They'll be worth more, when we're done with his training. Let's go home."

* * *

A casually-clad Echo, in black jeans and turtleneck sweater, was stretched out on his couch reading O. Henry's *The Gift of the Magi* from a book of holiday short stories when a smiling Omega suddenly appeared, elflike, in front of him. He jumped despite himself, then grunted and rubbed his stomach, which had pulled developing scar tissue with the muscle contraction.

"Shit! Damn, Meg, give a body some warning, huh?"

"Woops! Shoulda knocked. Sorry," she told him. "C'mon. India and Romeo are on their way over."

"For what?"

"In case you don't remember, SOMEBODY was in surgery on Christmas morning, so Romeo and India and I decided to wait until we could all be together to celebrate. So come on!"

"Meg...I'd really rather not..."

The smile disappeared.

"Oh. All right. I, um, I wasn't thinking, I guess. I'll...drop your gifts off later, then."

Omega followed her smile.

* * *

"Where's Echo?" Romeo asked, as he and India came into Omega's apartment with a flowering plant and armloads of packages.

Omega simply pointed at the back door; normally open—a habit the pair had gotten into over the months they'd been partnered, given the soundproof walls—it was now pulled almost closed, allowing only a scant couple of inches' gap.

"He's not coming?" India asked blankly. Omega shook her head, then shrugged.

"Nope."

"Did HE close the door?" Romeo asked quietly.

"No. I did. I...didn't want to disturb him."

"Well, I'm going to make him come over if I have to drag him bodily, dammit!" An outraged India started for the door.

"No, India, please." Omega laid a strong restraining hand on her friend's shoulder and met her eyes. "You couldn't anyway. You know that. Just let him alone. I understand, and it's all right. I do wish he would, but...that's just Echo. And I wouldn't want him to change, because then he wouldn't BE Echo." Omega went over to the tree and sorted through the gifts. "Here's Echo's gift from me, and here's his gift from the two of you that you brought over when he was still in the medlab."

"This is for him, too," Romeo said, holding up the plant as India deposited the rest of the gaily-wrapped packages under the tree.

"I...don't understand..." Omega said, looking at the potted plant.

"Remember I told you about Chase's favorite flower?" Romeo reminded her.

"Oh. Those are the same kind of flowers? Those stargazer lilies?"

"Yeah."

"Here, then. Lemme get that." Omega took the plant from him and carried it, with the other two presents in her arms, over to the back door.

* * *

Nudging the door open with her foot, Omega set the gifts down just inside Echo's apartment.

"Merry Christmas, Echo," she wished him softly as he looked up from the couch, and she quickly withdrew into her own apartment lest he get a good look at her wistful eyes and feel she was trying to pressure him.

* * *

He saw Romeo and India behind her, though, just before she pulled the door closed, and their frowning—nearly scowling—expressions were clear: *How could you do this to her?*

Echo sighed, put his book down, laced his fingers behind his head, and stared at the ceiling for a while, thinking about comments that had been made to him in recent days about his partner—by Fox, by Dr. Taylor, by Monkey—as well as the remarks his partner had made in the tribunal hearing regarding the wisdom of allowing one's past to inform one's future.

Then he got up and moved to the closed door, listening to the muffled, barely-audible sounds of subdued celebration from the other side. Glancing down, he saw the brightly-wrapped packages left for him at his feet.

"Damn," he finally said softly. Then he gathered up the packages and opened the door.

Romeo and India, off shift for the evening, were lounging comfortably on the floor around the Christmas tree, which was again the only light in the room. Omega rested on her belly, elbows on the floor, chin in her hands, denim-clad ankles crossed in the air behind her, sock feet above that. A huge platter of homemade chocolate chip cookies was in evidence on the coffee table, right in between a plate containing slices of Omega's special recipe fruitcake and a veggie tray, and the familiar scent of chicory coffee filled the air from the carafe on the corner of the table. They looked up in surprise as Echo appeared in the door.

"Does this mean I have to sit on the floor, too?" he asked, tone dry.

"Of course," Omega said, a twinkle appearing in her eye as she sat up. "No, really, it's okay if you want to grab the couch," she followed up, reaching for an empty mug and the coffee carafe. "I know your belly is still a little tender. It might be more comfortable that way."

Without a word, Echo moved to her side, folded his long legs and sat down on the floor with a soft grunt as scar tissue tugged, before depositing the gifts back under the tree. Omega handed him a cup of coffee.

"Here, hon. The way you like it. Want a cookie?"

Echo accepted the cup and the cookie, and listened as the others reminisced about Christmases past. Omega considerately, skillfully, steered the conversation around Echo, and he shot her an appreciative glance.

Omega and Romeo, however, compared family traditions, and they all listened as a very quiet and thoughtful Omega fondly reminisced about her birth family.

* * *

"They'd be proud o' ya too, ya know," Romeo told her, emphasizing the *too*, as India and Echo nodded. Omega looked around at them all, then sighed.

"Thanks. I'd like to think so." She chuckled once, self-deprecatingly. "You'd think, at my age, I'd..."

Echo laid a reassuring hand on her shoulder, and squeezed lightly.

"Don't go there, baby. Don't even worry about it. It's like I told you, Meg. You—WE—are going through a rough spot right now. We'll get through it."

Omega smiled at her partner, grateful for his faith and reassurance...his friendship. *We may not be like Romeo and India,* she decided, *but we've got something pretty special just the same. And if that's all I ever get, I'll still take it in a heartbeat.*

* * *

When a serious dent had been made in the cookies, only two small slices of fruitcake were left, a minuscule side salad was all that remained of the veggie tray, and the big coffeepot was almost empty, they began opening gifts.

Echo had already recognized the significance of the plant, and nodded his solemn thanks to Romeo and India.

India and Omega handed each other two small packages each. Opening them together, they laughed to discover identical gold chain bracelets in one, and charms that said "Sister" in the other.

"Do I detect Romeo's hand coordinating that one?" Omega said with a chuckle.

"Who? Me?" Romeo protested in mock innocence, grinning. Then Romeo handed Omega another small box. "Here, Meg, this one is from me." Opening it, Omega found a pair of gold stud earrings shaped like stars.

"Oh, you saw me salivating over these in the store!" she exclaimed.

"Yeah. I thought they were you. An' they're subtle enough, you can even wear 'em on duty. I already checked, an' Fox said they're fine."

"Thanks, Romeo, they're gorgeous. Here's mine to you, but you have to open it along with India's present for you."

"Now who's coordinating?" Echo observed.

"Just wait," India told him. "You're next."

"Oh, joy. I can hardly wait," Echo murmured, voice dry as dust in the Sahara.

Omega hit him in the shoulder.

"Ow!" he exclaimed, flinching away and grinning. "You really wanna go there, baby?"

"Behave," she told him, matching his grin. "Appreciate that we cared enough to coordinate, hush, and watch Romeo."

"All right, all right," Echo said, holding up his hands, as an amused Romeo and India watched the interaction. "Romeo, tear some paper, there, junior."

"Y'all done arguin' yet?" the younger man wondered.

"We weren't arguing," Omega said, looking innocent. "I'm just teaching him a little better social interaction, is all."

"The hell you say," Echo commented, snorting.

"Hush, you! Go, Romeo, before he smarts off again!"

* * *

When Romeo got the two packages unwrapped, he found the latest video game system from India, and a solid dozen games to go with it from Omega.

"Yeah, BAYBEE!! Best thing to come out of the Betelgeuse Treaty yet! WOOT!"

"Your turn," Omega told Echo, trying to keep a straight face. "Same protocol Romeo used."

* * *

Sighing longsufferingly, Echo pulled the packages in front of him and started ripping the brightly-colored paper. When he got enough of the wrappings off to realize what he had, the paper started tearing a little faster.

"Meg?! How in the HELL did y'all get your hands on the quantum light storage unit, WITH the new sound system? Neither one of 'em is even in production yet!"

"We called in a few favors," was all Omega would answer, grinning openly now.

"Off-planet favors," India amended. "Please note that the sound system has eight wireless speakers, and is across-the-board compatible..."

"Yeah. Not only the QLS plugs in, but your old system will, too," Omega explained. "It'll handle anything that'll plug into a standard USB port."

"An' we made sure that Alan Jackson album you like was in there," Romeo added. "Several Lonestar disks, too. Oh, and that Ercwlff album—you know, the chick from the Kallos system? Meg scoped out your music on the sly."

"And with ten terabytes of storage on that thing, I don't think you'll be fillin' it up any time too soon," Omega declared, grinning from ear to ear.

"Thanks...I think," Echo said with a nod, shooting Omega an amused look. "Maybe I've trained you a little TOO well, baby."

She grinned as she raised one shoulder in imitation of an Igor hunchback.

"You've created a monthter," she said in a feigned—and deliberately very bad—Transylvanian lisp. "No, sorry, wrong holiday." Echo rolled his eyes as Romeo and India broke up with laughter.

"Here's a couple of packages I don't remember," Omega said, reaching back under the tree to pull them out before reading the name tags. "Here, Romeo, this one's for you, and this is yours, India."

* * *

Romeo unwrapped the small, flat package to discover a sheaf of papers. Scanning them, he suddenly let out a whoop of delighted surprise.

"What?! What is it?" India exclaimed.

"It's an approved requisition for T-38 flight training!"

India looked at the document over Romeo's shoulder. She pointed at a section of the form.

"Look who initialled it as having submitted it for you," she said. The letter E showed under her fingertip. A gratified Romeo met the department chief's gaze.

"Thanks, man. This is cool!"

Echo shrugged, nonchalant.

"Figured it was about time you learned the right way to drive the Lexus, junior," he deadpanned. But there was a mischievous glint in his eye.

* * *

A curious India opened her package then, to find a single sheet of paper with a username and password.

"Huh? What's this?"

A somewhat apologetic Echo glanced at Romeo, then back at India.

"You know that you and I met...several times...before you helped out Romeo and then joined the Agency?"

"Um, no?!"

"Yes, we did. I...had to brain bleach you, each time. Take this to Special Operations. They can access and download all of those memory records for you, too, so you'll have 'em in addition to the ones of Romeo that Fox approved when you transferred out of the medlab." He shrugged. "They're no big deal, nothing Earth-shattering or anything, but you helped me out a couple times, and I thought you'd like to have the complete set back."

India stared down at the paper, then back up at Echo. Her amber eyes glistened; she opened her mouth to say something, but nothing came out.

"Oh, wow, Echo. You're all right, man," Romeo murmured.

* * *

Omega laid a light hand on Echo's shoulder for a moment. He turned his head to look at her, his face seeming expressionless—at first glance. But she thought she saw something in his dark eyes, and she smiled slightly.

Romeo reached under the tree and pulled out the last gift.

"Here, India. Merry Christmas, babe."

A puzzled India tore off the wrappings on the large, flat, oblong box, revealing the latest board game, *Alien Dissection*, which he'd acquired—on the sly—at the science fiction convention in the dealer's room. Everyone burst out laughing, even Echo.

"Of all the damn things to get an ER physician," Echo chuckled. "Romeo, that was priceless."

"Go ahead, hon. Open it up," Romeo said then, grinning.

Surprised, Echo leaned toward Omega and opened his mouth to say something, but Omega turned to him and laid a quelling finger across his lips, signaling him to watch.

* * *

India removed the lid of the box, and laid it aside. As she looked over the game board, something glittering caught her eye.

Reaching into the recess in the board where an alien appendage would normally go, India extracted the sparkling object and held it to the light. It was a star ruby ring in a gold setting.

"Oh...Romeo..." India wrapped her arms around him, and Omega unobtrusively rose and left the room, motioning for Echo to follow.

* * *

At the kitchen door, Echo glanced back, peeping out around the door frame.

"Does this mean they're engaged?" he murmured, turning toward his partner.

"No," Omega answered with a smile. "Not yet, anyway. It's a ruby, and most women prefer diamond solitaires for that..."

Peering out herself under Echo's arm, she saw the finger on which India had slipped the ring.

"Huh. On the other hand...so to speak..." She shrugged. "Well, I guess they'll let us know when the time comes."

Echo followed Omega's gaze, and raised an eyebrow. Omega grabbed his arm and tugged.

"Whoa. Lip lock. C'mon back in the kitchen, Echo, and let's give 'em a few minutes. I'll make a fresh pot of coffee."

Omega dumped the used grounds, and opened a cabinet to get a new filter.

"Blast and damn it," she said, standing on tiptoe and trying to reach the top shelf, hopping, but still not quite able to reach. "I have GOT to tell the delivery guy to quit putting the things way up there when he brings 'em in. I'm tall, but not THAT tall."

A hand extended over her shoulder and easily grasped the coffee filters. Pulling them down, Echo peeled one from the stack and handed it to her, then put the rest on the bottom shelf.

"Thanks," Omega said as she resumed preparing the coffee. As she worked, she remarked in an offhanded, conversational fashion, "So, was it very uncomfortable for you to be here with us tonight? I hope it wasn't too bad, Ace. I know I really appreciated it." She deliberately didn't look back at him.

Silence.

"Oh," Omega said softly, hoping the pain didn't show in her voice. "...I'm sorry. But I really liked your being here..." She turned around.

Echo was gone.

* * *

When the coffee had finished brewing, Omega carefully peeked out the door. Seeing that the coast was clear, she ventured out with the fresh coffee. Romeo and India looked up from where they sat beneath the tree, talking quietly.

"Where's Echo?" Romeo asked.

"He...left," Omega answered, deliberately oblique.

"So what did he get you?" Romeo pressed, curious.

"Well, uh..." Omega thought hard, trying to figure out how to make them understand.

"Meg," India said, sitting up straight, "Echo DID get YOU a Christmas present, didn't he?"

"He spent the evening with us when he didn't have to," Omega replied, calm. "He helped me meet some family traditions on Christmas Eve. And he TRUSTS me, guys. Completely. With his life. That's more than enough."

"Yeah, pretty lady, but still—"

"NO, Romeo, you don't understand," Omega interrupted him, struggling to come up with the words that would make them comprehend. "Look. Do you remember what I told you that day we went shopping? I said, 'Not all losses are material. And not everyone handles them the same way.'"

"I remember," Romeo said. "You were talkin' 'bout you an' Echo."

"Right. It holds true for GIFTS as well."

* * *

Romeo and India stared at her thoughtfully; her face was calm, relaxed, with no sign of hurt or disappointment.

"Okay, I guess I get it," Romeo decided.

"Me, too," India agreed with a sigh. "It isn't what I would have done, but I'm not you or Echo."

* * *

"Right," Omega murmured. "And I'm okay with it, guys, I swear. The things Echo DID give me mean more to me than all the gold and platinum and jewels in the galaxy."

"Meg...c'n I ask somethin'?" Romeo wondered, seeming a bit hesitant. Omega studied his face for a moment before answering, suspecting what was coming.

"Sure. What's up?"

"Do you...love Echo?"

Without hesitation, Omega responded, "Do I love you, Romeo?"

"Whaaa?"

"What?!" India chimed in. "Meg!"

"Hush, India," Omega soothed. "Y'all are family, guys. My family these days have the names Echo, India, Romeo...and Fox. What does that tell you?"

"That you love us, an' Echo, an' Fox, too," Romeo murmured. "But Meg...even after Fox didn't trust you?"

"He did, actually," Omega told them. "He and I had a little talk. He believed me, but there was a risk of him and Echo getting caught in a whole big..."

"Mess," India finished.

"Pile o' shit was what I 'uz gonna call it," Romeo said, pulling a face.

"Same difference," India said with a rueful grin.

"Pretty much," Omega agreed. "Anyway, Fox was trying to do the best he could to walk a fine line. Echo doesn't know it, but I gathered from various things that have been said by sundry people, that they even leveled an accusation of sorts against him. And we think that might have been the next step in the whole conspiracy—discredit Echo, or at least his memory, if he hadn't survived the gunshot; then go after Fox."

"A coup!" India exclaimed.

"Yup. Next step? A puppet leadership in the Agency. Probably with the Prime Minister pulling the strings."

"Damn!" Romeo cried. "I knew things were bad, but...wow."

"Yeah. Anyway, Fox told me directly, in front of Echo, that he did trust me, but that he had to..." she shrugged. "Maintain a, a distance, and do all the stuff he needed to do, so that paranoid agents didn't have a reason to accuse him of collusion with me in their imagined conspiracy. All while being sucked into one of their own, I guess."

"Okay. I get it now," India said, nodding. "You told me a little of it on New Year's Eve, but you just now said some stuff I hadn't heard."

"Yeah. Me, too," Romeo said simply. "So...yeah. We're fam'ly. You an' Echo, me an' India, an' Fox."

"And maybe Zebra eventually, if her relationship with Fox keeps going the way it's going," India added.

"Right." Omega smiled. "And I'm good with that. All of that."

"Us, too," India agreed, and Romeo nodded.

* * *

A knock sounded on the front door just then. When Omega answered it, an agent from the Deliveries service stood there, clipboard in hand.

"Agent Omega?"

"Yes?"

"Your equipment is on the roof. Sign here."

Automatically initialling the form, Omega pondered, confused. "But I didn't requisition anything..."

The agent shrugged, then disappeared down the corridor. Omega closed the door.

"Probably something Fox has got for Alpha Line," India commented.

"I guess I should go see what it is, in case it needs tending to..." Omega said, hesitant to leave her guests.

"Go ahead, Meg," Romeo said, looking at India with a gleam in his eye. "We'll be juuust fine, right here."

"If we're not here when you get back, we'll put things away and clean up before we leave," India added, amber eyes twinkling.

"I'm sure you will." Omega grinned at the two of them, fetched her shoes, and got her overcoat out of the coat closet.

* * *

A silent-as-the-tomb Echo had crept out past a completely-preoccupied Alpha Two into his own quarters, pulled his cell phone and triggered an app, grabbed an armload of outerwear from his coat closet, then made his way quickly up to the dark roof by a different stair than the one Omega normally used.

Now he stood in the snow, wrapped in black overcoat and muffler, gloved hands jammed deep in his capacious pockets, goggle glasses hiding most of what the muffler didn't cover, fading ninja-like into the deep shadows of an overhang. He waited patiently. It was only a matter of time.

He was rewarded with the sound of footsteps ascending the far stairwell. After a moment, the door latch clicked, and Omega stepped out onto the snowy roof.

Almost immediately, she began laughing, long and hard. In response, white teeth flashed slightly through the dark in a momentary grin.

* * *

A few feet from the stairwell door, and facing it, stood a rather nicely-built snow-woman, decidedly curvaceous of figure, with a silvery, sun-bleached straw braid of 'hair' hanging down her back, a classic carrot nose, a curving row of pink candies forming the mouth, and two bright blue faux jewels for eyes. But this snow being's face was tilted back, the 'sapphires' aimed up, to look at the sky.

"Somebody knows me entirely too well," Omega chuckled, when she could finally catch her breath. "And that...is a GOOD thing," she added as she stepped carefully across the icy roof to survey the snow-woman up close. As she glanced down, she paused and wrinkled her brow in puzzlement, espying several marks in the snow.

Across from her, unseen, brown eyes glinted with amusement in the shadows, observing her reactions closely.

"HOOFPRINTS?!" she exclaimed. Kneeling, Omega studied the prints in the snow with an experienced eye. "Hm. Deer. At least one big buck. Now how on Earth did he manage...??" Abruptly Omega suddenly remembered meeting a certain Arctic dweller back at Halloween, in Stockholm; a most particular famous denizen reported to dwell at the North Pole...and who had been driving a sled pulled by a reindeer. "Nick? Nnnooo. He didn't. Surely he wasn't REALLY...I thought he was just mistaken for him, like he was mistaken for Odin..."

She glanced up into the clear night sky and began laughing to herself again. "For all I know, my favorite mythological big guy in the RED suit really IS just another offworld pal of my favorite guy in the BLACK Suit."

* * *

Across the roof in the shadows, Echo's dark eyes grew jet-black as he listened, and his breath caught silently. He watched, gaze intent on his partner.

* * *

Omega stood and brushed the snow off her hands and knees. As she looked up, she went stock-still, staring in delighted disbelief.

"No...Echo, you didn't...oh, ECHO..." she breathed in awe. "It's beautiful."

The large black telescope looked almost identical to the one with which she had been observing when Echo had first encountered her, the one Kenny's brother Cartman had destroyed.

Neatly folded on the base was a tarpaulin cover, in urban camouflage print so it would blend in with the roof, carefully made to wrap around the entire assembly to protect it when it was not in use.

Omega ran visibly-trembling fingers over the tube, and began checking it out. She removed the tube cap, stood on tiptoe, and peeked down the tube at the primary mirror. Hooking the cap on the mount, she checked the clock drive and motor.

"It's already polar-aligned," she murmured. "I'm impressed..."

* * *

Omega flipped the switch that activated the drive, and a soft, steady hum filled the rooftop area. She glanced at the sky, surveying it thoughtfully, then at her wrist chronometer, and Echo saw her lips move silently as she mentally calculated.

Echo watched with fascination as a previously-unseen, though not unknown, side of his partner was revealed. Omega, dropping into what was obviously a professional observing mindset, expertly set the coordinates on the telescope, swinging it around on its yoke mount to point high in the southeast. Every movement was practiced and sure. She picked up the eyepiece case and opened it, considered, then selected an eyepiece and filter and slipped them into position, tightening the screws that held them in place.

"Orion Nebula, old friend, I'm back," she said to the heavens, and Echo could hear the smile in her voice.

She picked up the control paddle, checked the view in the finderscope, tweaked the telescope's pointing, and finally bent her head to the eyepiece. Echo heard a long, happy sigh, and somehow he knew that she was not really on the roof any longer.

The man known, even to his friends, only as Echo, smiled. Then, stealthy as any ninja, he made his way to the stairwell behind him. As the door closed silently, he glanced back once more to see his partner, happily absorbed at the telescope eyepiece.

"Merry Christmas, Omega," Echo whispered.

Author Notes

It's time to thank some people for their help in enabling me to produce the volume in your hands. In addition to the usual suspects—my husband, Darrell Osborn, who also did the cover artwork, and my parents, Steve and Colene Gannaway—all of whom are always supportive of my writing, there are a few other people who need naming, too.

First of all, there's Larry Bauer, one of my beta readers and the closest thing I have to a manager. He's also an old friend and colleague from my NASA days, and I Tuckerized him—at his request—in this volume. Larry, this book—this series—wouldn't even exist if it hadn't been for your idea.

Dr. James K. Woosley is another beta reader on this series, as is Evelyn Hively. Guys, your comments and editorial remarks are as invaluable as the brainstorming, and I appreciate you both immensely.

Nitay Arbel, formerly of the U.S., now hailing from Tel Aviv, has kindly assisted me with ensuring that Fox's Yiddish is up to snuff, and that's GREATLY appreciated!

And Ed Smith, my regular liaison at the LibertyCon science fiction convention in Chattanooga, TN, requested to be Tuckerized as well. The sequence I wrote for Ed's cameo is, in my humble opinion, one of the funniest classic comedy pieces I've ever written. Your mileage may vary, but the longer the sequence went on, the harder I laughed as I wrote.

Last but not least, there is my writing mentor, Travis S. Taylor. He's responsible for getting me started in this business in the first place, and a friend of quite some years' standing. So when I needed a well-known science fiction writer of note to be "something more than he seems," all I had to do was give him a call. He loved the idea, and thus became a character in this tome you hold, as well.

Much thanks to all, and I hope this book proves as fun to read as it has been to write!

~Stephanie Osborn

Huntsville, AL

August 2016

About the Author

Stephanie Osborn is a former payload flight controller, a veteran of over twenty years of working in the civilian space program, as well as various military space defense programs. She has worked on numerous Space Shuttle flights and the International Space Station, and counts the training of astronauts on her resumé. Of those astronauts she trained, one was Kalpana Chawla, a member of the crew lost in the Columbia disaster.

She holds graduate and undergraduate degrees in four sciences: Astronomy, Physics, Chemistry, and Mathematics, and she is "fluent" in several more, including Geology and Anatomy. She obtained her various degrees from Austin Peay State University in Clarksville, TN and Vanderbilt University in Nashville, TN.

Stephanie is currently retired from space work. She now happily "passes it forward," teaching math and science via numerous media including radio, podcasting, and public speaking, as well as working with SIGMA, the science fiction think tank, while writing science fiction mysteries based on her knowledge, experience, and travels.

For more, go to http://www.stephanie-osborn.com/.

A sneak peek at *Tour de Force*, Book 4 of the Division One series, by Stephanie Osborn!

Echo returned to his quarters later that morning from the unexpected meeting with Fox to come face-to-face with a gift. A huge, poster-sized full color print of the Orion Nebula was propped carefully in the recliner in his living area. Echo stood there studying it for a long moment. The gas filaments in the nebula were sharp and clearly defined, the colors vivid, the stars crisp and bright but not overexposed. The giant sheet of paper on which it was printed was high-quality photo stock. This was no off-the-shelf poster; this was the personal work of a professional astronomer. A skilled professional astronomer.

Thoughtfully he lifted the image and flipped it over to check the photographic paper. It was from the Agency photolab. He nodded to himself, the corners of his mouth curving slightly.

Wow. Just...wow. Somebody, he decided, *must have realized I was not happy about being thrown out last night, I think. After all, it wasn't like I tried to hide it. And I'll just bet this is an apology. A pretty cool one, too.*

He laid the photo back down with care and went to the back door. Upon seeing Omega's quarters empty, he shrugged, and headed into his own kitchen to grab some lunch.

* * *

Later that day, Omega returned to her quarters from running errands, and knocked on the frame of the connecting 'back door,' calling to her partner.

"Hi, Echo, I'm back..." Omega paused as Echo glanced up from re-reading H. G. Wells' *The Invisible Man* to look at her from his prone position on the couch.

Over the couch now hung the only adornment on Echo's walls, the Orion Nebula photo she had made and printed, which had, in the interim, been beautifully matted and framed in jet black. The overall impression created by the framing was that the nebula itself extended onto the wall, while at the same time it highlighted the beauty of the delicate colors. More, Echo's position on the couch seemed calculated to allow him to glance up at it whenever he was not actively reading.

She studied the framed picture silently for a long moment, startled but pleased, and he watched her reaction equally silently, with dusky brown eyes.

"...Did Fox call?" Omega finally finished.

"As a matter of fact, he did. It's not anything you have to worry about. But it DOES look like I'll be going off-planet for a couple days."

"Just you? What for?" She moved farther into the room, an odd, disturbed sensation running through her being.

"Yeah, it's a first contact, and they're scheduled to arrive in a couple of weeks; sorry about that. I know you're dying to do an exo mission. Especially since the Agency co-opted you just as you made astronaut. But the Cortians are new to us, the Pan-Galactic Council is eager to connect with 'em 'cause they're from the Sagittarius Dwarf Galaxy, and the situation's a little complex. Seems they follow a strict protocol in making diplomatic overtures. One of the rules they've laid down is one agent, and one only. They also had some interesting requirements regarding gender and physical ability."

"What? Physical..." Omega's eyes narrowed, and she frowned, as imagery of a particularly unpleasant nature popped into the back of her mind while Echo talked.

* * *

"What's wrong?" Echo asked, noting her expression.

"I...don't know," Omega admitted. "I've just suddenly got enough bells ringing in my head for a five-alarm fire. I don't like the sound of that, Echo."

"It sounded pretty routine to Fox and me." He shrugged. "Nothing really unusual."

"I don't think you should go."

"Why not?"

"Call it a hunch. Women's intuition. Whatever. Just don't go."

Damn, he thought, biting his lip. *I was afraid she was gonna take it hard. Especially coming so soon after the South American mission, when she's still tired. Hell, when we're both tired.* He pondered how to let her down easy.

"Meg, look. I know you'd love to go, but...you can't. I really am sorry. I'll try to arrange with Fox to get us both an offworld assignment as Alpha One as soon as I can."

* * *

She stared at him, shocked, then a little glint of anger kindled in the depths of her eyes.

"You think I'm trying..." Omega turned on her heel and stalked toward the door. Over her shoulder she said, "I thought you knew me better than that, Echo. You've sure preached about it enough in recent months. But damn, are you off this time, Ace."

Don't miss any of these highly entertaining SF/F books by Stephanie Osborn!

Division One series:
Alpha and Omega
A Small Medium At Large
A Very UnCONventional Christmas

Alpha and Omega by Stephanie Osborn

(ISBN: 978-0-9982888-0-2 ebook/978-0-9982888-1-9 print)

Dr. Megan McAllister was already a pretty unusual human—NASA astronaut, professional astronomer, polymath—when she encountered the man in the black Suit that night in west Texas. What Division One Agent Echo didn't know, when he recruited her to the Agency, was that she was even more special.

But he'd find out, soon enough.

Stephanie Osborn, aka the Interstellar Woman of Mystery, former rocket scientist and author of acclaimed science fiction mysteries, goes back to the urban legend of the unique group of men and women who show up at UFO sightings, alien abductions, etc. and make things...disappear... to craft her vision of the universe we don't know about. Her new series, Division One, chronicles this universe through the eyes of recruit Megan McAllister, aka Omega, and her experienced partner, Echo, as they handle everything from lost alien children to extraterrestrial assassination attempts and more. [First book in the Division One series.]

A Small Medium At Large by Stephanie Osborn

(ISBN: 978-0-9982888-2-6 ebook/978-0-9982888-3-3 print)

What if Sir Arthur Conan Doyle was right all along, and Harry Houdini really DID do his illusions, not through sleight of hand, but via noncorporeal means? More, what if he could do this because...he wasn't human?

Ari Ho'd'ni, Glu'g'ik son of the Special Steward of the Royal House of Va'du'sha'ā, better known to modern humans as an alien Gray from the ninth planet of Zeta Reticuli A, fled his homeworld with the rest of his family during a time of impending global civil war. With them, they brought a unique device which, in its absence, ultimately caused the failure of the uprisings and the collapse of the imperial regime. Consequently Va'du'sha'ā has been at peace for more than a century. What is the F'al, and why has a rebel faction sent a special agent to Earth to retrieve it?

It falls to the premier team in the Pan-Galactic Law Enforcement and Immigration Administration, Division One—the Alpha One team, known to their friends as Agents Echo and Omega—to find out...or die trying. [Second book in the Division One series.]

* * *

Burnout: The mystery of Space Shuttle STS-281 by Stephanie Osborn (ISBN: 1-60619-200-0)

How do you react when you discover the next shuttle disaster has happened...right on schedule?

Burnout is a SF mystery about a Space Shuttle disaster that turns out to be no accident. As the true scope of the disaster is uncovered by the principle investigators, "Crash" Murphy and Dr. Mike Anders, they find themselves running for their lives as friends, lovers and coworkers involved in the investigation perish around them.

* * *

Sherlock Holmes: Gentleman Aegis series by Stephanie Osborn:
Sherlock Holmes and the Mummy's Curse

Sherlock Holmes and the Mummy's Curse by Stephanie Osborn (ISBN: 1-51888-312-5)

Holmes and Watson. Two names linked by mystery and danger from the beginning.

Within the first year of their friendship and while both are young men, Holmes and Watson are still finding their way in the world, with all the troubles that such young men usually have: Financial straits, troubles of the female persuasion, hazings, misunderstandings between friends, and more. Watson's Afghan wounds are still tender, his health not yet fully recovered, and there can be no consideration of his beginning a new practice as yet. Holmes, in his turn, is still struggling to found the new profession of consulting detective. Not yet truly established in London, let alone with the reputations they will one day possess, they are between cases and at loose ends when Holmes' old professor of archaeology contacts him.

Professor Willingham Whitesell makes an appeal to Holmes' unusual skill set and a request. Holmes is to bring Watson to serve as the dig team's physician and come to Egypt at once to translate hieroglyphics for his prestigious archaeological dig. There in the wilds of the Egyptian desert, plagued by heat, dust, drought and cobras, the team hopes to find the very first Pharaoh. Instead, they find something very different...(First book in the Gentleman Aegis series)

Sherlock Holmes and the Mummy's Curse is a Silver Falchion Award winner.

* * *

Displaced Detective series by Stephanie Osborn:

The Case of the Displaced Detective: The Arrival

The Case of the Displaced Detective: At Speed

The Case of the Cosmological Killer: The Rendlesham Incident

The Case of the Cosmological Killer: Endings and Beginnings

A Case of Spontaneous Combustion

Fear in the French Quarter

The Case of the Displaced Detective: The Arrival (ISBN: 1-60619-189-7) by Stephanie Osborn is a SF mystery in which brilliant hyperspatial physicist, Dr. Skye Chadwick, discovers there are alternate realities, often populated by those we consider only literary characters. Can Chadwick help Holmes come up to speed in modern investigative techniques in time to stop the spies? Will Holmes be able to thrive in our modern world? Is Chadwick now Holmes' new "Watson"—or more?

And what happens next? [First book in the Displaced Detective series]

The Case of the Displaced Detective: At Speed by Stephanie Osborn
(ISBN: 1-60619-191-0)

Having foiled sabotage of Project: Tesseract by an unknown spy ring, Sherlock Holmes and Dr. Skye Chadwick face the next challenge. How do they find the members of this diabolical spy ring when they do not even know what the ring is trying to accomplish? And how can they do it when Skye is recovering from no less than two nigh-fatal wounds?

Can they work out the intricacies of their relationship? Can they determine the reason the spy ring is after the tesseract? And—most importantly—can they stop it? [Second book in the Displaced Detective series]

The Case of the Cosmological Killer: The Rendlesham Incident by Stephanie Osborn
(ISBN: 1-60619-193-4)

In 1980, RAF Bentwaters and Woodbridge were plagued by UFO sightings that were never solved. Now, McFarlane, a resident of Suffolk has died of fright during a new UFO encounter. On holiday in London, Sherlock Holmes and Skye Chadwick-Holmes are called upon by Her Majesty's Secret Service to investigate the death.

What is the UFO? Why does Skye find it familiar? Who—or what—killed McFarlane?

And how can the pair do what even Her Majesty's Secret Service could not? [Third book in the Displaced Detective series]

The Case of the Cosmological Killer: Endings and Beginnings by Stephanie Osborn
(ISBN: 1-60619-195-0)

After the revelations in *The Rendlesham Incident*, Holmes and Skye find they have not one, but two, very serious problems facing them. Not only did their "UFO victim" most emphatically NOT die from a close encounter, he was dying twice over—from completely unrelated causes. Holmes must now find the murderers before they find the secret of the McFarlane farm.

And to add to their problems, another continuum—containing another Skye and Holmes—has approached Skye for help to stop the collapse of their own spacetime, a collapse that could take Skye with it, should she happen to be in their tesseract core when it occurs. [Fourth book in the Displaced Detective series]

A Case of Spontaneous Combustion by Stephanie Osborn
(ISBN: 1-60619-197-7)

When an entire village west of London is wiped out in an apparent case of mass spontaneous combustion, Her Majesty's Secret Service contacts The Holmes Agency to investigate. Once in London, Holmes looks into the horror that is now Stonegrange. His investigations take him into a dangerous undercover assignment in search of a possible terror ring, though he cannot determine how a human agency could have caused the disaster. Meanwhile, alone in Colorado, Skye is forced to battle raging wildfires and tame a wild mustang stallion, all while believing that her husband has abandoned her. Who—or what—caused the horror in Stonegrange? Will Holmes find his way safely through the metaphorical minefield that is modern Middle Eastern politics? Will this predicament seriously damage—even destroy—the couple's relationship? And can Holmes stop the terrorists before they unleash their outré weapon again? [Fifth book in the Displaced Detective series]

Fear in the French Quarter (ISBN: 1-60619-202-7) by Stephanie Osborn revolves around a jaunt by no less than Sherlock Holmes himself—brought to the modern day from an alternate universe's Victorian era by his continuum parallel, who is now his wife, Dr. Skye Chadwick-Holmes—to famed New Orleans for both business and pleasure. There, the detective couple investigates ghostly apparitions, strange disappearances, mystic phenomena, and challenge threats to the very universe they call home.

It was supposed to be a working holiday for Skye and Sherlock, along with their friend, the modern day version of Doctor Watson—some federal training that also gave them the chance to explore New Orleans, as the ghosts of the French Quarter become exponentially more active. When the couple uncovers an imminently catastrophic cause, whose epicenter lies squarely in the middle of Le Vieux Carré, they must race against time to stop it before the whole thing breaks wide open—and more than one universe is destroyed. [Sixth book in the Displaced Detective series]

CPSIA information can be obtained
at www.ICGtesting.com
Printed in the USA
BVHW032133010321
601056BV00001BA/8